DEVIN'S DREAMS

D. C. WILKINSON

To my muses: the versions of myself that I was and will become. And to the passengers riding along with me on this cosmic stagecoach, among them and in particular, my dear friend and writing coach, Clifford Dean Scholz.

CONTENTS

I. Dragons and Swallows

Almost two months had passed since the last late-night disturbance. The end of the school year and the warmer days of summer appeared to have brought a measure of calm and tranquility to the Sharps' modest home in Kingston, New York. Outside, the gentle light of a waxing crescent moon bathed the rooftop. Inside, silence.

Then, Devin disrupted the peace.

"Mom!" he cried out as he stood in his parents' bedroom doorway, barefoot in his pajamas.

Lauren's face twitched. She raised her head and saw her seven-year-old son's silhouette. She reached for the bedside lamp and turned it on. "Devin? What's wrong, honey?"

"There are strangers in my bedroom," he said between sobs.

"Come here sweetie!" She sat up as he rushed over and threw his arms around her.

"What's going on?" Phil grumbled. He rolled onto his side, rubbed his eyes and glanced at the alarm clock on his nightstand.

"We're trying to find out," Lauren replied, gently running her fingers through Devin's messy blond hair.

Paige and Abbey, Devin's older sisters, quietly slipped into the room and sat at the edge of the bed.

"I guess we're having family time at two in the morning," Phil said in a raspy voice. He yawned, sat up and leaned back on the headboard.

Lauren wiped Devin's tears from his face. "Do you remember the last time this happened, Devin?"

"Yes."

"We checked your bedroom together, you, Daddy and I, and there was no one there."

"But, they were there *before* we looked!"

"Is anyone there now?"

"Maybe."

"So, where exactly did you see these strangers, Devin?"

"In a corner, on the ceiling."

Abbey and Paige giggled.

"Stop it!" Devin shrieked. "It's true!"

"Girls!" Lauren frowned. She held Devin's hands on her lap and continued. "Were you asleep when you saw them?"

"I—I don't think so."

"Were your eyes closed?"

"Yes, but I could see them! I swear, Mom!"

"What did they look like?"

"Hm… I'm not sure. But they *were* there!"

"How do you know?"

"There were shadows, moving…"

"Their shadows?"

"Yes! Behind a sheet."

"But, you could still see them?"

"There was a light behind the sheet."

"A light?"

"Yeah, b-blinking."

"You mean, flickering."

Paige started weeping. "I'm scared!" the 9-year-old whimpered.

"Don't be!" Abbey told her younger sister. "It's just one of Devin's silly dreams."

"Shut up Abbey!" Devin yelled raising his chin, face flushed. "*You're* silly! Mom, make her stop!"

"Please! Everyone, calm down!" Lauren pleaded. "Phil, will you? Let's get Paige and Abbey back to bed."

Phil drew a deep breath. "Okay, okay. Girls, come on, let's go." He climbed out of bed and walked them to their bedroom. Moments later he returned, settled back into bed, leaned on Lauren and whispered in her ear. "Can we please finish this tomorrow?"

"Just a couple more minutes, sweetheart," she said quietly, then faced her son. "So, Devin, did these strangers talk to you?"

"No."

"Did you hear anything at all?"

"A ring, at the beginning… after I closed my eyes."

"Like a telephone ring?"

"Uh-uh!" Devin shook his head.

"What kind of a ring?"

"Soft, then louder, and then…"

"Then, what?"

"It went away."

Puzzled, Lauren glanced at Phil. "A sound wave?"

Phil shrugged.

"What is a sound wave, Mom?"

"Never mind that, honey. What happened next? Did you say anything?"

"Nooo! I didn't! You and Dad always say never speak to strangers. Anyway, I couldn't talk… I—I couldn't move!"

"But you could see?"

"Yes. I saw everything! I swear!"

"What's *everything* Devin?" Phil asked. "What else did you see?"

"Everything in my room, Dad! My bookcase, my desk, my sailboat, my bed, *me*…"

"You saw *yourself?* How? You said your eyes were closed!"

"I dunno. Um, I—I was in the air… flying."

"Okay. Enough. You had a bad dream, Devin. That's all."

"No, I didn't! I didn't!" Devin shouted, his blue eyes welling up.

"Devin Sharp, I think it's time to get back to bed."

Lauren hugged Devin. "Honey, you'll be fine. I'll stay with you and read till you fall asleep, okay?"

Devin's face softened as he nodded.

Lauren rose, took Devin's hand and walked him to his bedroom.

"You like this one, right?" Lauren asked, sitting at Devin's side on his bed with *Harold and the Purple Crayon* in her hand.

"Yes! I love Harold!"

"Good!"

As Lauren read, Devin lay in bed scanning the surroundings. Hanging on the wall across from him, a collage of carefully arranged family photos made him pause. At its center was a picture of Lauren in a hospital bed holding her newborn baby boy in her arms, with Phil by her side. Around it, photos of

Devin's early childhood with Paige embracing him full of smiles, and Abbey next to her, vigilant and stern. Thumbtacked to a cork bulletin board by a bookcase, a world map dotted with multicolored pushpins stood out. Pinned on upstate New York, a paper cutout in the shape of a star with the word 'HOME' written in capital letters. Just as Devin's eyes shifted to a vintage model sailboat on a desk shelf, Lauren's voice began to fade. A muddled mixture of thoughts and emotions looping somewhere in his head dissipated, and the knot in his stomach finally relaxed.

Shortly after all the lights were off and the house had fallen into silence, Paige tiptoed into Devin's bedroom and gently tapped his shoulder.

"Devin?" she whispered. "Are you awake?"

"Yes," he answered softly. The moonlight drifted through a window and reflected on his face as he sat up. "What's going on?"

"I can't sleep."

"Sorry I spooked you."

"It's okay. And I didn't mean to laugh at you."

"I know."

"For you," she said, handing him a small flashlight. "I took it from Dad's old toolbox in the basement. He won't miss it."

"Thank you."

"So, where did you see *them?*" Paige asked looking upward.

"Who?"

"The strangers."

Devin switched on the flashlight and aimed it at a corner of the ceiling.

"Maybe they won't come again," she said, mustering a tepid smile.

Devin sighed. "I wish. But it's not like that... Let's go back to bed now or we'll get in trouble."

———>-☺-<———

A few hours later, a wooden dish clock above the fireplace in the dining room marked the time: 6 a.m. Two old-world prints of horse-drawn carriages flanked the clock.

In the adjacent living room, Phil and Lauren sat on a couch in their night robes, coffee cups in hand. A low wooden table separated them from their black-and-white Zenith TV tuned in to CBS. On the screen, a time stamp: Wednesday, July 16, 1969.

Good morning! It's three hours and thirty-two minutes until man begins the greatest adventure in his history, said anchor Walter Cronkite referring to the imminent launch of Apollo 11.

"If it wasn't for the launch special I could've used a couple more hours in the sack," said Phil. He set his cup aside and groaned as he stretched.

"I hear you," Lauren responded. "The kids are still in bed." She crossed her legs and stared blankly at the TV screen. "At least it didn't happen in the winter on a school night."

"What?"

"Devin's nightmare."

"It was nothing."

"*Not* nothing. You know he's had sleeping issues since he was a baby. Now this."

"Now what? This is not the same."

"You're right, Phil. He's no longer a baby. This time he gave us a full explanation."

"Well, you kinda quizzed him on it."

"I wanna know what's going on with him. Don't you?"

"Come on, sweetheart. It was just a bad dream. Nothing to worry about."

Lauren gave Phil a sidelong glance. "If you say so," she responded in a soft tone, raising an eyebrow. She brought her cup to her lips and took a thoughtful sip.

After breakfast the family gathered in front of the TV to watch the launch. Devin sat between Paige and Lauren, his eyes fixated on the old prints hanging on the wall.

"Mom, how long could horses go without water?"

"What horses?"

"The ones in the pictures," he said, pointing.

"Gosh, I have no idea, honey. A few hours, I suppose."

"I feel sorry for them," Paige said. "They were pulling so much weight!"

"They were workhorses, darling," Lauren responded, gently caressing her head. "That's how people moved around in those days."

"No trains or buses?" Devin asked.

"Not at that time."

Devin paused, his eyes quickly shifting back to the prints.

"How come there are no horses at the zoo?"

"Some zoos have wild horses," Lauren replied. "Just not the common, domesticated breeds."

"Dad, are we going to the zoo tomorrow?" Devin shouted out. "You said we would!"

Abbey aimed a long glare at Devin. Then she pounced. "Could you. Just. Be. Quiet."

"*You* be quiet!" Devin shot back.

Phil rose to adjust the rabbit ears on the TV. "Gang! We're about to watch history in the making here. Can we all try to pay attention?"

The countdown began.

Everyone fell silent.

An hour later, Apollo 11 had begun its journey to the Moon and Phil and Devin were out in the sun, on their knees, harvesting the fruits of a small vegetable garden tucked in a corner of the family's backyard. Lauren and the girls had stayed inside. In the background, a small transistor radio played all-time favorite pop hits.

"What's bugging you, Devin?" asked Phil. "You've been quiet."

"Nothing. Thinking…"

"About?"

"The zoo."

"Oh, right! I forgot you asked about it."

"Are we going?"

"Of course, we are!"

Devin brightened. "Goody! I really wanna see the birds. We missed them last year."

"We had no time, remember? We had to wait in line to see the Komodo dragons."

"I loved the dragons!"

"I know. You said you had a dream about them."

"Not about them. The dragons in my dreams were different."

"They were? How?"

"They were huge! They looked like snakes with big fangs. But they had claws and wings."

"They sound like dragons from China and Japan. Scary?"

"Yeah, at first. I thought they were chasing a bunch of little birds. Then I saw they were just playing with them."

"You must've seen them on TV or in one of your coloring books."

"No, I didn't."

"You didn't?" Phil responded, a skeptical look on his face. "You know, they only exist in stories."

"Huh…"

"How did your dream end, anyway?"

"It didn't. I still dream about them, sometimes."

"Hm… Well, tomorrow we'll make sure we see the birds, okay?"

"Yay!" came a spirited cheer from Devin.

Phil grasped the last ripe tomato, twisted it away from its stem and placed it in a small wicker basket along with the radio. "All righty! It looks like we're done here," he said, standing up. "Let's go in."

Devin followed him into the house.

The following day, after an hour slogging in the sweltering heat, Phil and Lauren trailed behind their kids on a gravel path leading to the Bronx Zoo House of Birds. Above them, a deep blue cloudless sky stretched endlessly, bathed by a bright midday sun.

"I'm thirsty!" Paige cried out.

"Me too!" Devin shouted.

"Come on, gang! We're almost there!" said Phil, tiny beads of sweat collecting on his forehead and along the length of his deep brown sideburns. "There are water fountains at the entrance of the building."

Once they arrived, Lauren brought the children together. "It's busy here today," she said, pushing a messy strand of red hair under her straw hat. "Let's make sure we stick together, okay?"

Everyone nodded.

After freshening up they stepped into the building. A bubbling cacophony of raucous chirps, tweets and wings flapping and fluttering engulfed them. Ahead of them, people chatted while waiting in line to move past each of the exhibits.

"Do you remember our first time here?" Phil asked Lauren as they strolled side by side along a raised winding boardwalk.

"How could I forget? It was our first date."

"Kind of a strange first date, right? The zoo?"

"I thought it was cute and different. And, I liked *different*."

"*You* were different," said Phil, a tender gaze directed at his wife. "Spunky.

But it was your curls and freckles that really turned me on."

Lauren smiled coyly, returning Phil's gaze. "The tiny mole on your left cheek drove me crazy."

"We were lookers!"

"And, romantic. We talked forever, remember?"

"Of course! We had ideals."

Lauren sighed. "True. But we were never as bold and defiant as the hippies are today. I admire their courage."

"There was courage in our idealism. We believed in education as a means to change the world. That's why we became teachers, right?"

"Well… the hippies think we're a part of the establishment."

Phil chuckled. "The hippies can think what they want. We know who we are. Did you forget our pledge to each other just before we got married?"

"Which one?"

"We swore we'd let our kids grow into their own values and beliefs based on their own life experiences, not ours. And not those of any particular religion or political something or other."

"Right. We also said we'd be fair and open-minded."

"Yes, we did. And we are."

Lauren lowered her head. "I hope so."

"What do you mean? We're *not*?"

"Honestly, sometimes I wonder if we're receptive enough. Especially with Devin."

"Receptive to what?"

"His head is set about certain things…"

"Like what?"

"Well, take his nightmares. He's adamant they're real."

"He's stubborn, and he's got a wild imagination. Did I mention his dream about the dragons and the birds?"

"You did."

"That's a child's fantasy at work, sweetheart."

"Even so, I'm afraid dismissing him is doing nothing but ignore the issue, Phil."

"Are you kidding? We've been listening to him since he was in the crib. There *is* no issue."

Suddenly, a call from Devin interrupted them. "Dad! What are those?" he shouted, pointing at a noisy flock of small, colorful birds perched on a tree inside a large cage.

Phil walked up to a sign. "Let's see…" he said. He read it and turned to Devin and the girls. "They're swallows from Java, an island in a country called Indonesia."

"They're so pretty!" said Paige.

"They're also very special," Phil went on. "They live near the water and feed on insects, seaweed and fish. Oh, and… they make their nests with their saliva."

Intrigued, Lauren chimed in. "Really?"

"Yup. And they're edible."

"The birds?"

"The nests. People eat them."

"Yucky!" Paige shrieked, sticking her tongue out.

Oblivious to his sister's reaction, Devin gazed at the birds speaking to himself as if under a spell. "They're so beautiful! Like the birds in my dream."

"Anyone hungry?" Phil asked. "It's lunch time."

Lauren made a face. "Not anymore!"

The kids giggled.

Phil smiled and led the way to the exit.

As the warmth and mellowness of summer waned, night breezes gradually arrived laced with the cool veins of autumn. The beginning of the school year came with its own rhythms and routines: Early mornings, scheduled meals, homework, TV time and outdoor play. Quiet time? Never. Then, like clockwork, summer collapsed into fall.

Mid-October brought landscapes blanketed with patchworks of yellow, orange and red leaves. Mesmerized by the sight of carved pumpkins, witches, ghosts and goblins on countless front lawns, Devin and Paige sat next to each other in a school bus, silently looking out the window.

"Decker and Van Der Zee!" the driver called out, bringing the bus to a full stop. He looked in the rearview mirror and saw Devin and Paige rising from their seats. As they stepped off the bus, they spotted their mother waving by the front door. They made their way up the walkway, dropped their lunchboxes and greeted her with hugs.

"What happened to your jacket, honey?"

"Nothing," Devin answered, looking down.

"Your sleeve is torn. It didn't rip itself, did it?"

"It wasn't his fault, Mom!" Paige cut in.

"I didn't say it was, young lady. But I'd really like to know what happened," she insisted. "Devin?"

"Nothing... Some kids started bugging me at lunch."

"Why? What did you say to them?"

"Nothing! I swear! I was minding my business."

"They just came at you out of nowhere?"

"Yeah! They tried to steal my lunchbox!"

"What did they say?"

"I dunno... They were loud. They called me names."

"What *names*?"

Devin shrugged, blushing.

"So how did your jacket get ripped?"

"They were tugging and pulling."

"Paige, did you see any of this?"

"They were nasty, yelling and laughing! They yanked his lunchbox, ran with it and tossed it in a garbage can."

Lauren turned to Devin. "For heaven's sake! Did they hurt you?"

Again, Devin shrugged.

"Yes, they did!" Paige shouted. "They pushed him and shoved him real hard. He was crying."

"Who are these kids, Devin? What are their names?"

"I don't know them, Mom!"

"There were two of them," Paige said. "One was really loud and mean. I think his name is Tommy. The English kid with awful breath and crooked teeth. Everyone knows him. He's a troublemaker! He kept yelling and calling Devin a sissy and a weirdo."

"What? That's awful! Were any teachers there?"

"Yeah, Ms. Murphy," said Paige. "She came over right away."

"I see. Well, I guess Daddy and I will be seeing her tomorrow first thing in the morning."

———>-☺-<———

Early the next day Phil, Lauren and Devin climbed the steps leading to the main entrance of Kingston Elementary. Behind them, a resplendent crimson sky spread out all around as the sun slowly rose above the city skyline. Minutes later all three sat at a table in a conference room across from Ms. Murphy, a petite, grey-haired, middle-aged woman wearing a pair of black thick-rimmed eyeglasses.

"Thank you for coming in today," she said. "I'm sorry your visit is due to such unfortunate circumstances."

"So are we," Lauren responded. "We're glad you were witness to what happened."

"I wasn't exactly at the spot where the scuffle took place," Ms. Murphy explained. "But I was on cafeteria duty and I rushed over as soon as I became aware of the situation. Devin was a bit shaken."

"We heard," said Phil. "So what measures did the school take?"

"Our counselor, Ms. Calhoun and I spoke to Tommy's parents when they came to pick him up. We've been working with the Bambridges for a while now."

Lauren's eyes widened. "Oh, so this is not something new." She turned to Devin. "When was the first time this happened?"

"When *he* showed up last year."

"Last year? And you didn't say anything?"

"No one believes me anyway…" Devin answered, his eyes stinging.

"What? Come on now! Who is this awful kid, anyway?"

Ms. Murphy cleared her throat. "Honestly, he's the leader of a small group of boys who've been quite a handful. In any case, yesterday we were told by his parents that they're moving back to England at the end of the month."

"At least that's a relief," said Lauren, placing a hand on her chest. "What about the others?"

"We're taking care of them. I'm confident things will improve from now on, Mrs. Sharp."

"Let's hope so."

Phil leaned forward. "It seems like Devin's habit of keeping to himself is becoming a bit of an issue lately."

"He's a quiet boy," said Ms. Murphy, looking at Devin. "And frankly, sometimes he comes across as being a bit timid."

"Yes, I remember we discussed this with you when he was in your class last year."

"Regrettably, Mr. Sharp, some of the boys can misperceive shyness as a weakness."

Devin scowled. "I am *not* weak!" he interjected, nostrils flaring.

"No, of course not, sweetie," said Ms. Murphy, her hand reaching out to him. He looked away.

Phil stared. "Take it easy. That's not what we're saying."

The bell rang.

Ms. Muphy rose from her seat. "We'll do our best to keep an eye on things," she said. "Please call if you have any further concerns." She turned to Devin and put a hand on his shoulder. "I'm sure you'll do great this year!"

"Thank you, Ms. Murphy!" Phil responded, as he and Lauren stood up.

Lauren smiled politely. "See you after school, Devin." She kissed his forehead and followed Phil out the door.

➤◉◄

Late October brought shorter days and tones of chilly gray to cities and towns along the Eastern Seaboard. A weekend afternoon filled with ominous forecasts of an approaching nor'easter had prompted Lauren and Phil to make a hasty run to the grocery store, leaving Abbey in charge. Alone at the dining room table she did her homework, her foot tapping along to Chicago's latest album on the family's record player.

Suddenly, a loud crash followed by bouncing and rolling sounds echoed through the house. Startled, Abbey put her pen down and rushed upstairs.

"Paige? Devin? Where are you?" she called out. Phil and Lauren's bedroom door was ajar. She peeked in and saw Devin sitting at the edge of his parents' bed in a loose-fitting negligee with a white towel wrapped around his head. On his lap, two Barbie dolls and a hairbrush lay unattended, as he watched Paige frantically attempting to gather a bunch of wooden beads strewn across the floor.

Abbey pushed the door open and stepped into the room. "What's going on?" she asked.

Jolted, Devin wobbled as he rose. The dolls and brush fell to the floor.

"Nothing," Paige replied, still on the floor. "Mom's necklace broke." A smudge of blue eyeshadow on her left eye and messy red lipstick on one side of her mouth accentuated the sheepish look on her face.

"I can see that!" Abbey responded, then turned to Devin. "Are you wearing mom's lipstick and jewelry, too?"

Devin's chin dipped as he discreetly nudged the dolls under the bed with his foot and took off his mother's bracelet and clip-on earrings.

Abbey sized Devin up. "Hm... you look taller." She moved closer and lifted his jeans above his ankles. "Oh, now I get it... You got mom's platform shoes on!" She giggled. "Wow! No wonder those boys at school called you a sissy."

"You're a jerk, Abbey!" Devin shouted, fighting back tears.

"That's mean!" Paige screamed.

Abbey's piercing gaze fixed on Devin. "We'll see who mom thinks is the jerk after she finds out about this!" She turned and left.

As Abbey started down the staircase Paige yelled: "Tattle-tale! Goody two-shoes!"

By the time Lauren and Phil got home, thick dark clouds had blotted out the sun.

"Damn. We beat the rain by seconds," Phil said as they walked in the front door and heard the wind and the downpour start beating on the house. Abbey walked up to help carry the grocery bags to the kitchen. She then proceeded to describe what Devin and Paige had been up to in their absence.

Sitting quietly at the top of the stairs Devin and Paige listened.

"Thank you, Abbey," Lauren said. "Now, could you please tell your sister and brother to come downstairs? We'll need a few minutes alone with them. You stay in your bedroom until we call you back, okay?"

"Sure."

Phil leaned on Lauren. "Are you sure we want to do this now?"

"Of course, I am. We need to nip this in the bud. We can't let mayhem happen in this house when we're away."

The couple walked to the living room and sat on the couch.

Shortly afterward Devin and Paige stood side by side in front of their parents.

"Please take a seat, both of you," Phil said.

"Abbey says you two were in our bedroom while we were out," Lauren began.

"Yes," Paige responded. Devin nodded.

"Could you please tell us what you were doing there?"

"Playing," Paige answered.

"Do you think it's okay to play with someone else's belongings without their permission?"

"No," said Paige. Again, Devin nodded.

"Do you realize some of the things you were playing with were *very* private?"

Paige lowered her head. "I'm sorry, Mom."

"Me too," said Devin.

"Okay, fine. But why did you do it?"

"It was a dare," Devin replied.

"Who dared who, and why?" Phil asked.

"We dared each other to dress up," Paige responded.

"So, you both made a choice. And, not a good one."

"We didn't mean to, Dad," Paige said, eyes glistening.

Phil stared at Devin. "So, what do you think would happen if *other people* found out about this?"

Devin shrugged.

"What if some of the boys at school found out? What do you think they'd say?"

Lauren squeezed Phil's hand.

"They'd tease me," said Devin, tearing up. "…and call me a sissy."

"And how would that make you feel?"

"Same way I feel when Abbey calls me that!" Devin cried out. He stood and ran upstairs.

"Young man, come back here!" Phil shouted.

Devin ignored him.

Lauren stood. "Paige, honey. Please go to your room. We'll call you when dinner's ready." She faced Phil. "Was that really necessary?"

"I didn't mean to upset him."

"But, you did! What was the point?"

"He needs to know that doing certain things could get him hurt out there."

"Looks like we're doing the hurting right here."

"That was not my intention, Lauren. But, you're right. I'll go talk to him."

"Thank you. I'll have a word with Abbey."

They went upstairs.

Phil tapped on Devin's bedroom door. "Devin, may I come in?" He waited a moment in silence. "Please? I just wanna talk."

"Whatever," Devin responded softly, curled up in bed, his back to the door.

Phil stepped in and sat beside him. "I'm sorry I upset you. I just wanted you to see that the things we say and do can have consequences. I don't want you to get hurt, ever."

"I know, but Abbey said things…" Devin answered in a hushed tone.

Phil took a deep breath. "I hear you. We all make mistakes, now and then. Mom and I will talk to her. I'm sure she'll apologize. When that happens, I hope you can forgive her."

"I'll try."

Phil gently touched Devin's shoulder. "Are we good?"

Devin turned around and nodded.

"Halloween is just around the corner. If you wanna dress up, maybe this year we can all go shopping for costumes. What do you say?"

"Sounds okay," said Devin, a hopeful note in his voice.

Phil stood, looked at Devin and smiled. "Hungry?"

"Uh-huh!"

"Then I better go help Mom with dinner. We'll call you when it's ready."

Alone, Devin settled in his bed and relaxed. Outside, bursts of wind-driven rain spattered the windows as the nor'easter continued to roll in. Looking up at the ceiling, Devin pictured himself in a Halloween costume. He closed his eyes just as a faint sound wave crept into his ears. Suddenly, he found himself standing on some kind of stage. A lavish robe felt soft and warm, a bulky wig weighing on his head. Candles twinkled on a chandelier while a host of fleeting shadows danced beneath it. *Strangers?* Not this time. He sensed he knew them and attempted to take a step forward. To no avail. He couldn't move.

A familiar voice sounded in the distance: "Devin! Dinner!"

Instantly, everything around him crumbled, then vanished in the ether.

Startled, he opened his eyes and realized he had been dreaming.

II. An Annoying Beauty

G rade school had been tough. Tommy was long gone, but random episodes of spiteful taunting had persisted. Even as time pressed forward, they left their mark, then morphed into a hazy blur of memories buried deep inside.

As Devin grew taller, his once golden hair turned a light reddish brown, and a voracious appetite for reading evolved into a daily habit. High school brought a measure of relief. He joined the Drama Club and felt, for the first time, he might have found a refuge and his tribe.

"Devin? Are you up?" his mother called from the bottom of the stairs.

"Yeah, I'm almost ready!" he yelled back from his bedroom.

"Remember your Dad and I are picking you up after school. We're seeing Doctor Kessler right after your session."

"I know, Mom. Thanks." Leaving his bed unmade and his homework still spread across his desk, Devin stepped into the bathroom, turned on the light and looked at himself in the mirror. *Good! No blemishes!* He splashed some water on his face and reached for a towel.

This was a special day. No after-school rehearsal.

Devin put a foot on his desk chair and tied the laces on his sneaker. He glanced at the *Bredenhoft*, his cherished model sailboat, still on the shelf where it had been since his parents had given it to him on his fifth birthday. Above it, a poster of a dazzling Maria Callas as Violetta in *La Traviata* flashed a smile at him. Drawn to the magic of the opera at just fifteen, Devin admired her.

Later in the evening, Phil and Lauren sat in a waiting room outside Doctor Kessler's office. Inside, Devin stared at a grand view of Kingston's Old Dutch Church through a large window behind the doctor's desk. Above the church's clock tower a white spire rose up to the heavens.

"Just a few minutes left, Devin," said Doctor Kessler, his rosy cheeks shining as he removed his eyeglasses and set them on his desk.

"Uh-huh… Okay," Devin responded, his mind elsewhere.

The doctor turned his head and looked out the window behind him. "Pretty sight, isn't it?" he asked.

"The church?"

"Yes. One of the gems in the Old District. Built when Kingston was just a small village in the colony of New Netherland."

Devin sat up. "I know. The Old District is all that's left of the village. I read about it in a book my dad gave me."

The doctor smiled. "Exactly. I forgot he's a history teacher."

"Right."

"You know Devin, we're surrounded by history," said the doctor, pointing to a brick fireplace across from his desk. "See that ebony bracket clock on the mantel? It's been in my family for centuries. I saw you looking at it a few times during our sessions."

"I think I've seen it somewhere…"

"Only here. It's an original. It belonged to one of my ancestors who came to America from Antwerp."

Devin gazed at it wistfully.

"It's a beauty. But a little annoying," said the doctor, rubbing one of his grey, bushy sideburns. "You see, it strikes on the hour."

"An annoying beauty? I love that! And I love antiques! My mom has some of my favorites."

"What are they?"

"Old prints. Of stagecoaches."

"You have an eye for the arts, Devin! Now, *that* you must take from your mom."

"Maybe. She's the art teacher."

"Speaking of teachers, how was your last report card?"

"I got all A's except for Phys Ed."

"Super! But what happened in Phys Ed?"

"Nothing. I hate sports, so I cut out on basketball a few times. I think I'll try bowling in the spring."

"Fair enough. And your Italian lessons with your next-door neighbor? How's that going?"

Devin gave the doctor a thumbs up and rattled off a sentence in Italian. "*La Signora Gentile pensa che sto bene.*"

"Impressive! But, what does that mean?"

"She thinks I'm doing good!"

"Great! Do you find it helpful at the opera? I know how much you enjoy your trips to The Met with your Drama Club."

"Yes. That's what got me thinking I should learn Italian in the first place."

"Still watching *Great Performances*?"

"Always. We never miss it."

"Why do you think the opera is so appealing to you?"

"I'm not sure…" Devin replied, eyes wandering. "The stage is like a magnet."

"Perhaps you'd like to be one of the actors or the singers?"

"Not that. But maybe work around them."

"Ah, that would be the job of a director, or manager. Something to think about in the future."

"I guess. Are we done now, Doctor?"

"We are! Grab something to read, if you like," the doctor said, pointing to a magazine rack. "It's your parents' turn next."

Outside the office, Phil and Lauren had been waiting for Devin to come out.

"How much longer do you think Devin will need therapy?" Phil asked. "It's been a while now."

"For as long as it takes," Lauren replied.

"As long as it takes for what?"

"For Devin to feel comfortable in his own skin."

"Maybe a change at home might help with that," Phil responded.

"What do you mean?"

"His routine. How many kids do you know who spend so much time watching TV with their parents?"

"There's nothing wrong with that, Phil."

"PBS?"

"He enjoys it!"

"Yes, I know… *Great Performances*."

"Don't you think that's extraordinary?"

"I'd say it's a bit unusual. Also, kids his age don't lock themselves up in their bedrooms with piles of books most adults would never touch. Isn't it time he comes out of his shell?"

"Seriously? It was us who instilled a love for books in him."

"True. But… The history of the opera? A biography of Jacques Rousseau? Henry Fielding's thoughts about this and that? Who the hell is Henry Fielding anyway, and why is Devin interested in him?"

"Because he's different, Phil. I wouldn't be surprised if one day we find out his IQ is way above average."

Just then, the office door opened and Devin emerged.

After greeting Doctor Kessler, Phil and Lauren settled into their seats and prepared to hear him deliver Devin's bi-annual assessment.

"Please help yourselves to coffee or tea before we start," the doctor said, motioning toward a modest self-service counter next to the fireplace.

"That would be lovely, thank you!" Lauren responded. She uncrossed her legs, gently pulled the bottom of her cowl neck sweater below her waist and rose from her seat.

"Phil?"

"None for me, honey. Thanks!"

"How's Devin doing these days, Doctor?" Phil asked when Lauren returned to her seat.

"Our weekly sessions continue to yield good results," the doctor began. "Devin is beginning to see things from a different perspective."

"But he's not out of the woods yet, is he?" Lauren asked.

"Not completely. But we're forging ahead. He has acquired new coping skills that are helping him deal with the sleep paralysis. Since then, he has stopped mentioning his hallucinations."

"Is he free of them?"

"Not necessarily. Though their impact is clearly diminished."

"At one point, he was convinced they were real," said Lauren.

"To him, they were!" the doctor responded. "In most cases, patients incorporate these episodic experiences into their psyches and learn to live with them as fully functional individuals."

Phil's corduroy jacket expanded as he took a deep breath. "So you're saying it's a chronic condition."

"It could be. And it could also completely disappear."

"Is there a chance it could get worse?"

"I doubt it. As I mentioned, Devin has already developed effective coping mechanisms that have allowed him to move forward."

"Good!" said Lauren with a hopeful smile. "Any specifics?"

"Absolutely!" the doctor answered. He opened a desk drawer, took out a thick file with Devin's name on the tab and pointed to it. "Devin's progress is longstanding and fully documented. Most importantly, he has already overcome much of the fear associated with his sleep paralysis. He is now fully aware this is a recurring event and knows what to expect when it happens. As a child, he didn't. So, naturally, he was frightened and traumatized by it."

Lauren sighed. "I've always suspected the source of his shyness was this trauma you speak of. Then, the taunting and teasing he suffered at school exacerbated it and caused him to withdraw even further."

"It's possible, Mrs. Sharp. These experiences in young children can often trigger a variety of subconscious responses that can result in unexpected behaviors. In Devin's case, they may have prompted him to build an imaginary fortress around him. Behind its walls, he probably felt safe and in control."

"Makes sense. And it's still there…" Lauren said, glancing at Phil. "It's what my husband calls his *shell*."

"We've been trying our best, honey," said Phil.

"Yes, we have. But if this make-believe fortress is his *safe place*, maybe we should not be so eager to nudge him to come out of it so fast," she said, with a twinge of self-reproach. "Not until he's ready."

Phil nodded.

Doctor Kessler leaned forward. "Of course! The good news is that Devin has come a long way. I've been a witness to how he gradually began replacing his fears with feelings of anticipation."

"I'm not sure I'm following you, Doctor," Phil responded. "What's this anticipation about?"

"As you're aware, Devin's sleep paralysis involves a pattern of recurring hallucinations during which he sees a sheet or a veil in a corner of his bedroom. Behind it he sees flickering lights and moving shadows."

"Yes, we know this."

"Here's the thing: the last few times he mentioned experiencing these episodes, he seemed to be developing an eagerness to see through this veil and find out who or what was behind it."

"And that's supposed to be a *good* thing?"

"Well, this means it no longer frightens him. I'd say that's an improvement!" the doctor insisted. "By the way, my theory is that his love for the opera may be related to this positive development."

"How?" Phil asked.

"I get a sense it's probably a useful tool for him. Think of the sheet or veil of Devin's hallucinations as the curtains on the stage of a theater. The curtains, unlike the veil, are always raised at the beginning of each act, so he can safely cross the invisible threshold that separates the audience from the universe of the stage that lies beyond them. The theater is a harmless, collective experience where he's not facing the unknown. It provides a way for Devin to forget himself and enter new worlds populated by characters inhabiting places and living in circumstances that are right in front of him, but completely separate from his own."

"I'll be damned. Of all things, it's the opera that's helping him."

"Yes! And, his Drama Club has become a great support network."

Phil nodded. "I know we're almost out of time. But if I may, just one more question."

"Certainly, Mr. Sharp. Go right ahead."

"When we first brought Devin to you a few years back we mentioned a concern about behavior that involved occasional dress-up games with one of our daughters, and sometimes by himself. At the time, you said it was normal."

"Yes, I recall."

"This went on for quite some time."

"For how long?"

"Oh, at least until he turned thirteen, maybe even longer."

"I see."

"He also rarely showed interest in playing with toys like trucks, footballs or GI Joes," Phil explained, then looked at Lauren. "Remember that Wild West playset model of a fort we got him for Christmas when he was seven or eight? It had plastic figures of army soldiers, cowboys and Indians."

"Yes. Of course, I remember it. He hardly ever played with it."

"Remind me please," said the doctor. "What kind of toys did Devin play with instead?"

"His sisters' toys," Lauren replied. "For a long while he seemed obsessed with two Barbie dolls that he named Johnny and Mark."

"He gave them *boys'* names?"

"He did! He insisted they were twins. He adored their long, brown hair. But he replaced their dresses with old rags until I stitched a few scraps of fabric together and made pants and shirts for them."

"He also had a model sailboat that he loved," Phil said. "He still keeps it in his bedroom."

"Well, it's great that Devin had a chance to play with a variety of toys and in multiple ways. Play is essential for children. It's one way they learn to interact with the world."

"And the dress-up games?"

"Dressing up is a common form of imaginative play. When kids dress up they create situations that encourage them to engage in problem-solving and promote the development of new vocabulary."

"At thirteen? Wasn't Devin a bit too old for that?"

"Let's not forget he has a keen interest in the theater. Costumes are an important part of it. Who knows? He may end up in that field someday."

Lauren smiled. "You're right. He might."

"Devin is a good kid! Celebrating and rewarding him for his accomplishments may be another way to encourage him to move forward. I hear he's been doing great at school and his Italian keeps getting better and better."

"Mrs. Gentile adores him. She's known him since he was little and she's been teaching him for free!" said Lauren. "Actually, we're also planning a special treat for his graduation."

"Oh?"

"A trip to London that includes a theater tour."

"That's still two years away, honey," Phil said. "And it's a family trip. We'll need to fill up our piggy bank to make that happen."

"Sounds like a wonderful idea!" the doctor said, rising from his seat. "I'm sure Devin will graduate with flying colors."

III. HER MAJESTY'S THEATER

R *epent! The End is Near!* read the placard held up by a graying woman, her eyes filled with conviction. A large wooden cross necklace hung prominently against her chest. Despite such dire warnings, Abbey's gaze remained fixed on loftier sights.

"That guy must've thought he was somethin' special!" she said, looking up.

"Who was he?" asked Paige. "Dad?"

"You girls should talk less and pay attention to our tour guide. That's Admiral Nelson," Phil replied. "He's a national hero."

"Where's Devin? I bet he could enlighten us about him," Lauren chimed in.

"He's over there," said Paige, pointing.

While Phil, Lauren, Abbey and Paige admired Nelson's Column in Trafalgar Square, Devin had ventured out on his own. A bronze sculpture of a man mounted on a horse at nearby Charing Cross had caught his eye. As he paused to read the plaque on its base, a young woman in a lavender blouse, jeans and white sneakers, approached him.

"Excuse me," she said, green eyes sparkling. "Sorry to bother you. Are you with the theater tour?"

Startled, Devin stammered. "Uh… Yes, I—I am."

"I thought I saw you on the bus. You were sitting by yourself in the back, right?"

"Yeah, I was. There's only so much I can take of my sisters' constant yammering."

"I totally get you. I like quiet. I'm Stella, by the way."

"Nice to meet you, Stella. I'm Devin."

"Cool coat of arms, eh?" she said, indicating the elaborate carvings on the stone pedestal in front of them. "And all that heavy armor on this guy. Impressive!"

"I was wondering about that…" Devin responded. "Armor, but no helmet? I mean, this guy was Charles I after all, the only English king who lost his head and the monarchy itself, all at the same time!"

"I know, right? A royal double whammy!"

Their giggles drowned in the roar of a red double-decker bus passing by.

"So, Devin, I'm guessing you're American?"

"Yes, ma'am! I'm a Yankee from Kingston, New York. But I'll be moving to the Midwest soon."

"Let me guess again. Going to school there?"

"Good call! I'll be starting at the University of Michigan in just a few days."

"Nice! I hear that's a great school."

"That's what they say. What about you? Where are you from?"

"Ottawa."

"A friendly Canuck paying a visit to Old Blighty."

Stella giggled.

"Are you in school?"

"Yes, I'm a Liberal Arts sophomore at the University of Ottawa."

"Awesome! What do you wanna do after you graduate?"

"I'm thinking my calling might be in the performing arts. I'm a bit of theater nut, you know?"

"It figures. We're on a theater tour. I was in my high school Drama Club and I love the opera, but I never thought of pursuing a career in this field. You must be super talented."

"Not really. I'd just like to be a part that scene. Have you chosen a major yet?"

"I'm working on it."

Stella glanced at her wristwatch. "We should get back to the bus. We're supposed to be leaving in five minutes."

"Oh, right. Thank you."

They headed for the bus. All around them, an urban symphony: engines revving, horns beeping and brakes screeching. The smell of exhaust fumes filled the air.

"How old are you?" Stella asked.

"I'll be eighteen in November. You?"

"I just turned nineteen."

"Here with your family?"

"Yeah, my parents. I'm an only child. They're over there," she pointed. "By Nelson's Column."

"So are mine. That column and those lions are colossal. They dwarf everything around them."

"I think that's the idea."

"My dad is the guy with the blue Yankees cap," said Devin as they drew closer. "My mom is beside him wearing sunglasses."

"Ha! Looks like they're talking to *my* parents!" Stella said. "They're the couple in khaki shorts and the maple leaf t-shirts. Are those your sisters standing there?"

"Yup. Paige and Abbey."

"They're not much older than you, are they?"

"Paige is twenty and Abbey twenty-two."

"Must be fun having siblings so close to your age. Do you all live together?"

"Not anymore. Abbey moved in with a friend last year. Paige is living in the dorms at Bard College, and I'll be moving away in a few days. Pretty soon, it'll just be my parents and Harold in the house."

"Who's Harold?"

"Our puppy," Devin answered, as they approached the tour bus. "He's a beagle."

"Aww! I love beagles! And I love that name!"

"So do I. My Mom named him after one of my favorite characters in a children's book."

"*Harold and the Purple Crayon*?"

"Yup. That's it."

"One of my favorites, too!"

Devin looked up. "Whoops! We should get moving. Everyone's in their seats already."

"Mind if I sit with you for a while?" Stella asked, before getting on the bus. "I'm enjoying our chat."

Devin blushed. "Huh… Sure!"

They boarded the bus, introduced each other to their families and took their seats.

Intrigued by Devin's new-found friend, Abbey leaned against Paige and whispered in her ear: "What's up with *that*?"

"What's up with *what*?"

"Devin and that girl."

"What about them? They just met."

"Well, they seem to have hit it off at the speed of light, haven't they?"

"They're just talking, Abbey. Chill out!"

"She's so bubbly and pretty. No jewelry and no makeup at all. Did you notice?"

"I did. But I doubt Devin cares about that."

"Why not?"

"Are you serious? He doesn't look at girls that way."

"So, what's he doing with her then?"

"I just told you! They're talking!"

After several stopovers on the City's West End and along the Strand, an avenue bustling with activity, the time for the highlights of the day finally arrived: Dinner at a historic restaurant on Fleet Street, followed by an opera at a famous theater.

By the time the bus had arrived at The Jolly Hanging Tavern & Inn, Devin's and Stella's parents had decided to share a table. Devin and Stella sat next to them and across from each other. The scene around them brimmed with a distinctive buzz: Baroque chamber music played in the background as patrons engaged in lively conversations. On the walls hung old prints and drawings of a bustling marketplace next to an imposing fortress.

"Check this out, Devin!" said Stella, reading from her paper placemat. "This joint has been around since the year 1720."

"Far out! This is 1979... so that makes it, what? Two hundred and fifty-nine years old?"

"Incredible. Did you hear the guide say that the guards and inmates from a prison nearby used to hang out in this place?"

"Yes. Strange. Apparently, they were allowed to go out. I wonder how that worked."

"I would've loved to have done a tour of that prison. Too bad it's no longer standing."

"Me too!"

After dinner, a young waiter with long sideburns and a cleft on his chin cleared the table.

"I hope you enjoyed the ginger cookies with your coffee," he said with a smile.

"We sure did!" Stella responded, glancing at the name tag above the pocket on the right side of his shirt.

"They're fresh. Baked in-house, from scratch."

"They were yummy!" Devin said, discreetly eying the waiter's toned physique.

Stella leaned forward. "Excuse me, Adam," she said, boldly addressing him by his first name. "I have a question for you, if I may."

"Sure!"

"Thanks. My friend and I were reading about the history of this tavern on the placemats and we were wondering if there might be a bit more to it."

"Like a fun ghost story or something, you know," Devin chimed in, making a scary face.

The waiter grinned. "Apparitions? No. None that I know of. But, the story goes there was a brothel upstairs."

"A brothel in a tavern?" asked Stella, eyebrows raised.

"It was a common thing in those days. Apparently, a madam by the name of Charlotte Hayes was running it. And this, while she was an inmate at a neighboring prison."

"Hayes? You're kidding. That's my last name! That just sent a shiver up my spine."

"What about the name of this place?" Devin asked. "Is there a story behind it? How can a hanging be *jolly*?"

"Well, from what I know, some of the prison wardens were not too kind to the inmates," the waiter explained. "At that time, torture before execution was rather customary in these parts, so it's quite possible that some of the condemned actually welcomed the noose at the gallows."

"Ouch… That's daaark! But thank you for the info anyway, Adam!"

"You're welcome! Enjoy the rest of your stay in London," he said as he gathered their dishes.

At the other end of the table, Abbey shot furtive glances at Devin and Stella while whispering to Paige sitting across from her.

"Tell me he's not flirting with her," she said, eyes alight.

"He's not."

"Well, I have a theory."

"What?"

"I think he's a late bloomer in the romance department."

"He's just drawn to her personality. That's all."

"So there! She's pretty and smart and he's falling for her."

Paige rolled her eyes. "You're delusional!"

The tour came to an end with a show at Her Majesty's Theater on Haymarket Street. The Sharps and the Hayeses stuck together. Devin and Stella sat together.

Stella held a playbill in her hands. "Should we take a look at this?" she asked.

Devin scoffed playfully. "Look at it?" he replied, already immersed into his. "I *study* these things!"

Stella grinned, opened her playbill and began reading. "Interesting! The name of this place keeps changing depending on the gender of the reigning monarch. It started as The Queens's Theater, then it became The King's, and now it's Her Majesty's."

"Yes. Very cool. And the performances began in 1705."

"Any thoughts about tonight's program?"

"It should be fun. *The Maid Turned Mistress* is a comic opera."

"Good," said Stella. "I've never seen one before."

"Me neither, except on TV. I also know a little from what I've read here and there. I'm kind of a geek that way."

"So, what are comic operas like?"

"They're musical spoofs that were originally performed during the intermissions. Eventually, they became so popular they took on a life of their own."

"I'm not surprised. Comedy is always popular."

"Let's hope we get some of that tonight," Devin responded as the lights dimmed and the curtains went up.

———➤☺◄———

A few days later, the Sharps had returned to the States and Devin had left for college. It was early September and the Michigan summer still hung on with brash bravado.

At the break of dawn on Devin's second day on campus, the sound of a key unlocking his dorm room door awoke him.

"Good morning!" said a lanky guy in an untucked shirt and faded jeans as he walked into the room carrying a suitcase. Somewhat befuddled, he stared at Devin sitting up in bed. "I'm Matt," he said, through long strands of blondish hair half covering his face. "Sorry to wake you. Looks like we're roommates."

"Morning!" Devin rubbed his eyes and watched Matt put down his suitcase. "I'm Devin. Need any help?"

"Huh… Nah, thanks man. I just got a couple milk crates and my stereo." He walked back out and brought them in.

"You're an early riser," Devin said, slowly getting out of bed while Matt started unpacking.

"Only when I have to. I should've been here yesterday for freshman orientation but my Volvo broke down."

"You didn't miss much," said Devin. He grabbed a pair of shorts and a t-shirt and pulled them on. "I can fill you in later, if you like."

"Sure, thanks!"

"So, you drive a Volvo. Nice!"

"It's ancient. You got wheels?"

"A Chevy Impala. I drove it from New York. Also ancient."

"Long trek. Must be in good shape if it's still running."

"So far, so good. Let's not jinx it, please!"

They both smiled.

Matt stored his milk crates filled with books and albums inside an open closet, then picked up a turntable and placed it on his desk.

"A Pioneer!" Devin blurted out. "High fidelity. That's a beauty!"

"Brand new. A gift from my parents, speakers and all. Don't worry, I won't be playing it when we're studying."

"Studying? What's that? No worries here!"

"Mind if I put one of the speakers on the top shelf of your desk? I'd be taking a bit of your space."

"Be my guest. I don't have much stuff anyway. I didn't even bring any of my albums with me. Just a few books."

"Oh yeah? What type of books?"

"The boring type, I guess. History and biographies, mostly."

"Not to me. I read all kinds of stuff. So, no albums, uh?"

"Nah. I—I *do* have plenty, though. Just not with me."

"Such as?"

"Well, that's the thing, it's chamber music, and um… the opera."

"Really? Wow!"

"Yeah, I know. That's why I didn't bring them. I don't wanna freak anyone out. But, don't get me wrong, I also like pop and rock."

"You're not freaking me out. I'm into rock, my sister likes punk, and my parents love country. Whatever floats your boat, dude!"

"Awesome! I guess I'd better jump in the shower and head for the dining commons. I don't wanna miss breakfast."

"Can I join you? I don't even know where anything is and I'm starved."

"Sure!"

A few weeks into the fall semester, Devin and Matt were still getting acquainted with each other. Lounging around in their dorm room late on a Sunday afternoon they found themselves engaged in casual conversation.

"You mentioned you write," Devin began.

"Bits and pieces. When I'm fired up."

"What's your muse?"

Matt opened a drawer, pulled out a small Ziploc bag with a few green buds in it and held it up.

"Pot? I've actually never tried it."

"You wanna?" Matt asked with an impish look on his face.

"Truth is, I've been curious about it."

Matt unzipped the bag, opened it and brought it up to Devin's nostrils.

Devin took a deep whiff. "Whoa! Pungent!"

"Good batch, man. Rare. Californian sinsemilla. No seeds." He began breaking up the buds then rolled a joint while Devin watched. "Perfect," he said, after sealing it. He flicked his lighter, lit it, took a quick hit and passed it to Devin.

Devin's lips twitched.

"Skittish?" Matt asked, sensing Devin's hesitation.

"Of course not!" Feigning resolve Devin took a drag and promptly started coughing and wheezing. Looking for relief, he grabbed a beer can from a small cooler on the floor, pulled the tab, took a gulp and wiped his mouth on his sleeve.

As Devin composed himself, Matt pulled a piece of paper from a manila folder tucked between the books inside one of his milkcrates. "Here," he said, handing the paper to Devin. "I called this one Jack in the Box. I wrote it a few months ago."

Devin held it up and read it silently.

Sometimes I wonder,
how many others
live in boxes like mine.
And in the evenings,
when I peek out,
I swear I can feel them
peeking back at me.
Then, when I sink back into my box,
I wonder
how many others have done the same,
and wondered,
and wrote this down.

M. Shultz.

"You know, I can relate to this."

"Yeah?"

A muted smile crossed Devin's face. "Sure. A clown trapped in a box. That could be me…"

"I wrote that when I was in a funk," said Matt, passing the joint back to Devin.

"An inspired funk, I'd say," Devin responded.

"I guess. There are far more powerful types of inspiration, you know…"

"Oh?"

Matt turned on the stereo, placed an album on the turntable, raised the tonearm and lowered the needle onto its outermost grooves.

"Have you read *The Teachings of Don Juan*?"

"Mm - mm," Devin replied, shaking his head.

"It's a story about a guy who finds enlightenment through the wisdom of a shaman."

"A sorcerer?"

"More like a medicine man."

"Ah…"

"So, the shaman serves this guy a brew he makes with peyote buttons."

"What's that?"

"A type of cactus."

"And then?"

"The guy drinks it and starts seeing things that make him wiser."

"Did you ever try this stuff?"

"Not me," Matt replied. "But uh, I've tried other stuff… Similar."

"Like?"

"Acid. It's pretty awesome."

"LSD?"

"Yeah."

"I read about it."

"Powerful stuff," said Matt. "Mind-warping. Some people swear they cross boundaries when tripping." Taking one last drag from the roach pinched between his thumb and index finger he held his breath and exhaled.

"What kind of boundaries?"

"They say they see things in places and times beyond our own."

Devin's eyes lit up, his mind racing.

"I could get some, if you're interested," Matt offered.

"I might." Images of the veil in his dreams flashed through Devin's head, sending waves of shivers running up his spine. "How long does a trip last?"

"A few hours."

"These are pills you pop?"

"Not pills. Blotters. Acid comes in blotters."

"What are they?"

"Tiny pieces of paper soaked in acid. Most have designs on them, like artwork."

"How do you get them?"

"Someone I know. Wanna give it a try? I could get some for next weekend."

"I guess. As long as it's just us doing it."

"Sure. It's your first time. I get it."

As the weekend rolled in, Devin and Matt walked leisurely across campus back to their dorm from a 7-Eleven. Each carried a brown bag with a six-pack of Stroh's. A cool breeze rustled the leaves as the evening sky waited for the sunset.

"Good thing we had a light dinner," Matt said. "We're in for a rollercoaster ride tonight."

"Are we?"

"It should be fun! You're not getting cold feet, are you?"

"Nah! Just asking."

"I bet you've heard about people who had bad trips."

"Yeah, I've read some stories."

"Well, you know, shit can happen to anyone who abuses any kind of substance. Even water can be lethal if you drink too much."

"Huh… Right. Except LSD is a chemical. Do you believe the rumors about the government feeding it to prisoners during the Vietnam War?"

"Could be. Who knows? Some say it's a truth serum. But all we'll do here is have some fun. Let's rock 'n' roll, eh?"

"Yeah, cool!"

After settling back in their dorm room Matt reached for his wallet and pulled out a small folded sheet of aluminum foil. He opened it and carefully lifted two tiny paper squares attached to each other by a tear-off perforation line. He pulled them apart and handed one to Devin. He popped it in his mouth and chased it with a gulp of beer.

"How long will it take before it kicks in?"

"Around twenty minutes."

Devin sat up in his bed and watched Matt roll a joint and play DJ. After a while, he glanced at his watch and looked around the room. For a moment, everything seemed anchored on terra firma. Then, a trail of color following the motions of his hands signaled something had changed… Soon, Matt's ramblings about the meaning of the Yin and Yang symbol printed on the blotters blended with the stereo music playing at half speed…

In the distance, a muffled heartbeat slowly turned into a faint sound wave softly humming its way into Devin's ears. His head dipped as he closed his eyes. A kaleidoscope of images swooped in, then quickly disappeared. Gradually, all sounds faded and deep silence took over.

Seconds later, as if suspended in a vacuum, Devin felt vertigo, suddenly finding himself hovering above a thin veil floating in the air. Under it, flickering lights chased moving shadows. Abruptly, a powerful gravitational force pulled him down into the veil below him. He plunged into it headfirst, folds whirling and spinning as they turned into a spongy rabbit hole. One last thrust hurled him into a place that looked like the backstage of some kind of playhouse, somewhere… And, he wasn't alone. Two men who looked like police officers stood next to him. By their uniforms and helmets Devin guessed they might be foreign. They seemed upset. Yelling, they slapped handcuffs on him.

Frantic attempts to make sense out of what looked to be sheer madness kept bouncing him back to the same simple questions: *Where am I? What is this?*

The men dragged him along a wide aisle between row after row of seats in what appeared to be the orchestra section of a large and magnificent theater. He resisted them as he heard himself shouting a name: "Vanneschi! Vanneschi!"

Undeterred, the men forcibly hauled him to the main entrance hall leading out to the street. A horse-drawn paddy wagon with the words 'WATCHMEN PATROL' painted on its side awaited. Before they shoved him into it, Devin quickly turned around and glanced at the name of an imposing red brick structure. A large slab of stone on the building's façade read: 'KING'S THEATER–Erected MDCCV.'

Once on the coach, Devin looked out the window. Astonished, he realized he was no longer in Michigan, or even in America…

IV. THE GOLDEN RUMP

L ooking out through the bars of a police paddy wagon, Devin swallowed hard as he took in an urban scene from another place and time. Suddenly, a strong smell of manure overwhelmed him. Passing by, there were countless carriages and stagecoaches, horses neighing and snorting, their hooves clopping on the cobblestones of a wide and busy avenue. High above, a tinge of pink on a thin streak of clouds spread across the sky.

Rows of nearly identical brick and stone terraced houses lined both sides of the road. Oil lamps hanging from iron rods at every door awaited nightfall.

For a moment, Devin's eyes shifted to the people in the street, leisurely strolling on the sidewalks and reveling in the summer sun. Awestruck, he observed clothing and hairstyles he had only seen in movies and history books.

Women wore low-necked gowns over elaborately embroidered petticoats embellished with lace and trimmed with ruffles. Most piled their hair high and carried folding fans. Metal buckles shone bright on their curved high-heeled shoes.

Men wore waistcoats, breeches, and stockings, their long hair brushed back from the forehead and tied with black ribbons at the nape of the neck. Many wore tricorns, and a few, top hats or periwigs with little curls on the sides and coated in white powder. *Actors?* Devin wondered.

Then, the wagon passed by a building that looked strangely familiar and memories came rushing in. Popping up, one after the other, were images of places Devin had seen on the trip his family took to England late in the summer of 1979. One in particular had registered with him. The tour bus had hit a traffic jam soon after leaving Trafalgar Square and had remained in the vicinity for a short while. Forced to improvise, the guide kept babbling on about an aged, tall and narrow structure. *St. Mary le Strand Church! That's it!* The name had stuck. He knew he was in London!

Devin's brief spell and visual extravaganza ended abruptly. A voice emanating from his own vocal chords stubbornly demanded to know the reason for his arrest and the wagon's destination.

"Quiet!" shouted one of the officers sitting across from him.

"Shut your trap!" barked the other.

Minutes later they arrived at the entrance of a large stone building not unlike a fortress. The wagon halted at the gatehouse. The officers yanked Devin out of it and pushed him into a small, dark, foul-smelling office.

A short middle-aged man with two chins and no neck stood beside a massive desk, his waistcoat buttons straining over his prominent abdomen. A commanding presence, he projected an air of self-confidence that seemed to cast an uncanny effect on those around him. The arresting officers and a young guard present in the room appeared conspicuously deferential toward him.

Some kind of authority... Devin speculated, watching the man adjust his periwig, a fine white powder falling from it onto his shoulders.

"Much obliged, constables!" the man said, revealing a set of stained and crooked teeth. "You have done well!" The officers bowed and stood in silence. He turned to Devin standing before him. "Ahh… Impresario! We meet at last! We were expecting you. Welcome to our humble establishment. I am Warden Thomas Bambridge. We hope you find Fleet Penitentiary to be a suitable accommodation during your residency here. Now sir, for the record, if you would kindly state your birth name, your age, and whence you hail."

Devin heard himself speak. "I believe you are already acquainted with who I am, Signore. Yet, perchance my Christian name eludes you, I am Giovanni Francis Crossa. I hail from the Duchy of Savoy and the Republic of Genoa. I first drew breath in the year of our Lord 1700."

"I see. You are aged fifty."

"Indeed I am. Now, I beseech you to expound upon the reasons that have led to my unwarranted detention."

Devin struggled to find meaning in the words he had just heard.

Giovanni? 1750? What's going on?

The Warden then proceeded to read from a parchment he lifted from his desk.

"Sir, you are hereby served official notice that you have been detained on charges of unlawful insolvency and bankruptcy, which under English law necessitates the execution of a warrant. To this end, one has been issued by order of the Magistrates Court, and signed by the Honorable Lord Henry Fielding, Justice of the Peace."

As he heard these charges, Devin felt anxiety and resentment building up within him. Casting a glance at a mirror on a wall he saw a middle-aged man with short greying brown hair, a full beard and blue eyes looking back at him. Suddenly, he sensed his consciousness slipping away, his self-awareness retreating deep into the recesses of Giovanni's mind.

Bambridge stared, arms folded. "Sir, are you listening to me? You seem distracted!"

Startled, Giovanni blinked and shook his head. "I—I *am* listening," he said, regaining full composure. "These charges are plain falsehoods! This is a charade! Who is my accuser?"

"The enforcement of our laws takes place in response to complaints to the court by victims of a crime. In your case sir, Mr. David Garrick himself, the renowned manager of The Drury Lane Theater, an honorable gentleman and a most esteemed member of society, has filed a complaint against you, in which he declares you beholden to him in the amount of £800. You may elect to reflect about a future private settlement with him, or proceed to a public trial. In the interim, you shall remain our guest here at the Fleet."

"Mr. Garrick embellishes the charges! I shall not allow my reputation to be tarnished by him! I will petition the court to have this transparent sham dismissed without further delay!"

"You may suit yourself, Impresario. In any case, I am certain you shall soon have an opportunity to confer with Mr. Garrick directly and come to a mutually convenient agreement. Meanwhile, may I recommend you collect yourself and remain calm? I assure you, we shall make every effort to provide for you, as long as you abide by our house rules."

"What *house rules* do you speak of, Signore?"

With a quick nod, the warden dismissed everyone in the room and took a seat behind his desk.

"Well sir, you see, until your case is settled, we shall need to make arrangements for your stay here. Therefore, it behooves us to arrive at a gentlemen's agreement. One based on mutual trust, that will secure your safety and comfort, in exchange for a reasonable garnishment."

"*Garnishment?*"

"Indeed. All of our residents are expected to honor a commitment fee of fifteen shillings for a fortnight. This is the rate for a solitary dwelling chamber, thrice-daily repasts, and beyond."

Setting all pretensions of gentility aside, Giovanni began yelling. "Fifteen shillings for a fortnight? You swindler! You mean to fleece me!"

Bambridge remained unruffled. "I assure you these fees amount to fair compensation for your lodgings, your daily repasts, water, blankets, candles and more." He leaned back in his seat, an imperious expression on his face as he waited for Giovanni's anger to subside.

A tense pause followed.

Finally, Giovanni spoke. "What about my lodgings? Where shall I stay?"

"If we come to an agreement, you shall be spared the Common Side...

Instead, you shall reside in a single chamber on the Master's Side of our establishment. You'll be free to come and go, mingle with others and receive visitors. Naturally, the more generous your contributions, the more privileges you shall have, Impresario."

"Whatever do you mean I shall be spared the *Common Side?* What is that?"

The Warden leaned forward, replying in a somber tone. "You do not want to know, sir. You see, the galleries there are packed full and least accommodating. It's six or eight souls to a chamber, sometimes more. Those wretched souls… May the Lord have mercy on them! Most are penniless, and so deprived of their most basic needs."

Giovanni's eyes widened, droplets of perspiration forming on his brow. Sensing weakness, the Warden carried on. "Regrettably, this is a ripe environment for jail fever and many will be pitted with it, and give up the ghost. Those who survive must rely on the sympathy of others to avert starvation."

"Christian benevolence?"

"Indeed. There is a grille built into the Farringdon Street prison wall where inmates from the Common Side beg alms from passers-by. And that's when they're not on the docks dredging the Thames. Few pay their garnishments that way, and even fewer will ever honor their larger debts. Yet, sometimes it can get worse…"

"Worse? How?"

"When the inevitable happens. When quarrels turn into fights, and fights turn into riots. Then, we have no other recourse but to march them to the dungeons."

Giovanni cringed. Moments later, the Warden had removed his cuffs and Giovanni had agreed to affix his signature on a special ledger.

Bambridge grinned complacently. "You are now committed to honor the House Rules and bear the expenses of a fortnight's lodging, your repasts, and general provisions." He then presented Giovanni with a ream of letter-sheets and a writing case holding a quill, an inkwell, a stick of sealing wax. "This comes with your privileges," he explained. "I am sure you shall find it useful."

Giovanni nodded.

"Your chamber is at ground level, just across the courtyard," the Warden continued. "A guard shall escort you."

"Obliged."

Soon after settling, Giovanni composed a short note. Before nightfall he handed it to one of the Warden's deputies. Written on its face, appeared the name and address of the intended recipient:

Francesco Vanneschi, Director
King's Theatre
Haymarket Street
London

The following day, just before noon, a knock on the door broke the stillness of Giovanni's chamber, interrupting his writing. He rose and opened the door.

"Pray excuse me, sir. You have a visitor," a guard announced. A tall and slender middle- aged man stood beside him, his long black hair in a braided pony tail.

The guard stepped aside and left.

With his chin up and chest thrust out, the man moved his right foot forward, placed his left hand on his waist, removed his tricorn and nodded cordially.

Giovanni bowed long and deeply then threw his arms around him. "Francesco! *Entra!* I am heartened by your sight!"

"I rushed to see you as soon as I received your note, Dottore!" Vanneschi responded, taking his coat off. Underneath it, a silk quilted waistcoat matched his breeches.

"Pray, allow me," said Giovanni. He took the coat and hung it on a wall peg. "Apologies. 'Tis rather stifling in here."

Both men stood facing each other.

"I brought a trunk with a few of your garments and other personal belongings," Vanneschi said. "I found it backstage, unattended. I thought it might be useful. A guard shall bring it to you presently."

"Much obliged! I meant to take it with me the last time I was there."

"Yesterday? I regret I was not on the premises. I hear you were calling for me when the watchmen apprehended you. I hope they were not too boorish."

"They were merciless! They barged in and grabbed me like a common criminal. They slapped handcuffs on me, dragged me out on the street and tossed me into their wagon."

"'Tis a shame you had to bear such indignity. The Warden apprised me of your predicament on my way in."

"I could never have imagined! Twelvemonths twice past when the two of us met in Genoa, all I hoped for was a new opportunity for my troupe here in England. Instead, I now find myself facing this absurd and most pernicious circumstance."

"Quite right. At the time, we were eager to explore new ventures. As for me, I had hoped that by bringing you and your troupe here I'd be ushering in a fresh new style of opera to the London stage. And begetting financial success to us both. Alas, our business, the theater, is never easy. Especially at these trying times, when foreign impresarios like us are not always welcome in these parts."

Giovanni sighed. "My folly. I confess. I allowed myself to be ensnared by the allure of the stage." He cast a downward look as he preened his moustache. "I could not resist the prospect of performing at a major venue while ensuring a fair and steady sustenance for my faithful players."

"Justifiably so. The enticement was significant. The contract you signed under my auspices guaranteed your company a series of engagements at none other than the King's Theater. Nothing to scoff at!"

"Yet, behold where it's got me... On reflection, perhaps I should have stayed at home. If I had, I'd be merry and free, travelling from town to town with my troupe, my beloved *Commedia dell'Arte*, and would not find myself in this quagmire."

"Oh, come now! Your success staging your burlettas was marginal. I offered you a chance to turn *Opera Buffa*, barely known here in England at the time, into a new sensation. Yet—"

"—yet, we could hardly compete with *Opera Seria*, which even now continues to be all the rage," Giovanni retorted. "'Tis a fact that traditional operas have always outshone their stunted comic cousins, and their disparate budgets have everything to do with it."

"Not entirely, Dottore. For the past nine years I have been fairly successful as a manager and director of the King's Theater, often with less than adequate resources."

"Well, you've had Lord Middlesex at your side, the proprietor of the theater, a high-ranking member of the English nobility and someone close to the Royal House of Hanover."

"I freely admit I am beholden to His Lordship. After all, it was he who brought me to London."

"I appreciate your candor, Francesco. I imagine my current situation must not be an easy pill for His Lordship to swallow."

Vanneschi took a deep breath. "Nor is it for me. Your predicament has become a rather public affair since the news of your detention and confinement was published in the dailies. A serious setback to the theater's reputation at this point could hardly be averted. There is even a chance that our royal benefactors may abandon us."

"I had no notion my departure would cause such a disruption."

"Alas, it has. All our prior disputes seem miniscule in comparison."

A knock on the door made them pause. Giovanni answered.

A young guard with long sideburns and a cleft on his chin stood in the doorway with a trunk at his feet.

Hmm… He bears a striking resemblance… Giovanni thought. *But, to whom?*

"For you, sir," he said. "Pray excuse the interruption."

"Obliged," Giovanni responded. "You may set it at the foot of my bedstead."

The guard stepped into the chamber.

"What is your birth name, officer?" Giovanni asked. "I have seen you a few times now."

"Adam Hawley, sir. Your servant."

Giovanni reached for a coin in a small pocket in his waistcoat. "Here's a farthing, Hawley," he said, handing it to him. The guard took it with a smile.

"May I offer to fetch coffee and the broadsheets in the morning, sir? I do this for the Warden and for others on the Master's Side."

"Aye. Eight o'clock will do."

"Glad to be of service. I shall be here at eight. A good evening to you, sir!"

"And to you!"

Hawley bowed and exited the chamber.

Giovanni cast a glance at the trunk by his bed. "I am much obliged to you, Francesco." Vanneschi nodded slightly.

"Should I wet a pot of tea?"

"Not for me."

"Pray let us sit by the casement then, and return to our discussion."

They sat opposite each other at a small table adjacent to a window with a view of the prison's vast courtyard.

"You and I are known for being bold," Giovanni continued. "Perhaps, in bygone days, this was the root of our trifling disagreements."

"Our differences were private, Dottore. And limited to the inner workings of our business: the cost of production, the actors' wages, the setup of certain acts, and the inclusion or exclusion of specific scenes."

"We were bound together in our venture," said Giovanni. "In the end, we always found common ground."

"Maybe then. Alas, at present your arrest is a public embarrassment."

"I must impress upon you, Francesco, I fully intend to clear my name!"

"I have every faith in you. And yet I confess. I wonder about the manner in which you intend to accomplish such a feat. Your letter alluded to a need for assistance."

"A thousand guineas would do. With that, I could settle with Mr. Garrick and be done with this most undeserving humiliation. I assure you, I would promptly reimburse you. My family in Genoa has the means. Of course, an expeditious return of my troupe to the King's Theater, under a new contract, would also permit me to make you whole, and quicker."

"One thousand guineas? That is out of the question! You must realize, Dottore, that your confinement places me in a somewhat uncomfortable position with His Lordship."

Giovanni frowned. "Pray enlighten me as to how my current personal affairs involve Lord Middlesex."

"Your present circumstances indeed affect his public image, and his connections to the Crown. Furthermore, your liabilities have cost him dearly already."

"Your words confound me, Francesco. I am a proprietor of a serious business. I shall not default."

"I trust your intentions are noble. Yet, at this time, I can only offer to defray the cost of your expenses for a fortnight. After that, I cannot guarantee any further allowances. As regards your return to the theater, lest you forget, you were banned since Prince William, the Duke of Cumberland, shuttered us, due to your impertinence."

"*My* impertinence?"

"Indeed! Have you forgotten your actions were the cause of our misfortune? Who in his right mind would insist on poking fun at the King in his son's presence and expect nothing would come of it?"

"It appears your memories do not match mine, Francesco."

"Do they not? Then, perhaps we should examine them further. Prince William was in the royal box on the night he witnessed a string of tasteless jokes play out on stage about his father, King George II."

"That much is true."

"Your troupe ridiculed His Majesty with lines about his ample hindquarters and his chronic flatulence. Then, as if that wasn't enough, one of your actresses playing the role of the King's mistress pretended to abet him with an enema!"

"Also, veritable," said Giovanni. "Save for one detail: We did not pen the lines of that libretto."

"The Golden Rump. You claimed it was anonymous and I believed you. I still do."

"Yet, in your eyes I was accountable."

"Well, was it not you who insisted this scene be a part of the act despite my doubts? Alas, I yielded, and to what atrocious end! You must recall how it triggered the audience's convulsive laughter and the duke's deep consternation."

"I do."

"What followed was quite the spectacle. The duke and his entire entourage rose from their seats for everyone to see and made an abrupt exit."

"Yes, I was a witness to that."

"Your lack of foresight caused our theater's reputation and its treasury to take a heavy loss. The next day, as you well know, we received the gravest of tidings: A letter from the Palace withdrawing their patronage and an order from the Court to shut us down."

"You forget I had no prior knowledge the duke would be attending the performance on that ill-fated night. The joy of laughter and amusement were my sole desires!"

"You defied the protocols and made us look like fools by insulting the King and embarrassing Prince William, one of our theater's greatest benefactors and a national hero."

"Prince William, a hero?"

"Quite right! You must recall that just four years past, in the spring of 1746, Prince William defeated the Scots and their allies at the Battle of Culloden. That alone made him immensely popular."

"I was not in this country at the time," said Giovanni. "Perhaps the newssheets I read when I was still at home misled me."

"How do you mean?"

"The Prince's status as a hero may be true here in England, but elsewhere… Have you ever wondered what the Scots think of him after Culloden? There must be a reason they call him the *butcher of Cumberland*."

"That should not be a matter of concern to us. We came here to try our fortunes, not to become embroiled in domestic squabbles. Moreover, we should never forget we are Catholics in a Protestant land."

Giovanni reached deep into his breeches' pocket and pulled out his snuffbox. He opened it, took a generous pinch of the brown grainy stuff from it, carefully slid his index finger off his thumb, brought it up to his nostrils and inhaled it.

"Lord Middlesex was furious!" Vanneschi carried on. "We could have lost it all! Had it not been for our appeals to Genoa's Ambassador to intercede with the Crown on our behalf, we might've never managed to get the theater re-opened."

"'Tis all true," Giovanni responded. "In the end, it was our mutual acquaintance, our compatriot and brother in our faith, the *ambasciatore* Renato Azzoni, who graciously agreed to reach out to the lovely *Principessa* and plead with her to hear our case."

"Indeed, that was the case, Dottore. The Ambassador and Princess Amelia were our saviors. And in barely a fortnight, we were back in business."

"*You* were. My troupe was banned."

Vanneschi shrugged. "His Lordship wouldn't see it any other way."

"I know. I was cast out in the cold."

"Yet, you survived."

"Only just. My only recourse was to borrow. That is how fate brought me to Mr. Garrick and then, this wretched place." He took out his snuffbox and helped himself to another pinch.

"I can see that, Dottore. Yet, I am not sure there is anything else that I could do."

"Perhaps there is…" said Giovanni. "I believe the Ambassador may be acquainted with my dear cousin Niccolo in Genoa, a person of means and influence."

"Say no more. You fancy *me* acting as your liaison to the Ambassador in hopes that he relays your current circumstances to your kinsman."

"If you would be disposed to oblige," Giovanni pleaded, "my cousin could render great assistance in hastening my release."

"I suppose I *could* do this, Dottore. I might even endeavor to procure a respectable barrister for you. Your legal encumbrances certainly demand one. However, I would only do this under certain conditions."

Giovanni leaned in, eyes alight. "Yes?"

"You must vow to never attempt to return to the London stage. Everyone is aware it was me who brought you here, and my reputation has suffered dearly as a result. I can hardly afford any more incidents involving you."

"My word of honor!"

"Then I shall hold you to it."

"You have my undying gratitude, Francesco!"

Both men rose and bid each other goodbye.

V. A PERSON OF CONSEQUENCE

B ent over a white basin set on a modest cabinet, Giovanni washed his face, picked up a towel and dried himself. After salting his teeth, he rinsed, combed his hair and sat on his bed. Glancing at a pile of candle stubs inside a pail by the hearth, he pondered. *Has it really been a week? Feels like a century...* He looked up and out of his chamber window and saw a light mist floating in the air. Beyond it, the sun rose steadily in a pink haze of clouds. It was early morning on the seventh day of his confinement at the Fleet.

Suddenly, a knock on the door startled him. *Hawley,* he figured. The young keeper guard had been fetching coffee for him every morning. He rose, put on a robe, and dashed to answer. An older gentleman stood before him, stooping slightly, a wooden walking cane with a fancy silver knob in one hand and a newssheet in the other. *A person of consequence,* Giovanni reckoned by the looks of the gentleman's fine garments, his fancy periwig and a gold ring with a large oval onyx on his left index finger. *Someone from the embassy, perhaps? Odd... He comes without an escort.*

The man bowed. "A good morrow to you, sir. Henry Fielding, your humble servant."

"And I, yours, Signore. I am Giovanni Crossa. Pray, pardon my appearance." He motioned for Fielding to come into his chamber.

Fielding stepped in. "Pardon *me*, sir! I have come unannounced and in the midst of your morning routine."

"Pay no mind. I see the Warden sent you by yourself."

"I know my way around. I visit on occasion."

"Fielding, you said? The name sounds familiar. Are you a court officer bearing news from Ambassador Azzoni?"

"Uh... No. I am here on my own accord. I am a barrister by profession and in the service of the court."

"I see. Signor Vanneschi entreated you to lend your counsel to me in matters concerning my welfare."

"I assure you, no one had a say in this."

"What is your business, then? To what purpose do I owe the pleasure of your visit?"

Fielding handed Giovanni a week-old copy of the police section of *The London Evening Post.*

Giovanni held it up and read the headline: "Italian Opera Impresario Goes to Gaol."

"As soon as I chanced upon this I took the notion that I might be of service to you," Fielding said, pointing to the paper.

"I never expected my personal affairs would ever come to be so very public," Giovanni responded.

"You've been in the public eye for quite some time now, Impresario."

"Aye… this past while has been a rather unusual time from what I am accustomed," Giovanni said. He pulled one of two chairs by the fireplace and offered it to Fielding.

They sat and faced each other.

"What is it in particular that appeals to you about my case, Signore?"

"This goes well beyond the particulars of your case, sir. For one, the new style of opera you brought to the King's Theater has not gone unnoticed. I have attended a few of your company's performances and I happen to admire your satirical prowess. There's courage in poking fun at the rich and the powerful."

"You say you admire me, Signore. Yet you allude to a most unfortunate occurrence that did not do me or my troupe any justice. I never intended to cause such an uproar. My company aims at providing a light diversion to the public. We meant no offense."

"Verily. Yet, you must agree that oftentimes intentions and actions are at odds with each other. Take *Orazio*, for instance, one of your company's most popular productions. Who could ever imagine such a bewildering last scene? An aspiring young singer and her music teacher, both innocents full of good intentions, wind up peddling their souls to a crook. And to what end? Their ambitions were nothing but illusions."

"I suppose so. I never paid much mind to it. In any case, you say you are a barrister?"

"Indeed, I am a servant of the law but also a brother of the quill. As a playwright I have penned a few political satires which I admit were savagely critical of our former prime minister, Sir Robert Walpole, may he rest in peace."

"You dared mock a prime minister, Signore?"

Fielding smiled. "Just as you dared mock a king on a public stage, sir. This may come as a surprise to you, but your case may be affected by one of my past actions."

"Whatever do you mean?"

"If your case goes to trial, the court's judgment may be tainted by your involvement in the King's Theater closure of a few years ago. After all, 'twas your company that staged *The Golden Rump*, was it not?"

"Aye. Indeed, that was the title of the libretto where I lifted the idea for the scene. 'Twas an anonymous pamphlet I purchased in the street."

"I believe you!"

"You do?"

"I *know* you did not author it."

"You seem so certain… How did you come to know this?"

"Because *I* am the person who penned it."

"*You*, Signore, wrote *The Golden Rump?*"

"I did. This is the very reason that brings me here today. Had you not staged that scene, the Palace would not have shuttered the theater, you would not have become an outcast and subsequently beholden to Mr. Garrick for accepting his offer for a loan."

"It appears you are aware of Mr. Garrick's role in this affair."

"I am well acquainted with your creditor. However, the circumstances surrounding this *affair*, as you term it, extend far back into the annals of time. Long before either you or he became entangled with it."

"I am not sure what you mean, Signore."

"You were not in this country yet when in 1737, the Theatrical Licensing Act, a most tyrannical law, was passed as a result of my criticism of Sir Walpole. Once the law came into being, political satire on the stage became virtually impossible, and playwrights like myself were viewed as suspect."

"What did you do then?"

"I gave up writing and became a barrister."

"You bailed out?" Giovanni asked, taking a pinch from his snuffbox.

"Far from it! My work on behalf of the poor and the social rejects has endured. I have long held that social inequities are the root of all evil. Every good Christian should manifest compassion for these forlorn souls who dwell outside the common flow, and endeavor to bring them into the embrace of the community."

"I see now… You think I am a social reject."

"Not so. Yet, here you are, sir, bankrupt and presently in jail."

"A bold statement from someone who knows so little of me."

Quiet tension ensued. Then, a knock on the door broke the silence.

"Compliments from Warden Bambridge," Hawley said, as soon as Giovanni appeared at the door. He held a tray with a shining silver coffeepot, two porcelain cups set on their saucers and a small dish with two gingerbread biscuits.

Extravagant comforts for an inmate... Giovanni thought, gesturing for Hawley to place the tray on the table.

Eyeing the biscuits, Fielding leaned forward. "Very nice, indeed," he said.

Hawley smiled. "Freshly baked."

"Obliged," said Giovanni.

Hawley bowed and left.

Fielding poured coffee into Giovanni's cup and then his own. "Pray forgive my forwardness, sir. I did not mean to be offhand with my comments about your present quandaries. I happen to be a self-made man with a lifetime of troubles and tribulations of my own."

"In what manner do you mean, Signore?"

"Where should I begin? As a young man I was accused of trying to abduct my cousin Sarah while she was on her way to church. This was a cheap fib made up by her father, my uncle, a morally corrupt man who had done her wrong in the way of touching her intimately. Then my dear first wife, Georgina, died after ten years of blissful marriage. Three years later I found love again in my most precious sweetheart, my second wife Mary. For this, I was condemned by the hypocrites, for she had been my maidservant and was with child at the time of our wedding."

"Two-faced buffoons!" said Giovanni.

Fielding took a bite from a biscuit and savored it. "Mmm! Delightful!" he said, lifting his coffee cup. He took a swig and carried on as Giovanni listened intently. "All of this commotion and no letup, for only a few years ago I penned a number of short pieces I called *The Female Husband* about a woman named Mary Hamilton, who tried to pass for a man in order to marry the woman she loved. Vilified by public opinion for it, she was prosecuted for the crime of deception, found guilty and sent to jail."

"Wherefore such a harsh penalty?" Giovanni asked, transfixed by Fielding's words. "Quite right. 'Twas clearly unwarranted. Love was her crime! The very reason I wrote about it in the first place. Anonymously, of course, like nearly everything I wrote during that period. Alas, someone found me out, and again, I became the bullseye for the double dealers' rage. Nonetheless, I have not once waivered in my commitment to come to those in need and offer them a respite."

"A noble stance, indeed."

"A lifelong cause! Even now, afflicted as I am, with gout and asthma, I persevere."

"You must be facing a rough go of it. Two ailments in the same stroke."

"That won't deter me."

"I marvel at your resolve. But why cast your sight upon me, Signore? You hold but a scanty acquaintance with my character."

"And yet, I am aware of plenty. If only I could reassure you that my intentions are honorable."

Giovanni looked askance. "Then perhaps you might care to shed some light on the nature of your acquaintance with Mr. Garrick."

"Certainly. He and I were never close associates. I made his acquaintance when he was an aspiring writer and an actor, long before he rose to prominence and wealth. At that time, he was far from being the object of so much adulation as he is today."

"Mr. Garrick is not the person he purports himself to be," Giovanni said. "There is a darker side to him that goes beyond all his conceit and affectation."

"Pray tell! I am not aware of it."

"'Twas he, who during the brief closure of the King's Theater, entreated me to join him in a limited engagement at The Drury Lane Theater, where he is the director."

"And you readily accepted, did you not?"

"I had no source of revenue, Signore! He made an offer I could not refuse."

"What kind of offer?"

"A substantial sum in the manner of a loan meant to defray the considerable cost of production. In hindsight, it was foolhardy of me to accept it. I should have known better."

"What do you mean?"

"I had misgivings. I feared some oddi might be afoot behind such unexpected kindness."

"You had qualms about a man who granted you a loan intended to save you from financial ruin?"

"His true intention was to bankrupt me and steal my troupe!"

"That sounds implausible. Why would he do that?"

"He aimed to throw a double punch at me and my compatriot, Signor Vanneschi, the King's Theater manager. We were his competition."

"How did you come to this conclusion?"

"His scheme became evident soon after the deal was done. He set out on a brazen campaign to publicly defame me while privately endeavoring to recruit my actors and my singers."

Fielding rubbed his temple. "Clearly, an unfriendly gesture on his part, but not at all unlawful. Now, with regards to the loan you took from him, I expect you signed a promissory note."

"Naturally. Neither Mr. Garrick nor I would have had it any other way. However, the interest he claims is vastly overblown."

"You shall have to prove this in court."

"That is my intent, Signore."

"All the same, your case won't be dismissed, and you shall not regain your freedom until you cancel your debt with Mr. Garrick."

"I gather. Yet, no settlement is possible before I hear from my family in Genoa."

"Then, it behooves you to become acquainted with the basics of how our justice system runs."

"Pray tell. I entreat you."

"Were you aware that in England a man can be made bankrupt by a declaration of a person claiming to be his creditor, and that the same person can act as the prosecutor?"

"I was not."

"Once charges are filed, the petitioner can present evidence to a grand jury and, if the charges are found to be credible, the case then goes to trial, unless bargaining between the parties leads to a settlement."

"Do most cases end in a trial?"

"Just the opposite, sir. Trials can be onerous. Everyone endeavors to avoid them. Under normal circumstances some reparation in coin or kind offered by the accused himself is agreed upon and all charges are promptly dismissed."

Giovanni heaved a deep sigh. "I see. Then, it stands to reason a lack of coin on the part of a defendant would bring about a trial."

Fielding nodded. "That would be an accurate assessment. Nonetheless, even during the course of a trial, a defendant like yourself could petition the Court to have his case postponed or dismissed. In your particular situation, even *before* the trial is set to begin, a deferral might be possible, perhaps for a few days. This would give you a chance to procure the financial help you require from your family in Genoa."

"What if I could not?"

"If you had no financial resources, then your accuser could take all your earthly possessions and leave you with nothing. Only after making your creditor whole would you be eligible to be released."

Giovanni stared at a wall. Pale and silent, the awareness of his predicament had finally sunk in.

"Bear in mind, sir," Fielding continued, "As a defendant, you have no right to object. Unless you have committed a felony by concealing your assets, or have friends or family that could support you, there isn't much you could do."

"I am concealing nothing, Signore! While I acknowledge I have an obligation to my accuser, this in no way compares to what he owes *me*!"

"How is Mr. Garrick indebted to you?"

"He took my troupe! That was how I earned a living!"

"Well, Impresario, did you really believe the members of your troupe would remain loyal to you even when you were unable to honor their wages? They may not have intended to desert you, but at the end of the day, everyone needs to make ends meet. 'Tis not unreasonable to assume that if Mr. Garrick offered them employment, they might not have been able to refuse it."

Giovanni shook his head. "I suppose you are right. My choice is plain. Either I acquiesce to Mr. Garrick's demands or bear the consequences. Alas, I do not expect to hear from my family for at least another week or a fortnight."

"I am fully aware of your dilemma," Fielding responded. "It appears to me that, at this point in time, petitioning the court for a deferral of your trial might be a most prudent course of action."

A slight nod from Giovanni signaled his approval.

"Good! Then, with your consent, I shall ensure a petition is entered on your behalf."

"Will you send word of the outcome?"

"Of course. I shall also speak to the Warden on my way out and appeal for his grace."

"Your kindness shall not be forgotten, Signore!"

Fielding picked up the copy of the newssheet he had brought with him, bowed, and headed for the Gate House.

"Your Lordship, how did you fare with the Impresario?" Bambridge inquired, as Fielding entered his office.

"Better than I expected," Fielding replied. "My goal is now fulfilled. The Palace will be pleased to hear he is in good health and spirits, and has been fully apprised of his rights. His safety and welfare are in the interest of His Majesty's government and the Crown. As I am sure you are aware, the Republic of Genoa's Ambassador is mediating in this affair. I am certain His Excellency will soon procure the funds necessary for his release."

Bambridge nodded.

"As previously agreed," Fielding continued, "you shall house the

Impresario in the Master's Side quarters at all times while he awaits to hear from his family. I expect there shall be no *pressure* applied to him at any time or for any reason. Are we clear on this, sir?"

Bambridge flushed, jaws tightening. *How audacious! My wardenship, my establishment, my pocket. Yet, he makes demands to protect this bankrupt Papist foreigner!*

"Sir?"

"Of course, my lord! I grasp your meaning."

"Moreover, be aware Mr. Garrick is fully acquainted with these particularly trying circumstances and is prepared to exercise patience."

"I assure you, my lord! The Impresario will be safe here, belly full and merry."

The Warden and the magistrate bowed to each other.

Fielding exited and boarded his carriage waiting at the door.

VI. THE DUNGEONS

A sudden gust blew Giovanni's tricorn as he strolled briskly through the prison courtyard. He dashed after it, picked it up, fastened it back on his head and kept on walking. Moments earlier, the Warden had summoned him.

The Lord has heard my prayers! Assuming help from his family had finally arrived, Giovanni imagined he would soon regain his freedom. As he drew close to the Gate House, warbling sounds seeping through the fortress walls caught his attention. *Swallows nesting by the Thames,* he figured. He paused and stared at the ramparts, his face shining in the morning sun.

They feed on insects, seaweed and fish, a voice whispered within him...

"Good morrow, sir!" Hawley called. "Such luck to chance upon you!"

Jolted, Giovanni gasped. "Apologies! My thoughts were wayward."

"I hope you're well and rested."

"I am. Though I admit that now and then I am afflicted by most peculiar visions that stir me up at night."

"Apparitions?"

"No, nothing sinister. Alas," Giovanni sighed, "sometimes I feel a tear in my mind, as if my head was split."

"Pray, forgive me," said Hawley, eyes lowered. "Pay no mind to my imprudence."

"Not at all. I know you mean well."

"I hear the warden awaits you."

"Aye."

"I shall not keep you then. Good day to you, sir!"

"And to you."

The door to the Warden's office was wide open. Giovanni breathed deeply and stepped in. He found Bambridge alone, writing at his desk. "Good morning, Signore!" he said, tipping his tricorn. "You sent for me."

Bambridge looked up. "Aye. 'Tis nearly a fortnight since the day of your arrival, Impresario. I trust our hospitality hath met with your approval."

"I have no gripe or grievance."

"Then, I suppose you are prepared to retain your lodging privileges."

"Uh… No news from the embassy yet?"

Bambridge scoffed. "Not a word."

"I am confident sufficient coin is on its way by now to cover my expenses."

"What proof of that can you offer?"

Giovanni handed him a letter.

"I see. From Vanneschi, your comrade from the theater," the Warden said, setting it aside. "I am familiar with its contents."

"I thought you might be. The seal was broken when it reached me."

"No need to be alarmed. All letters coming in and out are routinely sorted as a precautionary measure."

"Then, you are aware that Vanneschi has reached out to the Ambassador."

"Which in no way alters your arrangements here. At least, not for the time being."

"I assure you. My family shall deliver."

"Words are only words, Impresario. And I cannot run this establishment by words alone."

"Patience, Signore. I beseech you. The court—"

Bambridge's face soured. "—I've heard enough! I am aware the court has agreed to a deferment of your trial by ten working days. As for your living arrangements, should your financial situation remain unchanged, you shall be transferred immediately and will adhere to the rule of chummage."

"I have no notion what you are alluding to."

"Nothing that you could not bear."

"My preference would be—"

"*Your* preference? Clearly, this must be your first time in an English jail."

"My first and last, I pray," Giovanni responded, crossing himself.

"I imagined as much. Trust me, Providence has been on your side."

"Pardon me?"

"Have you not taken notice? This is no ordinary jail."

"I profess to know nothing about it."

"How could you? You keep to your chamber at all times."

"I pass the time reading the broadsheets and writing to my colleagues."

"I am mindful of it. You've had paper, ink, candles and every meal delivered to you since you set foot here. Not to mention exorbitant quantities of snuff. Your purveyor, someone by the name of Matthew Shultz has become a frequent caller."

"A true gentleman, indeed. I value his loyalty and constancy."

"You must realize these extravagant dispensations have been appended to your balance sheet, and shall not be extended if you are transferred."

Giovanni remained silent.

"Perhaps I could take a moment to enlighten you as to the true nature of life within these walls, Impresario. This may afford you a chance to see for yourself how very privileged you are. Come along!" The Warden walked out of the office followed by Giovanni.

"You must be aware that these humble abodes are intended for those unable or unwilling to discharge their debts," said the Warden, as the two men walked side by side across the courtyard. "No one leaves here until they have honored all their obligations. And that can take a while."

"Save for cases when the court intercedes to expedite the process, I would hope," Giovanni responded.

"By my knowledge, no court has ever interceded for anyone in a threadbare coat with empty pockets. In truth, few fated to the galleries in the Common Side could ever hope for such indulgence. By the by, the court is also charged with appointing wardenships like mine," the Warden continued.

"I suppose it also compensates you for your services, Signore."

"Nothing could be further from the truth. The court rarely makes disbursements to a warden."

"You mean you carry out your duties *ad honorem?*"

Bambridge chuckled. "You jest! Wardenships are bought and sold. Leased, if you will. The appointments from the court go to the highest bidders."

"I see. The Office of the Warden is your property."

"For all means and purposes, it is. And this penitentiary, my business venture. Mind you, running it is never easy. My earnings come through fees and garnishes collected from people who claim to be insolvent. A rather fiddly task… Then, of course, I am accountable for compensations to my deputies: the clerks, the turnkeys, the keeper guards and the night-watches. All fledglings in my nest with their beaks constantly open."

"I had no notion," said Giovanni.

Bambridge stopped by an open door. "This is the wash-house," he said. "The first of our sojourns."

They stepped into a large chamber and found six young women washing, rinsing and folding, a heap of cloths and garments by their side. Seeing the Warden come in they stopped at once and bowed.

"Pray excuse us," said the Warden. "Just passing by." A quick hand motion from him signaled them to resume their chores.

In silence, the two men watched the scene: A long wooden table and two deep metal washtubs made for three work stations. Scrubbing boards in hand and coppers filled with boiling water by their side, a pair of women washed, another pair rinsed, and a third couple stood at the table and folded dried linens that had been hanging from lines in the sun.

Leaning on Giovanni, Bambridge spoke quietly. "These wenches are also in my service," he said, his foul breath blowing on Giovanni's face.

Feigning a cough, Giovanni winced and turned his head.

"Without them, pests would be feasting on us all," Bambridge continued.

Giovanni nodded. "They are a Godsend, Signore."

"And quite the bargain!" whispered the Warden, starting for the exit. "They also make soap from ashes, oil, salt and tallow."

Giovanni followed the Warden back into the courtyard.

A few feet away they came across another open door. They stepped in and found themselves inside a chamber devoid of any occupants. Tables and chairs scattered throughout, a faint aroma of malt and hops in the air.

"This is the alehouse," said Bambridge as he and Giovanni surveyed the room. "The keeper must be in the cellar. Patrons don't come in till noon."

"Inmates?"

"Everyone with coin is welcome, Impresario. Same goes for the coffeehouse, the common kitchen and the chapel. And for a fair price, there's the infirmary, where the apothecary can dispense tinctures, potions and herbs to treat all kinds of ailments."

"Most helpful, indeed. I shall keep this in mind, Signore."

After a few more stops, Bambridge pointed to a nondescript entrance in a corner between the gun room and the Gate House. He walked up to it and pulled the door open. They entered a small antechamber. Mounted on a bracket on the wall, a small wrought iron oil lamp shed a dim light on the opening to a steep, spiral stairway.

"One last call," said the Warden, carefully removing the lamp from the holder.

"A stowage chamber, I presume?"

"In a manner of speaking…" the Warden replied.

Before beginning their descent, Giovanni glanced down at the slightly uneven stone steps on the narrow stairway. "An impressive fortress, this is," he said. "A world within itself. How many souls do you reckon make their home here?"

Bambridge paused. The lamp in his hand cast a tenuous light on his face in the midst of the encroaching gloom. "Three hundred by my last count," he answered.

"That many."

"And often even more. Some bring their families, you see."

"To stay?"

"Sometimes for weeks and months. But then, they come and go."

"The residents as well?"

"Indeed. Everyone in the Master's Side can step outside the premises. If only for a day, and always for a fee. Though, many choose to stay. You see, wrestling in the courtyard, playing tennis, ninepins, billiards and more, is altogether free."

"Remarkable."

"Oh, and then, if so inclined, some will indulge in the pleasures of the flesh."

"I beg your pardon?"

"The ladies of the night are a much-needed diversion."

"Here?"

"And in the taverns nearby. Even the clergymen swear by the joys and delights of their company." He turned around and started down the stairway.

"I would never have thought that men of the cloth were lodging here," Giovanni said, following Bambridge into the darkness.

"Are you taken aback? They are among some of our most sought-after residents."

"By whom?"

"By everyone! You see, their outstanding financial obligations do not preclude them from practicing their trade."

"How? Do they say mass and hear confessions at the chapel?"

"They do. And at a handsome profit! Moreover, young couples oft-times seek them out to tie the knot of wedlock. What about you, Impresario? Will *you* need one of them to marry you?"

"I'm a widower, Signore."

"Was it recent, Impresario, your wife going to her reward?"

"Five years ago. From the smallpox. Since then, I have sworn off love and marriage."

"Offspring?"

"Twins, Gianni and Marco. All grown up now. They sailed for the Spanish colonies in the South Atlantic long before the Almighty took their mother."

"Ah, spawn… They stick like glue, and for so long! You must be glad you're rid of them."

"Quite the contrary, Signore. I long to see them. I have visions of them on board the sail ship that took them away," Giovanni said, eyes glistening. "Their long, curly brown hair, flying in the ocean breeze."

"Comforting and yet unsettling for you, I suppose. Let us move onward now, shall we?"

Lost in his thoughts, Giovanni followed the Warden silently as they continued to descend lower and lower.

"We're close now," the Warden announced as they approached the bottom of the stairway.

Giovanni glanced at the shadows on the walls escorting them along as they stepped into what seemed to be a subterranean cavern. Clanking and rattling could be heard in the distance. *Irons dragging on the ground?*

As they approached a massive wooden padlocked gate, a blend of muffled whispers, whimpers and moans filtered through the cracks.

The Warden's keys jangled as he unlocked the gate. Suddenly, sharp and jarring sounds of whips lashing, wailing and screaming collided with the creaking gate as Bambridge slowly pushed it open.

A powerful waft of nauseating smells assaulted Giovanni's nostrils. Instantly repulsed, he covered his nose and mouth with both his hands. *Vile!* he thought. *The bowels of hell!*

"Here we are, Impresario! Welcome to the dungeons!"

"What is this awful stench, Signore?"

"The stink of rotten souls!" Bambridge replied. His eyes then quickly shifted toward a narrow corridor ahead. "Here's where we keep the miscreants who persist in breaking the House Rules. So that they may reflect on their sins." Leading the way, he advanced into the entrails of a labyrinth of tiny cells, all damp and dark, some empty.

Giovanni peered into one of the cells. "The black streaks on the walls… What are they?"

"Blood stains. Wild beasts must be tamed by the whip, which ere long, shall draw blood."

"How many are confined here?"

"A dozen. Sometimes more. Two to a cell, depending…"

"Ill-aired cells…" Giovanni said, speaking through his hands. "No casements, doors, washbasins or latrines. The hay on the ground must be for bedding, I presume. How can anyone endure this, Signore?"

"Endurance is *their* riddle to solve, not mine, Impresario. And yes, 'tis true, there's no way in or out but through a hatch."

"A hatch? Where?"

"Look up! There's one in every cell. On the ceiling. The guards use ropes to lower the beasts in. Then hoist their bodies out when—"

"—Lord Almighty! What did these hapless souls do to meet such awful end?"

"Chronic thievery, murder, mutiny and attempting to abscond, among others."

"I see. Egregious transgressions, indeed," Giovanni responded, a hint of apprehension emerging in his voice.

"Pray come along now, sir. There is a place I would like to acquaint you with."

"What is it?"

"The Strong Room, a most particular cell reserved for the unrepentant," the Warden explained, as they reached the last cell at the end of the corridor. Standing in front of it, they peered down through the bars at a large pit with a rack set up at its center. Surrounding it, barrels replete with thumbscrews, spikes, long nails, whips and more. In a corner, a cage filled with squeaking rats.

Next to the pit two hooded men lowered an inmate, bruised and bloodied, from a pair of manacles attached to a wall.

"That one is going straight to the rack," Bambridge said, leaning forward to get a better view. "We'll see how long he lasts…"

As the wails and screams began, Giovanni turned away from the grisly scene and faced the Warden. "What on earth did he do?"

"He plotted a revolt. He has accomplices, but he won't give them up. On that count alone, if he persists, he might just find himself having to give up his ghost instead. At the rack!"

Giovanni's forehead creased, his face pale.

"Perhaps you'd care to see the course of these proceedings," the Warden offered, pointing to the rack. "Such an effective tool! It slowly stretches the body until it tears the limbs from their sockets."

"Good heavens, no! I cannot bear the sight of this! But what about the rats? Whatever are *they* for?"

Bambridge cast a sideways glance at Giovanni, his mind turning and scheming. "Our little furry darlings are voracious," he said. "A rather helpful thing when all is said and done."

"How do you mean?" Giovanni insisted, tremors in his voice.

"They help clean up the mess, you see. By feasting on the flesh of those who would have otherwise had *them* for supper!" He let out a loud, sinister cackle that echoed in the darkness.

Giovanni broke out in a cold sweat. He palmed his forehead, fear pulsing through his hand. He staggered, took a step backward and stared at the Warden. *A demon!* he thought, as Bambridge's figure appeared to shape-shift like the shadows on the walls. He rushed to a corner, fell to his knees, slumped over and emptied his stomach on the ground. He wiped his mouth on his shirtsleeve, raised his head and looked up at the Warden once again.

Bambridge's merciless glare bore into Giovanni's eyes.

"You look a bit pallid, Impresario. Admittedly, this kind of excursion can oft prove to be wearisome. Still, worth it, I'd say. It puts things into perspective, does it not?"

"I—I must return to my chamber at once, Signore," Giovanni pleaded between rasping breaths. "I am unwell." Unsteady, he slowly propped himself up.

"Come, then!" the Warden commanded, walking toward the exit.

VII. RULE OF CHUMMAGE

V ivid images of the horrors he had witnessed in the dungeons flashed through Giovanni's mind. Laying on his bed in a stupor he stared at the ceiling, unable to eat or sleep for hours. *The bowels of Hell await me,* he feared, as the day drew to a close. An anxious, restless night followed.

Early the next morning a knock on his door broke the spell. He sprang up, threw his night robe on and rushed to open it. A courier handed him a letter and a small pouch. He tore the seal and read it.

My Dear Dottore,

It pains me to report to you that His Excellency, the Ambassador Azzoni, has not yet been able to reach your kinsman, the Marquis Niccolo, in Genoa. Still, he promises to persevere. I shall keep you apprised of any tidings. Meanwhile, pray avail yourself of 8s which should defray some of your personal disbursements.

Your Humble Servant,
Francesco Vanneschi

Giovanni closed his eyes and took a deep breath. As he exhaled, a sinking feeling overtook him. *My fate is sealed!* He looked inside the pouch still in his hands and tossed it on his writing desk. *Eight shillings. A pittance!*

A modest wooden bracket clock tick-tocked while he dressed. His mind raced from thought to thought as he went about his morning chores with his head down and shoulders drooping. All of a sudden, a hard knock rattled him. He raised his head and looked out his chamber window. A pair of steely eyes stared at him. Standing by the door, Bambridge flailed his arms demanding to be let in. Giovanni complied, his chest heaving.

"I'm here to collect!" the Warden announced, dispensing with all social graces. "Your comrade's courier insisted on making a delivery directly to your chamber."

"He did. To my surprise, you did not intercept it."

"No need. 'Tis plain, you've come into some currency," Bambridge responded, glancing at the pouch on Giovanni's desk.

"Alas, not what I expected," said Giovanni, carefully avoiding eye contact. "Particularly now, as I am aware I have no choice but to prolong my stay here."

Bambridge grinned. "A most unfortunate delay indeed, and such a nuisance for you, I am sure. Yet, your obligations are now due, sir. You're well-acquainted with the rules." He held out his hand. "Fifteen bob for a fortnight, without the supplementals."

"*Bob*?"

"Shillings, sir. Shillings!"

"Apologies. I can only make good on five, Signore. I assure you more should arrive shortly." Without warning, the Warden lunged forward, forcefully shoving Giovanni against the wall. Raising his arms in an attempt to repel him, Giovanni lost his footing and tumbled down to the floor. "You've gone mad!" he screamed.

Bambridge attempted to grab him by his arm and pull him up, ripping a sleeve from his shirt.

"I will not hear it!" the Warden shouted in Giovanni's face, lips curled up as spittle shot out through his teeth, a swollen vein throbbing on his forehead. "You make a grave mistake if you take me for a fool!" He snatched the pouch from Giovanni's desk and made a hasty exit, leaving the door open behind him.

Breathing heavily, Giovanni slowly rose to his feet and sat down on his bed.

Within minutes, Hawley appeared at the door.

"Sir? Are you all right?"

"I wish I could say so."

"You must pack your essentials at once. You are being transferred."

"Just now?"

"Warden's orders."

Fearing the worst, Giovanni quickly filled a small leather haversack with his bare necessities.

"Your sleeve," said Hawley, pointing to Giovanni's shirt. "Did *he* do this?"

Giovanni nodded. Faint sounds of a crying child resonated in the back of his head...

"Change quickly then, and off we go."

"And my trunk?"

"Never you mind, sir. I shall fetch it for you once you're settled in your new ward."

A moment later, they stepped out. Probing eyes gazed at them as they made their way around the courtyard's perimeter and alongside the ground floor chamber galleries. Then, Hawley stopped at an arched wooden door. He knocked and faced Giovanni standing beside him.

"Your new lodgings, sir," he said. He tipped his tricorn and left.

A middle-aged man wearing an oversized periwig and thick layers of makeup on his face opened the door and greeted Giovanni with an exaggerated bow.

"I've been expecting you, Dottore Crossa!" he said with a wide smile, a peculiar twinkle in his eyes. "Allow me to introduce myself. I am John Cleland, your humble servant. Do come in."

Slightly befuddled by Cleland's effusive welcome, Giovanni bowed and cautiously stepped into the chamber. "I'm glad to make your acquaintance, Signore," he said, a pungent scent instantly clashing with his nostrils. *French parfum?* Feigning to preen his moustache, he covered his nose while casting a side-eye glance at Cleland's colorful attire— a pink satin waistcoat over a cream shirt with pleated ruffles at the cuffs and collar, matching breeches and stockings, and a brick-red pair of high-heeled buckled shoes.

Cleland pointed to a modest desk. "You may place your bag next to my *escritoire*." Resting on it were six bottles of eau de cologne, three periwigs perched on their stands, and a powdering carrot.

Giovanni walked up to the desk, put his bag down and quickly returned to Cleland. "By what means did you become aware of my birth name?" he asked.

"The bully at the Gate House apprised me of your impending transfer," Cleland replied. Using a pair of tongs he picked up a tiny piece of coal from the fireplace and lit a long, white clay pipe pinched on the side his mouth.

"This does not strike me as the ward I thought I would be sent to."

"What would that be?" Cleland asked, a smoke plume billowing out of his mouth.

"Somewhere in the Common Side."

"*He* would not dare!"

"He wouldn't?"

"Behold: A fireplace, two bedsteads, a writing desk, a table, two chairs, and even a bathing tub! No dwelling chamber in the Common Side would ever boast such comforts."

"Is this what the Warden calls the *rule of chummage?*"

"Indeed, it is. We are now chamber *chums*, Impresario," a sanguine smile on Cleland's face. "Not too shabby for eight bob a fortnight."

"That is exactly what he took from me!" Giovanni responded. "And now, I am penniless!"

"You sound aggrieved."

Giovanni grimaced.

"Well then, this is the perfect time to rustle up some tea and put the kettle on!" Cleland responded cheerfully. "You must shake off this feeling at once, Impresario!" He put his pipe aside, pranced over to the hearth, placed a cast iron kettle on a square grill and stoked the coals beneath it with a fire iron.

Mystified by Cleland's exuberant gaiety, lisp and peculiar mannerisms, Giovanni watched silently.

"That shall be your bedstead, Dottore," Cleland pointed to a modest wooden bedframe. He set a teapot, two cups, a tea strainer, and a bowl of scones on a small wooden table across from the fireplace. "You may put away your belongings and freshen up, if you so desire. We shall avail ourselves of refreshments when you are ready."

Soon, a subtle aroma flowed from the spout of the blue and white ceramic teapot on the table, its belly pregnant with leaves steeping in hot water.

"I am obliged for your hospitality, Signore," said Giovanni as he and Cleland sat across from each other. "Now, if I may beg your indulgence. How did you come to know to address me as *Dottore?* Only my most intimate associates do."

"Word travels quickly around these parts," Cleland replied as he poured for Giovanni.

"I'm certain you're aware both you and I are not unknowns."

"You mean here at the Fleet?"

"Not only here, but in polite society. Your reputation has travelled well beyond the boundaries of the stage," said Cleland with a flash in his eye. "And 'tis no wonder. I have been to a few of your company's performances, which never disappoint."

"You are too kind. You do realize we've only had two seasons of engagements. The last one unduly interrupted by rather unforeseen events…"

"Of course, the newssheets were awash with it."

"Pray excuse my indelicacy, but how long has it been since your confinement?"

Cleland twiddled with a long double string of pearls around his neck. "Almost a year now," he replied, nonchalantly. "This is my second time."

"Twice you landed here?"

"Indeed. 'Tis been a curse! At first, I was accused by Thomas Cook, someone I once held in high esteem, of failing to discharge a long-held obligation. Oh, how he acted like a faultless gent at the beginning of our long partnership. So mellow and polite, just like the pink of courtesy. Alas, I learned too late he was a liar and a cheat. And very much adroit at his deceit."

"A square turnabout it seems. Pray tell, how did the two of you become acquainted?"

Cleland crossed his legs, picked up his pipe and lit it with practiced flair. "We are both writers and frequented the same environs. Indeed, the theater was one of them. Your delightful comic operas, included."

"It gladdens me to hear you found my company's performances agreeable."

"I did! The humorous side of life has always been my weakness. Your operas make me feel mirthful and gay. You are blessed with a marvelous troupe, Impresario!"

"Verily. Yet, 'tis not just the performers' talent that bears consequence. The whimsical wit of playwrights bequeaths the very means by which the actors can thrive upon the stage."

Cleland smiled. He took a drag from his pipe and blew the smoke upward, adding volume to the hazy brume hovering above his head.

"Do you speak *lingua Toscana*, Signore?"

"The language of Tuscany and the great Dante Alighieri? *Si, naturalmente,*" Cleland responded, with a perfect accent. "I delved into the pages of the Divine Comedy at an early age."

"Bravo! Then you can read a libretto! Some swear that operas are best appreciated when one comprehends the mother tongue of the masters who write them."

"I concur! I am also fluent in French, Greek, Latin and Hindi."

"My eye! You are a true polyglot."

"I detest saying so, but I do come from a family of wealth and means. In my tender years we moved among London's finest social circles. You see, my parents had high aspirations for me. They sent me off to Westminster School where I studied foreign languages."

"Marvelous. But, why Hindi?"

"Ah, yes… That came as result of an engagement I accepted with *The British East India Company*, which kept me in Bombay for 12 long years."

"Fortune smiled upon you, Signore! You attended a prestigious learning institution and traveled round the world. You must be proud!"

Cleland sighed. "I suppose so."

"Regrettably for me, I never had a chance to go to school," said Giovanni. "I was raised in a small village in the Alps, in the Duchy of Savoy, close to the border with France. That's how I learned my French. My kinfolk owned a small farm there. My siblings and I helped our elders with the daily chores and sold the produce at the local market on the weekends."

"Well, Impresario, if it makes you feel any better, I was born in London though my ancestral roots lie in Scotland, and as odd as this may sound, *that* made me a bit of a stranger in my own homeland. Then, my parents disowned me when I reached the age of twenty…"

"On what count?"

"Their professed loathing of my use of French fragrances, the blanc and rouge paint on my face, and my love for oversized periwigs, ribbons, pearls, and pins. Mind you, I have never been awarded a school title. In fact, I was expelled from Westminster."

"You were thrown out of school?"

"For misconduct, they alleged. I was notorious for my puckishness though I was certain my offence was none of that."

"What was your transgression then?"

Cleland replied without hesitation. "Being caught in the midst of a consensual carnal indiscretion with one of my male classmates. By then, everyone had taken notice of my lack of interest in the female charms and my steadfast refusal to pretend otherwise. I was not one of the *them*, you see. I suppose after a few beatings and a surplus of disgraces, they must have concluded it would be best to dispatch with me."

"Heavens! Did they intend to murder you?"

"No, no. Although, sometimes I feared as much."

"What did they do?"

"They reported me to the School Board for licentious behavior. They sent me off soon afterward."

"Such an unfortunate decision. 'Tis clear enough you did not coax anyone to lose their innocence."

"It gratifies me you see it in that light, Impresario."

————— ➤-◉-◄ —————

During a midsummer heatwave, the recently acquainted chamber mates found themselves spending considerable time together beyond the confines of their living quarters. They took leisurely strolls in and around the prison premises, often finding respite under the cool shade of trees or on benches in the courtyard. On one such occasion, while resting near a ninepins lane, they observed three players rolling their balls and placing friendly wagers. Following several rounds of play, one of the players, a tall grey-haired man, approached.

"Good day, gentlemen! Pray excuse me," he said with a quick tip of his tricorn. "I am Captain Wesley MacKinnon, your servant."

Cleland nodded. "Glad to make your acquaintance! I am John Cleland, and this is my chamber mate, Giovanni Crossa."

Giovanni dipped his head politely. He and Cleland remained seated.

"Taking in the fresh air?" asked MacKinnon.

"Indeed," Cleland replied. "The heat indoors is quite stifling."

"You watched our game, I noticed. Perhaps I could interest you in joining us. My companions and I bowl here routinely for merriment and farthings."

"I am most honored by your invitation, Captain," Cleland responded. "I'd be delighted. Alas, I lack experience."

"Me as well. I'd gladly take your offer," said Giovanni. "If only I had a farthing to spare."

"I see no encumbrance in any of that. We can begin with trial runs," MacKinnon insisted. "No wagers for a week."

Cleland and Giovanni glanced at each other.

"Fair enough," said Cleland. "I'm in!"

"And I!" Giovanni followed.

"Tomorrow at ten, then?"

"Agreed!" Cleland answered.

Giovanni nodded.

MacKinnon bowed and returned to his mates.

Cleland's gaze trailed him. "A nice chap, MacKinnon. And fair to the eye…"

"Nice and fair are useless traits when facing evil," Giovanni said as he caught sight of two keeper guards across the courtyard escorting an inmate in handcuffs and irons into the Gate House.

"What say you?"

"Observe. *That* could be me." Giovanni gave a slight nod in the direction of the unfortunate man. "Like him, I could easily be taken to the dungeons."

Cleland waved his hand fan to cool himself. "Nonsense. That could be anyone *but you*, Impresario. The Warden cannot touch you."

"What makes you so certain?" Giovanni asked, gazing at the colorful dragons painted on the folds of Cleland's fan.

"Lord Fielding keeps a watchful eye on him."

Giovanni wiped the sweat from his forehead, eyes fixed on the back-and-forth motions of the fan. The voice of a child whispered to him as the dragons on the fan came to life. *They were huge! They looked like snakes with big fangs. But they had claws and wings!*

"Are you all right, Dottore?"

Giovanni shook his head.

"Huh… Apologies. I drifted for a moment," he answered. "You were saying?"

"I was about to say I saw Lord Fielding entering the Gate House shortly after he called on you. I gathered he had words with the Warden regarding your arrangements here."

"*Lord* Fielding? I thought he was a barrister," Giovanni responded, reaching for the snuffbox in his breeches. "He told me so, himself." Quickly removing the lid, he took a sizable pinch of the brown and grainy substance, brought it up to one of his nostrils and breathed in.

"How peculiar… His Lordship is a magistrate, a Justice of the Peace. He has the power to decide your fate as well as mine."

"Then, wherefore pretend he was an ordinary barrister?"

"Clearly, his business here that day was to ensure your welfare. Yet, he must have felt he had to go about it incognito. You see, as a man of the law, His Lordship is expected to keep himself impartial."

"Naturally."

"He must have told the brute at the Gate House to keep his hands off you."

"Intriguing, indeed… A day or two after His Lordship's visit, Bambridge took me on a tour that ended in the dungeons."

"He does this to those he believes he can intimidate. Let us banish him from our thoughts and move on to merrier things, Impresario."

"I wish I could."

"We should go back inside and take some water," said Cleland. "There is also something I wish to present to you."

"What is it? One of your favorite color lip balms?"

Cleland giggled. "How witty of you!"

They stood up and returned to their chamber.

Once settled in and having quenched their thirst, Cleland reached inside a drawer on his writing desk and retrieved an elongated box. "One of my beloved keepsakes," he said, carefully removing its cover and revealing a gold-tipped black swan feather quill with a stand and an ink well. "'Twas given to me as a birthday gift by Thomas Cook when we were still mildly civil to each other. Here, take a look."

"Marvelous!" Giovanni said, as he held the quill and examined it. "A very tasteful gesture."

"Aye. At that time, we had not yet traded public accusations and defamed each other."

"A distressing time for you, I am sure."

"Quite right. Yet not as much as when I filed charges against him for attempted murder."

"Lord Almighty!"

"Oh, yes… Our partnership was very volatile. We were as passionate as we were vicious to each other. All the same, I relish the good memories, like those this beauty brings to mind whenever I behold it."

"Do you still make use of it?"

"Routinely. It's been my faithful muse. Even as lately as the span of two years past, I used it to put the final touches on my best-known piece so far: a novel that took eight years to complete."

"That's a long stretch!"

"'Twas! I started writing it in India in the year 1740 and finished it in 1748 here at the Fleet."

"What took you so long to get it done?"

"Frankly, I cannot say. Perhaps the subject matter… At times, it made my head spin."

"Ah! A tale full of twists and turns."

"And curls and curves, for it conveyed the *Memoirs of a Woman of Pleasure*, Impresario. In point of fact, that was the title of my novel."

"A lady of the night?"

"Indeed. Her name was Fanny Hill. Her adventures were at the center of my story."

"An original subject, I daresay."

"I wrote it on a dare! To prove that it is possible to try one's hand at penning pieces that contend with matters of the flesh without descending into crassness."

"Were you successful?"

"To an extent. I took pains to never submit to the salacious and the vulgar.

Yet, to those for whom a mere observation of a natural act registered on paper as an indecency, I failed, and miserably so."

"What do you mean by a *natural act*, Signore?"

"Mating, of course. An act that most would say, derives in sensual pleasure."

"A singular perspective... And then? What happened next?"

"The outcome was as predictable as it was inevitable, Impresario," Cleland sighed. "The usual hypocrites proceeded to brand me as a heretic, proscribed my novel, and arrested me and my publishers on charges of obscenity. Since then, debt has become a heavy burden. Thus, here I am once again at the Fleet, bankrupt and barely making it on the meager proceeds from a few other publications that still remain in circulation."

"*Obscenity,* you say? What kind of acts does Fanny Hill engage in to provoke such harsh indictment?"

"Nothing that warrants such absurd accusations, Dottore. Who's to know why a whore's fixation with the size of a dangling appendage should suddenly become noteworthy? Then again, I may have inadvertently mistaken the wit and disposition of some of my detractors."

"How so?"

"My novel also dared examine in some detail the delights of man to mankind basket making, which may have caused a scandal among some of the readers."

"Basket making?"

"Fornication, my dear sir! Fornication!" Cleland cried out.

"I admit your tale has tickled my fancy, Signore. I know I shouldn't but... would you happen to have a copy of your manuscript to spare?"

"You mean my Fanny has tickled your *tail*, Impresario?" Cleland chuckled. "Well, you're in luck for I do have a copy, and I shall be glad to loan it to you."

"Much obliged!"

"Oh, dear me! It's becoming unbearably hot in here," Cleland said, unfolding and waving his fan. Come to think of it, this might be a good time to take a stroll along Fleet Street and look for a tavern where we could refresh ourselves with a cooling draught to ease the heat. What say you, Impresario?"

"I would like that. Alas, I am destitute."

"I am not so different from you. I live from day to day. But never mind. Tonight's affair shall be my treat."

"I am so obliged, Signore!"

"My pleasure!"

They stood up, put their waistcoats on and walked out the door.

———>-◎-<———

The Jolly Hanging Tavern & Inn brimmed with a mixed crowd of patrons as Giovanni and Cleland walked in. The smell of tobacco smoke, beer and food filled the air. Prison keepers, night watchmen, jailbirds, travelers, and ordinary townsfolk engaged in noisy chatter, a festive, cheerful bustle all around.

A trio played the hurdy-gurdy, the flute and a snare drum. A small group of men and women sang ballads while a couple danced. Sitting at the tables, some played cards, dice and shovelboard, while others ate and drank.

"Merriment abounds!" said Cleland smiling, as they huddled at a corner table. "Just what we needed."

"What's upstairs?" Giovanni asked, as he scanned the room.

"Lodgings where travelers and others can indulge in unspeakable acts of deliciousness, Impresario…"

"Pardon me?"

"You see those painted ladies perched on the staircase?"

"I do."

"They await gentlemen callers to request the pleasure of their company… upstairs."

"Ah, there is a brothel in the garret."

"Nothing unseen or unheard of."

"True."

"Now, over there is a truly extraordinary sight," said Cleland, indicating a couple standing nearby. "Sir Alexander Cuming, the Baronet of Cutler, chit-chatting with none other than Miss Charlotte Hayes!"

"A nobleman in here?"

"Why not? One's station in life should not preclude anyone from enjoying a little jollity from time to time. Though to be fair, Sir Cuming is a peculiar case."

"How's that, Signore?"

"To begin with, he's been confined to the Fleet since the year 1737. That's thirteen years and counting."

"Remarkable! His liability must be tremendous."

"Who knows? I'm not privy to such detail. However, I have heard a few odd tales about his past."

Giovanni leaned forward.

"The story goes that in 1730 Sir Cuming sailed for the American colonies, apparently influenced by one of his wife's dreams. He declared his purpose was to explore the Cherokee homelands somewhere in the Carolina mountains. A few months later, an excerpt from his journal appeared in a London daily claiming he was made Chief by the unanimous consent of the Cherokee nation…"

"Hm… suspicious. Wherefore would the Cherokee do this?"

"Right. It seemed nonsensical. Yet, on his return to England he brought along seven Cherokee chiefs and was allowed to present them to King George II, at the Royal Chapel in Windsor. As he bowed, he laid his turquoise feather crown at the feet of the King. Then the chiefs, who were stark naked, save for the thin loincloths covering their privates, took turns laying down the scalps of some of their former enemies."

"Human scalps?"

"War trophies, Impresario. Symbols of their victories."

"Quite coarse! If at all veritable…"

"The courtiers were gripped in awe. There were deep sighs and loud gasps, and some of the ladies who were present fainted."

Giovanni shook his head. "What exactly did Sir Cuming do that landed him at the Fleet, and for so very long?"

"Reports from the colonies reached England accusing him of swindling the settlers of large sums of currency and property. By then he was deep in the mud and unable to clear his name, so the Palace proceeded to shun him. Eventually, the Crown charged him with fraud and a court placed him in permanent confinement at the Fleet."

"What about the beautiful signora chatting with Sir Cuming? Who did you say she is?"

"Miss Charlotte Hayes, Impresario. At age twenty-five she is thought to be one of the most prosperous brothel keepers London has ever known."

"'Tis easy to conceive how she achieved success at such an early stage in her life. She seems enchanting."

"And a force of nature! Her tall and slender figure is a magnet. And, she's no common whore. She mingles amongst the loftiest echelons, and she's very wise. She knows just how to invest the product of her labor. They say she has become the sole proprietor of some of the city's most luxurious brothels."

"Whatever is she doing here, then?"

"She's one of *us*, Impresario. An inmate."

Perplexed, Giovanni stared. "You said she was prosperous."

"Aye. Despite being bound to a common-law husband whose habitual gambling ensnared them in a labyrinth of debt."

"Pity," said Giovanni, just as a bubbly female server with a shiny smile approached and began rattling off the menu.

"Good day to you gentlemen and welcome to The Jolly Hanging Tavern! We have a full bill of fare to offer you: ale and wine, roasted mutton, savory pigeon, cabbage and sweet scotched collops. For the easier to please palates, we've got boiled eggs, sage cheese, and pork pies. Lastly, two sweet tooth pleasers: gooseberry pie and rice pudding. What's your fancy?"

"We shall take two pints of ale and two pork pies, my precious," Cleland replied.

Moments later, as the two chamber mates enjoyed their meal, Giovanni took notice of a well-attired man surrounded by a group of adoring damsels coming through the main entrance.

A familiar face… he thought. Yet, at a distance, he could not discern exactly who he was. As the man drew closer, a fuller image emerged. He tapped Cleland's shoulder and pointed politely in his direction. "Is this a vision, Signore?"

Cleland turned his attention to the evolving scene. "Oh dear! May God strike me dead if that's not David Garrick!"

As Garrick and his glamorous entourage made their entrance, Giovanni put on his tricorn, and dipped his chin down, hoping his presence would remain unnoticed. To his dismay, Garrick had already spotted him and walked swiftly toward him.

"Good afternoon, gentlemen! Pray pardon my intrusion," Garrick said, tipping his hat before turning to Giovanni. "What unexpected surprise it is to chance upon you, Impresario!"

"Likewise, Signore. Providence brings us together again."

"Quite so! Though I would have much rather seen you in court, and much sooner. It appears your Ambassador's intervention on your behalf has changed the timing of your trial."

Giovanni's jaw clenched. "I assure you, 'tis all in good faith. I shall discharge my obligations as soon as—."

"—I do hope so," Garrick cut in. "Otherwise, you can be certain you shall remain in residence at the Fleet a bit longer than you may have anticipated." Casting a glance at Cleland, he carried on, "On reflection, you might not mind it here at all. From what I see, you may have struck a special friendship to keep yourself amused."

"The gall!" Cleland muttered under his breath.

"Ah! *She* speaks…" said Garrick with a sneer. "A good evening to the turtle-doves!" He turned away and went back to his coterie.

Bastardo! Giovanni mumbled, face flushing. He finished the last of his ale in one large gulp and slammed the empty tankard on the table.

Cleland signaled the server to bring another round. "Let go of it, Impresario. He is not worth your grief!"

"I am mindful. And yet, his wickedness has soured my spirits."

"And me as well."

Just then a group of revelers nearby began singing in earnest.

"What are those lads singing so merrily about?" Giovanni asked.

"The Berkshire Tragedy Ballad," Cleland replied. "A much-loved song. Come now, let us join in!"

"Alas, I cannot sing. Besides, the words escape me."

"You will catch on! Come on!"

Giovanni acquiesced.

They stood and joined the singing party for a while.

Young men take warning by my fall
All filthy lusts defy
By giving way to wickedness
Alas! This day I die.

Upon returning to their corner, a fresh jug of ale awaited on the table. They promptly helped themselves.

"Such merriment," said Giovanni. He took a quaff from his tankard and went on. "But for a tragedy?"

"I do concede. It seems implausible."

"And to the cause of the calamity?"

"A lad made a promise to a lass he'd marry her if she would bed him. She refused, he persevered and, in the end, she yielded. When she found out she was with child she pleaded with him to fulfill his promise, but he rebuffed her. After much nagging on her part, he murdered her. Soon he was caught and sentenced to hang."

"I fear I missed the mark. How is this comical?"

"Well, the point of the ballad isn't *not to do murder*, but rather *not to do lust*," Cleland explained. "Still not comical enough to make it to the stage as one of your comic operas?"

Giovanni chuckled softly. "Lust is not the most egregious of the seven deadly sins. Greed and envy are. For they are likely to give way to greater evil. Pray, heed my circumstances, Signore. 'Tis David Garrick, my detractor, whose wicked greed keeps me in this bleak and miserable state."

"Let us behold the bright side of things, Impresario. If the brute in the Gate House thought you were worth nothing, he would not have hesitated to throw you at once into the Two Pence Ward, or even worse, the Beggars Ward!"

"What are those?"

"The lodgings in the Common Side. For those who stay there, life is but a veritable torment. Whereas for us, the swirl of day-to-day existence maintains its semblance of ordinary ease. That is, as long as we keep feeding the monster."

"That is exactly what concerns me, Signore. I fear I may not be capable of keeping him appeased much longer."

"I hear you. Those who use their trades to earn a wage are fortunate. The tailors, the blacksmiths—"

"—And the clergymen, I gather!" Giovanni interjected. "How I wish I could be one of them! Alas, my business is the theater."

"Well, you are not in the Beggars Ward yet, Impresario."

"Not yet… I imagine the place must be the most pitiful of sights."

"Aye. Those who give nothing, receive nothing. For them, their ward is but a death vault, beside the sink and dunghill where all the night soil is cast. Sometimes, even corpses find their way there to await the coroner and burial."

"Dreadful!"

Moments later, they rose from their seats and started for the exit. Dusk had fallen as they stepped out. They strolled leisurely through a marketplace past the dealers and traders putting away their merchandise. The smell of burning oil lamps and torches filled the air. One by one, candles and lanterns hanging over windowsills gradually lit up the neighborhood.

"Every now and again, I am overtaken by the notion that this is all naught but an ill-fated reverie," Giovanni said, wistfully. "Even worse, one from which I cannot wake…"

"Such sentiments visit us all on occasion, Impresario. Reveries can possess an air of enigmatic mystery."

"I concur. I've been afflicted with them all my life…"

"In all truth, you were the principal figure in one of my recent dreams," said Cleland.

"Really? Not a lurid one, I hope!" Giovanni joked.

"Do not flatter yourself! You're not my kind."

They laughed.

"'Twas rather uncanny…" Cleland went on.

"Your dream? In what manner?"

"It bore such striking resemblance to reality! We were riding in some sort of carriage when suddenly you felt unwell. You implored me to halt the carriage, and once I did, you climbed off and spewed your innards out."

"What then?"

"You returned to your seat. Then I awoke."

"A premonition?"

"I would not think so, Impresario. I do not count that as one of my mental powers."

Just before they reached the prison gate, the pair paused briefly at a rusty grate of thick metal bars built into an opening on a wall. Above it, an inscription: *Pray remember poor debtors, having no allowance!*

"This is the Grille," said Cleland. "Behold these ill-starred souls, pleading in desperation."

"Such a harrowing sight," Giovanni responded. "To see them in this wretched state, their arms stretched out, sticking through the gaps, begging for alms."

"Pitiful, indeed."

"I see some have tied strings to caps and boxes."

"That's how they angle for farthings," Cleland explained. "'Tis the only manner in which these forlorn souls can make it through another day."

Silently, they walked away toward the prison gate.

VIII. MacKinnon's Torment

S tanding by his chamber window, Giovanni watched a blanket of dark clouds slowly drifting in the sky. It was dawn on a day in late July and the air hung heavy. *Time's running out...* he mused, thoughts circling like vultures as he pondered when the Warden would strike next. Nearly four weeks had passed since his arrest and confinement at the Fleet, and a new fee was coming due. He closed his eyes and inhaled the rich aroma rising from the coffee in the cup he cradled in his hands. He took a sip and soothed himself. In the distance, thunder rumbled, a smattering of raindrops splashing on the ground.

Lifting his eyes to look out on the courtyard, Giovanni spotted his ninepins mate, Wesley MacKinnon, scantily clad, being dragged from his chamber by Bambridge and a guard.

"Rouse! Rouse!" Giovanni called out to Cleland, still stirring from the grasp of slumber. Rubbing his eyes, Cleland grumbled as he sluggishly sat up. "Lord Almighty, what is so urgent at this ungodly hour?"

"Come hither! Behold! 'Tis the Captain! He's in trouble!"

"MacKinnon?" Cleland rose from his bedstead and stepped up to the window. Together, he and Giovanni watched the Warden and his men walk away from the scene, leaving MacKinnon laying on the ground at the center of the courtyard.

"He bleeds!" Giovanni shouted. "We must go to him!"

A few inmates who had witnessed the assault from their chambers had begun gathering around him. Before long, Giovanni and Cleland had joined them in the courtyard.

"Here mate," said Cleland, handing MacKinnon a spirit flask. Rainwater and blood running down his face, MacKinnon took a swig from the flask and gasped. Cleland knelt to dab his head wound with a kerchief. "What on earth caused this bloody scuffle?"

"A fortnight ago," MacKinnon began, "my brother Peter died of the putrid throat." He paused, heaving and wincing.

"What of it?"

"The Warden caught wind of it and demanded higher fees."

"On what count?"

"An inheritance he fancies I've received."

"Did you submit to his demands?"

"I refused!" MacKinnon groaned while Cleland continued to press on his wound. "Now, he's enraged. Today, he broke into my chamber with a turnkey and a guard, and again endeavored to extort me." He paused once more.

Everyone held their breath.

Then, Cleland spoke. "What then?"

"I rebuffed him. That's when he pounced on me. His men held me down while he struck me on the head with a stick."

"Coward!" a man shouted.

"And a thief!" said MacKinnon. "He ordered his thugs to handcuff me and keep me down while he raided my chamber. He tossed the few valuables I own into a trunk and told the turnkey to haul it to the Gate House. He then locked me out and had me dragged out here."

"What now?"

"I am to stay here in the rain till he returns."

"Despicable! 'Tis plain this is intended as a warning to us all," said Cleland as he rose. "We must act!"

"Aye!" the men clamored.

"What scheme have you in mind?" Giovanni asked.

"We relieve the Captain at once," Cleland responded resolutely. "We raise a tent to keep him dry and bring him blankets, food and water."

Following Cleland's lead, the men wasted no time setting up a makeshift tent and gathering a bundle of provisions.

"Much obliged, comrades!" Still in handcuffs, MacKinnon remained under the tent.

As night fell, an approaching torch signaled Bambridge's return surrounded by a cadre of his men. Upon seeing the tent, he immediately ordered it destroyed and burned while repeatedly kicking MacKinnon in the head and midsection. His screams alerted the inmates in the galleries facing the courtyard, among them, Cleland and Giovanni.

"Are you now prepared to sign a new commitment with me, sir? Twenty-five bob a fortnight and you go back to your chamber."

"Never!" MacKinnon wheezed. "This is an outrage!"

"As you wish, then. You shall stay here through the night under no cover!" Bambridge yelled out, his voice reverberating within the fortress walls. "Beware! Anyone coming to your aid shall feel the sting of my whip!" He and his guards then walked away and disappeared under the cloak of darkness.

Cleland and Giovanni rushed out and carried MacKinnon into their chamber. They dried him and dressed his wounds.

"Captain, pray take my bedstead," Giovanni offered. "The Lord knows you need it more than I do."

"Obliged," MacKinnon mumbled. He lay down and promptly nodded off.

"A noble gesture, Dottore," Cleland whispered. "We shall take turns with my bedstead."

"Fair. No need to disrobe. We must be poised and ready, for our deed has now taken us on a most perilous path."

"I am aware of it," said Cleland. "Soon, word of the evil that occurred here today shall spread like wildfire, adding fuel to the tinderbox of smoldering rage that could explode at any time now. We should tread carefully."

"Let us rest now, Signore. We must rise and return the Captain to the courtyard before dawn or face the sword."

Hours later, the persistent crowing of a rooster stirred MacKinnon. A calm and quiet night and sheer exhaustion had kept everyone from waking at first light.

MacKinnon rose, walked to the window and looked out. "Mates, rise! Rise at once! He comes!" he cried out.

In the distance, Bambridge led a full detachment of armed men, brandishing muskets with bayonets as they marched through the courtyard.

Giovanni and Cleland sprung up and hurried to the window.

"We're finished!" Cleland said gravely, then turned to MacKinnon. "The sentinels must have noticed you missing. There is little we can do now."

The somberness of Cleland's tone set off an immediate reaction in Giovanni. "Lord help us! We're at the Devil's mercy!"

Upon reaching the center of the courtyard the Warden ordered a general search of the Master's quarter, ward by ward, one dwelling chamber at a time. He commanded his men to stab or shoot anyone who stood in their way, and to execute MacKinnon on the spot, if he resisted.

The guards quickly split in all directions.

Inside Giovanni and Cleland's chamber, the men sat counting their breaths as they awaited their fate, blank stares on their faces.

Languishing in the darkness of the moment, Giovanni wiped the sweat from his forehead and peered out the window. "I do not see them."

"I can hear them," MacKinnon responded. "I shall come out and surrender."

"I fear 'tis too late, mate," Cleland proclaimed with unmistakable finality.

The Warden and four guards stood outside the chamber.

"Open at once!" Bambridge shouted. No one answered. The guards kicked the door open and barged in. MacKinnon panicked. Though bound in handcuffs, he managed to reach for a fire iron and hurled it at them. They lunged forward and quickly brought him to heel.

Stepping up to MacKinnon, Bambridge spat in his face. "Clap double irons on him!" he ordered. "Then to the dungeons!" He turned to Cleland and Giovanni and shouted: "You fools! The Beggars Ward awaits you! Locked up. No food or water till I say so."

"Put an end to this savagery! I beseech you!" Cleland pleaded, as one of the guards began pushing and shoving him and Giovanni out the door.

"By what authority do you constrain me?" MacKinnon yelled at the Warden as the irons were affixed to his legs.

"My own!" Bambridge yelled back. "I require no one's permission to assert it."

"I demand to be taken to Lord Fielding!" MacKinnon insisted, face flushed and eyes ablaze with unwavering determination. "I am entitled to hear the charges filed against me!"

Bambridge scoffed. "You forget where you are, sir. I *am* the law within these walls." He then ordered the locks on the irons to be fastened.

MacKinnon screamed in agony, compressed flesh cutting off his circulation.

"You brought this on yourself! Your blasted stubbornness led you to your downfall."

MacKinnon shrieked amidst the sounds of bones snapping and popping, before he finally passed out.

Overcome with horror, Cleland fainted, collapsing on the arms of a guard standing beside him. Stunned, Giovanni watched the spectacle unfold before him like a slow-motion reel: Cleland's periwig slowly rolling down to the ground, his baldness exposed, and a wet spot expanding on his breeches just below his waist.

Outside, a rapidly growing mob of angry inmates carrying sticks and spikes had been gathering in the courtyard. "Justice! Justice!" they shouted, tossing pieces of furniture into a burning heap.

Upon hearing the uproar and unaware the gun room had been breached, the Warden walked out into the courtyard, issued an order to halt all searches, and re-directed his men to quash the agitators.

The troubles quickly spread to the Common Side, whose residents eagerly joined the throng in burning and destroying everything in sight. Soon, the shooting began and a full-blown riot ensued. Thick smoke filled the air, ear splitting sounds of shots being fired echoed off the walls as men screamed and writhed in pain on the blood-stained ground.

Amidst the mayhem, Giovanni and Cleland managed to clear out. While frantically looking for a place to hide, they lost sight of each other. Weak and unable to walk, MacKinnon had remained behind.

"Praise the Almighty!" Giovanni muttered, his gaze aimed at the sky. *His golden eye is blind today,* he thought. The sun, barely visible, conspired with the clouds and the smoke to keep him under cover. Just as he realized he had been meandering aimlessly, he felt a sharp stabbing pain on his left shoulder. He paused, reached for it, and felt a sticky substance slowly running down his chest. He looked at his hand. *Blood!* Falling to his knees, he made the sign of the cross and began praying. His head spinning, he prepared to surrender his soul when he felt someone's strong grip on his arm. *An angel!*

"Are you all right, sir?" asked a male voice.

"Who are you? I cannot see!"

"I'm Hawley."

"Hawley? You're a godsend! I've been shot!"

"The infirmary is in flames, sir."

"I'll bleed to death!"

"Pray, allow me," Hawley said, helping Giovanni rise to his feet. He carefully removed Giovanni's waistcoat and blood-soaked shirt and scrutinized the injured area. He took his own coat and shirt off, then used the latter as a bandage to stanch the flow from the wound. "You are fortunate, sir. The musket ball barely grazed you."

"Take me out of here! I beseech you!"

"Where to?" Hawley responded while covering Giovanni's torso with his waistcoat. "I have no notion where I could convey you." He put his own coat back on and continued. "And I'd be tempting fate. My own ruin, to be sure. If the Warden found out I abetted you, it'd be the end of me."

"I implore you! Pray take me to The Hops & Vines Tavern on Farringdon. Surely, the Good Lord will smile upon you."

"My liability is high, sir."

"My life is in your hands!"

A momentary pause ensued. Hawley closed his eyes and breathed in deeply. Then, without a word, he placed Giovanni's uninjured arm around his neck and shoulders, wrapped his own around Giovanni's waist, and carried him alongside the prison walls.

Every so often, they crouched and squatted in order to avoid detection.

Clutching onto Hawley, Giovanni prayed until they reached the Gate House.

"We're in luck, the guards have left their post," said Hawley.

They crossed the road and found an alleyway to sit and rest a moment.

"I'm feverish," Giovanni said, his voice weak and strained, face wet with perspiration. "I'm not certain how much longer I can stay awake."

"Pray tarry here, sir. I shall return to fetch you." Hawley walked back to the road and hailed an empty hackney that happened to pass by.

"Would you lend me a hand, mate?" Hawley asked the coachman. "I've got an injured gentleman in dire need of help."

"And then? Where to?"

"The Hops & Vines Tavern just up the road."

"That'll be tuppence."

"Double that, if you bring me back," Hawley responded.

The coachman jumped off the carriage and followed Hawley into the alleyway.

Within minutes the cab arrived at the tavern. Pale and shaky, Giovanni seemed to be fading fast. Hawley and the coachman helped him out of the carriage.

"'Tis the house that abuts the tavern on the left," Giovanni mumbled, catching his breath while gesturing toward a magnificent mansion.

Positioning Giovanni between them, Hawley and the coachman carried him to the main entrance.

Hawley knocked. A male servant appeared at the door.

"I won't be long," Hawley said to the coachman, who returned to the carriage.

"Good day, Signori," said the servant. "How may I assist you?"

"Sono il Signor Crossa del King Theater," Giovanni panted, his eyes half open. "Pray fetch the ambassador at once!"

"Of course, Signore. I shall apprise the Ambassador immediately," the servant responded. He helped Hawley bring Giovanni into a lavish parlor and sat him down on a sofa.

"I must return to my post without delay," Hawley said. "God save you. Farewell, sir!" He bowed and left.

Giovanni nodded off. Then, in the flutter of a heartbeat, he found himself immersed in a dark void. Out of nowhere, voices began seeping in.

"Careful now. He's frail," came a familiar female voice. "Carry him up the stairs to the guest chamber on the East wing. Bring a copper with hot water, fresh hand towels and a bottle of spirits."

"Our physician should arrive at any time, my dear," said a male voice.

"I shall sit by his side while we wait," she responded.

Moments later, approaching footsteps signaled a new presence.

"Will he be all right?" asked the female.

"'Tis a surface wound, my lady. He should be fine," an older male voice echoed in the distance.

Soon, all voices faded as a sound wave began trickling in. Giovanni's eyes stayed shut, his body motionless. Yet, somehow, he could see... Lush green velvet curtains had been drawn wide open on the sides of a large window. Above it, rosy-cheeked cherubs with golden harps danced in the clouds. The sun and the moon at opposite ends smiled at each other. *Heaven!* he thought. Then he realized he had been hovering just beneath a painted ceiling.

Below, an imposing post bed dominated the center of a palatial chamber. Resting on it, a middle-aged man looked familiar... Giovanni's focus then shifted to a dim flickering light filtering through the window sheers. As he approached, the sheers morphed into a thin, diaphanous, glistening membrane. Behind it, moving shadows, beckoning... All of a sudden, a powerful magnetic force pulled him into it, stretching and bending the slippery surface until he finally tore through.

In fragments of a second, Giovanni found himself facing four grand mirrors hanging next to each other on a vast white wall. Drawn to one of them, he slowly advanced and peered into it. A young man stared back at him with peculiar intensity. He instantly recognized him... Then everything went dark.

IX. Meeting Grandma

D evin awoke to the sounds of beeping horns and blinding headlights. He squinted, turned his head away from the windshield and looked out the window beside him. In the distance, a full moon rested on the treetops. Sitting at the wheel, Hal, an older friend, puffed on the last bit of a Kool Super Long cigarette.

"Where are we?" Devin asked, his eyes barely open.

"Still on I-94," Hal replied.

"Ah…"

"You took a nice nap there, Missy."

"Please pull over. I feel sick."

Hal put out his cigarette, turned the blinkers on and drove to the side of the road. Devin jumped out of the car, bent over, and threw up. When he returned, Hal handed him a paper towel and a bottle of water. He unscrewed the cap, took a few gulps and cleared his throat. "Sorry. Something I ate," he said.

"At school?"

"No. Matt and I went to a diner."

"Your roommate?"

"My *ex*-roommate."

"Did he bail out on you?"

"Nah. He moved in with his girlfriend. I got the room to myself now."

"About time you got some privacy."

"Yeah, I know."

"Did you ever come out to him?"

"You kidding? He's cool but, no. We never went there."

"Are you still messing around with that stuff you used to do with him?"

"No. That was a phase. Freshman year. I was experimenting."

"Good! So, are you still up for this tonight?"

"I'll be fine."

"Sure? We can turn back if you like."

Devin rolled down the window and took a deep breath. "No. I'm fine. Really. Detroit, here we come!" he bellowed, as Hal merged onto the highway.

"How long was I out for?"

"Half hour maybe."

"I was dreaming, you know."

"About?"

"I don't remember much. I just know I was."

Hal pulled out the car's lighter and lit up another Kool. "I bet you'd remember if it was a nightmare."

"And you know this because?"

"I get one every so often. It keeps repeating."

Devin perked up. "Seriously?"

"Yep. It's bizarre. I'm a drag queen in a jail somewhere, more concerned about my wig collection and my bottles of perfume than about being locked up."

"Sounds like a guilty conscience. What did you do to deserve jail, Grandma?"

"Some kind of karma, right?" Hal responded, blowing smoke out of the window.

"Yeah, a punishment for swishy fags!"

Hal chuckled. "Anyway, I hope this opera is worth the trip. You know, I'm not a connoisseur."

"It's *Rigoletto!* Of course it's worth it! But the tickets… They're so steep!"

"Forget that. You know I got you."

"You don't have to."

"I don't mind."

"You always say that."

"Take it as your graduation gift. It's close enough."

"Thank you. It's an expensive gift. You must be well-endowed."

"That's what they say," Hal responded, with a side eye wink.

"You're dirty."

"Well, if you meant money, let me remind you that I *do* work for a living."

"A thirty-five-year-old freelance writer with two houses, a Mercedes and a boat? Come on Hal, admit it. You lucked out when your wife divorced you."

Hal's cigarette tip glowed, red sparks flared. He inhaled, held his breath, then let a plume billow out of his mouth. "Say what? We were both on board with the divorce."

"Oh, so she knew about the Latin guy?"

"She knew about *me*, so there were no surprises. Our divorce had little to do with Mario."

"My fault. I shouldn't have brought it up."

"It's okay. I guess I never told you…"

"Told me what?"

"About me and my ex, Cheryl."

"Pray tell."

"We met in a kibbutz in Israel when we were very young. We were attracted to each other. She got pregnant. We both felt pressured by our parents to get married, and so we did. That's how things were in those days. By the time we realized we had made a mistake, it was too late."

"So, what happened?"

"Life happened. Nicki was born so we stuck together."

"For how long?"

"Ten years."

"So, your daughter was the reason you stayed on."

"Of course. She was our angel! The best that could've possibly come out of our marriage."

"Plus, your divorce settlement, right?"

"Really? What's gotten into you tonight, Devin?"

"Sorry. That didn't come out right."

"Yeah… Nobody's perfect. Remember you and Rick? That didn't go too well, did it? And, we know why."

"He was my first."

"I know. I introduced you."

"We had fun for a while."

"You hurt him."

"You mean that night at The Rubaiyat? I had no clue what I was doing."

"You shoulda."

"We were together for three months. It wasn't like a long-term thing."

"So, what? You walked out on him with someone else. And in front of all his friends. I was one of them. You humiliated him."

"Not intentionally. I was tipsy. And I apologized."

"Yeah, the next day."

"He forgave me."

"So did I."

"He wanted me to stay. But it was over."

"You could've been a little kinder."

"I learned my lesson, Grandma."

"I hope so," Hal responded. "Moving on to lighter things, how did you like that VHS tape you borrowed from me a few weeks ago?"

"Which one?"

"The one with Divine. She was hilarious in it."

"Oh right. *Fanny Hill: The Adventures of a Drag Queen*. You know, I never got around to watching it."

"You seemed so interested."

"I liked the title for some reason…"

"Watch it. It's worth it. It was a hit with the midnight movie circuit over a decade ago. Mark my words: one day it'll become a cult classic."

A few minutes later Hal pulled into a parking garage a few feet away from the Masonic Temple Theater in downtown Detroit.

Devin glanced at his watch. "We're early."

"How about a hot cup of tea? It'll help settle your stomach."

"Good idea."

They went into the theater and sat at a full-service bar in the main hall.

"Does this remind you of anything?" Hal asked while they waited to be served.

"The night we met, two years ago?"

"Exactly." Hal lit up once more, and they began reminiscing.

> ⊙ <

Devin and Hal had crossed paths in the late fall of 1981. It was Devin's junior year in college. He had arranged to meet a schoolmate at The Second Chance, a hip nightclub in Ann Arbor. He arrived early, took a seat at the bar, ordered a soda and took a look around. *Cool posters. Wow! Joe Cocker was here.* Within moments, a thirty-something guy sat beside him.

They glanced at each other.

"Excuse me. Are you here for The Ramones?" the guy asked.

Devin turned toward him, catching a whiff of his cologne. *Phew! Pungent!* "Uh… I had no clue they were playing here tonight."

"Did you have trouble finding parking?"

"Not really. I got lucky, I guess."

"You did. I bet in a few minutes there will be no parking spots anywhere near. By the way, the name is Hal. I come in peace." He lit a cigarette. The flickering flame of his lighter exposed a peculiar twinkle in his eyes.

Devin giggled. "Greetings, Hal. In this dimension, I go by Devin. A mere mortal."

"Nice to meet you, Devin. If not The Ramones, what brings your mortal presence to this realm on a Monday night?"

Devin cast a glance at the tassels on Hal's moccasins. "Meeting a friend, who's running late," he said. "And you?"

"I'm doing a feature story on The Ramones. I'm a writer."

"Cool. Who do you write for?"

"It depends. I freelance. I'm hoping *Rolling Stone* will take this piece." With a swift motion, Hal ran his fingers through his wavy brown hair, exuding an intriguing sense of style and flair.

"That's awesome! Good luck with that!"

"Thanks. I've been following this band for a while now. They're edgy. I kinda like that. They were even in a movie. Did you know?"

"No. What's it about?"

"A bunch of kids take over their school after their parents try to burn their rock records. When the police show up, the kids and The Ramones burn the school down."

"Whoa!"

"Pretty wild, uh?"

"But fun?"

"Well, all that burning and destruction spoiled it for me. It reminded me of the Comiskey Park riot in Chicago, with all those idiots burning disco records."

"I saw that on the news. It was odd."

"And creepy. That's how the Nazis started. Burnings books."

"True. But this was just a bunch of fools. Some people will burn Hansel and Gretel books, if you let them."

"That's the problem: We let them. They start with books or records and end up burning witches at the stake."

"I hear you. Joan of Arc was just nineteen when they burned her for her visions and her dreams."

"She was about your age, I guess."

"I'm twenty. You?"

"Thirty-three. Are you a student?"

"Yup. A junior, at U of M."

"And your major is—"

"Education."

"I knew it. You're well read. Hansel and Gretel…"

Devin giggled. "I'm also drinking soda. Not fair."

"Aging is not fair."

"Some things are ageless," Devin pointed to Hal's fancy wristwatch. "Vintage? The fabric strap is awesome."

"Thank you. It's a 1940 *Longines Art Deco*. A gift from my ex-wife."

"Nice!"

"Should we move?" Hal asked, indicating a table that had just been vacated in a quieter corner of the hall. "It's getting a bit crowded here."

"Sure."

They settled and continued chatting. Minutes later, during a lull in their exchange Devin became aware of Hal's intense gaze. He broke eye contact and blushed.

"Have you heard about the Rubaiyat, on First?"

"Is it a pub?"

"It's a fun dance club for queers and their friends. My partner and I go there every so often."

An awkward pause followed. Devin's heartbeat quickened. Though no longer an innocent, Hal's bluntness seemed unthinkable.

"Uh… A gay club?" Devin asked, struggling to keep his voice steady.

"Yeah, we should be there Friday night. Wanna join?"

"I—I don't dance."

Hal smiled. "Wait until you hear Donna Summer and you'll be cutting a rug in no time."

Devin took a deep breath.

"How did you know?"

"Know what?"

"About *me*."

"Oh… your feathers, I suppose. Plus, you kept looking at my shoes."

They laughed.

Feeling a weight had lifted off his shoulders Devin relaxed.

"So, you have a partner?"

"Yes. James and I have been together for five years. He's a nurse at the VA Hospital."

"Do your friends and family know about you?"

"They should. I don't hide. Do yours?"

"Only my friend Stella knows. And, she lives in Canada."

"Why her?"

"Long story. We met in England a couple years ago. We kept in touch. I had a feeling she might be interested in me and I just didn't think it'd be fair to lead her on. So, after a few letters and phone calls, I just told her."

"You did the right thing. How did she take it?"

"She was cool with it. We've been best friends ever since."

"And your family?"

"I doubt they'd be receptive."

"Opening up about these things is never easy."

"I get it. I've learned to keep stuff to myself since I can remember."

"You're not alone."

Devin smiled.

"So, will we see you on Friday?" asked Hal.

"I—I don't know…"

"Well, if you decide to join us, make sure you lose the flannel shirt and tennis shoes."

"I'm not used to dressing fancy."

"Don't overthink it. People will be checking out your backside before they ever notice what you're wearing."

"You don't say!" Devin responded with a mischievous look on his face.

"I should go," Hal said, rising from his seat. "I wanna try to have a moment with the band before they go on stage. They must be here by now."

"Nice meeting you, Hal."

"Same here," said Hal, handing Devin his business card. "Call me."

——————>-☺-<——————

Two years later, Devin's fortuitous rendezvous with Hal had grown into a full-fledged friendship. Taken with Devin's youthful charms, Hal had introduced him to his long-term partner and their friends, who quickly welcomed him into their midst.

"Feeling better?" Hal asked, just before the chandeliers and the sconces in the theater lobby flashed for the third time.

"Yes. Thank you. Tea always works for me."

"Good. I hope *Rigoletto* works for *me*. Three hours is a long time."

"I promise not to wake you if you fall asleep."

"I'll try not to. Let's go in."

Later that evening, on their way back to Ann Arbor, Hal broke the news that he and James would soon be moving out-of-state.

"Seriously? When?" Devin asked, bolting upright.

"In a few days. James just found out he landed a head nurse position in Fort Lauderdale."

"In a few days? I didn't even know he was job hunting."

"No one did, except for us. We kept it quiet. He didn't wanna say until he knew he got the job for sure."

"I get that. But why Florida?"

"We both love it there. You know that! We're sun worshippers, plus that's one of the gay Meccas in America."

"What will *you* do there?"

"I freelance, remember? I can work anywhere."

"Right. So, you *are* leaving."

"That's the plan. You will too. Your graduation is around the corner."

"Yeah, I know."

"Did you hear back from the schools you applied to?"

"Yup. I was admitted to Berkeley and Columbia."

"Both? Damn, that's terrific! Congratulations! Have you made up your mind yet?"

"Columbia. I'm a Big Apple fan. I'll be close to my family and only a subway ride from Broadway."

"Makes sense. Are you driving or flying?"

"Driving. It'll be warm by May. My clunker should survive the long trek."

"How long will it take?"

"Depends. Nine or ten hours with traffic and a couple stops along the way."

For a moment, Devin fell silent, his mind aflush with memories. Just two years back a random stranger in a bar had peeped inside his shell and saw a captive truth. He didn't hesitate to gently crack it open and rescue it in one fell swoop. *Nothing's been the same since then*, Devin thought, as Hal drove up to his dorm building and parked at the entrance.

"I guess this is it, then," Devin said. He turned to Hal and saw his own reflection in his eyes.

"I'll miss you, Grandma."
"Same here, Missy."
They hugged.
"Promise me you'll keep in touch," Hal said.
"I will."

X. THE BIG APPLE

T *hat should do it,* Devin thought, as he loaded the last piece of luggage into the trunk of his beat-up Chevy Impala. He checked his watch and jumped into the driver's seat a few minutes before midnight. Seven hours later and hundreds of miles behind him, the fused warm colors of dawn gradually began to emerge, sweeping across the eastern horizon.

Somewhere in rural Pennsylvania Devin pulled over at a rest stop and sat down for breakfast. While waiting to be served he reached inside his backpack, pulled out a roadmap and spread it out on the table. The smell of coffee filled the air. Oblivious to the animated chatter of a few early risers around him, he reviewed his trip details. *A few more hours and I should be in Midtown.* He had booked a room for a week, and planned to use the time to search for a shared apartment and a part-time job.

Devin counted on his parents to help cover his living expenses during his first month in the city. Just before leaving for Europe to celebrate their wedding anniversary, Phil and Lauren had sent him a wire transfer through a local bank.

Shortly after settling in at the Vanderbilt Y, Devin attempted to contact the bank. Day after day he persisted with repeated phone calls, only to encounter the same recorded message:

You've reached Manufacturers Hanover Bank. Our offices are currently closed due to extenuating circumstances. We apologize for any inconvenience. If you would like to leave a message, please include your name and phone number and we'll return your call as soon as possible.

As the week drew to a close, Devin began feeling a growing sense of urgency. Then, one last call brought a disturbing message: a fire at the bank headquarters on Wall Street had disrupted all operations until further notice. He riffled through his address book. Reluctant to burden his sisters and the few friends who might be able to help him, he envisioned himself stranded on the streets of the city.

On the eve of his last day at the Y Devin went out for a walk to clear his thoughts. One city block after another, he advanced at a brisk pace, feeling his feet bonding with the pavement. By the time he reached Central Park he had broken a sweat. He slowed down, then sat on a bench. Bending forward, he rested his elbows on his knees and buried his face in his hands, briefly retreating into a timeless space. In the distance, he heard sounds of passing footsteps and laughter. Rustling leaves prompted him to slowly raise his head. A light breeze caressed his face. The city hummed and whispered all around. He took a deep breath and exhaled. A sense of calm and peace enveloped him as he stood up and resumed walking.

The next morning, Devin awoke renewed and feeling hopeful. Within the hour, he found himself riding a train that took him to West Harlem. At 120th Street, he exited and made his way to the Student Affairs Office at Teachers College. As he entered, a young Asian woman sitting behind the reception desk greeted him with a courteous smile.

"Good morning!" Devin said. "I'm here to see a counselor."

"Hi! Did you have an appointment with Ms. Davis?" she responded, gently pushing her long silky black hair away from her face.

"I don't. I'm sorry. It's kind of an emergency."

"It's okay, I understand. Please take a seat." She handed Devin an intake form and a pen. "You can give this to Ms. Davis when you go in to see her. You're lucky her first appointment of the day was cancelled. She should be here any time now."

"Thank you. Is Ms. Davis the counselor?"

"Actually, she's the Office Director."

Within minutes, Devin was seated across from a greying, elegantly-dressed middle-aged woman, explaining his predicament.

"So, your parents are on vacation and you can't reach them?" Ms. Davis asked, holding Devin's intake form in one hand as she gazed at him over the rim of her reading glasses.

"They're overseas for their wedding anniversary and I have no idea where they're staying," Devin replied. "To be honest, even if I knew, I'd hate to disturb them. They've been planning this trip for quite a while."

"I see. What are their occupations, if I may ask?"

"They're school teachers."

"Both of them?"

"Yes."

"In public schools?"

"Yeah, they teach in the same high school in Kingston. My dad teaches history and my mom, art."

"Wonderful! I taught Spanish for thirty years in the city high schools here in New York, until I retired last year."

"Congratulations! But, you're back at work already?"

"Only on a temporary basis. Until they find a permanent replacement for my predecessor," Ms. Davis said, scanning the intake form. "So, Mr. Sharp, it looks like you're all set to start classes in September. Your application for a student loan has been approved. But you're here early and you have no place to stay?"

"My plan was to find a roommate and share an apartment somewhere in the city. But until the bank clears the wire that my parents sent me, I don't have enough for a security deposit."

"Have you considered applying for a part time job on campus?"

"I have. I picked up a form a few days ago. I filled it out and mailed it straight away."

"Okay. Let me check on that. I will also make a few phone calls and see where that gets us. In the meantime, you can wait in the reception area. I'll call you when I'm ready."

"I'm baaack!" Devin said to the girl behind the desk as he stepped out of Ms. Davis' office.

"That was a quick conference," she responded.

"I'm not done yet. Ms. Davis told me to wait here until she calls me back."

"Oh, okay. You're Devin, right? I read your name on the intake form."

"Yes. You?"

"Penny. Nice to meet you."

"Likewise."

Penny smiled. "We have hot coffee while you wait, if you like." She pointed to a small counter next to a Xerox machine.

"Thank you. I could use some caffeine right now." He walked over to the coffee station, poured himself a cup and took a seat next to Penny's desk.

"You're a new student, I take it," Penny said.

"Yes, I am."

"So am I. Taking any courses this summer?"

"Not yet. I won't be starting with classes till September."

"What's your major?"

"International Ed. And yours?"

"Neat. Mine is Psychology with a minor in Asian Studies."

"Coolness."

"Do you know if you'll be travelling for research?"

"I'm not sure but I hope so. I love travelling!"

"Me too!"

A few minutes later, the phone beeped on Penny's desk.

"It's Ms. Davis," she said. "She's ready for you." Devin stood up and walked back into Ms. Davis' office.

"Okay Devin, please take a seat. I have good news, and not-so-good news for you," Ms. Davis said with a slight smile. "Where should I begin?"

"I'll take the good news first, please."

"Fine. We did receive your application for employment and we happen to have a part-time position available right here at our office."

"Really? That's amazing! What is it?"

"Assistant to the Director. If you're interested Penny can give you all the details. She holds the same position. We just need another person to help out with basic office chores. Normally, we have two assistants."

"Wow. Are you offering me this right now?"

"I am. We have no other applicants. That is, if you can type, answer the phone, and file."

"I can. What are the hours?"

"We're flexible. When the fall semester starts we'll work your hours around your class schedule."

"I'll take it!"

"Can you start tomorrow?"

"I sure can. Thank you, Ms. Davis!"

"You're welcome. Now, about the *not-so-good* news... I contacted the Housing Office and I'm told there are no units available at the moment. They'll put your name on a waiting list, if that's okay with you."

"It is, but..."

"I know. This doesn't fix the issue of your accommodation. So, I took the liberty to make a personal phone call. One of my neighbors could possibly take you in, but only for one week. Maybe two, at most. She's a retired nurse and lives by herself in a three-bedroom apartment."

"Where?"

"On the Upper West Side. She won't need a security deposit. Interested?"

"Of course! I can't thank you enough!"

At last, an invisible door had swung open, marking the beginning of Devin's life in the Big Apple. In less than two weeks, the wire transfer from his parents had cleared and Ms. Davis had pulled strings to find a place to stay for him on campus.

"You're in luck, Mr. Sharp," Ms. Davis said on the morning she called Devin to her office to give him the details of his new living arrangements. "Your new shared apartment is a fully renovated two-bedroom in a beautiful walk-up building close to everything."

"Awesome! I'm so relieved."

"Well, two things worked in your favor. Because of the urgency of your situation, I managed to get the Housing Office to agree to give your case priority. Soon afterward, the last person living with your soon-to-be roommate reported he had no choice but to break his contract and move out."

"Do you know who my roommate is?"

"A full-time student. That's all I know," said Ms. Davis. "You'll get to meet him soon enough."

The following day Devin stood at the main entrance of a prewar red brick apartment building on Morningside Drive. A deep male voice answered the intercom. Minutes later he met Ben, a brown-eyed, twenty-five-year-old native of Long Island and a second-year student at Columbia Law School.

"Hi! I'm Ben," he said, standing at the door in his shorts and a sweatshirt. He reached out and shook Devin's hand. "Come on in!"

"Hi, Ben. I'm Devin. Nice meeting you."

"Just one suitcase?"

"The rest is in my car."

"I can give you a hand with that. I got a couple hours before I hit the gym. Can I get you something to drink? I got lemonade and bottled water in the fridge."

"Sure. Water's fine. Thanks."

"Make yourself at home," Ben said, pointing to an L-shaped couch in the living room. In front of it, a coffee table was covered with sports magazines and a small TV on a stand.

As Ben stepped into the kitchen Devin glanced at his towering frame before walking over to a large window in the living room. "Nice view of the park," he said, before he sank into the couch.

"It's a great neighborhood," Ben responded. He handed Devin a bottle of water and joined him on the couch. "Very safe and clean. Good for jogging."

"Good to know," Devin responded, the first impressions of his new roommate's character hatching in his mind. *Straight as they come*, he thought. *And, a jock.* "How long have you been at this apartment?" he asked.

"Two years. Since I got admitted to Law School."

"Cool. Must be tough. Then you gotta pass the Bar."

"It's not that bad. My Dad's a lawyer. My grandpa was a judge, and…"

"I gotcha. It's in your genes."

Ben chuckled. "Something like that."

Within a span of twenty minutes Devin had concluded that Ben's crew cut and square jawline were physical reflections of his somewhat distracting self-confidence and rugged masculinity.

———————>-◉-<———————

After a month sharing the apartment, Devin harbored no doubts: *We're a complete mismatch.* As a newcomer to the city, he spent most of his non-working hours at home reading, watching TV or chatting on the phone. In contrast, Ben's passion for sports, frequent workout routine and active social life seemed to keep him constantly on the go.

Then, on a quiet Thursday evening in midsummer, things took an unforeseen turn.

"Hey Devin! What are you up to this weekend?" Ben called, sitting at one end of the couch, his legs crossed and resting on the coffee table.

"Nothing. Staying home," Devin answered from his bedroom. "I got a paper due on Monday. You?"

"I got a free ticket for the opera."

Devin walked out of his bedroom.

"What?"

"It's for tomorrow night. My friend Donna can't make it. I thought you might be interested."

"Did you say *free?*"

"Yup."

"I'll take it."

"I thought you might."

"How come?"

"I heard the word *Rigoletto* when you were talking on the phone the other day. Sorry, I didn't mean to snoop."

Devin sat down on the couch. "No worries. I was just talking to my mom. So, you like the opera?"

"Not just the opera. Let me show you." Ben stood up and took a few quick strides into his bedroom. He returned with a small cardboard box filled with playbills from old Broadway shows.

"I save these."

"Wow! A law student, an athlete, and a theater buff. I'm impressed, mister!" Devin joked. "How did that happen?"

Ben stared down at his hands. "When my mom passed my family went through a rough patch. She had cancer. I was fifteen. It was just Dad, my sister and me in the house. The weekends were tough, with no school and no escape. Then, Dad decided to bring us to the city on Saturdays. *To change the picture*, he'd say. We'd begin with a walk in Central Park, then a quick bite, and we'd be off to the matinees at the movies or the theater. That's how it started."

"Sorry about your mom."

"Thanks. How about you?" Ben reached for a pack of bubble gum on the table, unwrapped a chunk and popped it in his mouth. "What got you into it?"

"The opera? Watching TV with my parents when I was growing up. I loved the feeling of forgetting myself while seeing all that drama from a sheltered space. I still do. I guess I'm a bit odd that way."

"Not that odd. Who doesn't like a bird's eyes' view of things once in a while?"

"True. So, is Donna just a friend? I thought she was your girlfriend."

"Yeah, we've been dating for a while. What about you? Are you seeing anyone?"

A cold chill ran down Devin's spine. In fractions of a second, an innocent question had shifted the earth under his feet. While frantically weighing his options, a memory popped up and struck a nerve: *I don't hide*, he remembered his friend Hal saying on the night they met. Suddenly, he felt a wave of courage surging through him. "Nah. I'm not seeing anyone right now," he said, his body thrumming with energy. "By the way, I think you should know, I'm gay. I hope that's not an issue."

"Not at all," Ben responded in a casual tone. "Maybe you should meet Meg."

Baffled, Devin stared. "Meg?"

"My sister. She's also gay and has a few friends you might be interested in meeting."

Devin froze. In an instant, reality had turned upside down. "Wow. Okay. Sure… I haven't had a chance to meet that many people yet." He sighed as a wave of relief washed over him.

"Meg lives in D. C., but she rides her bike to New York every so often."

"She rides a motorcycle? Awesome!"

"That's her thing. She belongs to this group who call themselves the *Motorcycle Mamas*. Do you know who they are?"

"No idea," Devin answered, still reeling from a rollercoaster ride of emotions. "Who are they?"

"They're a cool lesbian biker club that started in L. A. They're known for leading the pride parades in major cities. They're a sight to behold."

"No kidding."

"Meg says they're proud to follow in the tradition of true bra-burning gender-benders. You'll see what I mean when you meet her."

"Can't wait!"

In the early evening of the following day, the roommates sat together in the Paul Recital Hall at Juilliard School in Lincoln Center. Subdued lighting, red velour seats and walls clad with cherry wood surrounded them. Ben leafed through the playbill while Devin surveyed the chamber.

"Impressive for a small venue," Devin said.

"It's meant to be intimate. Keep in mind this is mostly used by grad students who practice their craft here. You'll see, they're just like pros."

"They're doing a burletta, right?"

"Yeah, a comic opera, according to this," Ben said, waving the playbill in his hand. "Short and sweet. The original was much longer and had a different name."

"What was it?"

"*Orazio,* the name of the main character."

Devin broke into gooseflesh. *Strange… Rings a bell.*

"A singing coach," Ben went on, reading from the playbill. "Maybe that's how the name of the production evolved into *The Music Teacher.*"

"Makes sense."

"Apparently, these operettas were one-act shows with just a few singers and musicians."

"Yes, I knew that," said Devin. "They were popular with travelling troupes that went from town to town."

"There you go. Just what the playbill says."

"So what's *The Music Teacher* all about?"

"It's about a pretty young woman who aspires to become an opera singer. She thinks she's ready for stardom but her teacher disagrees. A powerful impresario becomes infatuated with her and offers to make her famous. He persuades her to sign a contract and go with him. When her coach finds out, he tells her the impresario is a crook who can't be trusted. He then reveals *he* is in love with her and begs her to tear up the contract."

"Does she?"

"No. She refuses."

"So, the story doesn't end well?"

"Hang on. This is a comedy, remember? Comedies always end well."

"Oh, lemme guess: It ends in a three-way."

Ben chuckled. "You have a dirty mind, Devin. But you're right. She tells her teacher she loves him too, but she thinks all three of them need each other, so they should stick together."

"The lights are dimming," Devin whispered as the audience grew quiet. "*How* do they need each other?"

Ben leaned sideways and whispered back. "She claims they need the impresario for fame and fortune. The impresario needs a good singer. And she admits she still needs a teacher."

"Is that it?"

"Yeah, all three agree to work together."

"Ha… Not quite the happy ending I imagined."

Ben giggled as the curtains lifted.

An hour later, the music stopped. When the applause died down, Ben turned to Devin.

"How did you like it?"

"It was short and sweet as you said, but nothing special. Did *you* like it?"

"I'm not sure. For some reason something felt off."

"With the music?"

"No, with the plot. I was thinking there is nothing comical about people *peddling their souls to a crook.*"

Devin's eyes widened.

"Something I said?" Ben asked. "You look spooked."

"Nah. It's just that for a moment there, you sounded like someone else…"

"Huh?"

"Like a prosecutor or a judge. Someone I must've heard somewhere, I guess. I just can't remember."

"A haunting voice from a distinguished figure?"

"Yes, Your Honor!" Devin joked.

Ben smiled. "Judge Benjamin Fielding! I like the sound of that!"

They rose from their seats, walked out of the theater and headed home.

XI. THANKSGIVING MEDLEY

R ays of muted sunlight fell on a bonsai resting on the windowsill beside
Ms. Davis' desk. Standing over it, she watered it with measured sips from
a long-spouted can. A paper calendar was pinned to a bulletin board next to
the window. The top section showed a photo of a pumpkin patch and a red
barn in the background. At the bottom, the month of November was filled with
to-do notes and upcoming appointments.

"Come in!" Ms. Davis called, when she heard a knock.

Devin and Penny walked in.

"Good afternoon! Please make yourselves comfortable."

They sat across from her desk.

"Beautiful bonsai!" said Penny.

"Thank you! Yes, it's lovely. A gift from a friend. For peace and serenity,
she told me."

Penny smiled. "And for good luck. They're an Asian tradition."

"Good luck, too? Let's hope I can keep it alive then!" Ms. Davis put the
watering can aside and sat down at her desk. "I called to tell you that our office
will be assisting in the planning and coordination of a student trip to Asia next
year. It's a cultural exchange project with a university in Indonesia. I'd like
you to help me with it."

"I'd be happy to," Penny responded.

"Me too," said Devin. "When is this happening?"

"We're looking at spending spring break in Jakarta. Our goal is to take at
least fifteen students and one faculty member," Ms. Davis explained. "I was
asked to go, and I'm considering it. Since you're both enrolled in the
departments involved in sponsoring the trip, you could be a part of the student
contingent. That is, if you were interested."

"That would be awesome," Devin said. "I wish I could afford it."

Penny sighed. "Same here."

"Let's not get ahead of ourselves. This project is being financed by a grant,
so the students who are selected won't incur any expenses."

Penny's eyes lit up. "Oh my God! Really?" She glanced at Devin. "How do we register?"

Ms. Davis gave the pair a warm nod. "You'll just have to fill out an application and see how it goes."

"Is that it?" Devin asked. "What's the catch?"

"I'll know more after Thanksgiving. But I'm sure that at the very least, students will have to keep logs of what they learn at each stage of the trip."

"Sounds fair."

"Something else. I thought you might be interested in joining me at St. John The Divine this evening. Our school choir will be there singing Gregorian chants. I know it's short notice and the night before Thanksgiving, so I won't be offended if you have other plans."

"Thank you for the offer Ms. Davis," Devin said. "You can count me in. I'm free and I live just a few blocks away, as you know."

"I'd also love to join you," Penny said.

"Good! Let's meet at the main entrance around seven-thirty. It starts at eight."

That evening, Devin, Penny and Ms. Davis sat next to each other in the front row pews across from the altar at St. John The Divine.

Devin gazed up at the cathedral's high vaulted ceilings and the huge columns that supported them. "Wow. This is impressive."

"First time here?" Ms. Davis asked.

"I meant to drop by a while ago. I'm taking my time exploring the neighborhood."

"This is a landmark worth visiting, Devin. It's one of the largest cathedrals in the world. The acoustics are remarkable. You'll see what I mean in a moment."

"I've never heard Gregorian chants in person before."

"Some people find them hypnotizing."

"It was a Pope that came up with them, right?"

"Well, Pope Gregory the Great often gets credit for them, but they were created long after his time."

"The Pope who invented the calendar?"

"No. That was another Gregory, a thousand years later," Ms. Davis said softly as the lights dimmed, the singers took their spots on the choir riser and the audience fell silent.

Soon after the singing started, Penny noticed Devin nodding off. She nudged him gently.

He quickly snapped back, shook his head and turned toward her. "Sorry. I was miles away."

"Shh! Stay awake," Penny whispered. "You don't want to miss this, do you?"

An hour later, all three walked out of the warm, hushed sanctuary of the cathedral and onto Amsterdam Avenue, filled with blaring horns and blazing lights.

"How did you like it?" Ms. Davis asked.

"It was amazing. It kinda put me in a trance," Devin replied, pulling up the hood of his coat.

"It was lovely," said Penny. "Thank you again for the invite."

"My pleasure," Ms. Davis responded, hailing an approaching cab. "And, thank you both for your company. Happy Thanksgiving!" She climbed into the cab and waved goodbye before it whisked her away.

A cool breeze made Penny shiver. "Brrr! It's getting cold." She tightened the scarf around her neck.

"Taking a cab?" asked Devin.

"No. It's a long ride to Chinatown. It'll be cheaper and faster if I take the subway."

"Gotcha. I'll walk you to the station."

"I appreciate it."

They strode side by side on a chilly sidewalk.

"I'm glad you could make it this evening," Devin said.

"Me too. I wanted to be there for Ms. Davis. I think it was important for her. She's a widow, you know. No children."

"She mentioned."

"Besides, I'll be staying in the city with my family tomorrow. No pressure. You?

"Going upstate. But still, I also wanted to be there. Ms. Davis has been amazing to me."

"Were you really in a trance earlier? You sounded like you meant it."

"I'm pretty sure I was dreaming."

"What about? You just nodded off for a few minutes."

"Thing is, I rarely remember any details."

"Nothing at all?"

"Actually, this time was an exception."

"Cool! Wanna share? A few minutes in a dream can be a lifetime."

"I—I don't usually share about that kind of stuff," Devin said. "But uh...

Okay. Just this once, I guess." Then, he began: "It was nightfall and I was wandering around a beautiful town square somewhere in Old Europe. I saw horse-drawn carriages and age-old buildings all around. The whole thing was so vivid, it felt real. Suddenly, I heard echoes of melodies that carried in the air. I was drawn to them, so I kept walking until I found myself standing in front of a huge building. The doors were wide open. I went in and realized it was a church. I advanced through the nave toward the altar. It felt like I was floating. As I approached the pulpit, there was a choir of young boys singing. I sat in front of them and closed my eyes."

"And then?"

"You woke me up."

"Fascinating. I've had a few vivid dreams like that myself. I think there's something very special about them."

"I agree," Devin said, as they arrived at the entrance of the subway station.

"Maybe one day we could trade notes."

"Maybe."

"Happy Thanksgiving Devin!"

"Thanks! You too!"

Penny went down the steps of the station entrance and disappeared in the underbelly of the city.

———➤–◉–◄———

Early the next morning, Devin got up, showered, packed a duffel bag with his essentials and headed for the Port Authority. There, he boarded a Trailways bus going upstate. He had not seen his family since his return from Michigan.

Just before noon, the bus pulled into the Kingston bus depot. His dad was waiting for him.

"Hey pal! Good to see you! It's been a while," Phil said, wrapping his arms around him. "How was the ride?"

"Good, thanks. I slept all the way here."

They walked a few steps to the parking lot, Devin tossed his bag in the backseat of his dad's aging Ford Escort, and they drove away.

"Did you have breakfast?" Phil asked.

"I had no time. I'm starved."

"There'll be plenty of food when we get home. You know your mom. We got a 16-pounder in the oven!"

"Can't wait!"

Ten minutes later, as Phil opened the front door of the house, a medley of delectable smells invaded Devin's senses. Signaling a warm welcome, Harold, the family's beagle, jumped on Devin howling joyously and wagging his tail. Lauren rushed out of the kitchen wiping her hands on her apron. Standing behind her, Paige smiled, casually dressed in flare jeans and earthy colors. Beside her, Abbey watched the scene, hair done up, wearing long brown leather boots and a dress that reached just below the knees.

Lauren cradled Devin's face in her hands, nudged his cheeks and kissed him tenderly.

"There he is!" she said. "My gorgeous son."

"You got that right!" Devin responded.

She giggled.

Next, Paige and Abbey lavished him with hugs and kisses. Kyle and Frank, their long-term partners, greeted him with handshakes and slaps on his shoulder.

"Your bedroom is ready," Lauren said. "You go upstairs, drop off your bag and freshen up, if you like. Supper should be ready soon."

"Thanks, mom."

Shortly afterward, the Sharps had taken their seats around the dinner table. The warmth of the fireplace made the air soft and cozy.

Paige glanced over the holiday decorations in the dining room. "Everything looks beautiful, Mom!"

"And yummy," said Devin, eyeing the mouthwatering food on the table.

"Thank you. Daddy had a hand in this too, you know," Lauren responded, looking at Phil. She lifted the carving knife and held it out. "Honey, will you do the honors?"

"I'll be happy to, sweetheart." He rose, took the knife and began slicing the turkey.

"Mmm… Smells amazing!" Devin said, taking in the buttery aroma of the acorn squash drifting out of a bowl in his hand.

"Wait till you try the stuffing. Made with momma's love," Lauren said with a smile.

Abbey scrutinized Devin from across the table. "Looks like he's been grooming himself to death," she whispered in Kyle's ear. "Not one hair out of place."

"Please, Abbey. Not now," Kyle pleaded.

"So, what happened to your old Chevy Impala, Devin?" Paige asked, as she helped herself to a serving from a green bean casserole dish. "I thought you brought it back from Michigan."

"I sold it after I arrived. I couldn't afford to park it anywhere in the city. And, I was strapped for cash."

Abbey frowned. "I thought Mom and Dad were helping you."

Paige jumped in. "Didn't you hear what happened to the wire they sent him when they were in Italy? That freaky fire at that bank. What the heck! That was so screwed up."

"I know. That *was* screwed up," said Devin. "But I got it all sorted out in the end."

"Speaking of Italy, Mom and I have news," Phil announced. "We're going back next summer. This time, to Genoa and Turin."

"Northern Italy again?" Abbey asked, a tinge of surprise and annoyance in her tone.

"We fell in love with it," Lauren answered. "Venice and Milan were great, but one week wasn't enough. There was so much to see."

"That's wonderful!" Paige said. "You got a taste of it, and now—"

"—we want more!" said Lauren. She winked at Paige, lifted her wine glass and took a sip.

Paige smiled. "So exciting!"

"Thank you, sweetie."

"Cool! I may also be going on a trip next year," said Devin, wiping his chin. "I'm applying for a chance to go to Indonesia with a group of students during Easter Break. All expenses paid."

"Great! That's my boy!" Phil said. "When will you know?"

"In a few days, I hope."

Cheers followed.

"Well, Kyle and I also have an announcement to make," Abbey declared, swiftly shifting the focus of attention. "We're planning to tie the knot next summer. Now I guess we'll have to coordinate the wedding date with you guys, so it won't conflict with your trip to Italy."

"That's wonderful news!" Lauren responded. "Congratulations!"

"Welcome to the family, Kyle!' Phil boomed.

Paige rushed over to hug her sister, eyes glistening. "Oh, Abbey! I'm so happy for you!"

"Paige, no need for tears!"

"And we can talk dates later," said Lauren. "Now let's all raise our glasses and toast the newly engaged couple!"

Two bottles of wine lay empty and everyone had finished their second helpings when Lauren tapped her glass with a spoon. "Save some room for dessert everyone. I made your favorite pies."

"No pressure, though," Phil said, triggering giggles and chuckles.

Devin patted his stomach with his hands. "I'm so full! That was delicious."

"It warms my heart to see you enjoying a home-cooked meal again, Devin," Lauren beamed. "Last time was Christmas. Almost a year ago. Now if I may, how's my prized son doing in the love department?"

"It's closed for business at the moment, Mom," Devin quipped.

Everyone laughed.

"Not for long, I should hope," Lauren insisted. "Someday soon, and when you least expect it, love will find you."

Devin glanced at Paige, eyes pleading. "It'd be nice," he responded.

"Wouldn't it?" Abbey chimed in. "Maybe you'll settle down and start a family, too."

Kyle's eyes darted to Abbey.

Paige sprang into action. "What's the rush? Devin just turned twenty-two. Are you guys trying to marry him off already?"

Casting a tender gaze at Phil, Lauren responded. "Your dad was twenty-three and I was just nineteen when we got married."

Paige rolled her eyes. "That was another time, Mom."

"Besides, not everyone gets married," Devin blurted out, light tremors stirring in his stomach. "Not everyone can… or wishes to."

"Who would that be?" Lauren pressed on. "The clergy? Everyone *who*?"

Endless seconds followed as the pops and crackles from the fireplace reverberated in the air.

Devin cleared his throat. "All kinds of people. We're all different."

"Different how?"

"Honey, please," Phil said. "There's no need…"

"You know exactly what I mean, Mom. You've always known…"

"I see. Please excuse me." Glassy eyed, Lauren rose from her seat and walked toward the kitchen. Abbey and Paige followed her. A palpable chill had replaced the soft warmth Devin had felt when he came into the house.

"Well, now that everyone is done making their announcements…" Phil began, in an attempt to inject lightheartedness into the rarefied air. "How about some coffee and dessert?"

"That sounds wonderful," Kyle said. Frank nodded.

"None for me, thanks," said Devin, staring down at his napkin. Just then, Abbey and Paige came out of the kitchen with two serving platters.

"I was just coming for that," Phil said, pointing.

Abbey glared at Devin as she and Paige approached the table.

"We got it Dad," Paige said, then turned to Devin. "Mom's making coffee. Would you mind lending her a hand?"

"Sure," He got up and walked into the kitchen.

Lauren stood by the counter, taking cups and saucers from an overhead cabinet and placing them on a tray. Gurgling and bubbling sounds emanated from the coffee maker.

Devin approached. "I'm sorry, Mom."

"No. I am," said Lauren, moving closer and taking his hands. "I didn't mean to hurt you."

"You didn't. You caught me off guard. I was just wondering—"

"—why I needed confirmation?"

"I didn't know where you were coming from. I thought you knew."

Lauren sighed. "It's a mean world out there. Your dad and I have always wanted to protect you."

"I know that."

"You also know we love you and want you to be happy, don't you Devin? Nothing will ever change that."

"Thank you, Mom. That means the world to me."

They embraced and returned to the warm glow of the dining room. Soon, sweet treats and light music revived the holiday spirit and the smiles.

As the sun began to set, Devin stepped out to the porch. Abbey and Kyle followed.

Kyle extended his hand for a handshake. "Time to head home. You enjoy yourself this weekend with your parents, buddy. We'll see you again at Christmastime, I hope."

"Thank you, Kyle. I'll be here."

"Honey, you go ahead and start the car," said Abbey. As Kyle stepped away she faced Devin. "You just couldn't let it go, could you? You had to drag us all into your drama."

"What are you getting at, Abbey?"

"Oh, come on, Devin! You can't help making yourself the center of attention."

"Wow. Really? It's hard to believe that, coming from you."

"Seriously? You were always a spoiled brat. You and your stupid nightmares when you were a kid and your endless issues at school drove Mom and Dad crazy. For God's sake! They had to get you a therapist! And now this shit! Did you have to spoil Mom's Thanksgiving dinner with that nonsense?"

Devin took a step back. "Abbey, please stop. I'm just not up for this right now."

"Whatever. You should be ashamed of yourself! You're incorrigible." Abbey turned and made a beeline for the driveway.

"I'll take that as a compliment!" Devin bellowed, then walked back into the house.

———>-☺-<———

On Devin's last day in Kingston, as he packed his bag, Phil showed up at his bedroom door.

"What's up, Dad?"

"Nothing. I just wanted to mention we'll be with the Hayseses in Italy next year. Have you been in contact with Stella recently?"

"Of course! We write each other and talk on the phone every so often. What's the scoop?"

"We'll be meeting her parents in Genoa. We plan on staying at the same hotel and going on tours together."

"Sounds great. Will Stella be joining you? She never mentioned any of this to me."

"That, I don't know. This is all new, but I don't think so. Anyway, your mom and I were wondering if you might consider housesitting for us. It'd be only for a week."

"No problem. I got you guys. I don't expect to be taking any summer courses, so I'll be more than happy to take a break away from the city.

"You could bring a friend along, if you like."

"Maybe I'll ask Stella if she wants to join me."

"Good! You'll have plenty of time to plan ahead. Thank you, Devin."

———>-☺-<———

A week after returning to the city, Devin and Penny stood by the time clock at the office. Two minutes before five on a cold December evening, they waited to punch out and head home for the night.

"We're so lucky we were picked for the trip to Indonesia," Penny said.

"Yep. In a few months we'll be walking on the streets of Jakarta."

"I know! A once-in-a-lifetime experience."

"Hell yeah! Ten days at the bottom of the earth."

"Well, Australia and Antarctica are further south."

Devin grinned. "It's the end of the day and you're starting with me? What's gonna happen when we're stuck together in Jakarta?"

"I'll murder you."

"You would. I can see it in your eyes."

They laughed.

"You know, we could avoid a bloodbath."

"Oh yeah? How's that?"

"We should get to know each other better," said Penny. "Wanna grab a bite?"

"Tonight?"

"Why not?"

"Are you hitting on me?"

Penny giggled. "I know better. You're unavailable," she said, winking and smiling. "No need to explain."

"You got a special radar or something?"

"Maybe I do."

"Thank God for that! Everyone should get one."

"You like Thai?"

"I'm always open to new flavors."

"There's a pretty good place not far from here."

"Affordable?"

"It's fast but tasty."

"Let's go."

A half hour later they sat across from each other at a casual Thai eatery nearby. Around them, a lively mix of students and locals chatted while nibbling on delicious treats.

"Yummy! Whatever *Gai Pra Ram* is," Devin said, through a mouthful.

"You crack me up. You ordered chicken and steamed veggies from the menu."

"Just kidding! I love the peanut sauce."

"No chopsticks?"

"What for? The Byzantines invented the fork so people could easily shove large portions of food into their mouths. Easy access, baby."

"Barbarians."

"My people!"

"So, are we ever going to discuss this thing we have in common?"

"What *thing*?"

"Remember what we said the night before Thanksgiving after leaving St. John The Divine? You walked me to the subway and—"

"—Oh, right. Well, I don't think I've ever talked about that stuff with anyone at length. Except in therapy. And that was not my choice. I was a kid."

"At least you had someone to talk to."

"Not really. The doctor told my parents I suffered from hallucinations. So, in the end, I just quit talking."

"Same here. I was afraid people would think I'm nuts."

Devin shrugged. "Me too. Who knows? Maybe we are."

"If that's the case, we're not alone. I've been reading about it."

"What did you find out? I'm curious. I've had to live with this my whole life. It was really bad when I was growing up. It frightened me."

"What did?"

"Well, it's still happening… But I'm used to it now."

"What is it? It's okay. Tell me."

"Uh… Recurring dreams. Every so often, I fall asleep but it feels like I'm awake. I can't move, but suddenly I find myself floating in the air. I look down and there I am, lying in bed. Then, there's this veil in a corner of the room and I feel like there's a presence there."

"Oh, shit. That's heavy. And very scary to a little kid."

"You bet. But it's a rare thing now."

"Still scary?"

"Not anymore. Truth is, I kinda welcome the experience."

"Serious? How come?"

"I want to know more about that veil and what's behind it."

"Maybe what you see is a kind of threshold. Did you ever think of that?"

"It crossed my mind. Sometimes when I wake up I feel I've been somewhere…"

"It's not uncommon. There are people who have similar experiences."

"Really?"

"You're looking at one."

Devin tilted his head to one side, eyebrows arched. "Okaayy… So, what are *your* dreams about?"

"Like yours, mine are recurring dreams that happen once in a while. But there's no veil or anything like that. Once I'm in deep sleep, *boom!* I'm on the other side."

"What do you see?"

"It's weird. Sometimes flashing images, sometimes short moving scenes. Like old movie reels or something."

"*Old* movie reels? So, you catch glimpses of a time somewhere in the past."

"Yes. And not a happy time."

"What do you mean?"

"I wake up feeling sad, as if something awful happened to someone I know, or used to know."

"Someone in your family or a close friend?"

"Maybe."

"Male or female?"

"Female, almost for sure."

"Hmm… Sounds like a puzzle."

"It really is. That's why I keep a journal."

"I like that. Could be useful to connect the dots. I think I'll start doing the same."

"Good idea! Just so you know, there's a conference coming up in a few months sponsored by an organization called the American Association for the Study of Dreams. I've been thinking I should sign up."

"Where is it?"

"By Columbus Circle. Maybe you'd like to join me."

"Is this before or after our trip to Asia?"

"I believe it's just one week before we leave."

Devin slid his chair back. "Cool. Let's do this! Now I need to go. Sorry but I'm beat."

"Me too. It's been a long day."

XII. BELORA NIGHTS

Devin emerged from a bustling subway hub into the crisp air of an early spring morning in Manhattan. He looked up. Glints of sunlight shone on a marble statue of Christopher Columbus atop a rising column. He walked a few steps and stood at a crosswalk, hands tucked inside his coat pockets. Broadway buzzed with a steady stream of traffic as he waited for a green light. Just ahead, he saw his destination: A massive structure, the New York Coliseum, a conference and convention center.

I hope this thing is not a waste of time, he thought. *Saturdays are precious.*

A familiar voice derailed his train of thoughts: "Hey!"

He looked over his shoulder and saw Penny approaching from behind.

"Good morning, Devin! Perfect timing!" she said, brandishing her watch. She slipped her arm through his and squeezed him gently. "Excited?"

"Curious, more than anything."

"Me too. Can't wait to start learning from an expert."

The crossing light turned green. A few short strides and they reached the other side of Broadway.

"The speaker is supposed to be some kind of specialist, right?" Devin asked.

"Yes. In the study of dreams. He's a renowned psycho-physiologist. Doctor Stephen Haverhill."

Minutes later, Devin and Penny sat in the third row of a small conference room as people trickled in and took their seats. At the front and center of the room was a podium. To the side, by an exit, a young man stacked paperbacks on a small table. Next to it, a poster advertising Doctor Haverhill's most recent book was displayed on a floor easel.

Penny reached into her pocketbook, pulled out a roll of mints and held it out. "You want?"

"Thanks." Devin took a mint and popped it in his mouth. "Mmm… So soothing. I love wintergreen."

"Which brings to mind winter and the holidays. Where did they go?"

"I know, right? In just a few days we'll be in Jakarta."

"It's crazy," said Penny. "Sometimes I feel like someone presses a fast-forward button and suddenly everything speeds up by weeks or months in a few seconds. It's like falling off a time cliff."

"No kidding. I'm sure I fell off one of those a few times already," Devin joked. "I just have no clue how I found my way back."

Just then, Doctor Haverhill walked in and took his place at the podium. The murmur of the audience quickly died down and he began. "On average, a person sleeps twenty-six years in a lifetime, six of which are spent dreaming. Add to that daydreaming, and we begin to see a landscape where we find ourselves navigating a kaleidoscope of reveries that transcend the night."

An hour later, the doctor took a quick glance at his notes and delivered his final remarks captivating everyone's attention: "Everyone dreams. Even those who claim they don't, or can't remember what they dream about. For those who can, our studies indicate that in the REM sleep stage, almost every awakening yields a relatively elaborate dream report. More significantly, our findings point to the notion that the mind *never stops*. As we move between our slumbers and our daydreams, life becomes a blend of the conscious and the subconscious, where the boundaries between dreams and reality blur."

A smattering of applause greeted the doctor as he took a swig from a bottle of water and prepared for a brief question-and-answer session. After a light exchange with several members of the audience, he stepped off the stage and his assistant announced that the paperbacks on the table were available for purchase.

"I'm getting one," Penny said, as she and Devin rose from their seats. "You?"

"Absolutely," Devin replied.

They approached the table and bought their copies. As they walked out of the room, Penny skimmed over the blurb on the back of her book. "Fascinating stuff," she said. "I had no clue we have a gland in our brains that pumps a hormone that makes us go to sleep."

"Yeah, the *pineal gland*. I didn't know that either. What had me hooked was when the doctor mentioned the ancient Egyptians believed this gland caused an invisible eye to open up in their foreheads."

"Right. They called it the *Third Eye*. They thought it was a gateway to higher levels of awareness. Some Eastern religions still believe in this."

"Maybe they're onto something."

Penny pointed at a small crowd standing by an elevator. "Should we take the stairs?"

"Sure. After you."

As they began their descent their voices echoed in the stairwell.

"How do you know so much about this stuff?" asked Devin.

"I'm majoring in Asian Studies, remember? Eastern religions and philosophy are both required courses. And, in case you haven't noticed, I happen to be Asian."

"You're hysterical! Is your family religious?"

"Some. My parents are Tibetan Buddhists. So, yeah, that helps a little."

When they reached the ground floor they crossed the lobby and stepped out of the building. The street roared with the rush of cars and buses. The rattle of a subway train emerged from below, drowning out a wailing ambulance in the distance.

"The sunshine feels wonderful," Penny said, her face gleaming. "But all this noise…"

"City soundscapes. Part of the package with the Big Apple."

Penny scoffed. "A nuisance. Wanna sit in the park? We can chat for a while, if you like."

"Sure, I'd love to," Devin answered.

They walked over to Central Park and found a bench.

"Are you Buddhist like your parents?"

"No. I'm not religious. But I have my views."

"I'm curious. Is it okay to ask?"

"I don't mind. I guess I could say I'm a bit of an agnostic and a pantheist."

"Hmm… Help me out here, Penny. I know agnostics won't say whether or not there is a higher power, but I'm not sure what pantheists believe in."

"Pantheists think God is the universe with everything that's in it, including us. And, that's pretty much what I imagine."

A skeptical smile crossed Devin's face. "You think *we* are God?"

"Well, I'd like to think of God as a living tapestry with zillions of threads constantly changing into infinite patterns and designs."

"Wow. That's a mouthful, Miss Penny. And a very cool thought, I should add. Lemme guess: we're the threads."

"There you go. We're unique but inseparable from the larger fabric."

"That'd be radical! I mean, if people thought we were all part of the same being, we might be a little kinder to each other."

Penny nodded and smiled.

"Now, about your last name…" Devin began. "I've been wondering about it for a while."

"Right. *Valckenier*. I knew you'd eventually ask. Everyone does."

"Sounds familiar…"

"How?"

"It's a Dutch name, isn't it?"

"Yep."

"You know, Kingston, my hometown, was first settled by the Dutch. Some of the streets are named after the founders. Maybe that explains it."

"Actually, no one in my family knows exactly how we ended up with a Dutch name. My parents are from Taiwan, but my paternal grandfather is from Indonesia. He's ethnically Chinese but he's always claimed we have ancestors related to a Dutch colonial family. I think there's something to that."

"Maybe you can do some research when we're in Jakarta."

"I was thinking about that. It's one of the reasons I jumped at the chance to sign up for this trip. What about you? What made you go for it?"

"I love to travel. Plus, now that we know Ms. Davis will be the only school official coming with us, I almost feel a sense of duty to be there for her."

"Right. She needs us."

"I could keep talking with you for hours, but I've got to get going," Devin said, as he rose. "We can pick up where we left off during our flight next week."

"Absolutely! It's gonna be a long one," Penny responded. She walked to the curb and hailed a fast approaching cab. "Have a great weekend, Devin!"

"You too, Penny!"

➤◉◄

A few days later Devin and Penny sat across the aisle from Ms. Davis in the main cabin of a Pan Am 747 flight bound for Jakarta. Hours after leaving the mainland, Devin looked out the window as the aircraft cruised high above a dense gauze of clouds blanketing the Pacific Ocean.

"Have you ever been on such a long flight before?" Ms. Davis asked Devin and Penny. They shook their heads.

"Neither have I. The longest trip I took was to Russia a few years ago. The layovers were brutal."

"At least, you've come prepared," said Devin pointing to the books and magazines stuffed into the seat pocket in front of her.

She smiled. "I learned my lesson!" She then turned to speak to a student sitting next to her.

"What did *you* bring to pass the time, Devin?" Penny asked.

"A couple books, including the latest from Doctor Haverhill."

"I brought mine, too."

"We're on the same wavelength."

"Same boat, really."

"It's a jet, Penny."

She giggled. "Seriously, though, I don't know about you but I get the sense that this is not our first voyage together."

"I know what you mean. A déjà vu type feeling. I'm catching that vibe, too."

"Some researchers say they're quite common."

"Probably. Why should we be so special?"

"We're not," Penny answered. "Anyway, I'm glad I'm not keeping this stuff all to myself anymore. It's a relief knowing there's someone I can trust."

"Thank you. I feel the same way." Devin yawned and stretched. "Well, Ms. Valckenier, I'm fading fast." He peered one last time outside the porthole window and closed the scratch pane.

"I'm pretty worn-out myself," Penny sighed. "Unfortunately, I can never get any quality sleep on a plane. Have a good night!" She turned on her overhead light and reached for a magazine.

Several hours passed by before a stewardess announced the plane was preparing to land. Just before touchdown, Ms. Davis stood in the aisle and briefly faced the group.

"Hello everyone! I hope you enjoyed the flight. Please adjust your watches to the local time, make sure you have all your belongings with you when we disembark, and have your passports ready for immigration and customs. I've been told Jakarta International Airport is fairly large, so let's try to stick together. When we're ready to exit the airport, we'll be boarding a charter bus that will take us to West Jakarta University. After we check-in and get settled at the graduate student dorms, we'll re-group for lunch in the student cafeteria to review our program for the day. Thank you!"

Just before lunch, the group gathered around a long table in the university dining hall, abuzz with activity. The smell of food, the sounds of conversation and clinking silverware filled the air. Ms. Davis, Devin and Penny sat together. Standing at the head of the table, a slender young Asian male in an untucked white shirt and blue jeans put his hands together and bowed to the group, signaling he was ready to address them.

"Welcome to Indonesia, and to WJU! We're happy to have you as our guests," he said in perfect English, flashing a broad smile. "My name is Atmo and I'll be your tour guide for the duration of your stay here. How's everyone doing?"

Jet-lagged and hungry, students responded politely with "Great!" and "Super!"

"I can see you're a bit tired, but trust me, this will be worth it. By the way, I'm a grad student like you and I'm looking forward to showing you our campus this afternoon and our city during the coming days. Starting tomorrow we'll be going on the tours listed in your itineraries. We'll review those in just a moment. But before that, would any of you care to tell me what you know about Indonesia?"

Several students raised their hands.

"I'm impressed!" Atmo said, after a few shares. "You've come prepared. Are there any questions?"

Ms. Davis raised her hand.

"We know Indonesia is one of the most populated countries on Earth, but the traffic coming from the airport wasn't too bad today. Can we expect the same when we go on the bus tours this week?"

"You were lucky!" Atmo grinned. "I'm afraid you'll find Jakarta's traffic jams are some of the craziest you'll ever see."

In the following days, the group found the tour guide's prophetic words confirmed. Daytime tours frequently met with massive traffic gridlock. The long interludes stuck on the road in the oppressive heat without air conditioning tested everyone's patience. Yet, Atmo's amiable demeanor and the students' upbeat disposition consistently saved the day.

In the evening, the group would gather to review what they had learned from the day's activities before retiring to their rooms. A few resilient students, however, would occasionally go out on the town and experience Jakarta's legendary night life.

On the last Friday before returning to New York, Devin and Penny decided to venture out to a nightclub recommended by Luuk, a friendly, young Dutch tourist they had met at a flea market earlier that day. *Belora Nights*, he said, was a watering hole popular with locals and tourists alike, and an "unforgettable walk on the wild side." Intrigued by his description, Devin and Penny had agreed to rendezvous with him there later that evening.

Just before midnight, after a short ride from campus, a cab dropped off Devin and Penny a few feet away from the club's main entrance. As they walked toward it, they passed by a colorfully dressed group of young people hanging around, chatting loudly and smoking cigarettes.

Some of the women's clothing styles triggered Penny's curiosity. "Is it me or does this place look a bit like a red-light district?" she said quietly. "The dresses and the hairdos on these women… Wow!"

"Yeah. A bit out there," Devin responded. "But I love it."

As they entered the club, the blend of cigarette smoke and strong fragrances seemed overwhelming. They advanced alongside a large dance floor packed with people hopping and bopping to thunderous, pulsating music. Above them, an array of dazzling lights amidst a lush vertical garden, with hanging plants draping downward, wrapped with glittering ornaments.

Edging their way through the crowd, Devin and Penny navigated away from the dance area and the high decibels until they spotted Luuk, standing by a bar chatting with a girl. He greeted them with a radiant smile, white teeth sparkling. "*Hallo!* Glad you could make it!" he said, with a slight Dutch accent.

Penny approached, a friendly gleam in her eyes. "We couldn't miss our last chance to get out and see Jakarta at night."

"This is Flora," said Luuk. "Flora, this is Devin and Penny."

Dressed in a tight, sparkling green cocktail dress, pearl necklace, matching earrings and bracelet, Flora gazed at Devin and Penny before speaking in a low-pitched voice. "My pleasure!" With a grand, exaggerated gesture she took a drag from her cigarette, blew a column of smoke up in the air and flicked the ashes to one side.

"Beer, anyone?" asked Luuk. "The first round is on me."

"Thanks, Luuk!" said Devin. Penny and Flora nodded and smiled.

While Luuk talked to the bartender and Flora greeted an acquaintance who passed by, Penny cast a subtle glance at her, then leaned into Devin. "What's with all the makeup and the wig on this girl?"

"I noticed."

"You're closer. Check her out."

Devin's eyes followed Flora's jawline down to her neck. "Is that what I think it is?" he whispered.

"What?"

"On her neck."

Again, Penny quickly glanced at Flora over Devin's shoulder. "Gosh! That's an Adam's apple!"

"Looks like it, right?"

Flora popped herself on a bar stool, neatly crossing her legs, muscular calves and stilettos fully poised.

Luuk handed everyone their beers. "Skol! How's everyone doing?"

"Great!" said Penny. "Cheers!"

Devin gave Luuk a thumbs up.

Flora smiled, raised her bottle and took a gulp.

"You're here a few more days, aren't you?" Luuk asked.

"A couple," Penny replied. "We're leaving Sunday. We've been having so much fun. I wish we could stay longer."

"The flea market today was amazing!" said Devin.

"Glad you liked it. *Jalan Surabaya* is one of Jakarta's jewels. You can find all kinds of treasures there, from a gramophone to antique furniture, ceramics, old coins, whatever your heart desires. By the way, did you find the puppets you were looking for?"

"We did. At the stand you suggested. You know, we actually enjoyed all the haggling."

Penny giggled. "*You* did! And you were great at it. You saved a total of two cents!"

After a spin on the dance floor and a few drinks, Penny and Flora settled at a nearby table while Devin and Luuk remained seated at the bar.

"So, what brings you to Jakarta?" Devin asked, his eyes lingering on Luuk's auburn sideburns and goatee.

"It's a family tradition," said Luuk, catching a twinkle in Devin's eyes. "My folks used to vacation in Jakarta every year when I was a child. My father claims one of our ancestors was a high official in the company that built the first Dutch settlement here hundreds of years ago."

Out of the blue, subtle whispers of a name reverberated in Devin's mind: *Richard...* "That's so cool," he said. "We're visiting the Old City tomorrow. Our tour guide said it was called *Batavia.*"

"Yes, it was. Beautiful place. You'll enjoy it." Luuk took a swig from the beer in his hand then set it on the counter as he boldly surveyed Devin's chest and shoulders.

Luuk's probing eyes sent a tingling sensation through Devin's spine. "So *Belora* is a gay club, right?" he said. "I've been to a few myself, but I had never seen so many males dressed as females."

"Well, this isn't just a gay club," Luuk responded. "The way I see it, it's more like a wild tropical forest." He paused, gazed into Devin's eyes, and winked. "With all kinds of beautiful fauna…"

Devin snorted. He tossed back the remaining beer in his bottle and leaned in. "What about the Flora? Is she a *he*?"

Luuk broke into laughter. "She was born a *he*, but then she came to be herself as an adult. I've known her for years now and it wasn't easy for her to make the transition."

"How do you mean *transition?*"

"Since she moved out of her parents' home, she's been living as a female and fending for herself. She just turned twenty, you know. I really think that's brave."

"I agree."

"She's also very sweet and sociable." Luuk cast a long glance at Penny and Flora sitting across the bar engrossed in conversation. "Look at how quickly she's become acquainted with your friend."

Devin nodded, then waved at Penny.

Penny waved back.

"Luuk was right when he told us this would be wild," Penny said to Flora.

"*Belora* is a special place," Flora responded. "It's almost like a second home for people like me."

"You mean transvestites."

"Well, we're a lot more than just men who dress as women, if that's what you mean. We are the *Banci*."

Penny stared. "The *Banci?*"

"We were born male but are female in spirit. Some believe we come from a place between heaven and earth, so we see and feel things in different ways from other people."

"Do you?"

"Some of us do. We communicate with the spiritual world. We are messengers and healers."

"Now I get you. You're a medium!"

Flora grinned. "You could say that. Do you need a reading, darling?"

"You mean, right now?"

"Why not?"

"It's so noisy…"

"We can use a private room downstairs. I'm a regular here. The owners know me and they don't mind. What do you say?"

"I'd love to. Actually, I've been wanting to do this for a while."

"Let's go then." Flora rose and motioned for Penny to follow her. "We'll be right back guys," she told Luuk and Devin as she led Penny toward a staircase close by.

As they reached the bottom of the stairs, they walked a few steps along a dark corridor until Flora paused at a door, opened it, and flipped a light switch. In the center of the room, a single wire with a low wattage light bulb hung from the ceiling, flickering at intervals. They stepped in. The smell of mildew weighed heavily in the dense and humid air.

Penny scanned the room packed with chairs and tables stacked on top of each other. Piles of cardboard boxes overflowed with old decorations. "A storage area?" she asked.

"Yes, but it'll do," Flora replied. She quickly set up a folding table and two chairs across from each other. "Please have a seat, honey."

Penny sat down and crossed her legs, her hands cupped on the table.

"Is there anyone in particular you'd like to contact?"

"There is. Someone I know little about."

"So, this is not a loved one."

Penny shook her head. "I don't really know. It's just a someone in my dreams."

"Ahh… a visitation."

"Kind of. But definitely a constant presence... There's not much more I could add."

Flora extended her hands toward Penny's. "May I?" Penny nodded. She gently took Penny's hands into hers and closed her eyes. "Now it's your turn. Please close your eyes, go back to your last dream and focus on what you saw, what you heard, and what you felt. Are you with me?"

"Yes."

"Take your time. Then, when you're ready, silently ask this spirit who visits you in your dreams permission to make contact. I will do the same."

Meantime, at the bar, Luuk and Devin remained engaged with each other.

"Penny and Flora seem to have hit it off," Luuk said.

"By now, they must be trading makeup tips," Devin joked, his eyes fixed on Luuk's lush red lips. "You know, this place *is* fun. Thank you for inviting us to meet here."

"Nothing beats feeling free to be yourself, right? Did you know that in the Netherlands same-sex was legalized in the early nineteenth century?"

"You don't say!"

"We're a very open society," Luuk continued, holding Devin's gaze as he inched closer. He reached for Devin's hands and caressed them with his fingertips.

"Really… How open?" Devin leaned forward, tension building fast below his waist.

"Open enough to see no issue when men hold hands and kiss in public." Luuk leaned in, kissed Devin on the lips, then traced his jawline, grazing his cheek with the velvety brush of his stubble until he touched his earlobe. "There's a special lounge here I'd like to show you," he whispered warmly.

Devin's eyes lit up, heart pounding fast. "I'd love to see it."

"Follow me." Luuk rose, took Devin's hand and led him to a room tucked away in an inconspicuous corner of the club.

Penny and Devin walked out of *Belora* well after midnight. They hopped in the back of an orange *bajaj* rickshaw cab and headed back to the dorms. The streets were eerily quiet. The swollen arteries of the sprawling metropolis had been swept clear by a cool and gentle night breeze.

"I hope whatever you and Luuk did was fun," Penny said with a mischievous smile. "You were gone for quite a while there. How are we ever gonna get up?"

"We'll manage. And yeah, Luuk and I had fun. Check this out." He pulled a business card from his pocket and showed it to Penny.

"Well, well… He really likes you. You'll have to fill me in with all the dirty details."

"The audacity!"

They laughed.

"Do you plan to keep in touch with him?"

"I'd like to. He's a real nice guy and totally my type. He asked me to come visit him in Holland."

"Will you?"

"Maybe one day."

"Good!"

"How did it go with Flora?"

"Let me tell you, she's one of a kind. I feel like I learned more about Javanese culture from her than from all the tours. And then she told me about the *Banci*."

"What?"

"People like her. They're nothing like I had imagined. She said they're healers and mediums. And then she offered me a reading."

"Get outta here!"

"I'm serious."

"Did you accept?"

"Of course, I did! That's when we went downstairs. I swear I told her nothing about myself. And yet, she saw right through me."

"What did she tell you?" Devin asked as the cab came to a stop in front of their dorm.

"It's too much to go into it right now. I'm beat. I promise to bring you up to speed tomorrow."

XIII. GLODOK

"All aboard?" asked Atmo, facing the group as he stood next to the driver in the van that would take them on the last tours of the trip. Ms. Davis nodded and he continued. "Today our first stop will be Jakarta's Chinatown, one of the largest in the world. It's in a district called *Glodok*, settled during Dutch colonial times."

After reaching Chinatown, the group started with a tour of the oldest Chinese Buddhist shrine in the city.

"This is the *Vihara Dharma Bhakti*, a temple that dates back to the year 1650," Atmo explained standing at a pathway leading to a gate. The oppressive heat and humidity kept the nearby street vendors busy selling bottled water and hand fans to pilgrims who carried colorful umbrellas for shade. The air was heavy with smoke from food stands and burning incense.

As the group approached the main prayer hall, they passed by statues of Confucius, Buddha and several Taoist deities. People laid flowers and lit candles before them.

Inside the sanctuary, large pillars rose from the floor to support a high ceiling adorned with red hanging lanterns. On the walls, symbolic motifs in a myriad of vibrant colors with gold accents enhanced the splendor of the altar.

Devin and Penny paused to take in the surroundings as a handful of monks waved brass censers, wafting sweet scents as they circled around the chamber.

"There's so much peace here," Devin whispered, looking up at the billowing smoke rising in the air. Shafts of sunlight from above cut through the smoke, giving the chamber an ethereal aura.

Intrigued by the artwork on the pillars, Penny stared. "I wonder what inspired the artists who painted this landscape. Dragons and swallows frolicking in the sky?"

"Maybe they saw them in their dreams," Devin responded, visions from his childhood reveries swirling in his mind. "Speaking of, what did Flora tell you about *your* dreams last night?"

Penny swallowed hard. "Oh my gosh, Devin. I never expected to hear what she said. She told me she saw a young girl who's been at the core of my soul for many lifetimes, and who suffered a horrible tragedy."

"Wow."

"I know. I had the same reaction. I think she hit the nail on the head."

"Really?"

"Well, first she confirmed my suspicion that the presence I feel in my dreams is the spirit of a female, and that something very sad happened to her sometime in the past."

"Did she give you any details?"

"She said she heard the sounds of cannons booming and gunshots, and saw fire and blood all around her. And then water… lots of water, as in a drowning or something."

"Grim."

"I know. It sounds dark, but somehow, it feels real. Flora thinks one day this girl herself will tell me what happened to her."

"Mind blowing. I wonder if I could get some answers like that. Did you get her phone number?"

"What for? We're leaving tomorrow. I'm sure you'll find a good psychic when we get back to New York."

After lunch, the group headed for Jakarta's Old City. As soon as they arrived Ms. Davis stood up and spoke to the students before they exited the van.

"Welcome to the historic district of Jakarta! Please get your notebooks ready to capture your impressions of one of the most fascinating sections of the city. Pay close attention to our guide's words as he describes for us what this amazing site is all about."

Next, Atmo rose and faced the group.

"I suggest you try and imagine going back in time, seeing this place from a bird's eye view as a colonial hub and economic powerhouse for an entire region, with people from diverse backgrounds going about their business and living their daily lives, as their descendants do today. Once we get out of the van and before the formal tour begins, you'll have thirty minutes to explore the surroundings. Enjoy! And see you here later," he said, as the van door opened.

"So, this is Batavia!" Devin said. "So different from the rest of the city. Suddenly, it feels like we're in Europe."

"Yeah, it does," Penny responded, as they walked side by side around the main square snapping photos of the stately buildings around them. "Except to me, it feels a little different."

"Different how?"

"Weird. Like I know this place inside and out."

"Another déjà vu?"

"Something like that."

A while later, the group followed Atmo to the front steps of the largest and most imposing structure on the plaza.

"We're at the very center of what used to be the city of Batavia," Atmo said, as the students and Ms. Davis listened attentively. "The building behind us was known as the *Stadhuis* in Dutch, or Town Hall, in English. It was the Seat of Government for over three hundred years. All major decisions concerning the territories in the region were made here. Today, it houses the Jakarta History Museum." Within minutes, the group was inside scribbling occasional notes as they explored the exhibits.

Ms. Davis and Atmo walked together. Devin and Penny followed a few feet behind.

"The number of relics here is impressive," said Ms. Davis as they passed by several displays of costumes and artwork.

"Actually, there isn't much at all compared to museums in other parts of the world," Atmo responded.

"If you mean Europe, they have some of the largest collections of colonial era artifacts in the world."

"Of course. They hold the spoils of war."

Ms. Davis sighed. "I hope they help the new generations learn from the mistakes of our past."

As they entered the military relics hall, Penny stopped. "I'm getting chills," she said, her voice breaking. "I recognize these things."

Puzzled, Devin responded. "You *recognize* them?"

"Yes, especially the cannons…"

"From where?"

"My dreams."

Moments later, Atmo led the group to an open double door with a sign above it that read: *Heritage Reels Cinémathèque.* An older man with a long white beard wearing traditional clothing stood by the doors and greeted the group with a slight bow and folded hands.

One by one, everyone quietly filed into a small room, took their seats in front of a projector screen and prepared to watch a short Indonesian documentary with English subtitles about Batavia's history.

The film began by showing a series of old drawings of a garrison on the west side of the island of Java, as a female narrator explained that Batavia had been built by the Dutch East India Company with slave and prison labor in the year 1619. Its purpose, she said, was to provide safety for the families of company officials and a place where they could conduct business.

The region was an important source of food crops and building materials. Over the years thousands of people from different backgrounds and ethnicities settled in the area outside the original garrison. Among them, a large number of Chinese merchants and traders. Soon, the garrison become a fortress, then a village and a town which the Dutch named Batavia.

The narrator described how the town bloomed like a lotus flower, with beautiful buildings, meandering canals, and streets shaded with coconut trees. Alas, she continued, when economic activity declined, prosperity dwindled and gave way to unemployment and social unrest which peaked in the year 1740.

Tension grew against the Dutch authorities, especially within the Chinese settlements, which caused the government to begin massive deportations. The Chinese saw this as a provocation which led to an uprising that left several Dutch soldiers dead.

Suddenly, Devin felt Penny squeezing his hand. He leaned toward her.

"Are you okay?" he whispered. She nodded, her eyes fixed on the screen showing depictions of Dutch troops enforcing a general curfew in the Chinese neighborhood.

False rumors spread quickly among the townsfolk about a Chinese plot to murder them. Full blown raids on Chinese businesses and homes ensued. Before long, the Dutch forces joined the raiders and began firing their cannons in an all-out assault on the Chinese settlements.

Penny winced, eyes welling up with tears as she watched the re-enactment of the carnage that unfolded. One after another, the images on the screen showed the troops searching each and every house, shooting, stabbing or beheading anyone they found alive.

Only by suicide could the settlers evade the terror, and many chose that path. The few who managed to escape the searches and make it to the nearest canal were met by soldiers lurking in small boats, waiting to dispatch them.

"Let's get out of here, Devin. I can't take this any longer," Penny said, wiping her face with a handkerchief.

As they made their way to the exit, they could still hear the narrator describe, in detail, the full scale of the horror.

Within fourteen days, between October 9 through October 22, 1740 ten thousand ethnic Chinese had fallen by the sword. The mass murder pogrom destroyed an entire community. There were no more than five hundred survivors. In the month of November of the same year, the Dutch East India Company decreed that all of Batavia's ethnic Chinese who survived the massacre would be moved to a pecinan, or Chinatown, outside of the city walls, in an area known as Glodok.

Devin and Penny stepped out of the museum and into the blinding equatorial sun.

Devin squinted. "What just happened in there, Penny?"

"I need a moment," Penny answered.

They walked silently away from the main square until they found the merciful shade of a mango tree. Under it, a street side bird seller had built a makeshift shop. They handed him a few coins and sat on a pair of wooden crates, surrounded by countless birdhouses of different shapes and sizes hanging from branches and stacked on top of each other. As the birds chirped and sang, Penny began to unwind.

"Feel better?" Devin asked.

"Somewhat. What we saw in there shook me to the core."

"I hear you. It was intense."

"There's more to it than that. I think this is what Flora told me about last night," Penny explained. "I could almost hear the girl in my dreams speaking to me through the voice of the narrator in that film. I feel I saw what happened to her through her own eyes."

"Well, I guess that rules out reincarnation."

"What do you mean?"

"She couldn't be communicating with you if you were her, could she? Besides, if reincarnation is a real thing, I understand we're not supposed to remember anything about our previous lives."

"No, wait. Some people *do* remember. In Tibetan Buddhism, the Dalai Lamas always remember their previous lives. In fact, all of them are in a long line of reincarnations of one and the same person. They're all *him*, in different bodies, at different times. And, he remembers every one of them."

"But you and I are not the Dalai Lama, Penny. We can only remember bits and pieces of this and that. Nothing concrete."

"And yet, I feel there might be something else at play here…" Penny said, pausing for a moment.

"Like what?"

"What if these bits and pieces we remember were not just memories of past events but images of who we are right at this very moment, in another dimension?"

"Different versions of ourselves in a parallel world?"

Penny looked at Devin. "It's just a thought. Truth is, sometimes, I feel I am *her*, more than I am *me*. It's almost like I'm sleepwalking through this lifetime while the real thing is happening elsewhere."

"Do you think the girl in your dreams survived the carnage?"

"I wish I knew. But clearly, there were survivors. Glodok, Jakarta's Chinatown, is proof of it. I'll begin digging into this as soon as we get back. There must be a written record of this massacre somewhere. It was a major thing."

"You're right. There must be."

"Don't you think the two of us going through this thing together is also pretty strange? What are the odds?"

Devin shook his head. "Who knows? It's just another layer to this puzzle."

Penny glanced at her wristwatch. "We should get back."

They rose, gave the shopkeeper a nod and walked silently toward the main square.

Before rejoining the group, Devin stopped. "You know, I think there may be someone who could shed some light on what's been happening to us."

"Who?"

"Doctor Haverhill. His research is extensive. He could be helpful."

"It'd be great if he could. But how?"

"I'll write and ask him if he'd be willing to meet with us."

"Good! I like that!"

Back in the States, Devin quickly returned to his routine. School, work and the occasional weekend outings with Ben, his girlfriend, and sometimes his sister when she was in town, had become part of his limited social agenda.

"You've been on the phone an awful lot since you got back, buddy," Ben said, as Devin hung up the phone. "Those long-distance calls are gonna bite you."

"I'm not worried. I'll sell my body."

"I'll pimp you."

"Much obliged! So kind and thoughtful of you, Lord Fielding!"

"Glad to be of service, sir."

They laughed.

"Just so you know, these phone calls were long overdue. I promised both Hal and Stella I'd tell them all about my trip. Besides, Hal has been having a few health issues lately. I needed to make contact."

"What's wrong with him?"

"Acute bronchitis, he says. He's a heavy smoker, you know."

"Sorry for him. I hope he quits. You told me he's a good guy."

"He really is."

"So, what are you up to this weekend?" Ben asked.

"Not much. What's up with you?"

"Connecticut."

"What's in Connecticut?"

"Yale. Donna's alma mater. There's a special art exhibit she wants to go to. Wanna come?"

"You sure you want a third wheel?"

"Me? I don't care. It was her idea. Museums are not my thing. But yeah, I think you'll make it fun."

"Oh, I see... You need me."

Ben chuckled. "Maybe a little."

"What kind of art?"

"Nineteenth century paintings. That kind of thing. Donna said they're on loan from London's Tate Gallery. She's an Art History major, remember?"

"Of course. What is she planning to do with that?"

"She wants to become a curator."

"Very cool. So, when and where is this thing?"

"It's at the Yale Center for British Art in New Haven. We were thinking of going this Saturday."

"Sounds interesting."

"It'll be a nice day out. Donna will drive, and she said she'd treat us to lunch."

"Deal! I'm in!"

A couple days later, Devin sat in the back of Donna's car on the way up to New Haven. Sitting next to Donna at the wheel, Ben sipped coffee from a paper cup, windows rolled half- way down while music played on the stereo.

"Thanks for coming with me, guys!" Donna said, her curly brown hair ruffled by the warm air blowing in. "I need this for a class project, you know. So I'll be taking notes. I hope you don't mind."

"Not at all. I totally get it," Devin responded.

Ben grinned. "You said you're treating us to lunch, right?"

"Is that all you care about? You're a beast. I'll take you to Sally's Apizza, the best pizza joint in New Haven!"

"Hell, yeah!" Ben growled.

"Thank you, ma'am!" said Devin. "I love pizza!"

"You're welcome, Devin. And thanks again for the lovely puppet from Jakarta."

Ben scoffed. "He gave everyone a puppet. He paid two cents apiece."

"What? I told you I *saved* two cents after haggling with the shopkeeper. But that was worth hundreds of rupiahs."

"I know. I was just kidding."

An hour later all three walked inside a modern five-story building.

"Amazing skylights," said Devin, gazing up as they slowly advanced from one gallery to the next.

Donna lifted her eyes from her notebook. "It's a brilliant design. They fill the halls with so much natural light. They also make a perfect match with the concrete frames and white oak on the pogo walls."

"The architect must be a genius."

"Definitely. Louis Kahn. He designed the building in the early seventies."

"Showing off a bit?" Ben joked.

Donna made a face. "Shush, you troll!" She then turned to Devin. "You know, after I graduated from high school, I did an internship at The National Gallery in Washington, D.C."

"Awesome! What did you do there?"

"I was a PR person. I had to answer questions from visitors about the artwork on view."

"While shadowing a security guard, right?" Ben chimed in with a smirk.

"Yes, so? I'll have you know, security officers in art museums are required to have excellent communication skills. Speaking to visitors and writing reports is a big part of the job, and it's not easy. In fact, I know of several artists who worked as museum security officers before they became famous."

"My apologies, Madam Curator. I actually admire how much you know," Ben responded. He leaned on her and planted a kiss on her cheek.

Standing close by, Devin stared at a painting.

Donna took notice and approached. "*The Gate of Calais* by William Hogarth," she said. "Wonderful piece, isn't it?"

"Different. Looks like a caricature. I don't know why but it caught my eye."

"Makes sense," said Donna. "Hogarth painted it to mock the French. He was passing through Calais in 1748 right after the French had reclaimed the city from England after a long war. But that's all I know."

"Interesting. I'll try and read up on it later."

As the afternoon drew to a close, the trio headed back to New York City. Soft music played on the car speakers while they cruised down the interstate and chatted leisurely.

Donna passed a joint to Devin in the backseat. "Something else about *The Gate of Calais*," she said. "A print of it sold for five shillings in 1749."

"Must be worth a bit more than that now," Devin responded. He took a deep drag and held it.

"Oh yeah. A whole lot more."

Devin coughed, setting off a gentle wave of warmth, lightness, and a distinctive tingling sensation across the cortex of his brain. He sat back and slowly began losing himself inside his head. Feeling the weight of his eyelids, he nodded. Ben and Donna's voices morphed into a murmur while the music emanating from the stereo weaved itself into a fading sound wave. He closed his eyes and memories of his childhood home in Kingston came flooding in, blending with blurry images of a familiar farmhouse in a valley somewhere, surrounded by snow-capped mountains.

Suddenly, all images disappeared and Devin found himself alone. Beyond the windshield a faint light flickered, shadows behind it. Gliding toward them, he reached and touched the hard glass. Instantly, it turned into a gooey gelatin as a powerful force propelled him through it. In he plunged, the viscous substance sticking to his face and body. Landing on a soft surface, he felt paralyzed. Then, abruptly, reality collapsed, surrendering to darkness and deep silence.

XIV. THE AZZONIS

A ray of light eased in through a narrow gap between the drawn curtains of a large window and found its way to Giovanni, asleep on his back in a stately post bed. He squinted, instinctively reached for his left shoulder, tender and sore, and felt the bandages that covered it. Carefully propping himself up, he leaned back on the headboard and took in the surroundings: A sumptuously appointed guest chamber at Genoa's Ambassador's residence in London.

On a nightstand beside him, he spotted an issue of *The London Evening Post* and a crystal glass filled with water. Wincing, he stretched his arm out and pulled the paper into his lap. The date on the cover read: July 31, 1750.

A headline caught his eye: "Tea Drinking Opponent Speaks Up."

Jonas Hanway, a Londoner, argues that tea is pernicious to the public health, causes bad breath, ugliness and weakened nerves, obstructing industry and impoverishing the nation.

Giovanni chortled and continued leafing through the pages, then stumbled on an article that stopped him short. "Theatre Impresario Flees Jail." He began reading in earnest. The bloody riot at the penitentiary had left eight dead and twice as many injured. The Warden, Thomas Bambridge, hailed as a hero, was still in charge.

An inmate had escaped.

The fugitive is a slender man, standing at about five feet and five inches tall, of a pale complexion, with short greying brown hair and a full beard. Aged about fifty, he walks sideling, has a pensive aspect, and inhales a remarkable deal of snuff. He talks Piedmontese, French, and English. A reward of £50 is offered for his apprehension.

An editorial note laced with an unusual tone brought him to a pause: *Better he'd live in a garret at Turin, his pockets empty, but his mind serene.*

His pride hurt, Giovanni threw a strop. *My penchant for snuff offends them? What do they know about attics in Turin or my empty pockets?* While engrossed in his reflections, a young chambermaid quietly entered the room carrying a large wicker basket. She walked over to the hearth and placed it on the floor by its side. She picked up a fire iron and stoked the embers. Then, like a soldier on a mission, she marched to the window and drew the curtains open.

Sunlight flooded in.

Giovanni blinked and shielded his eyes with the paper in his hands.

Startled by the rustling sounds, the maid abruptly turned around and gasped. *"Mi-mi scusi!"* she stammered, surprised by the sight of Giovanni sitting up in bed. "Pray, forgive me, Signore. I did not knock. I thought you were asleep."

"No, no! Pardon me, Signorina!" said Giovanni, in a breathy voice, attempting to see her through the blinding light.

"I brought fresh towels and salts. They're in the wicker basket," she said, pointing. "The water's in the pitcher with the basin, by the privy. Her ladyship provided a change of uh… undergarments for you. They're in the trunk at the foot of your bed."

"Grazie mille!" said Giovanni.

The maid bowed and walked toward the exit. As she opened the door, a butler prepared to come in bearing a silver tray with a dome lid on it.

"Buon giorno, Signore!" he said upon entering. "Glad to see you're on the mend."

"Obliged."

"Would you care for morning repast?"

"Si. Per favore."

The butler set the tray on the nightstand. "His excellency shall see you in an hour."

"Is he aware I'm awake?"

"Not yet. I shall apprise him. His Lordship and Lady Azzoni have kept a watchful eye on you since you arrived two days past. They've come to see you daily, at noon and before supper. You were not fully conscious."

"I see."

"They've been keen on making certain you're well looked after, Signore. His Lordship even left some of his garments in the armoire for you."

"How gracious of him."

"Buon appetito!" the butler intoned, then exited the room.

Giovanni reached for the tray and placed it on his lap. A draped linen napkin bore the letter *A* embroidered in silk. *Such beauty and refinement*, he thought, running his fingers over it. *The 'A' must surely stand for Azzoni.* An hour later, he was finished with his meal and had completed his morning ablutions. He looked inside the armoire, pulled out a nightshirt and a banyan, and carefully put them on. He set the water pitcher and two tumblers on a small table by the fireplace, and sat there in quiet repose. For a moment, he gazed at the glowing embers until a knock on the door stirred him.

"Enter!" Giovanni called, pain radiating from his injured shoulder as he strained to raise his voice and stand.

A short, greying middle-aged man with an aquiline nose wearing a fancy blue waistcoat and matching pair of breeches stepped into the room and walked toward Giovanni.

Giovanni rose and bowed. "Your excellency."

"Ahh! How wonderful it is to see you up and about, Dottore!" said Ambassador Azzoni, drawing closer.

"My eternal gratitude for your hospitality, Your Excellency."

"Think nothing of it." The Ambassador gestured, inviting Giovanni to return to his seat. He then sat across from him. "Glad to see my dressing gown suits you."

"Like a dream!" Giovanni smiled, patting the soft damask of his sleeve.

"You have been convalescing for two days now."

"And yet, I feel I've been away for centuries…"

"Naturally. You've been in and out of it. How do you find yourself?"

"A bit weary but fine, just fine. I shall be eternally obliged to you and Her Ladyship. You saved me from death's grip. That monster at the Fleet wanted my head!"

"He still does," the Ambassador responded with a grave expression on his face. "And he is well acquainted with your whereabouts."

"He is?"

The Ambassador indicated the paper on the bed. "Have you had a chance to peruse the newssheets, Dottore?"

"I have."

"Everyone's aware you've absconded," he said, his sharp green eyes wide with restrained disquiet. "And those concerned could find you."

Giovanni lowered his head.

"We have no other recourse but to seek a pardon and safe conduct from the Crown," the Ambassador explained. "If we succeed, you may return to Genoa, or perhaps set forth on a new journey. Alas, the fact that you're a fugitive shan't make things any easier."

"I thought my cousin Niccolo would have provided relief for my bail by now."

"Indeed, he has. And graciously so. Without his support, appealing to His Majesty for mercy would not be possible."

"Does Lord Fielding have any say in this?"

"In different circumstances, he would," the Ambassador replied. "However, your elopement has increased your liability, which at this juncture, has rendered His Lordship's intervention superfluous."

"How do you mean? By what measure has my liability increased?"

"If you went before a Court, you would be facing new charges related to your status as a fugitive. In which case, Lord Fielding would be compelled to keep you at the Fleet without the possibility of bail, and until you go to trial."

Giovanni grimaced.

"Clearly, this makes our appeal to the King imperative," the Ambassador continued. "Do you now see what I mean, Dottore?"

"I do. In any case, I hope Niccolo was as obliging and kindhearted to your envoy, as you have been to me, my lord."

"He was. Only a few days before the riots, the Marquis received my emissary and was exceptionally sympathetic with regard to your financial needs. He even claimed to have obtained assurances from the Doge to be presented to the Crown in support of your cause. This should go a long way to persuade His Majesty to be merciful."

Giovanni's face lit up. "I am glad to hear of it!"

"Coincidentally, Arabella and I were introduced to your kinsman and his wife, Lady Carlotta, at a social engagement at the Doge's Palace a few years past," the Ambassador responded. "I believe Arabella still keeps up a correspondence with her." He lifted the jug on the table and poured himself a glass of water. "You recall my wife, Arabella, don't you, Dottore?"

"How could I ever forget her? Lady Azzoni has always been a ray of light, so charming and beguiling."

"She was enthralled by your company's performances. Nothing would afford her greater pleasure. That was the reason we came to your aid when the King's Theater was shuttered on orders from the Palace."

"I have always been deeply obliged for your patronage, my lord. As I am beholden to you for your timely intervention in bringing an end to that ill-fated affair."

"In all candor, 'twas Arabella who made turning the tide feasible."

"Oh? I had no notion Her Ladyship had played a role."

"Most certainly. She maintains a long acquaintance with Princess Amelia. Had she not appealed to Her Royal Highness, the theater might still be closed."

"I was unaware of Her Ladyship's ties to the Princess."

"Such liaisons are not always public, Dottore. Which again brings to mind your kinsman from Genoa. I hear you were engaged in a business undertaking with him. How did this come about, if I may ask?"

Giovanni reached for his snuffbox. "'Tis a rather long story, my lord."

"I'm eager to hear it."

"I was raised on a small farm in Pinerolo, a village at the foot of the Alps in the Duchy of Savoy. We were close to Turin and near the border with France," said Giovanni. He inhaled a dab of snuff and continued. "Since my early days, I labored with my parents selling our produce at the piazza market."

"Ah, you come from humble origins."

"I do. Yet, my father had designs for me. When I was aged but twelve, he started bringing me along on his sojourns to Genoa. There, we visited my uncle Pietro and his family in their lavish abodes. Niccolo was the elder of my cousins."

"I see."

"I had no inkling at the time, but my father was in earnest I should not end up as a farmer like him."

"You had a caring *papa,* Dottore."

"Indeed. He wished for me to learn a trade under the guidance of my uncle, then climb the social ladder."

"And he succeeded."

"I suppose. At sixteen, my uncle took me as his middleman in the family silk and timber trade with France. That is how I became a merchant."

"A suitable arrangement for everyone, it seems. Your uncle needed you at the border and you were there for him."

"Verily. I lodged with my family until I turned nineteen."

"And then?"

"I met my Antonia and together we raised our twins, Gianni and Marco."

"You were blessed."

"So we thought. Then our boys sailed for the Kingdom of Galicia, and from there to the New World."

"How brave and adventurous of them!"

Giovanni sighed. "Parting with them was not easy. We knew we might not see them again."

"A time to place your trust in the Good Lord."

"Amen. At last, our nest was empty and we could start anew in Genoa. By then, my uncle was gone from this world and Niccolo had inherited his vast empire."

"I gather you remained in your kinsman's employment all the while."

"I was his right-hand man!"

"In what capacity?"

"I was charged with overseeing the family's banking transactions. These were my beginnings as an impresario, Your Excellency."

"What kind of banking transactions?"

"We offered loans at substantial interest rates and we were paid back in gold."

"Marvelous!"

"This made my cousin's family one of the most affluent in Genoa, along with the Grimaldis and the Dorias."

"I was aware of that. 'Tis the origin of your kinsman's nobility that escapes me. If not by inheritance, how did Niccolo acquire his title?"

"With large contributions to the public purse, my lord. For it was Genoa's Great Council who bestowed upon him the title of marquis."

"Quite a natural path to the top, I daresay," the Ambassador responded. "I suppose that is how he began presenting himself at the Doge's Palace and demanded to be granted the privileges reserved for the nobility."

"That was indeed the case."

"How long did you remain in banking?"

"Until the smallpox plucked my sweet Antonia from my side."

"Such an unforgiving scourge. It has taken so many souls."

Giovanni shook his head. "Poisoned fate! I felt accursed! At one point I came to believe the year 1745 would be my last. But then a miracle occurred…"

"Pray tell!"

"The loss of my wife transformed me."

"How so?"

A knock on the door interrupted them.

"Entra!" the Ambassador called.

The housekeeper, a stout older woman dressed in black, stepped in and stood by the door.

"Pray mi scusi, Signori," she said. "From Her Ladyship. Midday repast shall be served at twelve o'clock in the *azzurro* dining hall."

"Grazie, Signora Gentile!" said the Ambassador. He turned back to Giovanni. "Before the thought eludes me, Arabella took the liberty of procuring new garments for you, Dottore. She will send them up to you."

"Her Ladyship's kindness is boundless."

"She is a kindhearted soul indeed," the Ambassador said, rising from his chair. "We shall see you shortly." He nodded, walked to the door and exited.

➤❖◄

At noon, Giovanni stood at the entrance of a grand dining hall. A footman welcomed him, bowing as he entered the chamber. He walked the length of an oval walnut dining table to greet his hosts, standing side by side, near an imposing black marble fireplace. *"Mio Signore. Mia Signora,"* he said, taking a deep bow.

"Benvenuto, Dottore!" Lady Azzoni responded, cheerfully. Her poise, high forehead and warm smile conveyed an aura of graceful benevolence.

A broad smile spread across Giovanni's face. "You look enchanting, *mia Signora!"* he said, gazing at her chestnut hair swept back and gathered in a bun atop her head, two delicate curls at her temples. "'Tis wonderful to see you again."

Lady Azzoni nodded. "Likewise! I am pleased to see you're healthy and strong again. You must be famished."

"My appetite is legendary."

"Then let us sit and enjoy," the Ambassador said, motioning invitingly for Giovanni to take a seat. He then pulled a chair and took his place at the head of the table.

Lady Azzoni gave the butlers a nod.

"A fine dining-chamber," said Giovanni, surveying the room while the butlers began their well-choreographed dance around the table. "The landscapes on the Delft tiles are magnificent."

"The Blue Dining Hall is our pride and joy," Lady Azzoni said, gently touching the silver pendant nesting on her chest. The pale skin of her hand drew a contrast with her purple high-necked dress. "I hope the main course is just as pleasing to you, Dottore. 'Tis venison and sirloin of beef roast with artichokes and French beans."

"It sounds delicious, Signora."

140

Raising his glass, the Ambassador proposed a toast. "To our esteemed guest's continued good health!"

"And to my esteemed hosts, a long and joyful life!" Giovanni responded.

They clinked glasses, sipped wine, and proceeded with the soup.

"Pray tell, how did you become a theater impresario, Dottore?" the Ambassador asked. "Earlier, you had begun to convey how the loss of your wife transformed you."

"Indeed. It all began when Niccolo and Carlotta invited us to join them at the opera. They had been faithful patrons of the theater for years."

"Of course," said Lady Azzoni. "We passed them on several occasions at the Teatro di Sant'Agostino, even before we made their acquaintance."

"Well, my Antonia was besotted with opera buffa and soon we both became devoted to it. After she passed, I thought I'd honor her memory by establishing a theater company exclusively dedicated to bringing comic opera to the stage. This is how my *Commedia dell'Arte* came to be."

"Extraordinary," said the Ambassador. "What about the financial aspects of your company, if I may inquire?" He lifted a spoon and began slurping up the soup.

"I gave up my commitments with Niccolo and invested my savings in my venture. By early 1746 I was all but finished recruiting and had a full troupe in place."

Lady Azzoni leaned forward. "Remarkable. How did you succeed in getting everyone on board so quickly?"

"I was blessed, my lady. And I offered fair wages, which swayed some of the most talented singers in the land to join me."

"Surely, you are alluding to Filippo Laschi and his wife Laura."

"To name but two! Although, without them we would have never been able to open in Milan with *Il Giramondo* that same year."

"We heard that was quite a sensation, Dottore," said the Ambassador.

"For a new troupe, it was!"

"I do recall the wonderful reviews," the Ambassador continued. "They raved about the Laschis."

"Of course! By most accounts, Filippo and Laura have always been exceptional. Redoubtable, if you ask me. We grew close to each other through the years. And now, we're just like family. Were you aware the three of us made the journey from Genoa to London together in the summer of 1748?"

"We read it in the news," the Ambassador replied. "Was the Marquis disappointed when you left him?"

"Not at all, my lord. By the time I decided to venture into the theater, Niccolo was already engaged in an official capacity in Rome. He had been named Ambassador to the Pontiff by the Doge."

"I gather you have not seen him in a while then."

"Alas, I have not. However, we exchange letters on occasion and our fondness for each other remains undiminished."

"A blessing indeed," said the Ambassador. "For your connection with him has proven quite valuable to you, under the circumstances."

Lady Azzoni cast a sideways glance at her husband, a slight hint of displeasure in her eyes. She then turned to Giovanni. "Surely, the Marquis must be aware that your calling for the theater has brought you good fortune through the years. Renato and I can bear witness to it," she said. "You must recall how we made your acquaintance."

"In Turin, I believe," said Giovanni. "At the Teatro Regio." He cut a piece of venison, lifted it with his fork and put it in his mouth.

"You have a faithful memory, Dottore. We attended one of your company's performances there in the autumn of 1747. In point of fact, the Regio was the place where we were presented to Her Royal Highness, Princess Amelia, seven years earlier."

"Such happenstance."

"Indeed! A bit odd as well. Nobody knew she was there."

"How did she avert the prying eyes around her?"

"She was in disguise. Veiled. And with no tiara. She sought privacy, you see. More so being unmarried, on her own, and far away from home."

"Then, with your leave, how were you acquainted with Her Royal Highness?"

"By chance! Renato and I happened to be seated with Lord Middlesex and his wife Lady Colyear, whom we knew from the theater. Naturally, Princess Amelia was no stranger to them. They were habitués at Court and instantly recognized her when they saw her seated in the box adjacent to ours."

"Ah! The quirks of fate!"

"Quite so. At the intermezzo, we went out to Piazza Castello to take the air and, to our thrill and delight, there she was, in a secluded corner with one of her ladies. Lord Middlesex introduced us, and she and I immediately took to each other."

"You had things in common, my dear," said the Ambassador.

"True. Our interest in the theater. Then her sojourn in Turin took longer than expected and we began paying visits to each other. In the end, we forged a lasting bond."

"A tried and unfeigned friendship," said Giovanni.

"And more! We became confidantes," Lady Azzoni responded. She took a sip from her glass and continued. "To such degree, that on one of my excursions to London, she surprised me with a most gracious offer."

"You whet my curiosity, my lady."

Lady Azzoni smiled. "She bid me to join the ranks of some of her closest associates: her ladies-in-waiting. This was a great honor considering she only kept but two, and I was bonded by matrimony. Aware I had no issue, she paid no mind to that. As such, after conferring with Renato, I accepted her offer."

"You made your move to London by yourself?"

"I did. I served in Her Royal Highness' household for the next two years, until Genoa's Doge named Renato Ambassador to the Court of St. James."

"Small world!" said Giovanni.

"Especially in polite society," the ambassador responded. "'Tis a most restricted circle."

Giovanni nodded. "On that matter, pray forgive my indiscretion for I remain intrigued by Lord Middlesex' association with Signor Vanneschi. They hail from such divergent walks of life. And yet, they have been in business together for so long."

"Indeed, they have," the Ambassador responded. "We have been acquainted with both of them for years."

"I cannot help but wonder how fate's design brought them together."

"They chanced upon each other in Florence, Dottore. During the summer of 1739. His Lordship had recently taken ownership of the King's Theater and was on a grand tour of Tuscany, looking for associates to assist him with his new venture. He ran into Signor Vanneschi and enlisted him as a librettist and deputy director. A few years passed and Lord Middlesex withdrew from overseeing the day-to-day affairs of the theater, appointing Vanneschi to replace him."

"Remarkable," Giovanni said. "I was only partially aware of that account."

Lady Azzoni signaled the butlers to begin serving dessert.

"What about you, Dottore?" the Ambassador asked. "How were *you* and Signor Vanneschi acquainted?"

"He knew Gaetano Guadagni, one of my castratos," Giovanni answered. "Through him, we established a connection. He was keen that I should bring my troupe to London and join him at the King's Theater. At first, I was not inclined to entertain such thought."

"What changed your mind?"

"He made a generous proposal."

The Ambassador grinned. "Ah! Temptation. Forever holding its sway."

Giovanni chuckled. "The Lord shall be my Savior. I merely hazarded a wager."

"You were brave!" Lady Azzoni chimed in. "And you succeed. Your performances drew the crowds."

"You are gracious, my lady. Truth is, comic opera was a novelty to the London audiences who were stirred by our performances."

"You had wonderful players."

"Indeed, we were fortunate. Alas, all that seems a thing of the past. Mr. Garrick took most of my singers and actors, and here I am now, in this disgraceful state."

"About *that,* Dottore," said Lady Azzoni. "I have succeeded in securing a private audience with Her Royal Highness, Princess Amelia. In three days' time I shall present your case to her."

"Will you?" Giovanni asked, eyes widening. "That is so very generous of you, my dear lady!"

"I shall appeal on your behalf, that she may intercede with her father, His Majesty. However, as I am sure you are aware, before anything is settled, we shall have to arrange to make a generous gift to Their Royal Highnesses, in the traditional manner."

"I shall be glad to contribute to that end, whatever you deem fitting."

"You are favored by Providence, Dottore," the Ambassador said. "The Marquis and indeed the Doge himself have shown considerable interest in your cause."

"Praise the Good Lord for His infinite grace!"

"Then, of course, there is the matter of how you would put your safe conduct to use, if we were able to obtain one."

"I have been pondering about that myself, and I have come to the conclusion that my prospects might be better beyond Genoa or even Turin."

"Where would you go, then?"

"I am partial to the Netherlands, my lord. An acquaintance of mine lives there. He is well aware of my plight and has vowed to lend his aid unto me."

"Who is this?"

"Sir Richard Westerbeek. He serves in the Court of Prince William IV of Orange."

The Ambassador raised an eyebrow. "An associate of your kinsman, the

Marquis, I presume."

"No, no. There is no connection between them. I have been Richard's acquaintance since my days trading in France and Savoy. At the time, we were competitors. We both contended for patronage from the neighboring residents, presenting our wares in the very same markets. I have always maintained a steady correspondence with him. Even during my residency at the Fleet."

"I see. Your mate rose to the loftiest echelons. Very wise, indeed."

"Pray excuse my keenness," Lady Azzoni broke in. "What is it you intend to do in the Netherlands?"

"My hope is to recruit a new troupe and resume honoring my wife's memory as soon as the Almighty shall allow it."

"I am glad to hear you have a plan. I shall convey this to Her Royal Highness and see where that takes us."

"Bless your heart, my lady! You're my angel of redemption!"

>-◉-<

Three times the sun rose and fell before a coach bearing Lady Azzoni delivered her to St. James' Palace. She emerged from her carriage in a salmon-colored mantua and a fine shallow-crowned ivory hat, daintily tied under her chin. Princess Amelia's First Lady-in-waiting greeted her at the main entrance and accompanied her to the Princess' drawing room. As the doors opened, a footman announced her arrival.

Robed in a muslin gown adorned with floral patterns, the Princess stood alone in the center of the room. Her dark brown tresses carefully arranged in small curls, and embellished with tiny white pearls nestled among them.

Surrounding her, and echoing the weight of heritage and lineage, hung a gallery of portraits of herself at various stages of her life, set among paintings of family members and ancestral figures.

Above, a grand crystal chandelier graced the heart of the chamber with a radiant glow, bestowing upon it an aura of opulence and splendor.

"My dear Arabella! How very pleasant it is to see you again after so long!"

"Likewise, Your Royal Highness!" Lady Azzoni said, rising from a deep curtsy. "I am so very grateful you have found the time to meet with me today."

"Pray be assured you are always welcome within these walls, my darling friend. Shall we take refreshments while we bring ourselves up to date with the events that have transpired in our lives since last we met?"

"It would be my pleasure," Lady Azzoni replied. She removed her hat and handed it to a servant.

The Princess led the way to a round table in an intimate corner of the room by two large windows. A deluge of natural light filled the seating area. On the wall between the windows, an oval mirror in an ornate gilded frame tilted slightly forward, reflecting the scene. Resting on the table, a silver tea service and a three-tiered porcelain tray overflowed with profiteroles, mini cakes, and scones.

Once the ladies settled, a butler poured their tea, then quickly moved away and stood at the ready.

"A small present in honor of our long-lasting friendship, Your Highness," Lady Azzoni said, handing the Princess a neatly wrapped gift box.

"How very kind of you!" said the Princess. She took the box, tore the paper wrapping, opened it and smiled. "Oh my! Such a pretty brooch! A golden harp, as in my coat of arms. How thoughtful of you, my dear. I shall wear it to my birthday ball at Hampton Court in a few days."

"I thought your birthday was in June."

"Indeed, it is. But this year, the public celebration is taking place in August. You and Renato shall receive an invitation shortly."

"We are most honored. We'd scarce dream of missing it! If I may, what made you choose to host the festivities at Hampton Court rather than here at St. James'?"

"'Twas not my delicacy, my dear," the Princess replied, taking a pastry from the tray. "My papa chose it as a special gesture to me. You see, in my youth, Hampton Court was my family's summer country home. So many fond memories…" she paused. "This is where I learned how to ride. At present, we only come to see the horses that are stabled there." She took a small bite from the pastry in her hand and wiped the corners of her mouth with a napkin.

"I am a witness to the passion you and His Majesty feel for your horses. Such magnificent and noble creatures."

"How are you and your family faring these days?" the Princess asked. "I hear you've been rather occupied hosting one of your former acquaintances from the theater recently."

"Admittedly, Your Highness," Lady Azzoni replied, her cheeks suddenly aflush. "We have been hosting Signor Giovanni Francis Crossa, the former Impresario from the King's Theater."

"Aye," said the Princess. "Someone who's no stranger to trouble."

"Well... He was being held at the Fleet, but since his departure from the facility, he has succeeded in meeting his obligations with his creditor and—"

"—his *departure?*" the Princess interjected, eyes level. "You mean to say *escape*, don't you, my dear?"

"He was injured during the riots and feared for his life, Your Highness. As one might expect, he sought to find a way to keep himself safe and out of danger. Somehow, he made it to our residence, where he's been convalescing."

"I see…" The Princess lingered for a moment, delicately tracing the rim of her teacup before bringing it to her lips.

Lady Azzoni continued, her words chosen and delivered with utmost care. "I assure you he is contrite, Your Highness. He prays the rosary for hours, beseeching divine forgiveness."

"It appears he is repentant."

"In a most genuine manner. Moreover, his kinsman, the Marquis Niccolo Crossa, who is presently Genoa's Ambassador to The Holy See, has expressed a keen interest in advocating on his behalf. Renato has also received word that the Doge himself is sympathetic to his plight."

"He seeks a royal pardon, I presume."

Lady Azzoni nodded. "This is the case, Your Highness. And safe passage, as well."

"Well, my dear Arabella, alas, this time it may not be so easy to persuade His Majesty to look the other way. This man has flouted our laws, and in a very public manner. The dailies have mocked one of our largest royal penitentiaries on account of his elopement. And then again, neither my brother, Prince William, nor my father, have quite forgotten the incident that led to the shuttering of the King's Theater not so long ago."

Lady Azzoni lowered her eyes. "Renato and I are terribly embarrassed about the circumstances surrounding this affair. We pray that His Majesty would find it in his heart to contemplate our endeavors to extricate the Impresario from this dreadful quandary by means of a traditional arrangement."

"Ah, now we come to the quick of it… What exactly would this *arrangement* entail?"

"My husband and I would deliver a letter penned by the Marquis, bidding His Majesty's clemency in this matter. Two hundred guineas would be part of the transaction, as a bond if you will, in exchange for a royal pardon and safe passage to the Netherlands. There would also be an assortment of personal favors from the Marquis, to be presented to the King once the signing of all required documents has been agreed upon."

"Well… Apparently, this *bird* has been fully cooked and is ready to be served. But, wherefore the Netherlands?" the Princess asked. "Why not his native land?"

"He wishes to revive his theater company in The Hague, where he claims he can bank on the aid of an acquaintance of his at the court of Prince William of Orange."

"A fortuitous twist," the Princess responded. "It appears the sheer magnitude of this man's resourcefulness deserves pause."

"I share your sentiments, Your Highness. Such is his character. All the same, in the end, he is the sole master of his fate."

"Our thoughts align, my dear. I shall speak of your endeavors on the fugitive's behalf to the King. And although I could not speculate as to what the outcome my intervention might bring, I promise I shall send word to you either way."

"My heartfelt gratitude for your graceful mediation, Your Highness!"

Two days later, the Ambassador and his wife sat on a sofa in the embassy parlor for afternoon tea. Across from them, seated on an armchair, Giovanni chewed on a scone, a porcelain cup and his silver snuffbox on an end table beside him.

"Can we persuade you to join us for a game of loo after tea, Dottore?" Lady Azzoni asked.

"I'd be delighted," he replied, his eyes following a footman who had just walked into the room bearing a tray.

The footman approached the Ambassador and bowed. *"Mi scusi. La posta,"* he said, presenting the tray with two sealed letters on it.

The Ambassador lifted the letters, and upon seeing the royal seal on them, immediately passed them on to his wife. "From the Palace," he said.

Lady Azzoni broke the seals and silently read the contents. Placing a hand on her chest, she cleared her throat and cast a gaze at her husband. "Good tidings!" she exclaimed with a jubilant smile. "We have been granted a private audience with the King and are invited to a grand fête: a royal birthday revelry. Both bestowed upon us on the selfsame day!"

Heartened by the news, Giovanni's eyes brightened. *The tide has turned!*

XV. An Audience With The King

Horses nickered and snorted as a coach bearing Ambassador Azzoni, his wife Arabella, and Giovanni rolled to a gentle halt at Hampton Court on a balmy early evening in mid-August. A footman escorted the couple to the Throne Room while a hall boy directed Giovanni to an adjacent chamber. There, he would await the results of the proceedings.

A hush fell on the courtiers as the doors opened and the Azzonis were announced. Attired in their finest, the Ambassador and his wife slowly traversed the expanse of the chamber, guided by a lush scarlet carpet leading to the throne set on a dais. In their wake, one of their servants bore a small gift box and a dainty silk pillow cradling a sealed letter.

Resplendent in his regal vestments, King George II observed the couple's approach. To his right sat Prince William, Duke of Cumberland, on his left, Princess Amelia.

Lady Azzoni swiftly identified the Countess of Suffolk, Lady Henrietta Howard, seated beside and inches behind Princess Amelia, a place of honor. *How she has aged!* thought Arabella of the Countess as she met the acknowledging glances of the two ladies.

An elderly man sat next to Prince William with two scrolls on his lap. His periwig tilted slightly forward, eyes obscured by thick-rimmed spectacles. The Ambassador took notice. *An auspicious sign!* he thought. *The Lord High Steward is here!*

As the couple reached the throne, the Ambassador set his right foot forward, removed his feathered hat and bowed in deep reverence to the monarch. Accustomed to the intricacies of courtly protocols, Lady Azzoni mirrored her husband, lowering herself into an extended curtsy.

The King addressed the Ambassador: "Pray state your business, Your Excellency."

"Your Majesty," the Ambassador began, "I bring tidings and offerings of good will from Genoa's Doge and the Marquis Niccolo Crossa, Genoa's envoy to the Holy See." He motioned for the servant to present the letter to the King. "The matter concerns the Marquis' kinsman, the Impresario Giovanni Francis Crossa, and the predicament that has befallen him."

"I'm aware who the offender is," the King responded, taking the letter. After breaking the seal and reading its contents, he turned to Lord Buckhurst, present in his role as Lord High Steward. "What business do we have with the Marquis?" he asked in a grumble.

"None, Your Majesty."

"Yet, he claims the Doge has endorsed his plea on behalf of his cousin."

"A rare occurrence, I daresay," Buckhurst responded.

"He also mentions he has remitted a sum that should suffice as a manner of a bond. And, upon reading his expressions of regret, uh… What say you, Lord Buckhurst?"

"I see no hindrance in the notion of a pardon," Buckhurst replied.

Suddenly, Prince William leaned in and spoke in the King's ear. "This rogue has flouted our laws since he's been here. Yet, a pardon would see him walk free as if nothing had happened."

"We cannot ignore the Doge," the King said softly. "We conduct business with Genoa…"

The Prince persisted. "And yet, can we turn a blind eye to what he did? A full pardon would not serve justice but subvert it."

"What, then?"

"A conditional pardon."

"What conditions do you propose?"

"That he never sets foot in England again."

"I see. A permanent banishment."

"Precisely."

The King's gaze turned to the letter still in his hand. "There is also a petition for a letter of safe passage."

"I'd take no exception to that," said the Prince. "Wherever the scoundrel goes is fine with me."

The King faced the Lord High Steward again. "It's settled!" he said. Then called on him to proceed with the formalities.

"What now?" Lady Howard asked Princess Amelia speaking in a low voice. "After so much ado, I'm still not clear what's been settled here."

"The Impresario will go free, my dear," the Princess answered. She glanced at Lady Azzoni, nodded and smiled reassuringly.

Holding their breaths, the Ambassador and his wife had remained standing, their eyes glued to the scene unfolding before them.

Lord Buckhurst rose and announced that the pardon had been granted.

"We are heartily obliged for your unfailing grace and mercy, Your Majesty!" said the Ambassador. He bowed, then handed him the gift box that he and his wife had brought with them. The King opened it. Inside, an eighteen-carat gold ring set with rubies and framed by two dozen rose cut diamonds on a miniature red velvet cushion. Surrounding the ring, two hundred freshly minted guineas.

During the proceedings in the Throne Room, Giovanni fidgeted with a rosary praying for a royal indulgence. As time elapsed, his mind drifted and he slipped into a reverie. Hovering weightlessly in a light mist, he saw a grand parchment unfurled on a small table. *A chart?* he wondered. Then, a familiar voice surfaced from within uttering mysterious words... *A few more hours and I should be in Midtown.*

Suddenly, the doors to the Throne Room opened. Startled, Giovanni leapt from his seat, his heart pounding. The Azzonis walked out, Lord Buckhurst by their side.

"Ah! Here he is!" said the Ambassador, approaching Giovanni. "Signor Crossa. Lord Buckhurst, the Lord High Steward." The men bowed to each other as the Ambassador returned to his wife, standing a few feet away.

Lady Azzoni slipped her arm under her husband's. "Let us take our leave now, my dear. We must not chance being late to the ball and vexing the Lord Chamberlain. He could assign our seats to someone else." She glanced at Giovanni and smiled. The couple then bowed, turned and walked away.

"Come along, sir!" said Buckhurst in a commanding voice. Giovanni followed. Together, they walked briskly along a grand hallway linking a series of ornate, stately chambers. Upon reaching its end, they entered a library. Here, Buckhurst pulled out two rolled manuscripts from his coat and laid them on a desk. "Behold your dispensation, sir. Two writs signed by His Majesty: A most benevolent pardon, and unencumbered passage to the Netherlands."

Giovanni closed his eyes and sighed. "Praise the Good Lord!" he said, his heart filled with gratitude.

Buckhurst continued. "All of it, on condition you leave England within a week's time, never to return."

"I see. I have been banished."

"A veritable fact, indeed," Buckhurst responded, carefully rolling up the papers and handing them over to Giovanni. "Here you are. Your Ambassador's coach shall take you back to his residence."

Giovanni nodded and hastily headed for the door. He walked out of the

Palace and prepared to board the carriage that awaited him.

"Where to, sir?" the whip inquired. "The embassy?"

"The Hops & Vines," Giovanni answered. "The tavern next door."

The whip nodded.

Upon arriving, he settled at a corner table, procured a writing case from the server and set out to compose two short missives. One, addressed to his esteemed colleagues Filippo Laschi and his wife Laura. Another one, to his long-standing acquaintance in the Netherlands, Sir Richard Westerbeek. The letters conveyed an account of his present circumstances and announced his impending journey to The Hague.

While visiting the Impresario during his convalescence at the Ambassador's residence, the Laschis had relayed their interest in returning to the continent with him. As a result, Giovanni now proposed they rendezvous with him at a familiar place in the port of Calais, across the English Channel, no later than the twenty-fifth of August. Full of hope and aspirations for a brighter future, the couple and Giovanni had lodged at an inn there, on their way to London in the spring of 1748.

After sealing the letters, Giovanni called on the tavern keeper to find a trusted post-boy to deliver them to the Postmaster General. "Have these dispatched at once!" he said, a sense of urgency laced in his words.

The keeper took the letters. "One bob and tuppence will do, sir."

Giovanni pulled a pouch from his waistcoat pocket and placed four coins on the table. "Here. Press on, now!"

———————▸◦◦◦◦◦◦◦◦◦◦◦◦◦◦◦◦◦◦◦◦◦

Not long after the Azzonis claimed their seats at The Great Hall in Hampton Court, the Lord Chamberlain signaled the yeoman to close the doors to the ballroom and let the festivities begin. The King and his family made their entrance and took their places facing the dance floor. Guests mingled and enjoyed refreshments. Around them, colorful tapestries adorned the walls while music played in the background.

"Such splendor!" said the Ambassador, contemplating the scene. His hand clasped a crystal flute filled with champagne.

"'Tis butter upon bacon, my dear Renato," Lady Azzoni responded, a flicker of a smile on her lips. "Without question, a dazzling spectacle."

For a moment, the Ambassador's gaze shifted upward to the peculiar carvings on the ceiling. "Those painted heads above are ghostly," he said, making a face.

"The eavesdroppers? Never mind them. Behold the view around us. All of London's upper crust seems to be here."

The Ambassador cast a mischievous glance at his wife. "No question. Personages of noble birth and virtue. Among them, the younger gents and damsels on the prowl…"

Lady Azzoni giggled. "I expect we shall have a marvelous time here tonight, my dear. We must avail ourselves of all the amusement and diversion."

"We are certainly deserving of it," the Ambassador returned.

"We are! Lending a helping hand to our long-suffering Dottore was quite a noble feat."

"Well put, Arabella." He leaned toward her and spoke softly. "Not to mention we did this while pleasing the Marquis, the Doge, and the royals as well."

"Clearly, the royals had the most to gain," she said quietly, a pained expression casting a shadow on her face.

"Is there something amiss? What grieves you, my dear?" asked the Ambassador with a quizzical brow.

She shook her head and remained silent.

"Perhaps, I should have mentioned that our success would have been quite unthinkable without your timely appeal to the Princess," the Ambassador continued. "She clearly holds you in high esteem."

"That may be so, Renato. Alas, this whole affair has left a bitter taste in my mouth."

"On what count? We succeeded!" He gently touched his wife's shoulder. "Without your intervention, our bid to save the Impresario may have never been contemplated."

Bringing her voice barely above a whisper, Lady Azzoni responded. "Indeed, we succeeded. Despite the deportment of those who sat in judgment in the Throne Room."

"How do you mean?"

"Let us take some air, my dear. 'Tis a trifle confining in here since they closed the doors." She took her husband's arm and led him away from prying eyes and ears.

They paused at a quiet corner of the hall.

Gazing at a tapestry on the wall, Lady Azzoni pretended to admire it. "The tapestries are endlessly distracting," she said. She took a quick look around and seeing no one near, she resumed. "Earlier today we witnessed how Prince William persuaded His Majesty to deny the Impresario a full pardon. Quite a repulsive spectacle. The Butcher of Culloden, a vile character, dispensing justice on a humble theater impresario condemned for bankruptcy and for merely attempting to save his own life."

"There is no use in dwelling on such vexing thoughts," the Ambassador responded. "What's done is done."

"Yet, I cannot bear the duplicity. 'Twas Prince William who had the King's Theater shuttered on account of the stunt that ridiculed His Majesty. His hand in this affair caused our Dottore to lose his livelihood. And all due to a minor indiscretion."

"Not so minor, my dear. To the Prince, his family's honor was on the line."

"On that score, Renato, there are certain intimacies you may be unaware of…"

"Whose *intimacies* do you speak of Arabella?" the Ambassador asked, surveying those gathered nearby.

"You may well be surprised, but the Hannovers are far from being without fault."

"You confound me. You have been the most loyal of friends to Princess Amelia, who has retained you as a close and cherished confidant for years."

"Indeed."

"What are you saying, then?"

Lady Azzoni drew closer to her husband. "Seeing the masquerade we witnessed in the Throne Room today, I find myself no longer willing to keep *any* confidences."

"Pray tell then, woman! I feel my head aching from the intrigue."

Slightly turning her head, Lady Azzoni's eyes fell upon a young boy standing by a fireplace. "Do you see that child by the hearth?"

"What of him?"

"His name is Samuel Arnold, Princess Amelia's love child," Lady Azzoni whispered. "He's standing beside Lady Howard, presently conferring with Lord Buckhurst."

"Princess Amelia's *love child?* Good heavens!"

"Please Renato, mind your tone."

"How audacious of her to bring him into Court!" the Ambassador responded, in a softer voice. "Pray tell, who is the begetter of this child?"

"A commoner by the name of Thomas Arnold. This has been her most guarded secret for the past ten years."

"How did she succeed in concealing her secret while she was with child?"

"The King sent her away to Turin on a longer than usual excursion. She was to partake in the daytime exploration of the sights and attend the theater at eventide. That was the plea for the journey undertaken."

The Ambassador frowned. "You jest! You mean to say her visit to Turin when we made her acquaintance was a ruse concocted by the King to conceal her gravidity?"

"Indeed so. Princess Amelia is the King's youngest child, and has always been his favorite. 'Tis not at all surprising he would wish to protect her."

"Pray, indulge me. Who is charged with raising this child?"

"His Majesty arranged for Lady Howard and her second husband to adopt him and raise him as their own," Lady Azzoni elucidated.

"Is the boy aware who his real mother is?"

"I am not privy to such detail. All the same, the Princess has never been a stranger to him."

"Ah. This explains why Lady Howard is so close to her."

"Well, there is more about that than meets the eye. Truth is, the Countess has been a long-lasting presence at Court. She has been around since the days the late Queen Caroline was Princess of Wales. Then, rumors abounded that while in her official role as Woman of the Bedchamber she quickly became the woman *at* the Prince of Wales' bedstead."

"I may have heard about that," said the Ambassador.

Lady Azzoni carried on. "When Princess Caroline became queen, Lady Howard remained in her service. And she also remained in the service of the King, as his mistress."

The Ambassador briefly delayed his response as he and his wife caught sight of Princess Anne, the King's second child and eldest daughter. Lady Azzoni knew the Princess well from her years at Court.

As Princess Anne walked by on the arm of her husband, Willem IV, Prince of Orange of the Netherlands, the Ambassador bowed and Lady Azzoni curtsied to the royal couple. Then, they resumed their exchange.

"If there was ever a pith of veracity in any of those awful rumors, it must have been awkward for Queen Caroline to cohabitate with the King's mistress," the Ambassador said.

"'Twas not. Everyone knew Queen Caroline was fond of Lady Howard."

"How could you be privy to such detail? This was long before your time at Court."

"Princess Amelia has always been my source."

"Even so. The Queen could not have been so blind."

"She was not. For she contrived it all!"

"The Queen approved of her husband's affair?"

"*Approve* and *affair* are not quite the right terms," Lady Azzoni replied. "After ten gravidities and eight live births, Queen Caroline was quite content with the King keeping a mistress she found affable and very much trustworthy."

"A courtesan!"

"Far from it! Lady Howard was blessed with all the social graces and proved herself to be quite helpful. The Queen set her to task, keeping a vigilant eye on her husband's every move, and making her report back to her. Besides, her bond with the King was genuine and lasted for years."

"How many?"

"Twenty, by my knowledge."

"Are Lady Howard and her husband raising Princess Amelia's child at Court?"

"Oh, no. The Countess has long been a widow and does not reside at Court since she retired in 1734. By the time her second husband had crossed over, her liaison with the King was a thing of the past."

"And yet, she was present in the Throne Room earlier."

"Of course. She's still welcome at Court on account of being a close confidant to Princess Amelia. However, her homestead is Marble Hill House in Twickenham. This is where young Samuel has been raised."

"Such a remarkable tale!" said the Ambassador, wiping his forehead with a handkerchief. "Still, I wonder. What really made you break your vow of silence, Arabella? After all, Princess Amelia aided our cause."

"She did. I harbor no ill will toward Her Royal Highness. Quite the contrary, I have a taking for her."

"Then, wherefore reveal her secret? And why now?"

"We both know why, Renato. Princess Amelia's secret is just one thread within a vast web of lies. I could no longer bear being a part of it, my darling. Not after today. Not anymore."

"I have every faith in you, Arabella. And you can place your trust in me. I won't breathe a word of this to anyone."

Just then, the King rose from his seat and trumpets sounded as he stepped forward to face the guests.

"His Majesty, the King!" the Lord Chamberlain announced. The Great Hall fell silent, the guests rose to their feet and faced the monarch.

"My lords, ladies and gentlemen," began the King with a broad smile. "I bid you all a warm welcome! 'Tis my privilege and pleasure this evening, to propose the first toast of the evening, in honor of my dear daughter Emily, Princess Amelia. On this joyous occasion marking her thirty-sixth birthday, I am impelled to express my feelings of pride and affection for one of the most respected and admired ladies in the land. I need not dilate upon the many good and generous qualities that make her who she is. You are all aware of her kind nature and her readiness to listen to the call of charity. I am certain I need say no more, but to convey my heartfelt gratitude to each and every one of you for joining me and my family in this celebration and this toast. Now let us raise our glasses and drink to the health, long life and happiness of my dearest child. To Princess Amelia!"

Everyone raised their glasses and cheered.

Standing in a corner of the ballroom, away from the center of attention, Lords Fielding and Middlesex engaged in a lively tête-à-tête.

"'Tis quite amusing to hear the King speak of the Princess as being predisposed to charity when, by most accounts, her interests lie exclusively in riding and hunting," Fielding whispered.

"Some would say there may just be a kernel of truth to that, my lord," Middlesex whispered back. "The vulgars have been going on about it for years."

"The vulgars? What could they know about a member of the royal household?"

Middlesex smirked. "Word has it that some time ago, a royal mare with a penchant for common breed stallions carried and birthed a colt from one of such dalliances."

"Surely, a galling fabrication!" Fielding grumbled.

"And yet so detailed…" Middlesex insisted. "They go as far as saying that although she never claimed the colt as hers, she kept him close to her stable."

"We are all sinners," Fielding declared, with composed demeanor. "To lend an ear to such hearsay coming from the rabble is preposterous."

"Pray forgive my lack of gravity," Middlesex responded, his face aflush. "In all truth, I harbor no animosity toward Her Royal Highness. Though, on reflection, I do perceive why others might have cause for it."

"What cause?"

"My sources tell me she has been influential in orchestrating the signing of a royal pardon for a certain fugitive… Should this hold any truth, it would set tongues wagging."

"You mean, your former associate, the impresario who eloped from the Fleet?"

Middlesex nodded. "He was a thorn in my side. I rue the day I welcomed him into my theater."

"Signor Vanneschi brought him to you, did he not?"

"He did. And to what end? He nearly ruined us! Now, I am told he got off scot free and will soon be on his way out of the country."

"I would not be so sure about that," Fielding countered. "The King may have granted him a pardon but he must have surely paid a pretty penny for it."

"What makes you think so?"

"Oh, just a hunch… Nothing is free in this age."

"What about his obligation to his creditor?"

"Mr. Garrick? He settled it several days ago."

"He did?"

"Indeed. All charges were dismissed. 'Tis public knowledge."

"I presume that might have carried some weight in His Majesty's pronouncement."

"Perhaps. Even so, the Impresario may still have other scores to settle."

"With whom?"

"I am a magistrate, sir. I am not at liberty to divulge any particulars."

"Say no more! My gut tells me this is something to do with Warden Bambridge."

"Your words, not mine."

"And yet, what recourse would the Warden have? A royal pardon has been granted."

"Anyone with fresh new evidence to sustain a grievance can petition the Court to issue an Order of Pursuit," Fielding explained.

"Ah… Now I see. Should this come to pass, the Warden would be free to unleash his hounds and pursue the Impresario wherever he may find him."

"I could not say. I refuse to engage in speculation, sir. However, I must credit you with possessing a rather fertile mind."

"I shall take that as flattery, my lord. If I knew any better, I'd venture that challenging His Majesty's discretion at this early stage would be rather untimely."

"You might be right about that."

———>◎<———

When the toasts ended, the King and Princess Amelia paid their compliments to high ranking courtiers, members of the nobility, foreign ministers and the circle of dancers awaiting to perform. Once the King was seated, the minuets commenced. At the end of the first set, and after the lingering applause, Lord Middlesex caught sight of the Azzonis returning to their seats. He dashed over to greet them.

"What a felicitous occasion to chance upon you, Your Excellencies!" he said, bowing.

The Ambassador and his wife nodded gracefully.

"'Tis ever our pleasure to behold your presence, my lord," the Ambassador responded.

Middlesex turned to Lady Azzoni. "You look radiant, my lady!"

"Obliged, my lord. 'Tis but a glow. You see, the minuet has brought on the vapors," she said, waving a folding fan.

"We have missed you at the King's Theater as of late. Your box has been vacant for a while."

"Arabella has been engaged with home duties," said the Ambassador, glancing at his wife. "And I with all the diversions at St. James'."

"Ah, but your devotion to the stage arts— Is it now a forlorn passion?"

"Not at all." Lady Azzoni replied. "Our fondness for the theater has not diminished in the least."

"Your gracious support has not escaped us," Middlesex responded. "We are indebted to you for your assistance in our effort to re-open a few months past."

"We are glad we could be of service, my lord. Your theater has brought boundless joy and delight to so many."

"Much obliged. We strive to please. But your resolve and verve are peerless! Even now, after having lost one of our troupes, you have endeavored to save its master…" Middlesex fired, impassively and without warning.

The Ambassador's eyes glazed. "We have our duties, my lord. We represent the interests of Genoa and her citizens here in England."

"Then, you might be interested to know that the Warden at the Fleet could still pursue your fellow citizen until he honors all of his outstanding obligations with him."

"I thought that had been settled."

"And I, as well. Yet, while speaking with Lord Fielding—"

Perplexed, the Ambassador and his wife looked at each other.

"I must take my leave now," said Middlesex abruptly. "I shall look forward to seeing you at the theater soon. 'Tis been a pleasure."

Silence came with a frosty nod from the Ambassador.

Lady Azzoni's stern look mirrored her husband's.

On their way back to the embassy, as they sat side by side on their coach, Lady Azzoni's lingering grimace drew the Ambassador's attention.

"What preys on your mind, my dear?"

"The poisonous tidings that Middlesex conveyed to us tonight."

"Perish those thoughts at once, Arabella. I beseech you."

"I wish I could! The notion that our endeavors to save our esteemed dottore were for naught weigh heavy on my heart. His travails might follow him to Europe!"

"It seems unlikely the Fleet's warden may seek to challenge the Crown's prerogative in Court," the Ambassador responded. "Ignoring the King's pardon seems a farfetched idea."

"The Warden may not see it that way."

"Fielding is aware Bambridge is corrupt."

"And yet, that would not preclude him from filing a complaint."

"I suppose not. Nonetheless, 'tis all too soon to tell."

"We know he is a zealot when it comes to garnishing his fees. He may fear that allowing an inmate to evade his obligations might tempt others to follow suit."

"He has done nothing yet."

"What if he did?"

"All we have is conjecture, my dear wife. Besides, our Dottore could always choose to settle with him, could he not?"

"Not without jeopardizing his future. He desperately needs what's left of what his kinsman sent him to start his life anew in Europe. Most of what he had went to the King."

"Pray let us leave all that behind for now, Arabella. We've done our part."

———>-☺-<———

Two days passed before the Ambassador and Lady Azzoni saw Giovanni out to the front of their residence and bid him adieu.

"We wish you an auspicious new beginning in the Netherlands, Dottore!" said the Ambassador, patting Giovanni on the back while a footman loaded his baggage onto a waiting coach.

"Obliged, Your Excellency!"

"May your journey to The Hague be safe and light!" said Lady Azzoni.

Giovanni bowed and kissed Lady Azzoni's hand. "My deepest gratitude for your thoughtfulness and generosity, my lady."

"Promise me you shall keep us apprised of your new troupe's whereabouts."

"You can count on it, *mia signora!*"

"Have a care!" she responded, dabbing her eyes with a handkerchief as she gazed at him tenderly.

Giovanni turned, climbed onto the coach and rode away.

XVI. JOURNEY TO THE NETHERLANDS

C hurch bells rang in the distance as Giovanni's carriage rolled into Charing Cross, a village between London and Westminster. He reached for his pocket watch. *Time for mass,* he thought, aware that observance that evening would not be feasible. He pocketed his watch and looked out the window. A busy town square sprawled before his eyes. Cobbled streets echoed with the rhythmic clip-clop of hooves while townsfolk promenaded amidst the aromatic blend of roasted chestnuts and the sweet scent of nearby bakeries.

The carriage rode through the square, then pulled into a bustling coachyard at The Golden Cross Inn, a prominent establishment. Giovanni stepped off, picked up his valise and walked into the inn's tavern. Behind him, a porter carried the rest of his baggage.

Once settled in the tavern hall, Giovanni procured an early morning seat on a coach to Dover and ordered supper. Following a satisfying repast and a pint of ale, he sank into a comfortable armchair by the fireplace and recounted his plans of the forthcoming voyage:

Cross the Channel.
Rendezvous with the Laschis in Calais.
Sail to The Hague.

Before long, the murmurs of chatter around him turned into a faint hum, and the warmth radiating from the hearth gently coaxed the Impresario to surrender to the embrace of slumber.

Moments later, he opened his eyes. *Strange... Not a soul around.* Flickering lights in a corner of the room caught his attention. *Burning candles,* he figured, before realizing they were reflections on the surface of a mirror suspended in the air. *Peculiar looking glass...* he thought, as shadows danced around it, then vanished behind swirling flames.

As one image dissolved, another one emerged out of thin air: a freestanding black rectangle. *A door?* Rising to his feet, Giovanni moved toward it and touched it. A soft, slick surface met his hand. Cautiously, he pushed into it. His arms and torso followed. The structure crumbled as he hobbled. "A thing not of this world…" he mumbled as he quickly righted himself, anchoring his feet on the ground.

Standing still, Giovanni's gaze swept his surroundings. For a moment, a large blue void engulfed him. *Heaven?*

Suddenly, a massive column began surfacing in the vicinity. Rising steadily, it materialized, guarded at its base by four colossal bronze lions.

Perched atop the pillar, a statue of a man looked out and over an emerging urban landscape. An empty sleeve was pinned against the right side of his chest. On the left, his hand grasped the pommel of a sword pointing downward. *Without a doubt, a most revered soul,* Giovanni mused. *A saint, perhaps?*

As structures continued to appear one after another in the distance, strange sounds began seeping in. *Tolling bells, horns and trumpets herald the arrival of Our Lord,* thought Giovanni, while tooting and screeching gradually filled the air. Then, a whole town square swarming with activity took shape before his eyes. *Cast steel coaches riding along flat roads… Chariots for the angels!*

An oversized red stagecoach roared past him. *No horses harnessed to it. Such a peculiar sight…* Gazing at the passengers looking out from a row of windows, he pondered: *The souls of those who've heeded the Lord's Call?*

Painted on one side of the stagecoach an image of a young girl caught his eye. Brandishing a contoured brown object in her hand, she flashed a radiant smile. Next to her, in large printed letters, intriguing words: "Coca-Cola. Delicious and Refreshing!"

A few feet away arose a statue of a man on horseback supported by a pedestal. In full armor and holding a baton in one hand and the reins of his horse in the other, the man struck a proud and noble posture. *Who is this?* As Giovanni approached to read the inscriptions on the pedestal, a familiar voice echoed in the ether.

Charles I… the only English king who lost his head and the monarchy itself, both at the same time!

Just then, something prodded him. He raised his head and saw the King staring down, his baton poking him on the shoulder.

"Sir! Sir! Awake!"

As he stirred, a porter stood before him, nudging him.

"Pray sir, arise! Your coach is leaving!"

Heavy-eyed, Giovanni struggled to his feet. The porter lifted his belongings and they headed for the coachyard.

After a day's journey, Giovanni arrived at the Customs House in Dover. He walked into the Packet Office and purchased passage on the next sailing ship departing for Calais. On his way out, he looked up at the sky. *No clouds. Such a blessing!*

Upon boarding, a crewmember showed Giovanni to the sole passenger cabin on the ship. He stepped into it and drew the curtains open. Peering out on the sea from his porthole, he listened to the waves lapping gently at the vessel's hull. He took his coat off, sat on his bunk, and brought a bedsheet to his nostrils. *Mm... So fresh!* He smiled, removed his shoes and lay down.

Soon after leaving harbor, the wind picked up. The ship heaved and swayed as she rolled on the waves. Abruptly, an unforgiving breaker pushed her up, then brought her crashing down. Giovanni's stomach turned. "Mercy me!" he cried out. He bent over a slop bucket, wincing in agony.

Six hours passed before reaching land. Still lightheaded, Giovanni stepped ashore, found the nearest bench and rested there. After a while, his dizziness abated. Looking around him, he spotted a French newssheet by his feet. He reached for it and instantly took notice of the date: *3 Septembre, 1750.* Confused, he shook his head. *I'd wager my last farthing we left Dover on the twenty-second day of August!*

A cool breeze brought a moment of clarity. *Ah! Now it comes to me! The pagans in England follow the Julian Calendar. Catholics in Europe, Pope Gregory's.* Relieved, the Impresario rose, called for help with his belongings, and made his way to the Calais Customs House.

Having dutifully attended to all requisite protocols, Giovanni availed himself of a coach and proceeded to the Lion d'Argent, a venerable inn nestled in the heart of Calais. There, he hoped to rendezvous with his travel companions. Alas, after taking lodgings for the night and making inquiries with the innkeeper, they were nowhere in sight.

After two days awaiting their arrival, Giovanni's colleagues remained conspicuously absent. *What could account for their delay?* Tidings had reached him that a vessel bound for The Hague had moored at the harbor, prompting a sense of urgency and unease.

On the eve of their intended departure, while sitting at a table in the tavern's hall, Giovanni weighed his options. Should the Laschis fail to appear, he reckoned he would have no choice but to sail alone. Such ruminations occupied his mind when unexpectedly, a gentleman clad in the finest attire approached.

"Bon jour, Monsieur!" he said with a thick English accent. *"Parlez vous anglais?"*

"Indeed, I do!" Giovanni nodded. The appearance of this worldly presence put a swift end to his fretful disquiet.

"I believe our paths may have crossed in the recent past," the man explained. "And now again…"

Giovanni peered into the man's face. "Ah, yes! Are you perhaps the sketch artist I once came across by the harbor, here in Calais?"

"I am, indeed! William Hogarth. Your servant."

"And I yours. Giovanni Crossa. Pray join me." He gestured for Hogarth to take a seat at his table.

"If memory serves," Hogarth began, "we chanced upon each other two years past, when I was on my way to Paris."

"Verily. And I was on my way to London. I caught sight of you drawing a sketch of the Gate at the port."

"I was! And keeping my own counsel…"

"Quite right. You were. And then—"

"—and then destiny took a fatal turn and two French soldiers charged me with spying and proceeded to detain me."

"My recollection of the scene remains quite vivid," said Giovanni. "It caused such a commotion."

"Right you are, sir. A commotion it was! And for me, quite a perilous circumstance. As you may also recall, this was shortly after the war had ended. The soldiers suspected I was an agent of the Crown, sketching the port's fortifications to report back to England."

"I do recall."

"You sir, were brave, for upon seeing my distress, you reached out and offered to carry my easel and my drawing tools to the wagon they were about to toss me into."

Giovanni nodded. "Alas, the soldiers refused me."

"Of course! They believed my artwork was evidence I had committed a crime. I was much chagrined when afterwards, I came to realize I never tendered my gratitude for your kind gesture."

"There was no need, Signore."

"I assure you, your kindness did not go unremembered." Hogarth signaled the tavern keeper who brought two pints of ale to the table.

"No good Christian would have failed to do the same."

"And yet it was you who came to my rescue." Hogarth raised his tankard. "Here's to your kindness, sir!"

"And to your health!" Giovanni responded. He took a swig and wiped the foam from his moustache with the back of his hand. "I hope your captors did no harm to you, or kept you long."

"They did not. All the same, 'twas a nuisance. They dragged me to the governor's, and he refused to discharge me until I proved myself to be a veritable artist."

"How did you fare with that?"

"I took the canvas I had been working on and drew the soldiers who arrested me."

"You put them in your picture?"

"I did. And bearing ghastly countenances, in rags, scrawny, and famished. Gawking at a gigantic piece of beef that had just landed at port."

"Extraordinary. You mocked your tormentors to their faces, and yet they set you free."

"Their folly! The simpletons did not detect either my jest or my disdain."

Giovanni chuckled. "Was the beef real?"

"Positively! And destined to be roasted at this very inn, The Lion d'Argent. The selfsame place where I was lodged at the time I was seized."

"Ahh! The whims of fate," said Giovanni, shaking his head. "And now? What brings you here again, Signore?"

"A vow I made to myself once I returned to England."

"May I inquire what that was?"

"Certainly. To convey my heartfelt gratitude to the proprietor of this establishment. 'Twas he who so graciously extended his hospitality without charge upon my release by the governor."

"A kind gesture, to be sure."

"Indeed. And one I was unable to return until yesterday. Two long years after this vexing affair."

"How did you square with him?"

"I presented him and his wife with an engraving, crafted by my own hand, of the original canvas that saved me in 1748."

"Very thoughtful of you. Did it meet their approval?"

"They found it comical. Especially when they heard how I baptized the original."

"How did you name it?"

"*The Roast Beef of Old England,* though as of late it has come to be known as *The Gate of Calais.*" Hogarth rose to his feet and pointed to a framed engraving hanging above the mantel of a fireplace across the hall.

"Naturally. It appears to be a faithful depiction of the gate at the port," said Giovanni, gazing at the artwork. "Save for the soldiers in their humorous poses."

"'Tis one of my grotesques," said Hogarth, smiling. "Meant to be whimsical."

"I am piqued. Why the allusion to *Old England*?"

"Because Calais was English for well over two centuries. And deemed by many to be the Crown's brightest of jewels. We may have lost it at war, but the old time English dwellers of these parts never turned tail and ran. Many things remained as they once were. Take the gate at the port. 'Tis still adorned with our glorious English arms. This very inn as well, The Lion d'Argent, is English."

"Then, wherefore the French name?" asked Giovanni. "Should it not be called The Silver Lion?"

"No one minds the name. 'Tis a good place to lodge while one's in transit. By the by, what brings *you* back to these parts?"

"I am on my way to The Hague, looking for new business ventures."

"From?"

"London. Two years I spent there before destiny brought me back to the continent."

"London did not suit you?"

"Not after a coxcomb I cannot abide filed a complaint against me that landed me at the Fleet."

"A coxcomb?"

"Vain as they come! Someone by the name of David Garrick."

"The actor turned theater Impresario?"

"One and the same. He fancies himself a fashionable dandy, strutting about all puffed up and full of himself."

"Oh, you must be the Impresario from Turin whose case was in the broadsheets a few days ago. I hope the warden spared you the whip. He has a dreadful reputation."

"Bambridge is a most wicked man! Before he and his thugs could lay hands upon me, I was forced to elope."

"I believe you! I am persuaded his devious ways will one day become his downfall."

"Time and tide will tell," Giovanni grimaced, images of the dark, recent past preying on his mind.

Following a few more minutes of animated talk, the men took their leave, bidding each other adieu.

Before retiring for the night, the Impresario stepped out for a leisurely stroll. As he walked, he watched the last few coaches pass by, the soft glow of the sun fading behind the silhouettes of buildings nearby. Around him, sailors caroused while the night crews lit the oil lamps and the torches.

On his return to the inn, Giovanni heard singing somewhere in the neighborhood. Intrigued, he followed the source. As he drew closer to it, he saw a cathedral, its front doors wide open. He walked in and advanced through the nave until he reached the chancel. There, stood a boys' choir on a wooden riser. Their tender voices seemed familiar… He took a seat in the front pews and closed his eyes.

For an instant, chants echoing through centuries swept him away elsewhere, triggering a lucid vision: People in odd-looking garments and hairstyles sat in orderly rows within a high-vaulted chamber. Oblique lights of peculiar intensity shone down from above. And yet, there were no candles…

Giovanni's spell came to an end when a clergyman gently tapped him on the shoulder. "Pray wake, Monsieur! Evening prayer has concluded."

Startled, Giovanni opened his eyes. *"Merci, merci! Je suis désolé!"* he responded. He rose and quickly made his way toward the exit.

A silver moon graced the heavens by the time Giovanni arrived back at the inn. Stepping into the main hall, he caught sight of a young couple signing the guestbook. He paused to take a closer look. The man's long, deep brown sideburns and a mole on his left cheek left him no doubt. It was Filippo, pale and slender, accompanied by his spunky, red-haired wife, Laura.

Giovanni dashed up to greet them. "At last, you have arrived!" he exclaimed, breaking into a wide smile.

The couple turned towards him. Filippo's voice cracked with emotion. "Dottore! You're here! Praise the Lord!" He removed his tricorn and bowed.

Laura nodded. Giovanni kissed her hand. "I landed in Calais but two days past," he said. "I can put my mind to rest now. I trust all is well."

"A thousand pardons for the delay!" Laura responded, her travel bags by her feet. "Filippo was taken ill. We had no choice but to remain in London until he came around."

Giovanni patted Filippo on the back. "I am glad to see you're well."

"Grazie, Dottore! 'Twas the putrid throat that kept me down. But by the grace of Providence, Laura's nursing care, and a special tincture from the apothecary, I am now on the mend."

"Good! I was preoccupied with the prospect of having to sail to the Netherlands without you."

"Sailing?" Laura repeated. "We were considering the diligence."

Giovanni paused. "Um… A six-horse stagecoach thronged with foul-smelling passengers in this sultry weather?"

Laura hesitated. "'Tis true. Yet…"

Giovanni insisted. "Travelling at four to five miles per hour, the diligence would take seven to eight days to reach The Hague. A rather hazardous venture."

"How do you mean?" asked Filippo, eyebrows arched with concern.

"Carriageway heists. We must not forget, we carry all of our troupe's possessions with us, including our cherished costumes. Richard, my Dutch comrade, assures me that sailing will be safer and faster than travelling by land."

"I do not mean to dodge, Dottore," said Laura. "Yet, the hour is late and we are weary. Perhaps by the morrow, when we are fully rested, you could assuage our doubts."

"Of course, my dear Laura. Pray forgive my eagerness. I fear I have not been myself as of late. A night's rest will do us all well. We shall discuss our travel arrangements in the morning. I bid you a good night, my friends."

➤·◉·◄

The following day, over morning repast, Giovanni succeeded in persuading his travel companions to join him on the *Bredenhoft*, a Dutch merchant ship docked at Calais and bound for Vlissingen and The Hague. Three hours before noon, they found themselves alongside a handful of other passengers on the ship's boarding ramp.

As they reached the main deck, they encountered a dapper young man wearing a black tailcoat over a white waistcoat, knee breeches, and a dark blue tricorn matching the color of his eyes. *"Welkom aan boord! Ik ben Kapitein Dienke van Der Zee,"* he said, tipping his hat with one hand while gesturing with the other for the passengers to move forward.

After the formalities of introduction were concluded, Giovanni wasted no time in bringing up his acquaintance, Sir Richard Westerbeek. Upon hearing the name, the Captain's demeanor took a visible turn. With striking alacrity, he became keenly deferential, offering to conduct a tour of his ship as soon as the trio had settled into their cabins. Shortly afterward, they rendezvoused with him at the wheelhouse.

"I trust all is in order with your accommodations," said the Captain. "Should there be aught you require, do not hesitate to acquaint one of my officers."

"You're most gracious, Captain!" said Laura, face glowing.

Filippo leaned forward. "Your ship appears to be in excellent condition," he observed.

"Flawless!" Giovanni chimed in, casting a sweeping glance around.

The Captain smiled proudly. "Indeed! She's at the apex of her kind. She was built just four years ago by the best of our shipwrights in Amsterdam. Pray, accompany me." He led the group out of the wheelhouse and onto the main deck.

As they ambled along the deck, the Captain pointed to the cannons aimed seaward. "She's fitted with six of these iron beauties, dozens of cannon shots and as many barrels filled with gunpowder. Aside from the Good Lord, this is our only protection against the Bugis." He then walked toward an open trap door leading to the lower deck.

"Who are the *Bugis*?" Giovanni asked.

"Pirates," the Captain replied. "Natives of Sulawesi. They claim they're seafarers and merchants, but in truth, they're ruthless warriors."

"Was the *Bredenhoft* ever attacked by them?"

"Never! Praise the Lord! Yet, we are painfully aware they could be lying in wait anywhere, to strike and pillage, given the slightest chance!"

Peculiar... thought Giovanni. *Native vultures preying on foreign sharks.*

"How long have you been at sea?" Laura inquired, following the Captain down the steps, her husband and Giovanni close behind her.

"Seventeen weeks today, ma'am."

"A long voyage, indeed!"

As they reached the bottom of the steps, the Captain lit a torch and advanced deeper into the hold area, revealing dozens of chests lashed and stacked up against the hull. "We've been to the East Indies and now return with 850 tons of cargo, most of which is stowed right here," he said.

Laura directed her gaze at the chests. "What's inside of them?"

"A sizable treasure in copper coins, silver ingots and golden ducats," the Captain replied. "Come along! There's more!" He then entered an area packed with barrels.

"More treasure?" asked Filippo.

"Of a most valuable kind, sir. These barrels are loaded with food, water, and provisions."

Filippo nodded.

The Captain paused at a gate. "Beyond this point," he said, "we have stalls and coops for chickens, pigs and sheep."

Filled with curiosity, Laura leaned forward. "You keep livestock on board?"

"'Tis of the essence, ma'am. We can only keep salted meat in barrels for so long. A few months and it will spoil and go to waste. It behooves us to keep our crew strong and healthy."

"Of course," Laura responded.

The Captain turned around and led the group back up the stairs. Once assembled on the main deck he paused and cast a glance at a hatch, a few feet away from where they stood. "Also," he said, "on this voyage we're carrying *human cargo*, which also requires sustenance."

"Passengers? In the cargo hold?" Giovanni asked.

"Slaves. Twenty-five females from Java."

Filippo felt his wife squeezing his arm, her mouth agape. "I—I didn't… I—I hadn't… a notion this was a slave ship," he sputtered.

"My dear sir, the *Bredenhoft* is a merchant ship," the Captain responded swiftly. "These are survivors of a tragic shipwreck off the Cape of Good Hope, in Southern Africa. They were being transported there from Java, when their ship went down."

"Frightful!" Laura cried out.

The Captain continued. "'Twas fate. We were anchoring at port when our lookout espied them in their bare skin by the shore."

Laura cupped her hands over her mouth. "Poor souls!"

"Verily. After docking, my Christian faith compelled me to acquire all twenty-five of them."

"From whom?"

"From the surviving officers who claimed them as their own," the Captain explained.

"What do you intend to do with them?"

"Why of course, they shall be sold as servants to the households of our company officials. I am certain this shall result in immeasurable benefits to them, as they will be treated far better in Europe than elsewhere." With this, the Captain brought the tour to a close. He walked Giovanni and his colleagues to their cabins and retired to his quarters.

XVII. ABOARD THE BREDENHOFT

A candle in a chamberstick burned in the center of a table at the *Bredenhoft's* dining mess as Giovanni sat waiting for supper to be served. The Laschis had excused themselves on account of Laura feeling seasick. *Poor thing!* he thought, as he watched the candle's tenuous flame wavering. *I know precisely how that feels.*

Lost in thought, the presence of two young servers waiting on the tables nearby had largely gone unnoticed.

Until one of them approached.

"Excuseer me, mijnheer," the server said softly in Dutch.

Giovanni blinked. Before him stood a young female, clumsily disguised as a man. *Odd... Females are barred from the crew.*

Loosely clad in black breeches, a white long-sleeved shirt buttoned up to the neck, and a brown round knit cap covering her head, the server recited the menu.

Captivated by her youthful, sun-kissed face, her words slipped past him. *Almond eyes. A stewardess from the Indies?* he pondered.

"Sir?" she repeated in English. "Will it be pickled salmon or gammon?"

"Uh… Apologies! I—I was distracted," Giovanni stammered. "I'll take the pickled salmon, if it's not too spicy."

"There's been no whisper of displeasure with the fare," she said, her brown eyes catching a glimmer from the candlelight.

"Then that settles it." He lowered his eyesight and spotted a tattoo of a colorful tiny bird on the back of her right hand.

"Shall I fetch you some ale as well, sir?"

"A stout porter, if you please." Giovanni's eyes shifted to the nape of her neck as she turned and walked back into the galley. Before long, she returned with a tray bearing food, ale, utensils and a linen napkin. She set it down before him and moved on to the next diner.

Within a half hour Giovanni's dish was empty and the server was back once again. "Anything else I could proffer you, good sir? Mayhap, a sweet treat?"

"None for me. Just a query, if I may."

"Of course," she responded lifting his tray.

"Pray forgive my forwardness. Your tattoo... It caught my attention." He pointed to the little bird inked on the back of her hand.

She smiled. "'Tis a swallow."

"Assuredly, a mark of significance," Giovanni responded.

"Verily. In my homeland, swallows are believed to be messengers from lost loved ones."

"Heartwarming, indeed."

After retiring to his cabin for the night, Giovanni's mind kept circling back to the image of the swallow on the back of the young female server's hand.

⟶ ▸◉◂ ⟵

The following day, just after morning repast, the *Bredenhoft* docked at Vlissingen.

"I am glad you feel better," Giovanni told Laura as they sat at a table with Filippo in the dining mess.

"I am sure I wouldn't, had I not refrained from having supper last night."

"A wise decision indeed."

"Will you be joining us for a stroll around town, Dottore?" Filippo asked, as he and Laura rose. "I believe we shall be anchored for the day."

"They say Vlissingen is a charming village," said Laura, adjusting her hat.

"Maybe at a later hour, my esteemed colleagues. Presently, I crave coffee."

Moments after Filippo and Laura left and the mess emptied out, the same young server from the previous night stood by Giovanni's table.

"Was the repast to your liking, sir?"

"Very much so. Although I fear I must trouble you again. This time, for coffee."

"'Tis no trouble at all."

"Something else…"

"Of course."

"You are a female… Yet, your attire—"

"Captain's orders. I have no choice."

"May I introduce myself, ma'am?"

"By all means, sir," she replied, a baffled look on her face.

He stood and bowed. "Giovani Crossa, your servant."

"My name is…" She paused. "Shane. While I'm on board."

"And when you're not?"

She blushed. "Sheina. I am glad to make your acquaintance."

"Likewise, Miss Sheina," he smiled, sitting back down.

"I shall return forthwith, sir." She walked away. Giovanni's eyes followed.

Within minutes, she re-emerged from the galley. "Here you are, sir. Arabian coffee."

"Delightful. Uh... apologies for distracting you from your chores. I thought perhaps you could spare a brief moment of your time."

"I am glad to be of service."

"I am new to sailing, you see," Giovanni said, twiddling with a napkin on the table. "And curious about the crewmembers' menu."

"The lower ranks get porridge for our morning meal. Then thrice a week, for midday repast and supper we get a bowl with boiled salt meat, peas or sauerkraut, and a small biscuit. We all get the same victuals and eat at the same time."

"And the other days of the week?"

"We get dried fish. Sometimes cheese."

"No fresh fruit or vegetables?"

"Rarely."

"Do you partake of your meals here at the mess?"

"The mess is reserved for sailors and passengers, sir. The Captain takes his meals in his quarters with a few of the high officers. Warrant officers take their meals in the gunroom. And the lesser hands like myself, wherever we can find an empty spot, but only after all galley and scullery chores have been completed."

"Is the food any good?"

"The meat is fair, but the porridge, not so much."

"And the biscuits?"

"They're hard and dry. And that's when they come without weevils."

"Dreadful! Would it be presumptuous of me to entreat you to join me for supper at eventide, after you've discharged your duties? I would very much like to treat you to a proper meal."

Sheina stared. "Alas, I must decline. I fear it would not be proper."

"My intentions are honorable, Signorina. 'Tis just a meal. Pray indulge me just this once."

"You are kind and thoughtful, sir. For that, I am much obliged. Yet, I must beg your forgiveness. I could never... Not without the Captain's knowledge and consent."

"I beseech you. Leave the Captain to me. I assure you, he shall consent."

Sheina dropped her gaze. "If you insist… I yield and place my confidence in you, sir."

Victory! An intense rush of energy surged within Giovanni's core. "Shall we convene here at the hour of seven then?"

"Pray forgive me. I cannot promise to be punctual."

"Marvelous! Around the hour of seven it is."

Back at his cabin, Giovanni took pains grooming himself for the evening. He combed his hair again and again, carefully trimmed his beard and smoothed his moustache. Glancing one more time at a small looking glass in his privy, he smiled. *Flawless!*

He polished his shoes and matched a pair of breeches, a shirt, a neck cloth and a waistcoat. Pocket watch and snuffbox in place, and he was ready. With a brisk step he proceeded toward the mess. A peculiar vigor coursed through him. He had not felt this way since the days he first laid eyes on his beloved Antonia.

The mess was empty and dimly lit but for a few candle stubs on the arms of a solitary chandelier. Giovanni sat at a table and waited in subdued anticipation as waves lapped against the vessel's hull, soft vibrations reverberating all around.

Within minutes, Sheina appeared, still dressed in her day labor garb, a tray with food, ale, and an oil lamp in her hands.

They took seats opposite each other, their faces lit by the lamp.

"I brought the best that I could find from this evening's bill of fare, sir. Charred fish, peas, goat cheese, freshly baked bread, butter, and wild berry tart."

"Delightful! To your health!" said Giovanni, raising his tankard.

"And yours!" she responded, raising hers.

"You must be glad we sail for The Hague in the morrow, Signorina," Giovanni said. "It shall be payday when we make land. I presume you are employed by the Dutch East India Company, like the rest of the crew."

"Not me. I am here on account of Captain van Der Zee's grace and kindness," Sheina responded, as she began to avail herself of the food on her plate. "He approached me at the port of Good Hope. Upon learning I speak several tongues, he offered me employment in exchange for passage to Europe."

"To labor in the galley?"

She nodded. "And to act as interpreter."

"For whom?"

The slaves. You see, I speak their mother tongue."

"You speak well in Dutch and English, too."

"You are too kind, sir. I am humbled by your words."

"Do you hail from Java, Signorina?"

"Aye. From Batavia."

"Yet, you are not—" Giovanni stopped abruptly.

"— a slave?"

"Apologies. I—I did not mean to imply…"

"Oh no. *My* fault, sir. I confounded you. We all hail from Batavia. We are survivors of a shipwreck. But that is the extent of what we have in common."

"I see." Giovanni picked up his tankard and took a healthy quaff. "Whatever happened to the ship that sank?"

"We had just arrived at the Cape of Good Hope," Sheina began through a bite. "I was on deck with my Dutch family awaiting our turn to board the ships' tenders that had come to take us into port. There were also hundreds of slaves crammed in the cargo hold below deck."

"Ah, that *was* a slave ship," Giovanni observed.

"Aye. 'Twas indeed. There were very few ordinary passengers on board, my family among them."

"What about the slaves below deck?"

"Their destination was the same as ours: Good Hope. Alas, only a handful made it there. Their fate was sealed even before the ship went down."

"How do you mean *before?*"

"The conditions below deck were frightful. The males were shackled at all times. Poor ventilation made the heat and humidity unbearable, and the air foul. We were all aware of their suffering."

"How? Did you see them?"

"We could hear their cries."

"And the females?"

"Some were free to roam within the cargo hold, and sometimes even on the main deck with their children. We heard them talk about the meager rations and the squalor. And we were also witness to some awful things that happened right before our very eyes."

"Pray tell. What did you see?"

Sheina put down her fork and knife, a grave and sober look on her face. "How sickness led to death. Every now and then, crewmembers hoisted corpses from below and dumped them overboard."

"Ghastly!"

"And some of the officers were merciless. They ordered public beatings and floggings at the slightest signs of defiance."

"What on earth could account for such malice?"

"My elders said that the officers were often ruffians recruited from the prisons."

"Inmates?"

"A handful, I believe. Most had been the wardens' hired thugs."

"Ah! Demons who learned their evil trade in dungeons," Giovanni responded, reaching for his snuffbox. "What about the sailors?"

"Indigents, I heard. And some, freed slaves."

"They must have found sailing the high seas a better choice than roughing it on land."

"Perhaps, but not by much. We witnessed their distress. Weeks and months out on the open deck. They had no shelter. The cargo hold was taken, replete with slaves."

"A tragic tale inside a tragic tale," Giovanni said, inhaling deeply, his nostrils filled with snuff.

Sheina nodded. "Sadly so."

"How did the ship go down? And, how did you and the others survive?"

"It all began when a female slave was accused by an officer of stealing a piece of chicken from him. The captain had her hanged from the ship's yardarm with a drumstick stuck in her mouth."

"Lord Almighty!"

"He ordered all slaves to march in chains before her dangling body."

"Such nauseating cruelty!"

"'Twas plain he intended to lay bare the fate that would await them if they ever attempted to mimic her actions. Just then, a group of armed sailors became enraged at the spectacle and started a revolt."

Giovanni shook his head. "A mutiny."

"Indeed. The rebels unshackled some of the slaves and a frenzied rage erupted. The officers and other crewmembers put up a barricade on the upper deck and the shooting began. A spark then caused a barrel of gunpowder to ignite and blow up, making a hole in the ship's hull where water began pouring in. Everyone panicked." Sheina paused, took a sip from her tankard and continued. "A few rebels succeeded in getting off the ship. Alas, most were overcome by the officers who, realizing the ship was sinking, ordered them below deck and nailed the escape hatches shut before abandoning the vessel."

"Pray tell, how could you see all of this? Where were you?"

"On the upper deck, hiding behind the officers."

"All by yourself? Where was your family?"

"In the mayhem, we lost sight of each other."

"What then?"

"As the ship began to sink, an officer took pity on me and lowered me into a boat tender, filled with female slaves. We were then brought into port."

"Did they ever catch the rebels who escaped?"

"Most of them were captured and executed on the spot. Only the female slaves who did not partake in the riot were spared and put on board the *Bredenhoft*, which was anchored at port and ready to sail for the Netherlands. 'Twas then, at the harbor, that Captain van Der Zee caught sight of me."

A brief interlude ensued. Giovanni and Sheina sat silently, the food on their plates barely disturbed. The flame of the oil lamp on the table wavered gently as shadows twirled in their midst.

"Your story stirs me, Signorina," Giovanni said, gazing into Sheina's eyes.

Sheina dipped her chin and cast a downward glance. "How I wish this were naught but a figment of the mind or a mere vision!"

"I am no stranger to visions," Giovanni responded. "By your words, I sense there is a great deal more we could confide in each other. Perhaps, a new encounter between us might prove propitious."

"Alas, I see no chance for that, sir. We are due at The Hague by noon tomorrow. No time to talk."

"Before morning meal, then?"

"To what end?"

"Our paths have crossed by happenstance, and yet somehow I feel the hand of fate entwining us. I must confess, your presence and comportment, Signorina, strike me as exceptional."

Sheina blushed. "You flatter me, sir. Perhaps, in excess. Especially, considering we have only made each other's acquaintance in the past few hours."

Pray, come to the mess at half-past six," Giovanni insisted.

"I am grateful for supper," Sheina said, rising. "It shall not go to waste."

Giovanni nodded. "My pleasure, Signorina."

Sheina placed the dishes on the tray and lifted it.

They bowed and bid each other good night.

Upon retiring to his cabin, Giovanni found himself tossing and turning in his bed, circling thoughts keeping him awake. *She is so young and fragile! She is in need of me! Who else could she turn to? Of course, she shall be there tomorrow!*

———⟫-☙-⟪———

The following day, Giovanni came to the mess a half hour before morning repast. The room was empty. Within minutes, Sheina emerged from the galley.

They bowed.

"Good morrow to you, ma'am!"

"And to you, sir!"

"'Tis best I say this now," Giovanni began. "I—I am aged fifty."

"And I, twenty-five. Is this significant to you?"

"I could be your father."

"Then, you'd be my *third*, sir."

"How do you mean?"

"I am born of Burmese and Chinese field laborers who settled in Batavia in the year 1725."

"I was under the impression your family was Dutch."

"I have had two families since birth, sir."

"*Two* families?"

"Aye. The year 1740 bore witness to my parents' demise. A most grievous event when I was aged barely fifteen."

"My deepest sympathy. How did such tragic incident occur?"

"During an uprising in Batavia. Thousands of Chinese settlers died at the hands of the Dutch and their allies. My parents among them."

"How did you make it out alive?"

"My little brother and I were taken in as household servants by a Dutch company official. We labored for this family, the Valckeniers, for the past ten years. This is how I came to learn Dutch and English."

"I gather 'twas the Valckeniers who were on the ship that sank off the Cape of Good Hope."

"Aye, sir. Our household master, Officer Diederik Valckenier, withdrew from active service and resolved to make a move to Southern Africa. He took his family and all of his belongings, including slaves and servants, and boarded the ship that sank on account of the riot."

Giovanni reached for his snuffbox. "I take it they did not survive."

Sheina looked down, eyes swelling with tears. "I wish I knew! I never saw them again after the shipwreck. I pray they still remain alive somehow, though I may never find out."

Giovanni's eyes glistened. "Oh, the cruelty of fate! You have been made an orphan. Not once, but twice. I see how Captain van Der Zee's proposal to take you on the *Bredenhoft* afforded you considerable solace."

"The Captain has been my saving grace! I have no possessions or abode. Our fortuitous encounter at the harbor in Good Hope allowed me to survive. All on account of his benevolence."

"And the Lord's compassion! You are a virtuous soul, and a person worthy of life and dignity."

"Alas, a person with no voice or writs to establish my identity, sir. Anyone could shackle me and claim their dominion over me, without recourse for objection."

"Then, what happens upon our arrival at The Hague? Has the Captain offered to keep you in his service?"

"No, sir. I shall have to fend for myself."

"Mercy! A frightening prospect. Especially for a young lady on her own. The world has been exceedingly unkind to you, my child! We must convene here once more before we disembark. A manner may present itself by which I, and even others, could extend a helping hand to you."

Sheina's eyes sparkled. "My gratitude a thousandfold, most gracious sir!"

They bowed to each other and parted.

Giovanni walked from the mess to Filippo and Laura's cabin and knocked on their door. Laura answered. "A fair morn to you, Dottore! Pray come in. Already prepared to partake of the morning repast?"

"Good morning my fair Laura! I am here to request your company. May we speak before morning meal?"

"You seem afflicted," said Filippo standing behind his wife.

"Nothing of the sort. Although I find myself in need of counsel on a rather pressing matter."

"We are here for you."

Moments later, under a clear sky and a cool breeze blowing, Laura and Filippo joined Giovanni on the main deck for a stroll. After relaying Sheina's story with solemn demeanor, Giovanni stopped and faced his colleagues. "What if I proposed to her?" he asked. "I find myself impelled to offer her succor. Should she accept my suit and take me for her husband, I would be able to ensure her safety and well-being."

Laura gasped. "Youth can be charming," she said. "Indeed, this girl is a sight to behold. She could be telling the truth. Yet, it could all be a fib. She has nothing to lose. If you propose now, she could take you for a fool."

"Oh woman! Pray, shake off this gravity!" said Filippo. "Let us not forget what our dear Dottore could gain from this: A loving companion, a partner in life, and a young, beautiful woman who could take care of his natural needs for many years to come! Nothing to scoff at, I daresay."

"I am merely advising caution, my dear," Laura responded. "Men are easily beguiled by women's outer beauty. A marriage proposal at this time seems premature. She might not be interested in it."

"Quite right," said Giovanni. "Still, if we lend credence to her words, and I do, how else could one provide protection and relief?"

Laura paused, bringing her hand to her forehead.

"May I speak plainly?"

"Most certainly!" Giovanni answered.

"Have you considered making her an offer of employment?"

"In what capacity? She's not a singer or an actress."

"Our troupe could use a seamstress. Someone to mend our costumes, make new ones, brush and powder our wigs, wash and iron, and even cook and clean, in exchange for meals and lodgings."

"The thought never occurred to me... I suppose my sentiments hindered my better judgment."

"You may always present your intentions in due time, Dottore. Once you have had a chance to gain a more intimate acquaintance with each other, and allow your affections to ripen."

"I see the wisdom of your counsel, Laura. I swear sometimes I hear my mother's voice in yours, as if I were a little boy back in Savoy. I shall extend an invitation to Sheina to join our troupe the next time I chance upon her."

Moments before the *Bredenhoft* made landfall, Giovanni looked for Sheina in the dining mess, the galley and the scullery. To no avail. She was not there. He walked to the ladies' quarters, stood outside the cabins and waited for a moment. No one came out.

Passengers and sailors gathered on the upper deck as the ship angled to dock. The Laschis stood among them, their baggage and Giovanni's by their side. The sounds of splashing waves and crying seagulls filled the air.

Growing increasingly anxious, Giovanni rushed to the wash room, one last place to look for Sheina. He walked in and spotted her folding bed linens. "Signorina!" he said. "I have been looking for you!"

"Apologies," Sheina replied. "I was tasked by the Captain to finish laundering before we disembark."

"I gathered. I shall not keep you. I have been pondering about the nature of your predicament and I thought you might consider an offer of employment with my theater company. I am told by my colleagues that we need a seamstress."

"A seamstress?"

"Indeed. More like a tailor. Someone who can sew, but who can also cut fabrics and fashion and craft garments. Is this something that might interest you? We have plenty of costumes that need mending."

"I do know how to sew, sir. I learned from my mother. I have crafted my own garments since I was a child."

"Then, would you contemplate my offer? Should you find it amenable, you may also lodge with some of the ladies in our troupe."

"Oh, kind sir! How could I ever refuse?" Sheina responded, quick tears rising to her eyes. "I am forever beholden to you!"

Reaching for her hands, Giovanni held them between his and gazed into her eyes.

"You have suffered unspeakable duress, my child. You must repose your trust in me. I shall endeavor to provide for your welfare. You owe me nothing. 'Tis the world we live in that is in debt with you!"

XVIII. A TRUSTED MATE

A thin veil of clouds softened the afternoon sunlight as the *Bredenhoft* anchored at Scheveningen Harbor in The Hague. Giovanni and the Laschis disembarked, sat on their trunks within sight of the ship's gangplank and waited for Sheina to come down. As time elapsed, the sun cast off its hazy shroud bearing down on them with unyielding tenacity.

Waiving her hand fan, Laura grew impatient. "How long must we wait for the girl? This heat weighs heavily on me."

"Pray forgive me. I cannot say," Giovanni replied. "She's on board with the rest of the crew on captain's orders. I fear she must remain there until all chores are completed."

Laura sighed.

A few minutes later, a coach rolled up to Giovanni and his colleagues. The body of the carriage bore intricate carvings and fancy decorations.

"Mijnheer Crossa?" the coachman called.

Giovanni rose to his feet. "As I live and breathe!" he replied.

The coachman dismounted, walked up to Giovanni and bowed. "A ride has been furnished for you and your associates by Heer Richard Westerbeek," he said. "His Lordship is expecting you at Huis ten Bosch Palace, a short distance away."

"Marvelous! How did Sir Westerbeek learn of our arrival at this very hour? I dispatched a letter to him with the particulars of my journey a mere seven days past."

"The winds have favored us as of late, sir. His Lordship must have reckoned you might be on the *Bredenhoft,* which was expected to make landfall during the course of this week. He is privy to our fleet's whereabouts from missives that reach him at all times. I have been sent to fetch you for the past few days."

"Blessings!" said Laura, taking Filippo's hand as she rose. The couple walked up to the coach and climbed in.

Before the coachman had finished loading the trunks onto the roof of the carriage, Sheina had joined the group.

"Ready to depart, ladies and gentlemen?" the coachman shouted after everyone had taken their seats.

"Aye! Ride out!" Giovanni hollered. Sheina sat beside him, head down and hands cupped on her lap. Sitting across from them, Laura and Filippo observed Sheina, now dressed as a female, with unabashed curiosity. Mesmerized by this novelty, Giovanni cast sideway glances at her.

"Apologies for the delay," Sheina said in a soft voice as the coach started moving to the sound of hooves clomping and horses nickering.

"There is nothing to apologize for, my dear," Laura responded. "You were not afforded the liberty of choice. I do hope that in the end, you were able to garner the wages promised by the Captain."

"I did."

"I'm glad to hear it. You might consider setting some of it aside for fabrics for new garments. I could lend you a hand with that when we settle."

"Much obliged, ma'am."

As the carriage wheels lumbered along, Filippo turned to Giovanni. "I was unaware you had such esteemed associates among the Dutch nobility, Dottore," he said, eyebrows raised.

"Sir Westerbeek? He is among them, but not *of* them. We have been acquainted with each other since he was only *Richard*, and I, *Gio*."

"In Savoy?"

"And France as well. We were young and trying to make a living. He was a merchant in the service of the Dutch East India Company, trading silk from Asia. I was doing as much on behalf of my uncle Pietro."

"You were competitors."

"We were."

"How did you chance upon each other?"

"At a roadside tavern. We engaged in a lengthy tête-à-tête while imbibing, which led to a mutual accord to fairly apportion the neighboring markets."

"A wise move. You pre-empted any potential feuds, quashed your rivalry and turned each other into mates."

"Quite remarkable!" said Laura.

Sheina's eyes rose and met Laura's as she heard her timely observation. Laura smiled subtly and nodded in return.

"Within a few years' time," Giovanni continued, "I found myself in Genoa, engaged in my family's banking ventures. By then, Richard had returned to the Netherlands and had taken a new role handling his company's maritime commercial interests. Still, we wrote to each other and, whenever Providence allowed, we met in person."

"Did he ever attend any of our troupe's engagements?" Laura asked.

"More than once. And since our early days in Turin."

"Strange," said Filippo. "We never chanced upon him."

"And yet, he saw you both on stage many a time. Our performances delighted him so much that at one point he proposed to become our benefactor. This, of course, was contingent upon our choice to journey to Amsterdam or The Hague."

"I gather, in the end, you took him up on his offer."

"I did. Though, only recently. I wrote to him while at the Fleet, and expressed my willingness and readiness to do so. He wrote back and mentioned there were Dutch ships bound for the Netherlands that frequently anchored at Calais. I thought that was a blessing!"

"Whence did Richard come to so much opulence and power?" Laura asked.

"By his assiduous endeavor, he ascended to the rank of director and became one of his company's principal shareholders. Since then, he has amassed a considerable fortune."

"What about his title? By what means did he become a *Sir*?"

"During Richard's tenure as director, Prince William IV of Orange bestowed the honorific title of *Jonkheer* onto him, for his services to Amsterdam, his birthplace and his home. Since then, he has been known as *Heer* Westerbeek."

"He must be much appreciated by the Prince," Filippo noted. "I daresay, not everyone in possession of a title can make a royal palace their abode."

"Richard is Prince William's right-hand man," Giovanni explained. "The Prince needs him close by."

"It looks like we've arrived," Laura said, after the coach halted at one of the palace's side entrances.

A pair of footmen stood at the bottom of the steps.

Giovanni was first to emerge from the coach.

"Mijnheer Crossa?" a footman asked.

Giovanni nodded in acknowledgment as Laura, Filippo and Sheina stepped out behind him and waited for the coachman to unload their baggage.

"Welkom!" said the footman, bowing. "Pray accompany me, sir." He led Giovanni up the stairs and into a small, lavish drawing room. "Pray, take ease," he said gesturing toward a finely carved beechwood chaise longue. "Heer Westerbeek will join you shortly."

"And my associates?"

"They are in good hands, sir. My mate shall see to their needs." He bowed and exited.

Blue silk brocade, Giovanni mused, running his fingers over the plush upholstery on the sofa. He sat, crossed his legs and reached for his pocket watch. *Not a hair's breadth past two. Yet, weariness assails me.* Behind him, two large windows overlooking a flower garden flooded the chamber with light. He cast his gaze about: A white tea table adorned with floral designs graced the space between the sofa and a pair of armchairs. A few feet beyond them, a white marble fireplace stood out. Four Delft Blue vases rested on its mantel. On the wall above them hung a large portrait of Sir Westerbeek.

While Giovanni awaited his host, Sheina and the Laschis had been shown to an open space downstairs adjacent to the kitchen and the servants' quarters. There, they sat in silence around a weathered table, trunks by their feet.

Within moments, a stout middle-aged woman clad in black entered the room, followed by a housemaid bearing a water jug and three tumblers on a tray. A white linen day cap with delicately ruffled edges framed her face and indicated her rank. "Good afternoon," she said with a slight nod. "I am Margriet van den Berg, the housekeeper." She gave a quick, stern gaze at the group, lingering for a moment on Sheina, before signaling the maid to set the tray on the table. "Pray slake your thirst. Then I shall guide you to your appointed quarters."

Meanwhile upstairs, a tall man in a dark blue velvet waistcoat and beige breeches had stepped into the drawing room carrying a roll of parchment and a small writing box. An unmistakable aura of wealth and authority enveloped him. His ash-grey periwig and stylish buckle shoes accentuated his imposing presence.

Upon seeing him enter the room, Giovanni rose and bowed.

"Ahh, Mijnheer Crossa, my dear Gio!" the man said with a smile. "*Welkom* to Den Haag!" He quickly placed the parchment and the writing box on the table and locked him in a vigorous embrace. "How was the journey from Calais on the *Bredenhoft?*"

"I am delighted to lay eyes upon you once again after so long, my friend! The voyage could not have been any better. 'Twas safe and swift. You were quite right to forewarn me in your letter about travelling by land. It would have been foolhardy to do so."

"And the captain? Was he agreeable?"

"Exceedingly so. Especially once I mentioned your name."

"I'm glad to hear it!" Westerbeek responded. "He is well compensated for his services by our company, and indeed our country." He took a seat on the couch and gestured for Giovanni to join him.

"I am pleased you heeded my advice and sailed on one of our ships, rather than travelling by land, Impresario. Carriageways can be perilous."

"I concur. This explains why so much merchandise is now shipped everywhere,"

"Are you aware that our fleet has grown to well over 2000 ships? 'Tis the largest in the world. Larger than the fleets of England and France put together."

A footman came in, approached and bowed. *"Excuseer me, Mijnheers.* Refreshments," he said. He carefully set a silver tray bearing a crystal decanter and two glasses on the table and stood by. Westerbeek waved his hand and he exited.

"We shall pour our own poison and drink to the old days," said Westerbeek with a puckish smile. A glimmer of amusement flickered in Giovanni's eyes.

They poured their cordials, clinked their glasses, and downed a few healthy gulps before resuming their exchange.

"Did I hear you say your country now lays claim to a fleet exceeding 2000 vessels?" Giovanni asked. "An outstanding feat for a small nation."

"Relatively small," said Westerbeek. "Yet, central. Like the great city of Rome was to the ancients. I can assure you that at present, the United Provinces of the Netherlands are at the very center of a large maritime empire."

"Of course, of course!" Giovanni nodded, his snuffbox in hand. "Your beautiful country is, indisputably, a major power in Europe and the world."

"A veritable fact. Our merchant ships are everywhere."

"Are you still engaged in the East Indies trade?"

"Not in a personal manner. I no longer travel as I did in my youth. Rather, I am charged with overseeing our company's operations from the homeland. Pray trust me, I'm all the better and happier for it! Prince Willem has been very generous to me."

"I can see that!" Giovanni responded, wiping a trace of tan powder from his nose. "You are here at Court, in the Royal Palace, no less."

"I am here at His Royal Highness' behest, Dottore. I come whenever I am summoned. Yet, my homestead is in the heart of Amsterdam."

Giovanni nodded.

"Now, if I may, let us turn our attention to the purpose of your presence here today. You must be eager to learn the reason that compelled me to send for you so promptly upon your arrival."

"Aye. In all truth, I am intrigued."

"It unfolds that we must set your troupe's opening tour into motion without delay."

"There is nothing more I could wish for! Alas, my troupe is not complete.

I have only brought Filippo Laschi and his wife Laura with me from London."

"Who else did you have in mind?"

"Well, while in Calais, I wrote to Francesco Bianchi, Eugenia Mellini, Maria Consoni, and Giustina Moretti, among others. They are all much celebrated singers and actors I am hoping to recruit."

"I have seen most of them on stage and I'm aware of their outstanding talents," Westerbeek responded. "Regrettably, we simply cannot wait until we hear from them."

"How could we proceed without them?"

"I am contemplating sending for all of them at once."

"Fetching them, you signify?"

"Verily. That is precisely my design. I have taken the liberty to procure adverts for your upcoming engagements in the *'s-Gravenhaagse Courant*, and have also printed the librettos you posted to me before you left England at a bookshop owned by one of my acquaintances."

"Wherefore such haste? We've had no chance to confer about dates or venues."

Westerbeek cleared his throat. "Your first engagement shall take place three days from today before a private audience. Then, within a week's time you shall gather your troupe and prepare for opening night at The Koninklijke Schouwburg Playhouse at Korte Voorhout. You shall start with *La Serva Padrona* and alternate with *Gismondo* through the end of September."

"A *private* audience performance in three days?"

"Private indeed!" Westerbeek responded, with a note of flourish in his voice. "Their Royal Highnesses, Prince Willem and his wife, Princess Anna, have expressed a keen interest in attending at least one of your troupe's performances here in Den Haag."

"I beseech your pardon. Alas, my troupe is not complete," Giovanni repeated.

"That should pose no obstacle," Westerbeek insisted. "Their Royal Highnesses shall be pleased to see a short version of *La Serva Padrona*."

"How short?"

"Two singers and an actor shall suffice. Laura Laschi as the soprano, Filippo as the bass, and we should have no trouble procuring an actor to play the mute."

"Aye. However…"

"Come now, Dottore! You know this piece does not require much. The main event of the evening shall be entrusted to Maestro Händel, the Princess' protégé. Your troupe will enter during the intermezzo."

Giovanni paled slightly upon hearing Händel's name. "My eye! Do you imply that we shall find ourselves partaking of the stage with the great George Friderick Händel?"

"You shall! The Princess has been a lifelong supporter of his, and at present he happens to be her guest at the State Apartments."

"Such an extraordinary privilege! May I inquire as to where this singular performance will take place?"

"Right here, at the Palace," Westerbeek replied. "Where else?"

"Of course."

"After completing your tour in Den Haag, you shall go on to Amsterdam. There, you shall commence a new round of engagements beginning the first week of October."

"I see. You have booked us already. But where?"

"At *Bergenvaarders Kamer* on the west bank of the Amstel River, a mile away from the city. You shall have to erect your own stage in a stable, Dottore."

"We excel at such endeavors. As you are aware, we were on the road for years in our early days. But wherefore outside the city?"

"Alas, the City Theater in Amsterdam holds a monopoly on theatrical productions, and it has banned all travelling acting troupes from performing within city limits."

"Pity!"

"Well, let us put all of that aside for now and proceed to review the deed that lists all of your troupe's scheduled engagements while you remain in the Netherlands," Westerbeek said, reaching for the scrolled parchment and writing box.

"What is the nature of this deed?"

"'Tis a Letter of Agreement I have prepared for you and Prince Willem's High Steward," Westerbeek replied, unfurling the parchment on the table. "Written in Dutch. A royal requirement for all official records. It contains all the details we have discussed here today. Once you put your name to it, I shall take you to the Orange Hall, where your troupe will perform in just a few days' time." He opened the writing box and handed Giovanni a quill.

"Alas, Dutch is not a tongue that I command," said Giovanni. "But you know that. Yet, I shall affix my signature with the utmost delight, my trusted mate. No need for an appraisal." He dipped the quill in the inkwell, signed the deed at once and stood to shake Westerbeek's hand.

"Wonderful! Pray come with me," said Westerbeek. He stood and led Giovanni out of the drawing room and into a hallway for a short stroll down to the Orange Hall.

"What a fine place this is! Both inside and out," Giovanni said, marveling at the artwork on the walls and ceilings, and the busts and statues along the way. "The Palace and the park are stunning."

"Most certainly, Huis ten Bosch is a magnificent place."

"When was it erected?"

"Over a century ago."

"'Tis extraordinary how it still remains in a such perfect state."

As they drew close to a row of large windows, they stopped to admire the views of the manicured gardens and the woodland in the distance.

"Were you aware that Huis ten Bosch means *House in the Woods*, Dottore?"

"It befits reason. 'Tis an oasis of comfort and elegance in the midst of a forest."

They resumed their stroll, and Westerbeek continued, "About your travelling companions… They are welcome here at the Palace until the conclusion of your tour of Den Haag. I have arranged for them to stay in the servants' quarters, while you take one of our guest chambers. As for the rest of your troupe, they shall have to secure their own accommodations, whenever they arrive in the city."

"I am much obliged to you, my dear friend."

"In all honesty, 'tis Princess Anna who has the final word on who comes in and out of the Palace. Minstrels are no exception," said Westerbeek, stopping just inside an open double door and peeking in. "Well, here we are. This is the Orange Hall, and we're in luck. No one is here."

"Intimate and luminous," Giovanni observed, as they stepped in. Surveying the room, he briefly paused to admire a small ceramic tile with a pink lotus flower design, discreetly placed on a wall in a corner of the room.

"A gift to the Princess from one of our captains upon his retirement from service a few years past," Westerbeek said. "I was there when he presented it to her. He said it was from Java. A symbol of purity and beauty."

"A most beautiful piece!" Giovanni said, as an image of a smiling Sheina flashed across his mind.

"You must be mindful, she is aware of who you are."

Giovanni's eyes shifted to meet Westerbeek's. "Who is?"

"Princess Anna! Her sister was a patron of your theater."

"Of course! The lovely Princess Amelia."

"Besides, you must admit, you kept yourself in the public eye during much of your stay in London."

Giovanni chuckled softly. "You mean, in the eye of the storm…"

"Regardless, the Princess loves the opera."

"Still, I have no recollection of her ever being in the audience."

"I cannot say she was. Yet, when I mentioned your troupe was on its way to Den Haag, she did not hesitate. She promptly conveyed her desire to welcome a performance within these very walls."

"I am honored!" Giovanni responded. "Pray forgive my ignorance. I had no notion she was married to Prince Willem."

"They were joined in wedlock in 1734, long before you arrived in London."

"Where did the wedding take place?"

"At St. James's Church on Piccadilly Road, in Westminster. 'Twas a most public affair."

"I do recall that road quite well," said Giovanni. "I found myself there many a time, at the drapers' shops, searching for fabrics, ribbons, buttons and piccadills for my troupe's wardrobe."

"Piccadills?"

"Lace collars to adorn the ladies' costumes."

"I see. Well, Princess Anna and our dear Prince Willem exchanged their wedding vows in the neighboring church."

"I thought the Princess' name was *Anne*."

"Indeed, before her union to our Prince, her name was Anne of England. King George II's second child and eldest daughter. Then, when the royal couple made their home here in the Netherlands, her name was styled as *Anna* van Hannover, or *Anna* of Orange."

Giovanni nodded, his attention drawn to a raised wooden platform. "May I?"

"Pray proceed! That is the reason we are here."

Giovanni stepped onto the platform, turned to face an imaginary audience, and strode across it. He repeated this several times from various angles.

"Do you approve, Dottore?" asked Westerbeek.

"This will do very well indeed," Giovanni replied, stepping back down.

"Marvelous! You shall find the acoustics in this chamber are also quite impressive. The royal family and their honored guests find this an utmost necessity."

Giovanni leaned forward. "On that point, perhaps you might wish to divulge a bit more about the hopes and wishes of our esteemed sponsors."

Westerbeek lowered his voice. "After two stillbirths and the death of a third infant child in 1746, the Princess finds comfort in music and the opera."

"I partake in her sentiments. Laughter and music can be healers. Hopefully, our opera buffa will bring a smile to Her Royal Highness. You may rest assured we shall do everything within our power to meet her expectations."

>-◉-<

On the appointed day of their performance, Giovanni's troupe had grown to include a half dozen players. In preparation for the evening's presentation, they had gathered in the Orange Hall for the final rehearsal. Dressed in his most formal attire, Giovanni had arrived early and was fully engaged with his lead singers and musicians.

Soon, several courtiers began trickling in. Giovanni vaguely recognized one of them, a gentleman in his late thirties, seated in the second row. *A well-favored gentleman,* he thought. *Save for that slouchy cap that betrays him.*

Moments later, a footman at the door announced the arrival of the royal family. Everyone rose and faced Prince Willem and his wife as they made their entrance. Holding hands, they advanced through the center aisle toward the stage, courtiers bowing and curtsying. A short procession followed them: two of their children and a governess, Sir Westerbeek and his wife, and a man in his sixties, Maestro Friderick Händel.

Sitting on a stool beside a harpsichord in a corner of the room, Giovanni could hear Prince Willem address his wife as *my dear Annin* while she responded to him lovingly as *Pepin.*

"You sit here, to my left, my sweet," Princess Anna said gently to her daughter.

Aged seven, mayhap? Giovanni pondered.

Beside the girl, a toddler sat on the governess' lap.

The heir apparent. Giovanni gathered, from the gasps of admiration and delight he had drawn when he entered the chamber. *Another Willem. His father's namesake. Aged two, if that.*

Seated next to the governess, Händel gazed at an open music score on a stand, his violin and a bow already on the dais. He rose and walked up to the stage. The chamber fell silent as he faced the audience. "Good evening," he began after a deep bow. "A recent composition, in honor of Their Royal Highnesses." To everyone's delight, he proceeded to play a violin sonata.

Many *bravos* and *huzzahs* followed after each of several pieces, one of which was dedicated to Johann Sebastian Bach. "A fellow composer," Händel said, "who has recently fallen gravely ill, according to the journals."

Giovanni fanned himself with a libretto, eagerly awaiting the maestro's exit from the stage. Several rounds of applause came and went before Händel retired to his seat and Giovani and his players stepped upon the dais and bowed before the audience.

Standing between Laura and Filippo, Giovanni spoke in French as he delivered a brief explanation of the plot, a traditional courtesy in smaller settings. "*La Serva Padrona* means The Maid Turned Mistress," he said in a full, clear voice. "'Twas penned by the celebrated composer Giovanni Battista Pergolese." Indicating Laura, he continued: "This is about how a young and fair maidservant, Serpina, succeeds in duping Umberto, a wealthy older bachelor, into marriage." Here Giovanni gestured toward Filippo, who threw his hands up in the air and gave a sigh, drawing laughter from the audience.

"With the intention of arousing jealousy in Umberto and compelling him to seek her hand, she pretends to be engaged to Vesponte, a youthful and endearing mute," said Giovanni, turning to the actor standing next to Laura. "Umberto cannot abide the notion that Serpina would choose to marry a silent charmer over him." The actor winked. The audience erupted into laughter.

"Serpina goes away, hoping that her scheme will goad Umberto into a frenzied state, which in the end comes to fruition," Giovanni concluded. He stepped aside, the music started, and the performance got underway.

As Giovanni watched the play unfold, images of Sheina fluttered in his mind, at times blending indistinguishably with Serpina's character. Then, transfixed by Filippo's act, he pictured himself as a gullible old man like Umberto, and imagined his emerging sentiments for Sheina may go unheeded or unreturned. Conflicted, he listened to Filippo deliver Umberto's speech at his moment of confusion:

"If what she told me is true... poor thing, she's but a simple servant! And yet, what if I were not her first? Would I still marry her, then? How mad you are! Enough! It cannot be! Irresponsible thoughts, vanish at once! Oh Lord! I burn inside with passion. Pray free me from this torment!"

A loud *bravo* from the man with the slouchy cap sitting in the second row caused Giovanni to shift focus. Discreetly, he laid eyes on him as long-lost memories began to resurface:

A wealthy lady in Savoy... Madame, Madame... de Warens! Aye! That was her name! A long-time dweller of the town of Chambery. And a most loyal client, indeed. She seemed possessed by a burning passion for fancy fabrics. I sold her heaps! And he, so young and fair to the eye, answered her door unfailingly. Could this be him? A footman from Savoy at a Dutch royal palace?

Soon, the intermezzo ended with a sustained round of applause. Giovanni and his players took a bow.

Such turnabout! Giovanni mused, heartened by the audience's response. *From the bowels of hell, I come… To this!* A fleeting nod of acknowledgement from Maestro Händel as he passed by on his return to the stage sent a wave of euphoria over him, as if a younger soul from an inner realm had taken hold of his being…

Just before the music resumed, Giovannni showed his players out as they quietly exited the hall. Mindful of his duty to garner his troupe's wages from Sir Westerbeek before the evening ended, he stayed behind.

After Händel's performance concluded, Giovanni observed Prince Willem stand up and walk toward the exit accompanied by Händel. Princess Anna remained engaged in what seemed to be an animated exchange with Sir Westerbeek and his wife. Then unexpectedly, she turned her attention toward *the footman from Savoy.*

She called on him. "Monsieur Rousseau, please join us!"

Rousseau? Is that his name? Giovanni wondered.

The man approached and bowed. *"Votre Altesse Royale,"* he said. "'Tis been a delightful evening. A magnificent supper and now this exquisite treat. I am infinitely obliged for your gracious invitation."

"I am pleased you found the entertainment enjoyable, Monsieur."

"I relished every moment of it. What an extraordinary privilege to hear Maestro Händel play in such an intimate setting!"

The Princess smiled proudly. "I was just saying how blessed I am to have been taught singing, harpsichord and music composition by the Maestro in England," she responded.

"How wonderful!" said Lady Westerbeek.

"The opera buffa at the intermezzo was also a very welcome whimsical indulgence," said Rousseau. "I am a long-time enthusiast and, I assure you, this troupe delivered an outstanding performance."

"We have been fortunate," said the Princess, glancing at Sir Westerbeek. "I believe they are only here for a short time,"

"Just passing through," Westerbeek responded. "They have been travelling the world for years."

The Princess turned to Rousseau. "Perhaps you'd like to make the acquaintance of the company's proprietor. I believe he may still be here."

"It would be my pleasure, your Highness."

Westerbeek leaned forward. "Pray allow me to introduce you then," he said, gesturing for Rousseau to follow him. He and Rousseau excused themselves, left the Princess with Lady Westerbeek and approached Giovanni, standing nearby.

"A quick word if I may, Dottore," Westerbeek said. "There is someone here who would like to make your acquaintance."

"Most certainly!"

"I present you Monsieur Jean Jacques Rousseau."

"Your servant, Signore. My name is Giovanni Crossa."

Both men bowed.

"I've delighted at your troupe's rendition of *La Serva Padrona,* Monsieur," said Rousseau.

"Merci beaucoup!" Giovanni responded. "Your first time seeing it, Monsieur?"

"Certainly not. In point of fact, 'tis one of my most beloved comic operas. I can certainly identify with Umberto's sentiments."

"Pray tell, how so?" Westerbeek asked.

"He is an ordinary man coping with ordinary matters," Rousseau replied. "Affection and desire, and everything in betwixt that concern the common folk in their everyday lives."

"Indeed, Monsieur! Yet, would *you* regard yourself as an ordinary man?" Westerbeek asked.

"Most positively!" said Rousseau. "Particularly concerning the matter of desire!"

All three men burst into laughter.

"I see," Westerbeek continued. "Then, would it be fair to say, that you deem it proper for amorous liaisons to form between those of gentle breeding and those of humbler stations in life?"

"I do. And most emphatically so. I am persuaded Umberto and Serpina had every right to experience *both* affection *and* desire," Rousseau responded, again drawing laughter.

"Pray pardon me, Monsieur," Giovanni said, addressing Rousseau. "You bear a striking resemblance to an individual from my past acquaintance."

Rousseau raised his eyebrows. "Do I?"

"I was a silk merchant in Savoy many, many moons ago. One of my esteemed clients in Chambery went by the name of Madam de Warens, and—"

Rousseau's face turned crimson as he cut Giovanni off. "—You mean, *Baroness* de Warens, Monsieur. Of course, you were the silk man! I was Her Ladyship's steward for many years. One of my duties was to greet the visitors who came to her door."

"Remarkable!" said Westerbeek.

"*Excusez-moi, s'il vous plait.* I shall take my leave now," said Rousseau. "'Tis been a pleasure making your acquaintances, Monsieurs." He bowed abruptly, turned and walked away.

"He appears to be vexed," said Giovanni. "Perhaps I should have held my tongue."

"Not at all. Never mind, Dottore! Everyone at Court is well-acquainted with Rousseau's occasional emotional outbursts. I have a slight suspicion you touched upon a sensitive spot when you mentioned the Baroness. She is known to have been his mentor, his benefactor, and the person who initiated him in the matters of affection and intimacy when he was but a youth."

"There seems to be nothing unseemly on that count," Giovanni responded, somewhat befuddled.

"Yet, he'd rather not be reminded of that part of his life."

"Pray forgive me. I do not grasp the source of his displeasure."

"'Tis on account of her morals, Dottore. After the Baroness furthered his education and turned him into the man he is today, *now* her morals distress him."

"What about her morals?" Giovanni insisted.

"Tongues have wagged for years about the time Rousseau and the Baroness cohabitated within the confines of her abodes in Chambery," said Westerbeek quietly. "She is said to have indulged in a rather close companionship with both him and another personal attendant."

"A malicious tale, to be certain!" Giovanni responded.

"In all likelihood. And a source of discomfort to Monsieur Rousseau," Westerbeek explained. "The truth of the matter is, most hold the Baroness in high regard as a woman of benevolence, refined sensibilities and elevated intellect."

"What about *him*? Who is this man, Jacques Rousseau?"

"You jest! Everyone knows him. He is a rising luminary in the realm of philosophy."

"Then, the Baroness' kindness and acumen have been demonstrated by her success in bringing out the best in him," said Giovanni.

"In the matter of success, Dottore, Their Highnesses were greatly pleased by your troupe's performance this eve."

"Splendid!" Giovanni beamed.

Westerbeek reached into his waistcoat pocket and handed Giovanni a pouchful of coin.

"To that point, my dear friend," he said, "The Princess would like your troupe to return for a longer performance, as soon as it is feasible."

"We shall be glad to oblige!"

XIX. A PROPOSAL IN ANTWERP

"Time is a thief! A twinkling of the eye and the world becomes a specter of its former self," said Sir Westerbeek as he and Giovanni strolled around the gardens of his home in Amsterdam one cool afternoon in late October. Surrounded by the peak colors of autumn, they advanced at a leisurely pace, the sound of leaves crunching softly beneath their feet.

"A ghost, if even that!" Giovanni responded. "Within a few days' time all this splendor shall be nothing but a memory."

"Which brings to mind our contract," said Westerbeek.

"I am aware it expires in a fortnight."

"Have you devised a scheme for what's ahead for you, Dottore?"

"I shall be journeying to Antwerp and Brussels as early as tomorrow."

"Seeking new venues for your troupe, I presume?"

"Faithfully."

"A wise and sensible decision. How long do you intend to stay there?"

"A week or two at most."

"May I propose you leave Filippo in charge during your absence?"

"That is precisely what I have contrived. He is a longstanding acquaintance. My trust in him is steadfast. By the by, I shall be journeying in the company of Signorina Valckenier."

"Your seamstress?"

"She is a great deal more than that…"

"Ahh! A mistress! You have surrendered to the tender charms of a delicate and exotic flower!"

"She is no mistress to me."

"Forgive my indiscretion. I do believe you might have mentioned how you made her acquaintance aboard the *Bredenhoft*. Yet, nothing beyond that."

Giovanni sighed. "I have not said much to anyone. Even she is unaware of my sentiments toward her."

"Oh? You harbor sentiments for her?"

"Aye. Sentiments I can no longer conceal."

"Then she will know, sooner or later."

"And so, she shall."

"You seem resolved. A mere reflection if I may: Few of our company officers return home with their native companions. And fewer still ever present them in polite society."

"I would never subject her to such trials. Besides, my present social standing excludes me from that lot."

"Not entirely. Your craft has brought you right into the midst of genteel circles. If nothing else but to divert them."

"And that is the extent of it. I do not seek to mingle."

"Be that as it may, the fact remains you're in a foreign land with unfamiliar roads that may be full of perils... Things could tip and turn rather swiftly and without warning."

"I am painfully aware. I learned that lesson well in England."

"Then, you can count your blessings. You are all the wiser for it!" said Westerbeek, patting Giovanni on the back. "Moreover, you're not alone. Our friendship has stood the test of time. To honor it, I shall provide you with a handful of letters addressed to a select few of my acquaintances in Antwerp and in Brussels. You and your lady companion will be safe should you choose to lodge with them. The letters shall serve as means of introduction."

"I am eternally obliged to you, my friend!"

"My pleasure. Now, if I may be candid..."

"Of course. Pray, indulge me."

"A word of advice: While in the public eye, it may be wise to use discretion at all times. If I were you, I would continue to profess that your inamorata is just your company's dressmaker. Anything beyond that might draw unwanted attention."

"Your advice is well taken. 'Tis plain to me, you seek a noble purpose. You mean to shield us. I shall make certain we heed your counsel."

"One final note, Dottore," Westerbeek continued. "The royal family expects one last performance at the Palace before you make your departure."

"You can rest assured, we shall deliver. Once our last engagement in Amsterdam is done, we shall return to The Hague."

———>-☾-<———

The next morning, Giovanni and Sheina boarded a coach that would take them to Antwerp, in the Duchy of Brabant, deep in the Austrian Netherlands. While the coachman finished loading their trunks, Sheina watched Giovanni carefully place a wooden box under the vacant seat in front of them.

"Is there treasure in that box, Dottore?" she asked.

"One could say so," Giovanni replied. "In our times, a man on the road would put his life in jeopardy without it."

"Pray tell, what is it?"

"My dragons, my dear. A pair of them. And a few balls, as well."

"Pistols!"

"A necessary evil. Mind you, I've never had to put them to use," Giovanni responded, making the sign of the cross.

"And by the grace of God, you never shall, my good sir."

In three days' time, Giovanni and Sheina arrived at a stately townhouse on Grote Goddaard, a street not far from Antwerp's main square. Upon their reception by a footman, Giovanni promptly handed him a letter addressed to one *"Dhr. Hans Kessler."*

"From Sir Richard Westerbeek," Giovanni said as he and Sheina stepped into the residence's foyer, baggage in tow.

"Dank u, Mijnheer," the footman responded. "I shall pass it on to the master straightaway." He bowed and withdrew into the house.

Moments later, a short and stout elderly couple appeared at the foyer. The footman and a woman dressed in black stood behind them. The older male, wearing a slightly tousled periwig and a thick pair of spectacles, introduced himself as *Mijnheer* Hans Kessler. Then, turning to the woman beside him, he presented her as his wife, *Mevrouw* Klara Kessler.

Giovanni bowed to the matronly woman attired in an ice blue satin gown, a fancy cream neckerchief and a net cap.

"This is Mrs. de Vries, our housekeeper," said Mrs. Kessler, indicating the woman behind her. Then she called upon her: "Pray show the girl to one of the scullery maids' vacant rooms."

Mrs. de Vries nodded and motioned Sheina to pick up her bag and follow her downstairs.

Mr. Kessler then directed the footman to take Giovanni's baggage and show him to one of the guest rooms upstairs.

"You are in luck, Impresario!" Mr. Kessler said as the footman reached for Giovanni's trunk. "We intended for a delayed supper. Six o'clock, should your appetite incline."

"Much obliged!" Giovanni responded. He then followed the footman to his room.

A few minutes before six, Giovanni checked his pocket watch, proceeded downstairs and found his way to the dining parlor. As he walked in he saw Mr. Kessler sitting with his wife at one end of an oval mahogany table under a large solid brass chandelier. Opposite the table, a stone fireplace warmed the room.

As Giovanni approached, the couple rose to greet him.

"Pray join us, Impresario!" said Mr. Kessler, looking at Giovanni over the rims of his spectacles and gesturing invitingly for him to have a seat at the table.

"My pleasure!" Giovanni responded. He loosened his jacket and sat across from Mrs. Kessler.

"Pray excuse our attire," Mrs. Kessler said, glancing at Giovanni's stylish sheer cuffs and white knotted neck cloth. "We were not expecting guests for supper."

"You're too kind, Madame! I admit I am new to the formal dining protocols here."

"Never mind protocols, Impresario. 'Tis just us," she responded as she tucked a lock of grey hair under her cap.

During the course of the meal, an ebony bracket clock resting in an arched alcove next to the chimneybreast caught Giovanni's attention.

"I see you've spotted one of our family's prized heirlooms, Impresario," said Mr. Kessler, his rosy cheeks shining as he smiled.

"Hard to miss!" Giovanni responded, transfixed by the sight.

"Indeed! 'Tis a beauty. But a little annoying," said Mr. Kessler, rubbing one of his grey, bushy sideburns. "You see, it strikes on the hour."

"'Tis a remarkable contraption!"

"I gather from Heer Westerbeek's note that you're headed for Brussels," Mrs. Kessler said, as a butler replenished her glass with red wine.

"Aye. First time there."

"Will you indulge in exploring the surroundings? You might find the town is very quaint, if you do."

"We are here on business."

"You mean you and your servant. Or is she your slave?"

"*Mademoiselle* Valckenier is neither my servant nor my slave, Madam."

"Oh? Then, to what end is her presence here with you, may I ask?"

"She is our company's dressmaker. Her purpose is to assist me in the selection of fabrics I shall be procuring in Brussels."

"I see…" Mrs. Kessler responded, her right hand resting on a fold of her elaborately embroidered neckerchief. "Pray forgive me, I was unaware a low-born would possess such skills."

"We are blessed to have her!" Giovanni said, forcing a smile. "Costumes are essential to our craft, Madame."

After his hosts retired for the evening, Giovanni crept into the servants' quarters, carrying a candle in a chamberstick. Seeing a feeble glimmer of a light under one of the doors along a narrow corridor, he took a chance and knocked on it gently. A soft female voice answered.

"Who's there?"

"'Tis me, Signorina!" Giovanni replied in a low voice. "Signor Crossa!"

Sheina cracked the door open.

"Pray pardon the intrusion," he said softly, their eyes sparkling in the candlelight.

"You're not intruding, sir. I was awake," she whispered.

"I have devised a plan for the forthcoming days," he said in a low tone. "I thought, perhaps you might care to partake in the details."

"Obliged. I would. But now?"

"I promise it shall take but a brief moment. Pray come with me."

Sheina nodded, tiptoed out of her room, and followed Giovanni down the corridor and into the kitchen.

As they entered, Giovanni cast a quick, sweeping glance around the room. A few embers still glowed on the firedogs in the hearth's spacious brick recess. He picked up a small log from a rack, carefully placed it on top of the embers and puffed at the fire with a bellows until sparks sprouted into flames.

Across from the fireplace, glazed earthenware jugs and bowls rested on a bench. A host of copper pots and pans hung from wall hooks and pegs above them.

The house was silent as a light breeze flowed in through a half open window, re-awakening a wide range of aromas, from rosemary to nutmeg. Sheina and Giovanni sat next to each other at a long, rustic table.

"Did you take supper?" Giovanni asked, his eyes falling on Sheina's silky black tresses, draping to her waist.

"I did."

"With the maidservants, I suppose?"

"By myself, sir. They and others stood and withdrew from the table as soon as the housekeeper bid me to be seated."

Giovanni grimaced. "Appalling demeanor. I am aggrieved by it."

A pause ensued.

"Their comportment eludes me," Sheina said, her eyes fixed on the flames shimmering in the hearth. "They know nothing of me."

"If they knew half as much as I do about you, they would scarce harbor such spite," Giovanni responded. "I count myself privileged that I have glimpsed great beauty in the quiet chambers of your heart."

Puzzled, Sheina stared. "Something tells me this is not entirely about Brussels…"

"You're quite right. 'Tis not."

"Pray tell then, sir. I beseech you. You have yet to disclose the true reason why you brought me along on this journey."

"Apologies. I could not… I wasn't ready," Giovanni said as he leaned forward and gazed deeply into Sheina's eyes. "And yet, I knew that distancing ourselves from familiar surroundings might be somewhat beneficial."

"In what manner?"

"That we may have a chance to discern our sentiments toward one another."

"Sir?"

"Pray forgive my immodesty. I should have bit my tongue. How bold of me to have presumed you might have sentiments for me! An old goat, twice your age and never far from trouble. You see, I must admit. This is no passing fever. I have been smitten with you from the moment I laid eyes upon you. And now this…"

"What, sir?"

"I feel I've loved you for a thousand years."

Sheina's breath trembled. "I—I am deeply honored. I would have never thought a gentleman like you might deem me worthy of such noble sentiment."

"Hush, my angel, hush!" Giovanni responded, inching closer toward her.

Their hands gently reached for each other, lips meeting for the first time.

"I must conclude our sentiments are mutual," Giovanni said, still holding her hands.

"My heartbeat echoes your own," she said softly.

"Your words, my dear Signorina, bring forth a joy I have not felt in years."

They kissed again.

"Now if I may," Sheina began. "About that old goat… Buddhists say our souls are timeless and our age meaningless."

Giovanni glowed. "Does this mean you wouldn't mind taking this old man for your husband?"

Astonished, Sheina stammered. "Ar-Are you p-proposing, sir?"

"Indeed, I am."

Sheina's eyes filled with tears. "I have been a serf all my life. No man of consequence has ever set his eyes upon me in this high-minded manner. And yet, here you are. You want me for your wife."

Giovanni gently wiped the tears from her face. "You are a rare and most precious gem, my dear," he said. "Wherefore would I not want you for my wife? The query that remains here is only one: will you take *me* for your husband?"

"I shall! With unwavering certainty, good sir. Your heartfelt proposal bestows upon me a great gift that I cannot refuse." They kissed and held one another in a close embrace.

"Pray take heed. There is no longer a need for you to address me as *sir*," said Giovanni. "Not in private."

"How shall I address you, then?"

"As *Gio*. This is how those who are closest to my heart have always known me."

"Birth names carry so much weight…" Sheina said, the hearth's soft glow mirrored in her eyes.

"Weight?"

"The weight of time, my elders claimed. In Java, people believe our ancestors' mark their presence when our parents confer our names upon us. *We* are *them*, to some extent and measure. And so shall our children be us in the future."

"Your reverence for those who came before you, and those still to come, reveals the untainted essence of your soul, my child."

"You are gracious. As your wife and partner in life, I shall endeavor to honor your expectations."

"My dear Sheina, you exceed all that I could have envisioned."

"As do you, Gio. Perhaps, destiny has had a hand in this. I recall a powerful emotion coursing within me when we first crossed paths as I beheld my own reflection in your gaze."

"I give you my word, our sentiments aligned. Even in those early moments, you stirred me to my core. 'Twas as though a force within me whispered this was no chance encounter."

"We have so much to learn about each other," Sheina said, rising. "And yet, the hour is late."

"Aye. We must be rested for tomorrow's journey."

Giovanni walked Sheina to her room. They embraced once more and bid each other good night.

The following day, as Giovanni and Sheina's carriage left a cloudy

Antwerp behind, Giovanni examined their journey route on a parchment on his lap while Sheina peered out the window. Having passed the last row of red-brick houses, a greener landscape emerged just as the clip-clop of the horses picked up, filling the silence.

"Shall we keep our betrothal to ourselves?" Sheina asked.

Giovanni lifted his eyes. "For now, it would seem wise to do so. Save for our closest acquaintances."

"Do you mean Laura and Filippo?"

"And perhaps a few others, like Sir Westerbeek. Until we are joined in holy matrimony, we shall have to continue to present ourselves in public quite discreetly, as if you were just one more member of our troupe. Alas, in the eyes of many, our union will be regarded as a one-of-a-kind…"

Sheina lowered her eyes. "I see. Have you contemplated a time and place for our nuptials?"

"I aspire to a wedding ceremony within the span of six to eight months," Giovanni replied. "Whether in a Dutch church or elsewhere."

"If we were in Batavia, there would be a few temples readily available to us," said Sheina, with a nostalgic twinge in her voice. "Were you aware 'tis quite ordinary for Dutch men to marry native women in Java? Yet, few of them ever take their families with them when they retire to Good Hope or return home to Europe."

"A curious practice. Regardless, I am not Dutch and we're not in Batavia."

"If we were, our wedding ceremony would certainly be very public," Sheina continued. "Even the most modest of ceremonies have dozens of guests. There is always a long procession in the streets, filled with music and puppets with painted faces and headbands made of coconut leaves."

"Puppets? For what purpose?"

"To ward off evil. They represent the spirits of deceased ancestors. They are tall and hollow, and there is always a pair of them, male and female. They hop and bob to the sound of happy tunes at the head of the parade, offering their blessings to everyone around them."

"And the bride and the groom? Where are they?"

"In the midst of it all, wearing bright garments and flower crowns, signifying inner and outer beauty, wisdom and honor. The bridegroom rides on a horse and the bride is carried on a covered litter with a carved white swan on top."

"Fancy that!" Giovanni said. "Alas, I cannot promise you a crown or a parade, though mayhap I can persuade Laura and Filippo to carry our puppets for one day!"

They laughed.

"We need no big ceremony or procession," said Sheina with a demure smile as raindrops began sprinkling on the carriage windows.

Giovanni nodded. "Quite right," he responded. "All we need is the Good Lord as a witness of our affection and commitment to each other."

"Pray forgive my keenness, my dear Gio. Who do you believe is *the Good Lord?*"

"God, of course!" he responded without hesitation. "As a Christian and a Catholic, I was raised to believe in the Bible, the Holy Trinity and the Church in Rome. God in Heaven, Jesus His Son, who came to the world to save us from our sins, and the Holy Spirit. My Antonia and I brought up our twins to believe in this. Yet, I admit, after she passed, I no longer had much time for any of it. What about you? Who is God to you?"

Sheina sighed. "Alas, a muddled subject. As a child living with my parents, we practiced Buddhism. Then, during my time with the Valckeniers I was introduced to Christianity. My views draw from both traditions."

"Is it two Gods then, you believe in?"

"Like you, I took for granted what my elders taught me. My parents believed Buddha was a man who, through much sacrifice, came to enlightenment."

"Through martyrdom?"

"Self-imposed afflictions, lengthy isolation and deprivations of the flesh."

"I see. Voluntary tribulations."

"One might say that. What unfolds is a story that he found a path that led him to the truth about the mystery of life. People began to follow him, hoping to learn from his teachings and eventually attain a likeness to him."

"Then, he was much like Jesus."

"In a manner, I suppose."

Giovanni broke into a wide smile. "Our beliefs are not so different after all!"

Sheina nodded and smiled.

Giovanni rubbed his beard, an inquisitive brow arching as he spoke. "Save for one aspect: if Buddha was a man, then who do Buddhists think was the Creator?"

"My elders said there is something called the *cosmos*, where all beings exist in a gigantic *time circle* with no beginning and no end."

"They spoke in riddles. How could you grasp what they meant?"

"My mother made it plain. She said all living things dwell on different floors of the same building. The building is the *cosmos*."

"The land of the living? What about death? Pray tell, what were you told about that?"

"I was told that when a being perishes, it will be reborn into another one, anywhere in the cosmos. And this continues on forever. That is the *time circle*."

"A bewildering notion, indeed."

"Is it? Jesus himself lived, died, then lived again, or did he not?"

"He did. Yet, not in different bodies."

"Pray forgive my ignorance. Then wherefore does the Bible say the Holy Spirit is in oil, fire, wind, water, and even wine?"

"Verily. A mystifying truth. More significantly, does this imply you would not mind our wedding ceremony to be held in a Roman Catholic church?"

Sheina smiled. "I would find joy and delight in joining you in holy matrimony anywhere, Gio!"

A day after Giovanni and Sheina returned to Amsterdam, all ten players of a now fully reconstituted troupe had gathered outside a large barn at *Bergenvaarders Kamer* on the outskirts of the city. There, under a web of grey clouds, they eagerly awaited to hear from the Impresario about where they would be headed next. A month earlier they had built a stage inside the barn at record speed, and they had been performing there ever since.

A chilly breeze rolled in as Giovanni stepped up onto a wooden box. Wasting no time, he tightened down his tricorn, buttoned his coat at the collar, and addressed the group standing before him.

"Miei cari amici," he began in his usual style. He then proceeded to lavish praises on his singers, actors and musicians for their contributions to their long-running series of successful engagements in the Netherlands.

After a few minutes he took a deep breath, adjusted his scarf and continued. "Also, my deepest gratitude to Filippo Laschi, who attended to our affairs while I was away in Brussels."

Giovanni's words drew applause as he pointed to Filippo and Laura, who stood directly in front of him. "We shall soon be journeying back to The Hague for one last performance at the Palace, after which we will depart for Brussels."

Inquisitive eyes stared at him in anticipation.

"I'm delighted to announce I have secured a lucrative contract there for a number of appearances at the prestigious Theater de la Monnaie."

Sustained clapping and cheering ensued.

"We shall start out early tomorrow for our final engagement in The Hague. I beseech you to make all necessary preparations," he concluded. As the members of the troupe filtered back into the barn, he stepped down and called Filippo and Laura to join him in a private chat.

"Where is Signorina Valckenier?" Laura asked.

"She is reposing at the ladies' lodge," Giovanni replied. "Our return trip from Brussels made her weary."

"Of course. 'Tis a long journey."

"Concerning the Signorina…" said Giovanni. "There is a matter of substance I must convey to you."

The Impresario's composed manner and choice of words drew the couple's full attention.

"I extended a marriage proposal to her," he said. "And, she graciously accepted."

Laura gasped.

"We thought you should be first to be apprised," said Giovanni. He pulled up the collar of his overcoat and stared at Laura.

"Auguri! Auguri!" Filippo cheered, in a frantic attempt to cover his wife's obvious faux pas.

Giovanni smiled. "I am glad you approve!"

"You hardly need anyone's approval, Dottore," Laura responded, aware of her husband's glare. "Affection and commitment should suffice. Pray indulge my curiosity. When did you propose?"

"Last week, in Antwerp. I could delay it no longer."

"You did well!" said Filippo, feigning a grin.

"Pray keep these tidings to yourselves, I beg of you. I shall announce our betrothal to the rest of the troupe in due time. Let's take our leave now. I feel raindrops in the air." He tipped his hat and walked away.

The wind picked up as a light, cool drizzle started falling. Laura and Filippo hastened over to a waiting coach. Holding on to her bonnet with one hand and clutching her handbag with the other, Laura stumbled before reaching the carriage.

"Careful!" said Filippo, extending his hand for support. "The ground is slippery already." He opened the carriage door. Laura stepped onto the footboard and climbed into the cab. Filippo followed.

"Whatever made him do this?" Laura asked once they were both comfortably seated.

"He's smitten with her," said Filippo. "Nothing we could say would make a whit of difference."

The carriage set into motion.

Laura sighed. "Pity. He's blind to how this union could bring the pair of them a heap of untold grief."

"A union that could only come to be, *if* they ever found a church willing to wed them," Filippo responded in a grave and sober tone.

Heavy rain started bearing down on the coach.

"I hope they can find solace somewhere," Laura said, wistfully. "They scarcely had a courtship, did they?"

Filippo grimaced. "How could they? Alas, in people's eyes, she shall forever be his servant, even when she becomes his mistress."

XX. UNFINISHED BUSINESS

Warden Thomas Bambridge stepped off his carriage and hastily proceeded toward the main entrance of the Magistrates' Court on Bow Street in London. As fate would have it, he skidded on cobblestones slick from an early morning fog, nearly losing his balance. "Good Lord!" he muttered. He quickly righted himself and marched onward at a slower pace.

Breathing heavily, he climbed the steps of an imposing building, crossed its threshold, and walked into the hallowed sanctuary of English justice. He strode through paneled corridors lined with portraits of dignified sobriety, until his sturdy boots found the office of Lord Henry Fielding. He removed his tricorn and rapped firmly on the door.

"Enter!" Bambridge heard. He turned the knob and stepped into the chamber.

Seated at his desk, Fielding's eyes lifted then quickly returned to the unfurled scroll in his hands. Behind him, a portrait of King George II. To his right, the Standard of the Realm. To his left, a scarlet robe and a black scarf hanging on the back of a walnut valet stand. Beside the stand, a full white bottom bench wig was displayed on a small table.

The Warden approached the desk and bowed. "A good morning to you, my lord!" he said, hands holding his hat below his belt line.

Fielding raised his gaze over the rim of his reading glasses and nodded slightly. "'Tis been a while…" he said. "A pressing need, I presume. What else might warrant an unannounced call upon my office?"

"Apologies, Your Honor. I humbly seek your backing and support in bringing one of the Fleet's former inmates and fugitives to justice."

"A fugitive, say you?"

"Indeed. The Papist rogue, who but a few months past, succeeded in absconding on account of his connections."

"I presume you allude to the theater Impresario who, in recent times, was granted a pardon."

"Aye. Alas, despite failing to discharge the obligations he accrued during his stay at my humble establishment."

"Are you implying the pardon did not contemplate your claim?"

"I had no chance to submit one, Your Honor. You do recall that under your directives the subject was afforded all manner of privileges. In point of fact, I ensured he was treated like royalty!"

Fielding drew a deep breath. "How much is this *royal treatment* worth to you, sir?"

"By my tallies, twenty-five sterling."

"Hm… A rather extraordinary sum, wouldn't you say? The Impresario lodged with you no longer than a month."

"And yet, he led a rather lavish lifestyle, my lord! In and out privileges, a private dwelling chamber, three meals a day, coffee, tea, ale and wine all on the same account. Then there was firewood, candles, stationery wares and ink brought to his door. He had laundresses and maidservants at his beck and call, not to mention Mister Matthew Shultz, his purveyor of snuff. He delivered his vice without fail twice weekly. Oh, and his blessed correspondence! He had post boys come and go, dispatching heaps of it just about every day!"

"I presume you are in possession of letters of receipt that can validate the accuracy of your claim."

"I am."

"Then it behooves you to submit them to this court without further ado," Fielding said. "That is, if your intent is to recover your losses."

"Indeed, that is my purpose," came the Warden's eager reply. "And to that end I've brought them with me." He pulled a ledger out of his knapsack and handed it over. "Here you are, Your Honor."

"You waste no time, I see."

"I am also well apprised of where the subject can be found quite readily."

"Where is that?"

"In the Netherlands."

"Enlighten me, sir. How did you come to learn his whereabouts?"

"One of my men inquired with a servant at the residence of Genoa's Ambassador. He was keen to cooperate after I summoned him to see me at the Fleet, and—"

"—Pray say no more!" Fielding cut in, eyes glaring with disdain. "I beseech you to refrain from elaborating any further. How you elicit anyone's cooperation is your business, sir. In any event, I shall examine the evidence and should my findings verify your claim I shall present it to Lord Buckhurst, His Majesty's Lord Steward."

"To what end?"

"'Twas he who served the King's pardon to the Impresario. His assurances shall be required for further dispensation."

"And then?"

"You shall receive word from this Court, in due time. Should the wind blow your way, you could proceed to solicit an Order of Pursuit and Capture. If you so desired it."

"Oh, I would! I stand poised and ready to undertake a journey to the Netherlands and seize him."

"We shall see how things unfold."

"Pardon my keenness, Your Honor. When should I expect to receive notice, then?"

"In due time," Fielding repeated. "Patience is a virtue, sir. And that should suffice. Now, if I may, I do have other matters to attend. I bid you a good day!"

➤⊙◄

Within a week, the early light of a cool morning found Bambridge settled at his desk reading the headlines on a broadsheet, a hot cup of coffee by his side.

At last! Westminster Bridge is done, he mused. *That gaggle of buffoons at the House of Commons are now steps away from the taverns and the bear pits in Lambeth.*

A discreet rap on the door punctuated the Warden's ruminations. He put the paper down and answered. "Come!"

Hawley stepped in and bowed.

"What is it?"

"The post, sir." Hawley walked up to the desk and placed a handful of letters within arm's reach of the Warden.

At once, Bambridge began rummaging through them. One bore the Seal of the Court. "Hmm… from Lord Fielding," he muttered. He picked it up, tore the seal, and began reading it silently.

Hawley remained standing by the desk, awaiting his dismissal.

Suddenly, the Warden's eyes lit up. "The Palace has consented!"

"Sir?"

"The Lord Steward has approved the issuance of an Order of Pursuit and Capture."

"Against who?"

"Against one of the birdies that flew out of his cage during the riots. You must have come across him at some point." He lifted his coffee and slurped.

Hawley shuddered as he recalled his role in aiding the Impresario's escape. "The theater man?" he asked, stoned-faced.

"That is the one. His days of liberty are numbered. Ere long, we shall pursue this rascal to The Hague."

"*We?*"

"You shall be joining me in this expedition."

"Me, sir? I—I am certain I'm ill-suited for the task."

"Nonsense! Since the riots, you've shown yourself to be one of my most reliable deputies."

"But my family, sir…" Hawley protested.

"They shall not be affected," the Warden reassured him.

"Do you seek to bring the Impresario back to London?"

"We might have to. Though it may not come to that."

Hawley sighed. "What next then?"

"Before we set out on our journey, I shall negotiate an arrangement with the Dutch to allow him to serve time at one of their facilities. That is, unless he meets all of his financial obligations before our return to England."

"Have you set a date for our departure?"

"I expect we shall be sailing shortly. I trust you will ensure we carry all necessary firearms and interrogation tools with us."

"I shall load our travel trunks accordingly, sir."

Before long, Bambridge had secured all necessary writs and had set forth on his mission to the continent with Hawley at his side. Upon their arrival at The Hague, they were promptly escorted to see the warden of Gevangenspoort Prison.

As they stepped into the Dutch warden's chamber, a potent smell of tobacco assailed them.

"*Welkom* to Gevangenspoort, Warden Bambridge!" said a broad-shouldered, middle- aged man, standing behind a weathered oak desk with a pipe in his mouth. "I am Hugo de Groot. Your servant."

The Dutch Warden stood six feet tall, with short red hair and piercing brown eyes. A window behind him overlooked the prison's courtyard. A few feet away, to one side of the room, a small framed portrait of Prince Willem of Orange IV graced the mantel of a modest brick fireplace.

"Pray have a seat," de Groot continued, settling in his chair, a brass spittoon by his feet.

"Much obliged!" Bambridge responded. He removed his tricorn, nodded, and sat across from de Groot. "I am honored to make your acquaintance, sir."

"As am I!"

"This is my deputy, Adam Hawley," Bambridge said, pointing. Hawley tipped his hat and remained standing by the fireplace.

"We received your letter a few days past," said de Groot, loading his pipe and packing it down tightly with a stopper. "It may interest you to know, we have located the subject in question, and have issued a warrant for his arrest."

"You proceeded with remarkable alacrity. We are beholden to you."

"We are glad to be of service."

"And your decision on the matter of his apprehension?"

"We shall execute our warrant and conduct the arrest. The subject will be in our custody at all times."

"Of course, of course. 'Tis your jurisdiction." Bambridge said, watching de Groot place a tiny piece of white birch tinder over a sharp shard of flint he held in his hand. Picking up a set of steel pipe tongs from his desk de Groot began striking down the flint with it.

"Verily," de Groot responded, catching a hot spark on the tinder. "We shall strive to make the process smooth as silk."

"Your confidence lends credence to your words," said Bambridge, captivated by de Groot's deft use of the pincher end of the tongs to hold the tinder up while gently blowing on it.

As the tinder burned, he carefully laid it on the bed of tobacco in the pipe bowl.

"I am pleased we see eye to eye on this," said de Groot. He drew on the pipe until a wisp of smoke finally blew out of his mouth. Then, as he took one puff after another, small grey clouds rose in the air and slowly expanded across the room.

Hawley began coughing. His face reddened. Bambridge glared at him, prompting de Groot to stand and unlatch the window behind him, leaving it ajar.

A cool fresh breeze drifted in. Relieved, Hawley relaxed.

"What about the interrogation?" Bambridge asked.

"You shall conduct it here, in our *examineerkamer*, the examination room," de Groot replied, returning to his seat. "In my presence."

"If you insist. I gather the first floor of this building is quite well suited for such purpose."

De Groot cleared his throat, lifted the spittoon by his feet and spat into it.

"Our sharp interrogations chamber?"

"I hear 'tis one-of-a kind," Bambridge responded with a grin.

"Aye. 'Tis studded with a vast collection of devices intended to persuade suspected criminals to cooperate with our investigations."

Bambridge coughed out a raspy guffaw. "Ahh... Very well then. We're rather proud of our own *first floor* chamber at the Fleet," he said.

Hawley looked down, a grave look on his face.

"We've heard about your dungeons, sir..." said de Groot, raising an eyebrow. "You do realize, the subject is a client of Prince Willem. His company has been engaged by the Palace as of late. He also has a high-status ally in Heer Richard Westerbeek, one of the Prince's closest associates."

"What, then? You must be mindful of the fact the English Crown is fully behind this operation."

"We are. An operation that precludes the use of our first-floor chamber as well as any of the conventional interrogation tools normally at our disposal."

"Then, what warranties can you provide that this miscreant will make good on his unmet obligations?"

"We shall furnish you with all the aid and support that you require to ensure you attain your goals."

"Such as?"

"Intelligence. We believe there is someone who may prove to be an asset to your cause..."

"Pray tell. Who would that be?"

"A person of interest," de Groot replied. "A female."

"I see. A paramour perchance?"

"Much in the same manner, we believe. In any case, she's a low born."

"An intriguing circumstance, indeed."

"You and your associate are welcome to come along and witness the subject's apprehension."

"May I inquire when it will take place?"

"At eventide tomorrow. Once his company's engagement at the palace has concluded."

———➤☙◄———

The following evening, just before sunset, Warden de Groot, one of his bailiffs, Bambridge and Hawley sat inside a patrol paddy wagon hidden from view behind one of the gate towers outside palace grounds. Using handheld telescopes, de Groot and Bambridge observed the activities occurring at the

Palace's main entrance.

"I count ten carriages queued up by the steps," Bambridge said, keeping his telescope fixed on the scene.

De Groot took a deep drag from his pipe, gasped and wheezed, then spoke in a raspy voice. "I gather six coaches await the royal guests, and four the players. The guests will come out first. Then, Mijnheer Crossa and his troupe shall follow. We must establish which of the carriages he boards."

In short order, the royal guests began exiting the Palace and boarding their respective coaches. One by one, the carriages proceeded through the gate.

"No one riding in those coaches seems to have noticed our wagon," Hawley observed.

"He comes now!" Bambridge shouted, his telescope glued to his eye.

"Indeed! That's him!" De Groot confirmed. "He's boarding the first carriage. Three others are with him. Two females and a male."

"Who are they?" Bambridge asked.

"The Laschis, man and wife. They're well known members of his troupe. Papists from Turin, like him. And his Achilles heel... His mistress."

Bambridge's eyes widened. "Oh, is that her?"

"Aye. We believe he smuggled her into the Netherlands. She may have escaped slavery in the East Indies. She shall be seized as well."

"How amusing! A fugitive protecting a fugitive. 'Tis clear now why there's no need to put your *first floor* to use, to get at him."

As the coach carrying Giovanni approached the gate, de Groot and his bailiff stepped out of the wagon.

"Halt!" they shouted, intercepting the carriage, gun barrels aimed at the whip.

"What is transpiring? Why the commotion?" Giovanni called.

"We are being detained, sir!" the coachman responded.

"A heist!" Giovanni cried out. He reached for a wooden box under his seat, opened it, and pulled out a pistol.

Terror swept across Laura's face. "By the grace of God! No!"

"Pray, I beseech you!" Sheina cried out. "There is no need for that!"

Raising his hands Filippo pleaded. "Dottore! Let go of your dragon!" Giovanni put it down just as the coach doors flung open and all three faced a bailiff with a blunderbuss aimed at them.

"You two, step out at once!" he shouted, indicating Giovanni and Sheina with his gun barrel.

"What is the meaning of this?" Giovanni growled as he and Sheina emerged from the carriage.

Laura leaned on Filippo and gripped his arm. "Is this a robbery?" she asked, her voice trembling.

"'Tis the *polizia, cara mia*," Filippo replied. "They are after our Dottore and the Signorina."

"Move on!" the bailiff ordered the coachman.

De Groot stepped forward. "You are under arrest!" he declared.

"This is a terrible mistake!" Giovanni yelled out. "On what grounds are you detaining us?"

"There are two outstanding warrants for your arrest, sir. One in England and one in the Netherlands," de Groot answered. "You shall be served tomorrow. Meantime, you and your slave will spend the night at Gevangenpoort Prison. We shall refrain from cuffing or shackling either of you, as long as you cooperate. Now, on to the wagon!"

"She's not a slave!" Giovanni screamed, wringing his hands. "Why must you arrest her?"

Sheina reached for Giovanni's arm and touched him gently. "Let us keep our composure, my darling Gio."

"You two! Be quiet!" de Groot roared.

The couple climbed into the paddy wagon.

Suddenly, Giovanni found himself face to face with Bambridge and Hawley. He paled, shivers down his spine. "You, again! Why?" he asked, incredulous.

"Ah! We meet again, Impresario!" Bambridge replied with a smirk. "Isn't it uncanny how unfinished business always finds a means to rear its ugly head?"

"What unfinished business do you speak of? I received a pardon from King George!"

"*That* was a wrong which has now been righted. Morrow shall grant us ample opportunity to deliberate upon the finer details of your current predicament."

As the wagon started its journey to Gevangenpoort Prison, a fleeting instant saw Giovanni and Hawley's gazes converge in mutual acknowledgment.

The next day, Giovanni sat opposite Bambridge and de Groot at a table in the prison's examination room. Hawley stood behind them.

Bambridge produced the warrants for Giovanni's arrest. "Pray behold," he said, pointing at two scrolls spread out on the table. "This one bears the signature of the esteemed Lord Henry Fielding. And this one was signed by a magistrate right here at the Court of Holland."

"And the reason for these warrants?" asked Giovanni. "All my obligations were discharged and I was granted a pardon."

"Alas, your memory fails you, Impresario. The pardon applied to your elopement. As for your debts, you only settled those you had accrued with Mr. David Garrick. You still owe a considerable sum to me, from obligations you acquired while you were consigned to my custody."

"You're well aware I paid my dues in full!" Giovanni protested. "I owe you nothing!"

"Not so. As your warden, even after you absconded, I honored the debts you incurred with all those who provided you with goods and services not covered under the customary commitment fee. All letters of receipt have been submitted to the court in London."

"Which court? I demand to review the evidence you speak of."

"Indeed. You may, if you so wish. During the course of a trial. If you insist, you shall be returned to England and to the Fleet, where you shall remain confined until a trial takes place, which could take weeks, or even months. Then again, you could save yourself much grief if only you settled with me at once, Impresario."

"What about my seamstress? Wherefore was she detained? She has no part in this. I implore you to release her!"

"She's here for quite a different reason," de Groot interjected. "We believe she's a fugitive slave from the East Indies, though she denies it. Yet she has produced no papers that can prove otherwise. And we suspect that, you sir, smuggled her into the country."

"That is utter rubbish! Your accusations are groundless. I demand to see a barrister!"

A tap on the door interrupted the proceedings.

"Ja?" de Groot called.

The door opened.

"Excuseer me," said a bailiff. "A matter of some urgency."

"What is it?"

"Sir," said the bailiff, his eyes indicating Giovanni, Bambridge and Hawley.

De Groot rose, walked across the chamber and drew closer to the bailiff at the door.

"A visitor is looking for you," whispered the bailiff. "A certain Heer

Richard Westerbeek."

"You must excuse me," de Groot said to Bambridge. He exited the room, closing the door behind him.

Turning to Giovanni, Bambridge stared hawkishly. "Well, Impresario," he said, his face creasing. "Here we are. With a great deal to discuss…"

➤◉◄

Meanwhile, Westerbeek sat in de Groot's chamber awaiting his arrival. Soon enough, the two men were facing one another.

"Directeur," Westerbeek began. "I was made aware of Mijnheer Crossa's apprehension by his colleagues, Filippo Laschi and his wife Laura. I am here to inquire about his well-being and how this woeful circumstance came to be."

"The Impresario is in good health, my lord," said de Groot. "We could not dismiss the English warrant against him. 'Tis legitimate. If you care to peruse it…" He began shuffling a pile of scrolls on his desk.

"That will not be necessary. I trust it is. Nonetheless, what are the charges?"

"The Impresario has outstanding financial obligations with the Warden of the Fleet penitentiary in London," de Groot explained. "When that is settled, I assure you he shall go free."

"With all dispatch, I would hope," Westerbeek responded. "You must be aware that Prince Willem would not wish Mijnheer Crossa's difficulties to become a public affair. His company has been in the service of the Royal Household this past while."

"Verily, I am confident this grievous juncture shall come to its conclusion by day's end."

"What about Mijnheer Crossa's fiancée?" Westerbeek asked.

"Fiancée?" de Groot repeated, eyes wide. He took a draw from his pipe and continued. "We harbor a suspicion she might be a fugitive slave."

"On what basis, may I inquire?"

"She has no papers, my lord."

"Was there a warrant issued for her arrest?"

"We did not believe one was necessary."

"You did not? Then, it appears 'tis *you* who has no papers. You have detained her without justification. Should you choose to persevere in this dubious undertaking, I'd venture any court would perceive her failure to prove that she is a free woman, as equivalent to your inability to prove that she is a fugitive slave."

"Save, she cannot justify her presence here," de Groot insisted.

"Nonsense! I am well aware who she is. One of our captains, Dienke van der Zee, picked her up after a shipwreck at Good Hope. I shall have him submit a sworn affidavit to your office verifying her account. And that, I suppose, should suffice."

"Our views align, my lord," de Groot responded, lowering his eyes.

Westerbeek rose. "I am certain Mijnheer Crossa won't hesitate to bail her out while awaiting to hear from the Captain." He replaced his hat and exited without further ado.

<hr />

Back in the *examineerkamer*, Bambridge had ordered Hawley to find the cell chamber where Sheina had spent the night and deliver a message. Alone with Giovanni, he stood menacingly over him flailing his arms while he shouted. "You Papist swine! You are as stubborn as you are obtuse! Do you not perceive the advantages that would accrue from reaching an expeditious settlement with me? Should you decline, I vow to you I shall take pains to ensure you rot in jail and forever part ways with your Batavian whore!"

One flight above the examination room, Hawley had found Sheina's cell, a few steps away from de Groot's office. Seeing the door had been left ajar, he drew closer and peeked in. A Dutch bailiff stood in very close proximity and face to face with Sheina.

"Back off! Back off!" she shouted, his body towering over her.

In a flash, the bailiff shoved her against a wall. She shrieked. He covered her mouth with one hand while ripping her chemise with another. She bit his hand and kneed him in the groin. Enraged, he screamed at her, "You! Devil's whore!" and slapped her across the face. Within seconds, he had flipped her around, planted one knee on her backside, bound her hands with a cord he pulled from his belt, and pinned her to the wall.

As the bailiff began pulling down his breeches, Hawley barged in, pulled him off of her and punched him in the face. The bailiff hit the ground. Startled, he shook his head. Quickly recovering, he rose to his feet and took a swing at Hawley. A fierce fight ensued. Sheina bolted to the door, ran into the hallway and screamed for help.

Hearing her screams, de Groot dashed out of his office and came running. Sheina pointed to her cell. He rushed in and found the two men on the ground in a bloody scuffle. He drew his pistol and aimed it at them. "Disengage at once!" he commanded in a deep, loud voice.

The men complied.

"You! To my chamber!" he ordered the bailiff, who promptly exited the cell, hands covering his nose, his shirt bloodied. He then instructed Hawley to follow him back to the examination room.

On their way out, Hawley paused to take his coat off and place it over Sheina's shoulders. Still shaken, she covered herself and stood in silence. Hawley informed de Groot what he had witnessed. Between sobs, Sheina confirmed his account. De Groot apologized profusely and swore his bailiff would be disciplined.

As Sheina composed herself, Hawley approached.

"Pray excuse me, ma'am. A word from Warden Bambridge."

Baffled, Sheina looked at him, her arms folded.

"The Impresario is rebuffing the Warden's entreaties," Hawley said, as de Groot looked on. "Should he persist, he might be brought back to England, where he would face certain trouble."

"Trouble?"

"A court of law and jail time to be sure."

Again, Sheina broke into tears.

"I did not mean to cause distress, ma'am."

"'Tis not you, sir," Sheina responded between sobs. "I fear I've brought a curse on him."

De Groot stepped forward. "Warden Bambridge believes you might be able to persuade Mijnheer Crossa to acquiesce to his demands, thereby assisting the Impresario in retaining his liberty," he said.

Closing her eyes, Sheina placed her hand on her forehead and drew a breath. "Pray forgive me. Alas, I am much confounded and aggrieved. I have no notion what message I could convey to him."

———— >◉◄ ————

Still alone with Giovanni, Bambridge's attempts to force his hand continued unabated.

"Your choice is plain!" he shouted, lifting a scroll from the table. He unfurled it and read its contents.

"'Tis a vile piece of rubbish posing as a contract," Giovanni fumed. "You mean to take possession of my property and collect my future earnings."

"Not so. Placing a lien on your assets is the only guarantee I can rely upon."

"What is the tally, then?"

"Twenty-five sterling."

Giovanni's eyes blazed, his voice thick with anger. "You shameless cheat!"

"The Court does not concur with your assessment."

"The Court knows nothing of this wretched nonsense!" Giovanni said, picking up the scroll and waving it in the air. "You are delusional if you believe you could compel me to surrender all of my music scores, costumes and stage props."

"Well, those are your assets, are they not?"

"I shall never agree to a scheme that would deprive me of the tools I need to earn a livelihood. Without them, my company would perish."

"What could you offer instead?"

Giovanni paused. Images of Sheina dressed in rags and begging alms whirled through his mind. "It grieves me to admit it, but I see no other choice than to yield to your deception. I shall provide you with a banknote for the sum you claim I owe you. I do this in my faith that the Almighty shall render His judgment upon you when your hour comes to stand before him."

"At last, you abide by reason, Impresario!" Bambridge snarked, his yellowed teeth showing in a crooked smile.

Within the hour, Giovanni stood outside de Groot's office. Minutes earlier he had settled his debt with Bambridge and covered Sheina's bail. In return, all charges against him had been dropped and de Groot had signed for their release.

Giovanni checked his pocket watch. *Where is she?* He looked up as he heard footsteps. A turnkey approached, Sheina at his side. Her eyes rose to meet Giovanni's.

"By heavens, what has befallen you my dearest?" Giovanni touched the red marks on her cheeks.

"Nothing, my good sir. Pray do not trouble yourself. My sleep eluded me last night. That is all. Pray let us take our leave now."

Giovanni placed his arm around her, and together they proceeded past the sentinels and out into the open air.

The following day, three carriages, one behind the other, made their way along the rough and winding roads that led to Brussels. The sound of heavy rain pelting the coaches blended with the swishing and splashing of the horses' hooves on the muddy ground.

Sheina and Giovanni sat side by side, holding hands, opposite Laura and Filippo. Laura's head rested on her husband's shoulder while she catnapped. Sheina gazed at the raindrops trickling down on the window, a hint of sadness reflected in her eyes.

"Pray be aware, Dottore," said Filippo in a hushed tone, "Laura and I apprised Sir Westerbeek of your predicament as soon as we were able. He professed his intent to intercede on your behalf at once and without hesitation."

"It would not be surprising if he did. He is a worthy mate," said Giovanni, reaching for his snuffbox. "I am relieved this ordeal is finally over."

"The Lord heard our prayers and supplications," Filippo responded, still minding his manner and his voice.

"I have been blessed with good colleagues like Richard, you and Laura, my dear Filippo. Naturally, there have been others. Crucial allies, like Ambassador Azzoni and his lovely wife. And even a few saving angels. Did I ever mention it was Hawley, the Warden's trusted guard, who had a hand in providing aid and relief when I escaped from the Fleet? I had been badly injured. Without him, I fear I would not have made it out."

"A brave and noble man, indeed. He's fortunate he was never found out."

"Quite right."

Sheina turned toward Giovanni with a start.

"Is something amiss, my dear?" he asked.

"Not at all."

"Then why the tears?"

"They're tears of joy, my darling Gio."

"You weep from joy?"

"I do. The notion that there are such virtuous people in the world fills me with happiness."

Several days later, the troupe had settled into their new lodgings in Brussels. On the day of their opening engagement, Giovanni and Sheina sat on an old trunk backstage at the impressive Theater de la Monnaie, preparing for the final rehearsal.

"Your eyes look heavy," Sheina said. "You seem weary."

"I am. Heartily weary. Filippo and I tarried until the wee hours last night. Tying up loose ends before today's performance."

"Effort is as noble as it is praiseworthy, my good sir. Yet, only if we're mindful not to let it weigh too much on our toil-worn bodies."

Giovanni looked up from the notes he had scribbled on the libretto in his hands. "Once our business in Brussels is done, perhaps the two of us could rest a while," he responded.

"A holiday?"

"Why not? Perhaps we should consider embarking on a journey to Rome."

"Wherefore Rome?" Sheina asked, needle and thread in hand.

"'Tis the Eternal City, my dear. A magical place. Besides, Niccolo, my kinsman, happens to reside there. He is Genoa's Envoy to the Pontiff. A powerful man with countless liaisons. We could entreat him to aid us in finding what we need."

"A cleric?"

"Aye. One who would consent to bless our union. In our absence, Filippo could again take the reins and lead our troupe to Liege, Brescia and Turin, our upcoming destinations."

"Quite a sensible scheme. Filippo is an experienced hand."

"On our return, we could re-join them in Turin."

"Do you suppose we might encounter the Pope during our stay in Rome?" asked Sheina with mischievous eyes.

"Who can say?" Giovanni replied. "Mayhap, he could well be the one presiding our nuptials at Saint Peter's!"

Sheina giggled.

They rose and joined the actors and musicians on the stage.

While Sheina inspected every costume for imperfections that might require last minute mending, Giovanni made the rounds with Filippo ensuring that all the props and everyone's position matched the carefully arranged stage configuration.

"You are the keenest of observers, Dottore!" Filippo said, seeing Giovanni scrutinizing the chandeliers and the oil lamps. "Every detail gets a close second and third look from you."

"Such things may seem trifling," said Giovanni. "However, they are crucial in making a performance a success. 'Tis my charge that nothing goes unnoticed."

"Nothing ever does!" said Filippo with a smile.

"You are acquainted with my motives. Our audiences are used to seeing Opera Seria, with all of its spectacular productions," Giovanni explained. "Alas, their standards are too costly for smaller troupes like ours. I confess, I dread appearing unpolished in the eyes of a discerning public. They knowingly invest in a considerable admittance fee and expect grandeur in return."

Filippo threw his arms out, palms open. "Our financial constraints have never deterred us from dazzling the eye, Dottore," he said, reassuringly. "You need not burden yourself with such qualms. We shall not disappoint."

Giovanni nodded. "I appreciate your confidence, my dear colleague." He stepped off the stage and sat down in the front row before giving the signal for the rehearsal to begin. Fatigued from the hectic week that had just passed, he struggled to remain alert. As the music started, his eyes gravitated toward the distant features on the scenic backdrop. There, the illusion of depth made the artwork in the landscape appear to vanish at the horizon.

Gradually, the music faded and a familiar sound wave replaced it. Surrendering to the weight of his eyelids Giovanni nodded off. Instantly, he found himself hovering above an empty stage, gazing at a shimmering light rising at the edge of the skyline. As if gliding through the air, he slid toward it. Drawing closer, he witnessed a rotating four-sided crystal pyramid emerge from a hazy brume, each of its triangular sides a misty window. Floating behind each one of them, vague, shadowy figures swirled in a vaporous miasma.

As Giovanni looked on, the mist began to clear, revealing a face behind each window. In the first one, a blond, blue-eyed boy no older than seven seemed uncertain and mystified. In the second, a scruffy old man appeared lost and disheartened. A concave mirror in the third, revealed a wide view of the theater's ample auditorium: a full house, patrons in their seats, balconies and boxes replete with eyes glued to the action on the stage. Behind the fourth and last, a young fellow bristled with energy, his piercing gaze a mystery…

Sensing his consciousness fading, Giovanni heard the echo of a female voice.

Gio… Gio—vanni? Yes! Giovanni! That's what I'm hearing! Does that name ring a bell?

XXI. Venus

D evin opened his eyes to a Michigan Wolverines banner attached to the ceiling overhead. Everything else in his bedroom had remained the same since he had left for college. He yawned and sat up on the edge of the bed. *Three chandeliers, four candelabra, and two wall sconces,* he mused, as if taking inventory of the puzzling images spinning in his mind. He shook his head, stretched his arms and rose. Shuffling over to the window opposite his bed, he paused to contemplate the view of the patio and the backyard beyond, teeming with the colors of summer.

Basking in the warmth of the sun, Harold, the family beagle, looked relaxed and contented amidst a cluster of terracotta planters overflowing with flowers. A fond smile tugged at Devin's lips. *Lucky dog,* he thought, ambling toward his closet. As he reached for a towel, he spotted an old shoebox on a shelf. He grabbed it and looked inside. A pair of Barbie dolls lay next to each other, dressed in boys' clothes. *The twins!* He gazed at them with tender eyes before returning them to the box.

Stepping out of the bathroom after a quick shower, Devin put on a t-shirt, slipped into a pair of shorts and sneakers, and dashed to the kitchen downstairs. Around the breakfast table, Ben, Donna, Meg and Stella chatted leisurely over tall glasses of lemonade, sunlight reflecting on their faces.

"Good morning and happy 4th everyone!" Devin said flashing a smile as he entered the room.

"Good *afternoon,* sleepyhead!" Donna responded.

"Sorry. I was beat, guys," Devin apologized. He then turned to Stella. "You made it!"

Stella rose. Devin approached.

"It's so good to see you, Devin!" A tight embraced ensued.

"Ditto! When did you get in?"

"About two hours ago. Meg and I pulled into the driveway at the same time."

"How was the drive from Ottawa?

"Good! Long lines at the border, though. As expected."

"Of course. Especially on holidays," said Devin, moving toward Meg for a fist bump. "And how was *your* ride from D. C., Miss Meggie?"

"Thrilling! I had a blast with Harriet between my legs!"

Raising his eyebrows, Ben looked at Stella. "There she goes... My Lady Godiva freedom-rider sis!"

Stella smiled.

"Harriet, huh? That's what you call your Harley Davidson now?" Devin asked.

"Hell yeah!" Meg nodded, a puckish look on her face.

Devin glanced at the table while pulling a box of cereal and a bowl from a cupboard.

"Did you guys have breakfast yet? There's bacon and eggs in the fridge."

"We raided your freezer and found a box of waffles," Donna responded. "We had them with a special maple syrup Stella brought you from Canada."

"Awesome. Thank you, Stella!"

"And, we're all properly caffeinated," said Meg, raising her *Motorcycle Momma* travel coffee mug.

Devin gave Meg a thumbs up then grabbed a gallon of milk from the refrigerator. "I saw Harold out back, napping," he said. "Did he get breakfast?"

"Yes sir," Stella replied. "And he's been duly pampered and fussed over."

"Thank you. He's used to that. My parents spoil him."

Stella peered out the window. "He's adorable," she said. "I can see that your parents lavish tender care on their plants and flowers, too. Those white dahlias in the patio are gorgeous!"

"That's all my mom's doing. Dahlias are her favorite," Devin responded through a mouthful of Cheerios. "My Dad minds the vegetable garden."

"Dude, we should get going with the cookout," said Ben. "What time did your sisters say they were coming?"

"Around two. No need to rush, though. By the way, Kyle and Frank are also coming."

"Your sisters' beaus?" Donna asked.

"Yep. Kyle is with Abbey, and Frank with Paige."

"What about Penny? Is she coming?" Stella asked. "I've been looking forward to meeting her since you mentioned the trip you took to Asia together."

"I asked her to join us but she couldn't make it."

The phone rang.

Devin walked over to the nook below the staircase next to the kitchen and picked up the handset. A few minutes later he rejoined the group. "That was my mom calling from Italy to wish us all a happy Fourth of July," he said.

"Cool!" said Stella. "Did she mention my parents?"

"Yes. They're all checked in and ready to rumble. I told her to let them know that you arrived here safe and sound."

"Thank you, Devin."

"So, how's school going? Still working on your Master's?"

"Oh yeah! Full steam ahead. I'm planning on pursuing a doctorate after that, as well."

"A doctorate? Wow! So, what happened with your acting? The last time we spoke on the phone you said you were involved with a theater group."

"I was, and I enjoyed it. Then I found out how the Italians turned the performing arts upside down during the Renaissance and found my passion for research."

"Ben also has an interest in the theater," said Donna. "It's odd how he and Devin, both closet opera fans, ended up together after the university paired them at random."

"A stroke of luck," Ben said. "You know, opera doesn't often come up as a topic in the locker room."

"Come on, Lord Fielding! You're a law student," said Devin. "Don't shortchange yourself."

"No, seriously. For a while, I almost started thinking of it as a secret vice."

"And yet, here I am, my sweet Ben," said Donna grinning. "Your loyal girlfriend, despite your crippling personality flaws."

Everyone laughed.

"Says the Art History major!" Ben quipped. "Can you imagine anyone taking art seriously?"

Chuckles followed.

"How about you, Meg?" Stella asked. "What's your passion?"

"Honestly? Boobs and bikes," Meg replied nonchalantly.

Everyone froze.

"What can I say?" she went on. "I'm a probation officer. I'm into stuff that's far from the arts and academia."

"Au contraire, my dear sister. You are a living masterpiece!" said Ben with a wink and a smile.

"And sculpted, too!" she shot back.

Ben smiled and rose. "How about we start getting that fancy grill ready, Devin?"

"Sure thing. Let the good times roll!"

An hour later, a delicious aroma wafted through the air, teasing Harold's hypersensitive nose as he scrounged around while Devin and Ben minded the burgers and hotdogs on the grill.

"Harold!" Devin called. He held up a piece of burger on the tip of his fingers prompting Harold to jump for it.

By the time Devin's sisters and their partners arrived, a table on the patio had been set and Prince's *Purple Rain* played on a boom box in the background. Drinks in hand, everyone chatted and mingled animatedly.

Abbey, Kyle and Meg stood together.

"That's an awesome bike!" said Kyle, admiring the shiny Harley parked on the driveway nearby. "Is that Ben's?"

"Nah, it's mine," Meg replied. "Pretty cool, eh?"

"It's a beauty! Looks brand new."

"It is. I traded in my old one for it just yesterday."

"Wonderful. A Fourth of July treat to yourself?"

"Yeah. Kinda. I had a bit of a spontaneous orgasm when I heard the Supreme Court ruled the Jaycees now have to let women in. So I ran to the dealer and got me my new Harriet."

"Uh… Right. I heard about the Jaycees on the evening news. So, what's the scoop on that bike?"

"It's a limited edition 1984 Disc Glide, better known as the Willie G. Special," Meg rattled off, pride laced in her tone. "I rode it here from D. C."

"Fantastic! How long was the trip?"

"About six hours. I took the longer scenic route."

Standing next to Kyle, Abbey watched and listened, her puffed up hair resting on giant shoulder pads.

"Come 'n' get it, folks! It's chow time!" Devin shouted out from the grill.

"Excuse me, but I'm starved!" Meg said.

Abbey's hawkish eyes followed Meg as she walked away. "Is she for real?" she said, drawing closer to Kyle. "I mean, look at her! What's with that tank top and the leather vest? A tub o' lard wearing tight jeans and no bra?"

"Come on, sweetheart!" Kyle responded. "Not everyone can be a Twiggy. Besides, who cares what anyone is wearing?"

"Who cares about her spontaneous orgasms? She's in public for God's sakes! She should look and talk decent. Plus, all that bragging about her new bike… Lord!"

"Please let's not do this, Abbey."

"Ugh! And that awful haircut. Jeez! She might as well call herself Greg instead of Meg! Why do they feel a need to show off like that? It's disgusting!"

"*They?* Come on honey. Let's grab a bite. You'll feel better."

Soon, everyone had taken their seats around the table.

"Good?" Ben asked. He lifted his burger from his plate and took a bite. Accolades for the chefs followed.

"How long will you be staying, Devin?" asked Paige.

"About ten days. My furry buddy here needs me until Mom and Dad come back," Devin replied, patting Harold on the head.

"Oh good! I thought you might take him with you to New York."

"No, no. Harold and I will be hosting for a while," Devin winked, gently elbowing Stella sitting next to him.

Stella smiled. "I promised I wouldn't leave until he showed me Woodstock."

"I plan to," said Devin. "It should be fun. Anyone who wants to come along is welcome. We'll probably be heading over there tomorrow around noon."

"Too bad we can't stay," Donna said. "Ben and I love Woodstock. But one of my friends invited us to see a special exhibit at an art gallery in SoHo tonight, and we just can't miss it."

"Did you say Andy Warhol will be there?" Ben asked.

"Yes. But apparently, the exhibit is all about the work of one of his new protégés. I believe the name is Basquiat, or something like that. There's been a buzz about him lately. Meg, you're welcome to join us if you like."

"Aww... I appreciate the thought, but I pass," said Meg as she tossed an empty beer can into a trash-can with a sideways flip of the wrist. "My friend Kelly is expecting me in the Village before I head back to D. C. Sorry, I won't be able to stay for Woodstock, either."

Abbey looked at Kyle and rolled her eyes.

By the time the gentle hues of dusk began to fade, Ben, Donna and Meg were already well on their way back to the city, and the few remaining guests prepared to leave.

"It's always good to see you, Devin!" said Paige, hugging and kissing her brother as she and Frank stood by the front door.

Frank tapped Devin on the shoulder. "Feel free to holler if you need anything, buddy. We're just minutes away."

"Thanks guys. I appreciate it."

Abbey and Kyle approached Devin next.

"Great cookout and great company," said Kyle. "Thanks for the invite! Can we expect to see you in late August for our Big Day?"

"You can count on it. I'll be there!"

Abbey grinned. "Oh good! We were wondering, you know. We're still waiting for your RSVP."

"Sorry! I promise I'll mail it to you as soon as I get back to the city."

"Have you picked your plus-one yet? And by the way, should we expect a *he* or a *she*?"

Devin flushed, a visceral reaction brewing as his jaw tensed. "Um, yeah. About that... I was thinking of bringing Meg with me, you know."

A stifled gasp squeaked out of Abbey's lips. "Wha... Your roommate's sister?"

"Yeah. And, we'll be crossdressing. No worries, though. I'll be wearing my best wig and tiara, the tightest cocktail dress I own and the sexiest pair of high heels you've ever seen. As for Meg," Devin went on, "I'll make sure she's in a three-piece suit and tie, classic men's dress shoes, and a nice fedora."

Kyle burst into laughter. "Good one, Devin! Can't wait!"

Abbey's breath caught in her throat. She swallowed hard. "Oh Devin, that's hilarious!" she blurted out, lips curling nervously into a half-smile. "We'll see you soon!" She turned and scurried after Kyle, already walking toward their car.

<hr />

The following day around noontime, Devin and Stella set off for Woodstock. The sun blazed overhead with a bright white light, the heat and humidity steadily rising.

Seated at the wheel of his parents' Jeep, Devin rolled down the window. "Sorry, Stella. The AC is shot."

"It's okay. It's a beautiful day out there and I'm prepared," she responded, brandishing a tube of sunscreen. She squeezed a dab onto her fingertips, turned the rearview mirror and carefully applied it to her face.

Devin scanned the panoramic views as he drove at a leisurely pace. "You know, the Catskills is an amazing place," he said. "Magical in a way."

Stella peered out the window. "I can see that. Beautiful. There's also majesty here."

"Oh yeah. Absolutely. Did you know it was Dutch explorers that gave the name to this region? Catskills in Dutch means cat creek. The word *kill* means creek."

"Cool! I had no idea."

"Yep. Dad says there were plenty of mountain lions around when the Dutch arrived here in the 17th century."

"Was Woodstock a Dutch settlement?"

"I don't think so. What I do know is that the town is nowhere near the location of the famous rock festival."

"Right. I knew that."

"By the way, Woodstock is where my parents met."

"At the festival?"

"No, long before that. They were born and raised here."

"Sweet!"

A few minutes later, Devin turned onto Tinker Street, Woodstock's quaint main strip, and drove to a parking lot near the village center. Soon he and Stella found themselves mingling with tourists and locals, zipping in and out of patchouli-smelling shops packed with merchandise appealing to art and nature lovers, nostalgic older hippies with their families in tow, and a sizable number of Buddhist converts.

During lunch at a quaint local diner, they sat outside by a creek under a canopy of trees, water bubbling over rocks.

"It's so peaceful here," said Stella, marveling at the surroundings. "I almost feel like there's a special energy here."

"Yeah, I feel it, too."

"Perfect for meditation, I suppose. I wonder if that's what brings the Buddhists here."

"Maybe. I hear they built a monastery somewhere."

"Very cool."

"I'm glad you like it here. Sorry we can't stay much longer. Harold is waiting. But maybe we could make one last stop at the purple house we saw earlier on the main strip next to the library."

"What is it?"

"A psychic shop."

"You're kidding me, right?"

"No. Actually, I'd like to give it a try."

"What for?"

"Penny got a reading from a medium in Jakarta and it was amazing. I've been itching to do this ever since."

"Really? What did the medium say?"

"Long story. I'll fill you in later. C'mon! It'll be fun!"

"Fine. But you'll owe me. The next time you come to Ottawa…"

"Deal! Fair is fair. Let's go!"

Devin and Stella arrived at the purple house with the sun still high and relentless. They climbed the steps to the front door and rang the bell. On the porch, a log bench with two rocking chairs and a small rustic table looked like props purposefully set on a centuries-old stage. Around them, potted plants and flowers rested on a creaky deck. Above the handrails, hanging windchimes tinkled in the air.

A tall, slender black woman in her early thirties answered the door. Beside her stood a Harlequin Great Dane puppy with piercing blue eyes matching the color of her turban.

"Good afternoon!" she said, tossing a light lavender pashmina over her shoulder. Beneath it, a loose kaftan adorned with rich, colorful patterns gracefully flowed over the contours of her body. "Are you here for a reading?"

"Yes we are, ma'am!" a sprightly Devin replied.

"Well, come on in, then. Welcome! My name is Venus and this is Nixon, my housemate," she said, flashing a friendly smile while gently scratching the scruff of his neck.

"I'm Devin and this is my friend Stella," Devin responded. As they stepped into the house they caught a whiff of fresh tangerines and apples in the air. A ceiling fan hummed softly overhead.

Nixon came to Stella, tail wagging.

"May I pet him?" she asked.

"Of course! He's harmless and craves attention."

Stella knelt. "Hello gorgeous!" she said, throwing her arms around him and returning licks with kisses.

"Nice to meet you both," said Venus. "First time?"

Devin nodded.

"My rate is $30 for a session. One person at a time. Sorry, I don't do couples."

"That's okay. We're not a couple," said Stella, rising to her feet. "You go first, Devin."

"Sure."

"Great! Stella, feel free to take a seat and get comfortable," Venus said, pointing to a plush green couch across from a stone fireplace.

"Thank you!" Stella took a seat and picked up a magazine from a nearby rack. Nixon jumped on the couch and lay next to her.

"Please follow me," said Venus, her clogs lightly rapping the hardwood as she led Devin into an adjacent room. In the middle of it stood a round see-through glass table and two white armchairs opposite each other. Above the table, a bright beam from a spotlight pierced through its center.

Devin quickly surveyed the room. "Awesome wallpaper!" he said, glancing over walls covered by a universe of stars and galaxies.

"Welcome to the *Celestial Lounge!*" Venus responded. "Please have a seat and excuse me for a moment. I won't be long." Moments later she returned bearing a small, four-sided crystal pyramid. She carefully set it at the center of the table, directly under the spotlight. She took her seat, leaned forward, and leveled a captivating gaze at Devin.

"This is *The Seer*," she said. "It represents the prism of time. In geometry, it's a tetrahedron: a triangle with four faces that are exact copies of each other. For our purposes, these faces symbolize life in its four main stages, infancy, adolescence, middle age and advanced maturity."

"Interesting. What's it for?"

"It's an aid that will help us identify some of the forces that have shaped your life journey so far. Ready?"

"I am."

"Pick any face of the pyramid and look into it for a moment. Then, close your eyes and let the world inside of you slow down." Devin complied. She then closed her eyes and remained silent briefly.

With her eyes still closed, she spoke again, softly and calmly.

"You are a manifestation of a long line of male energies that have cut into the fabric of the universe. Among them, there appears to be *one* who stands out, someone who remains active in one of your past lives… and continues to maintain a very special connection with you."

Devin opened his eyes. "An *active* past life? How?"

Venus' response came swiftly. "The universe is a living entity with countless faces. It vibrates like a string at an infinite number of frequencies, each within its own dimension. Most of us are tuned into just one of these frequencies. But there are a select few, who can tune into others…"

"Who?"

"You, Devin. You and… Gio… Gio—vanni? Yes! Giovanni! That's what I'm hearing! Does that name ring a bell?"

Devin felt shivers down his spine. "Yes. That name *does* ring a bell," he said. "Is this some kind of ghost?"

Venus smiled, her eyes still closed. "Not a ghost. But perhaps, another version of yourself in another place and time."

"What? Who is he?"

"A middle-aged man. A businessman. Show business maybe. Involved with actors and singers. I hear music all around him…"

Devin scratched his head, brows furrowed. "And the *special connection* between us? What's that all about?"

"The string that tethers you to him, and stretches over hundreds of years, is still vibrating," Venus answered.

"How? And why is he in my dreams?"

"*That*, only you or he would know. And who's to say it's *he* who's in *your* dreams, and not the other way around?"

"That's so far-out. I'm not sure what to make of it."

Venus remained quiet, her eyes moving beneath her eyelids.

Devin leaned forward. "Maybe I should ask about my love life before we run out of time. Are you picking up anything on that front?"

Devin watched as Venus raised her head and breathed in deeply.

"Actually, I see a very clear and compelling image."

Instantly skeptical, Devin wondered. *An image of what? The girl of my dreams?* Certain this would be the moment he found out she was a fraud, he feigned enthusiasm while masking incredulity. "Pray tell. I can hardly wait," he said.

Then, to Devin's astonishment, Venus proceeded to deliver a much different vision from what he had expected. "In just a few months, a special *man* in his mid-twenties will come into your life," she said. "Short in stature, fair skinned, with clear blue eyes and a huge heart. He will become your teacher."

"One of my professors?"

"No. He will teach you how to give and receive love," Venus explained. "And he will also show you a whole new world in the process."

"Where will I meet him?"

Venus paused. "I'm not sensing his presence anywhere near…" she said. "Ah… Water. I can see now… He comes from afar, possibly from across the ocean."

"Anything else?"

"Um… A shiny metallic disc painted on a canvas."

"What?"

Venus remained silent, a serene look on her face. A moment later, she opened her eyes and told Devin his time was up.

"Wow! I never expected to hear such a detailed glimpse into my future romantic life from someone I've just met. Not to mention your insights about my special connection to the past."

"I'm glad I could help."

"What about the disc you brought up at the end?"

"Never mind that. A blurry detail. Most likely insignificant. Now please tell your friend to come in."

"I will. Thank you so much."

Stella got her reading next.

Devin sat quietly on the green couch, his mind reeling from all the startling revelations. Lost in thought, time slipped away. Before long, Stella emerged from her session. They bid their farewells and started back to the parking lot. As they strolled along the main strip they traded notes.

"Did you believe her?" Stella asked, after Devin shared his experience.

"Kinda. She seemed so certain."

"Are you ready to meet your other half, then?'

"Are you kidding? I'll be twenty-four this November. I've *been* ready. But I'm hoping she was wrong about that."

"What? Why?"

"She said I'm supposed to be meeting this guy in a few months."

"That's a good thing. Isn't it?"

"Well, I just don't wanna wait so long."

Stella chuckled. "Patience, my friend. A few months will go by quickly. You shouldn't complain. What she told you is way better than what she said to me."

"What did she tell you?"

"She said that in a previous life I was a high-class whore living in London."

Devin broke into laughter. "She actually said that?"

"Not exactly. But I got the idea when she mentioned I was a very smart and wealthy *madam* with very bad luck."

"How so?"

"I had a lousy husband who gambled all my money away and landed me in jail."

"No way!"

"She even told me that my name was Charlotte."

"Wait a minute… *Charlotte?*"

"Yeah. That's what she said."

"That's incredible! Don't you remember what happened in London, at that historic tavern where we had dinner with our parents on the day we met?"

"Vaguely."

"The waiter told you about a *Charlotte Hayes* who ran a brothel inside the tavern. You freaked out when you realized she had the same last name as you. Then, you joked about it and said maybe you were her ghost who came back to haunt them!"

"Oh my gosh! I had completely forgotten about that!"

"The waiter even mentioned she was an inmate at a nearby prison called The Fleet."

"Holy shit! You're right! This woman, Venus, is for real!"

"This is so odd," Devin said. "Think about it. Penny, you and I are somewhat linked to these phantoms in our pasts."

"Penny, too? A bit spooky, if you ask me."

"This is nothing. Wait until you hear her whole story…"

Over the next few days Devin and Stella caught up with each other during long chats driving around the Catskills, discovering its natural treasures and occasionally stopping in the quaint little towns nestled in its mountains and valleys. Then, on the eve of Stella's return to Ottawa, they sat by a firepit in the Sharp's backyard roasting marshmallows and listening to the thrum of crickets under a starry sky.

"Will you tell your parents what Venus said to you?" Stella asked.

"Definitely not," Devin replied. "They never understood that part of me."

"Which part?"

"My dreams," said Devin. "They don't believe they're real."

"So, you don't talk about it."

"Not to them. There's no point."

"And what about your love life?"

Devin snorted. "I have none. Although if someone special came along, like Venus said, I wouldn't hide him."

"You shouldn't have to."

They paused and gazed at the flames and sparks rising from the fire.

"I'm so glad I came to see you, Devin. I feel this visit has been both an adventure and a grand reunion."

"Same here. We should do this again soon."

A few days following Stella's departure, Lauren and Phil arrived back from their vacation. As they sat in the living room sipping coffee and swapping tales, they presented Devin with a thin, rectangular gift box, elegantly wrapped in crinkled brown wax paper.

"Guys! You didn't have to do this!" said Devin as he began carefully removing the peculiar wrapping. "Let me guess. Some kind of fancy chocolate?"

"No, but it's something up your alley," Lauren responded with a warm smile. "A small gesture to thank you for your time here while we were away."

Devin took off the lid and gently lifted what seemed to be an aged, delicate booklet from the box. He held it in his hands and stared at it. "If this is what I think it is… it must've cost you a fortune!"

"We were told it's an original," Phil said.

"Precious! An eighteenth-century libretto of a *drama giocoso*. My Italian isn't perfect but I'm pretty sure this means it's a comic operetta."

"Just what they told us," Lauren confirmed.

"The score is by Gaetano Latilla and the title is *Madama Ciana*," Devin said, still examining the cover.

Phil pointed at the box. "That's not all. Look inside. It comes with a pamphlet."

Devin gently pulled out a yellowed leaflet. "Yes, it's here. Looks like an ad for the performance. I won't swear by my translation, but I'll give it a try." He then began reading it aloud.

Opening engagement
Saturday February 15, 1766
The Carignano Theater
Turin

Devin paused. The date, the name of the theater, and the city felt strangely familiar. As he continued reading, the last few words resonated louder within him.

By the acclaimed
Commedia dell'Arte Crossa

"How did you find this?" Devin asked, lifting his eyes to his parents.

"By accident!" Phil replied. "We took a day trip to Turin, and while visiting the historic district we passed by a bookstore that caught our eye. It specialized in rare publications. We went in, and there it was! It had your name written all over it!"

"The store clerk claimed he was an expert in vintage music scores," Lauren recalled. "He told us that *Commedia dell'Arte* was the name they used to refer to all travelling acting companies at the time, and that *Crossa* was probably the surname of the man who managed this one in particular."

"Amazing!" Devin said. "Thank you once again. It's a wonderful gift."

XXII. The Dream Doctor

A week's worth of mail waited on Devin's desk when he returned to the city. Sifting through it, he came across an envelope containing a flyer announcing an upcoming book-signing event in Lower Manhattan. The featured author was Doctor Stephen Haverhill. The address of the bookstore had been circled, and a short-handwritten note appeared beside it: *Let's meet here!* signed with the initials SH.

The following morning, during lunch break at the school cafeteria, Devin briefed Penny on his visit to the Woodstock psychic.

"Sounds like that woman hit the nail right on the head," Penny said.

"She did. But I still have so many questions," Devin responded. "Maybe this will help." He handed Penny the flyer he had received in the mail.

"Doctor Haverhill wants to meet you?"

"He wants to meet *us*. I mentioned you when I wrote to him."

"How cool is that?"

"I know! Right? I'm thinking he could help us sort things out. Wanna join me?"

"Are you serious? Of course I do! I've got my own questions brewing."

"I thought you might. By the way, how's your research going?"

"Well, it feels like my efforts finally paid off."

"What happened?"

"Just last week I received a letter in response to an inquiry I submitted to the National Archives Office in the Netherlands."

"What was your inquiry about?"

"I asked if they had any information about an individual with the surname *Valckenier*, who may have been employed by the Dutch East India Company in Batavia between 1730 and 1750."

"And?"

"They said yes! They told me their records show a Dutch military officer by the name of Diederik Valckenier served an extended tour of duty in Batavia, which included the year 1740, the year of the massacre."

"Wow! That's sooo amazing!"

"Of course, he had to have lived there with his family, within the fortified city walls. All officers at that time did." Penny explained. "Unfortunately, there's no proof of that."

"Right. But at least you now have a solid lead that your last name may have originated from this Dutch family in Batavia."

"Exactly! And, this could be the family that took the girl in my dreams into their home, as a servant," Penny said. "This was not uncommon. Also, at that time, servants and slaves frequently took the names of their masters."

"So, if you are related to this girl, she must've had at least one brother who had a male offspring down the line. That's how your name was preserved for generations."

"Makes sense. I wish my father knew more about his ancestors," she sighed. "But he doesn't, which means I'll just have to keep digging."

A few days later, amidst torrential rain, Devin and Penny made their way to the legendary *Mystic Manuscripts* bookstore downtown. There, they joined a line of fellow dream research enthusiasts, waiting their turn to get their books autographed by Doctor Haverhill. As they reached the front of the line, they stepped forward and introduced themselves. Devin presented the doctor with the flyer he had received in the mail with his note and initials.

"Thank you for braving the weather!" Doctor Haverhill said with a smile. He then signed their books. "I should be done shortly. There's a coffee shop across the street. Should we meet there in say 10-15 minutes?"

"Around seven?" Devin asked.

"Perfect."

Devin grabbed his book. "See you in a few."

"Seven on the dot!" Doctor Haverhill said to himself, glancing at his watch. He closed his umbrella and stepped into the coffee shop, immediately spotting Devin and Penny sitting across from each other in a booth not far from the entrance. They waved. He waved back and walked toward them.

"I didn't realize he was so short," Penny whispered as they watched him approach. "Early 40's, you think?"

"Maybe."

Devin and Penny rose to greet him. They shook hands, he took his raincoat off, hung it on the booth's hat rack along with his umbrella, and sat next to Penny.

"Thank you for taking the time to meet us, Doctor Haverhill," Devin said.

"This is my colleague, Penny Valckenier."

"Of course! I remember the name from your letter, Mr. Sharp."

"Pleased to meet you, Doctor," said Penny.

"Likewise!" The Doctor nodded slightly, then turned to Devin. "I've been getting an extraordinary amount of mail lately, especially after my latest publication, but I distinctly recall your letter, Mr. Sharp. You presented a rather unusual set of experiences that may be highly relevant to my research."

"I'm glad you think so."

A waitress came over and handed the doctor a menu. "Good evening! Can I start you with anything to drink, sir?"

"A cup of black tea will do for me."

"Sure! Coffee refills for the lady and the gentleman?"

They declined.

The Doctor tucked his shoulder-length salt and pepper mane behind his ears, and adjusted his eyeglasses. "I appreciate the letter," he said. "Not everyone has the patience to write things out."

"We had no one else to turn to," Penny sighed.

"I hear you. Perhaps we should begin by going over the core experiences that motivated your interest in my research."

Over the next few minutes, the Doctor sipped on his tea while listening to Devin and Penny as they took turns explaining how their recurring dreams fueled their interest in exploring the subject.

"Both your experiences merit a closer look," said the Doctor. "Just thinking about the soundwaves that you hear just before you fall asleep, Devin, I wonder if they may be related to what we call *theta waves*."

Devin leaned forward. "What are theta waves?"

"They are brain waves. They may appear when we're drifting off to sleep or just before we wake up. They can also occur when we're awake, but in a very deeply relaxed state of mind."

"Interesting. I always felt they were real. The veil and the shadows, too."

"I understand."

"Sometimes I wonder if the veil might be some kind of threshold." Devin said. "I mean, the type of thing that would allow someone's mind to enter into another time and place."

"Not enough rigorous research has been done to confirm or deny anything that would lead to such a conclusion," the doctor responded. "Nonetheless, a few individuals have reported crossing what they believe is some kind of *portal* while in a trance-like state, similar to a lucid dream."

"What do they say happens once they're on the other side?"

"Some claim they are transported into what they believe might be another dimension. Yet, very few can ever recall what they see. And if they do, it's usually just fragments."

"That's been our experience, too!" Penny said. "This is the reason we keep journals."

"Outstanding!" said the doctor. "If you're interested in digging deeper into this, you might consider participating in one of our research projects. Lately, we've been trying new data gathering strategies. If you decide to join us, your personal information will never be made public, and you'll be fairly compensated for your time and effort."

Devin and Penny exchanged glances.

"I'd love to," Penny said to the Doctor.

"So would I," said Devin. "By the way, any ideas what *the other side* might be like, Doctor?"

"I could not speculate about something we know so little about. What I can tell you is, some theorists back in the fifties and sixties suggested that there may be many worlds or dimensions, each in a separate bubble of space and time, perhaps next to each other. We just don't know."

"So, at least in theory, crossing over from one dimension to another might be a real thing, right?"

"In theory, yes. I suppose," the doctor answered. "In fact, there are individuals who claim to be capable of doing this at will. The intelligence services of some countries, including our own, are rumored to actively recruit them for their own purposes."

"I heard about that somewhere," said Devin, thinking of his former college roommate.

"Psychics?" Penny asked.

"That's right. Also known as clairvoyants or mediums by the general public. The government refers to them as remote viewers. They're supposed to be capable of seeing things outside the normal range of human perception."

"Superhumans," said Devin.

"Not really. Their skills can vary. Some can only view contemporaneous events, while others can see into the past, or even the future."

"So where do *we* fit in?" Devin asked the doctor, shooting a quick glance at Penny.

"So far, we can only catch glimpses of objects and events that appear to be in the past."

"That's about it," Penny chimed in.

"Well, if that's the case, you may have an extraordinary cognitive skill known as *retrocognition*," the doctor said, picking up his teacup and taking one last sip. "It refers to an uncanny awareness of past events that could not have been learned by normal means. Again, there has been very little experimental investigation of this particular skill. So, we cannot ascertain that it's real."

A playful grin spread across Devin's lips. "Bummer! And here I was, deluding myself into thinking I had special powers!"

Doctor Haverhill chuckled as he glanced at his watch. "I'm sorry. It's getting late. I should get going," he said, rising and reaching for his raincoat.

"Just one more question, if I may?" Devin asked.

"Sure. A quick one, please."

Devin and Penny slid out of the booth.

"Thank you, Doctor," said Devin. "Okay, so here it is: Could there be more than one version of ourselves in different dimensions?"

The doctor smiled. "Well, that's a biggie. I'm not a physicist but here's my answer: Why not? In theory, anything is possible." Taking his umbrella off the hat rack the doctor continued. "In fact, there may be infinite versions of ourselves leading different lives everywhere in the universe, at this very instant."

"So, if *anything is possible*, travelling between dimensions, at least in theory, is also a possibility, right?" Devin insisted.

"Yes, but probably not a risk-free possibility. Some theorists believe that there may be certain distortions or disturbances that could occur if a threshold were crossed."

"Why?"

"They suspect there's an invisible thread linking all particles. They call this *particle entanglement*. The state of one particle is dependent on the state of another, even if they are separated by large distances, like a domino effect."

"You mean, like when going from the present to the past, or vice versa?"

"Precisely. They speculate that if *any* interdimensional movement ever took place, it would likely cause changes that would affect people, places and things, even if ever so slightly. Now, I'm sorry but I must go," he said as he walked out the door.

"What kind of changes?" Devin persisted, as he and Penny followed the doctor out onto the wet sidewalk.

"Think about it," the doctor responded as he walked briskly toward the curb. "If time travel were possible, every time you ventured into your own past, you'd be changing something at your destination just by virtue of being there. Whatever that something may be, it could also trigger changes in the present. And not only *your* present, but everyone else's."

Wide-eyed, Devin stared at the doctor. "Wow. Mind-blowing!"

"They're just theories, Mr. Sharp. And at this point, they're closer to fiction than to science."

"Still, fascinating," said Devin. "Thank you so much for your time, Doctor Haverhill."

"You're quite welcome! It was fun chatting with you both tonight. I have your phone numbers and mailing addresses, so you'll be hearing from me as soon as we begin recruiting for our next research project. I'd be delighted if you decide to join us." Spotting an approaching cab, he stepped out on the street and flagged it.

"So long!" said Penny, as a bulky Chevrolet Caprice pulled to a stop. The doctor hopped into it, closed the door and waived through the glass before vanishing into the night.

XXIII. THE FORT

A chilly Friday night in late October had kept Devin at home. Sitting on the living room sofa, he leafed through an issue of *The Village Voice*. Ben was away for the weekend and he had no plans to venture out. Then, an ad for an off-the-beaten-path club downtown caught his eye. *Could be fun,* he thought, gazing at a Tom of Finland drawing of a muscular biker featured in the ad. He got up, jumped in the shower, quickly groomed himself, and headed out.

An hour later he emerged from the 14th Street subway station in Chelsea and checked the time on his watch. *Quarter to midnight.* He proceeded toward Little West 12th. As he drew closer he ran into a long line of buff and rugged men hanging around on the sidewalk. He approached a tall guy in a full leather outfit.

"Excuse me," he said. "Is this the line for The Fort?"

"Uh huh," the guy replied, a thick cigar jutting out of his mouth.

"Must be kicking in there."

The guy shrugged. "Doors open at midnight," he growled, sizing Devin up through puffs of rising smoke.

A few minutes later, Devin climbed a set of narrow stairs and faced a tall beefy bouncer with a horseshoe moustache, wearing a cop's uniform. A giant notice printed in bold letters hung on the wall behind him.

> *DRESS CODE & HOUSE RULES*
> *Black leather & Western gear.*
> *Levi's & uniforms.*
> *Tank tops, T-shirts & flannel shirts.*
> *NO colognes or perfumes.*
> *NO suits, ties, dress pants, or dress shoes.*
> *NO designer ANYTHING!*
> *NO preppies, disco queens, or crossdressers.*

"ID!" demanded the bouncer.

Devin reached for his wallet and pulled out his driver's license.

"Your *club* ID, sir."

"Sorry. I don't have one. First time here."

"This is a members-only club, pal," the bouncer responded with a tinge of impatience in his voice. "It's forty bucks for a temp pass."

"Sure." Devin took two twenty-dollar bills from his wallet and handed them over.

"Here," the bouncer said, giving Devin a pass. This gets you in, plus one drink."

Left with nothing but a subway token, Devin took the pass and advanced toward the entrance. With one foot in the door, he felt someone behind him grab his shoulder. He turned around and looked up.

Pointing to the notice on the wall, the bouncer stared at him. "See this?" he said. "Make sure you stop by the coat check and drop off your jacket. It's only black leather in here. You're wearing brown. And next time, lose the dress shoes or you won't get in."

"Oops. Pardon me," Devin responded, flashing an awkward grin. "I didn't know." He then stepped into a large, dark, windowless hall, its walls black and bare. As his eyes adjusted to the purplish-blue lighting he looked down and saw a thick layer of sawdust covering the floors. *Cool! Looks like snow.*

Carrying his jacket folded under one arm, he walked around until he found the coat check. "Which way to the bar?" he asked the attendant.

"Stick with the guy in the turquoise feather headdress and you'll find it," the attendant replied, indicating someone passing by dressed in faux Cherokee regalia. Instantly, snapshots from a peculiar dream raced through Devin's mind: A colorful fellow bowing to a king in a grand chamber. Seven tribal chiefs wearing nothing but loincloths stood behind him...

Acting as a moving beacon in the dark, the turquoise feather headdress led Devin to a Western-style saloon. There, a handful of guys hanging by the bar engaged in lively conversation. On display, a distinct brand of masculine flamboyance: leather pants, chest harnesses, arm bands, caps, ring collars and, to Devin's surprise, a remarkable amount of facial hair. The smell of weed, beer and sweat filled the hazy air.

Above the bar, hanging on a string from one end to the other, a dozen jock straps dangled like trophies. Devin shook his head and chuckled. *A sight to behold.*

In the back of the bar, a large vintage mirror graced the wall above the liquor shelves with a bunch of flyers scotch-taped on its glass. One of them stood out. *A nickel if you're hung and can prove it!* Devin smiled.

A shirtless bartender in black leather chaps, boots and a red handkerchief around his neck took his order. While waiting to be served, Devin spotted a stranger staring at him from a corner of the room. Moments later a short, clean-shaven twenty-something had made his way toward him and stood a few feet away.

"Oh my!" he said, approaching with a smile. "No leather, chains or spikes?"

"I know, right?" Devin replied, also smiling. "You too. I guess we came to battle with no armor."

"Looks that way. But what the hell. We're newbies here, right?"

"Oh yeah. First time for me."

The blue-eyed stranger cast a sideways glance and leaned in. "We're lucky they let us in."

"No shit! The dress code here is something."

"I'll say! I heard even Elton John was turned away one night."

"Really? That's a quite the tale. I wouldn't doubt it, though."

"I'm Milton, by the way. The embodiment of tales untold."

Devin giggled. "I'm Devin. Nice to meet you, Milton. Do I hear a British accent?"

"You've got it. I'm from London. You?"

"I'm a recent transplant from Upstate New York, trying to make it in the urban jungle."

"Nice! Have you seen The Fort, yet?"

"I thought this was it."

"No, no. It's up on the roof. I took a peek a few minutes ago when I first got in. I had to find out if the rumors were true…"

"What rumors?"

"Come with me, and you'll see what I mean."

"Okay."

Milton started toward a dimly lit staircase leading to the rooftop. Devin followed him. As they reached the top steps, a mix of electronic sounds began to filter in.

"Cool music!" said Devin as they emerged from the staircase and began exploring.

"It's Jean Michel Jarre. I love his stuff."

"Never heard of him. Is he big?"

"Oh yeah. Especially in Europe. He creates these magical moods that can put you in a trance."

"I think I'm in one of those already… This is amazing!" Devin responded, as they stood before a re-creation of an Old West fort.

Hell's Gate, a sign read at the entrance. *To those who enter here: Abandon all clothes!*

"That's pretty bold," said Devin.

"It's optional, I hope," Milton responded with a mischievous look.

A playful grin lit up Devin's face. "What are you afraid of?"

"I'm British. We don't disrobe unless the situation absolutely demands it."

"Oh yeah?"

"Certainly. And even then, it's usually accompanied by a lengthy apology and an invitation to a cup of tea."

Devin burst into laughter, with snorts in the mix. Milton began giggling with unrestrained abandon. "You're contagious, you know," he said, wiping his eyes.

"One of my many talents."

An exotic playground began to take shape as Devin and Milton stepped inside a labyrinth of nooks and niches partitioned by latticework and lit by torches strategically placed along the structure's outer walls.

Advancing through a maze of open stalls, they heard panting and moaning, the smell of sex and poppers in the air. As they passed by an alcove they saw a couple of half-naked cowboys making out. Inside another recess, a hardhat and a lumberjack inspected each other's tools…

They walked a few more steps and encountered a group of men in uniforms role-playing as sheriffs, guards and inmates, experimenting with bondage and discipline in an oversized replica of a Wild West jail cell.

Devin leaned into Milton and whispered. "I thought Halloween was a few days away."

"You're quite the cracker," Milton whispered back.

"If you mean I'm funny, I think you found your match."

A wry smile played on Milton's face. "Ready for a refresher? My treat."

"Sure. Thanks!"

They returned to the downstairs saloon and sat at the bar.

"So, are you a tourist?" Devin asked, while they waited for their drinks.

"No. I'm here for work. What do you do?"

"I'm a grad student at Columbia. I also work part-time in an office on campus."

"Fantastic! How old are you?"

"Twenty-three. But only for a few more days. I turn twenty-four in November. You?"

"I'm twenty-six. College wasn't a choice for me. Couldn't afford it. So I enlisted in the Royal Merchant Navy as soon as I turned sixteen."

"Mm… A Navy boy. Was it fun?"

"Oh yeah! Every port was an adventure, if you know what I mean."

"I can imagine. You know, my parents couldn't afford paying for my college either. I got scholarships and took some loans."

"When will you graduate?"

"Next year in May, I expect."

"And then?"

"I'll be looking for a full-time job."

"Looks like 1985 will be a big year for you."

"I hope so!"

Time drifted as Devin and Milton indulged in their tête-à-tête. The music and surrounding chatter had gradually receded into a distant hum by the time the house lights flicked on and off.

"Last call!" the bartenders announced on the loudspeakers.

"Hungry?" Milton asked.

"Always."

"How about breakfast together?"

"I'd love to, but I'm broke."

"Let's go to my place."

"Thank you but…"

"Come on! I make a mean omelet. No strings attached. I promise."

"Promises already? Well, well… Thing is, I only have one subway token."

"We'll take a cab. I'll cover it."

"Thank you. Sounds good! Where's your place?"

"On the East Side. Fifth and 77th."

"Fifth Avenue? Faaan-cy!"

———————➤-◉-◄———————

As Devin and Milton walked out onto the street, a light cool drizzle brushed their faces. They hailed a cab and rode uptown along Madison Avenue. Gazing out the window, Devin contemplated the aura of the city at night: endless glistening sidewalks, the inviting glow of 24-hour cafes and deli markets, some with stalls brimming with flowers.

"So, how did you like The Fort?" Milton asked.

"It's pretty wild! I didn't know it was a sex club. Did you?"

"I had a rough idea."

"Not me. All that raunchy role-playing caught me by surprise. I was amazed at how those guys live out their fantasies with AIDS going around and everything."

"It's a private club. Anything goes."

"I get it. Freedom. Gotta love it, right?"

"Oh yeah! Studs strutting their stuff without any inhibitions. Very hot, indeed. And they were making a point."

"Were they? What point?"

"That we can be as macho as any straight bloke cursing at a football match," Milton replied. "Unlike some of the stereotypes out there."

"That's a good thing, isn't it?"

"Sure. Except for the need to exclude certain people to prove it."

"Like who?"

"Disco queens, crossdressers, cologne lovers... You read the House Rules."

"Well, they let the Cherokee in," said Devin. "On account of his loincloth, I'm sure." They laughed.

"They had no choice. He's the club's owner."

"Serious?"

"Yes. Sir Alex Cumming. He's an English eccentric."

"How do you know him?"

"He's one of my employer's acquaintances."

"Oh really? Small world," Devin said, as the cab pulled over at the entrance of one of the most exclusive addresses in New York City. "Did you know it was the drag queens in the sixties who had the balls to fight back and change history?"

"Of course, I know! Stonewall. Those queens were brave."

They got out of the cab and walked into the building.

"Good morning, Milton!" said a doorman in a uniform.

"Good morning, Steve!"

They proceeded through a grand lobby and stepped into an elevator.

The doors opened on the 12th floor.

"This is it," Milton said. "It's one apartment per floor. This is the service entrance."

"You work here?"

"Yes. My employer is away and the rest of the staff are off for the weekend."

They walked across the pantry area and into an expansive kitchen.

"Wow. State-of-the art, and the size of my apartment."

"Take a seat, if you like," Milton said, indicating the stools around the island. He washed his hands, grabbed a skillet from a cabinet and placed it on the stove.

Devin sat and watched. "Are you the chef?" he asked as Milton opened the refrigerator door and retrieved a bottle of milk, four eggs, a bag of shredded cheese and a stick of butter.

"No, no. Chefs aren't live-in staff," Milton replied. "I am the butler."

"Are you kidding me? An English butler, like in the movies? Who's your employer?"

"Julienne DeGrasse," Milton answered. He cracked the eggs into a bowl and tossed the shells into a trash bin. "She's a philanthropist, originally from the Midwest."

"How did she find you?"

"Through an employment agency. She was looking for an English butler with experience and the right credentials."

"Obviously, you qualified."

"Over-qualified, the agency said. I had been recently employed by the royal family."

"What? The British royal family? Are you messing with me?"

"Why would I?" Milton began beating the eggs, pausing to add a pinch of salt and pepper and a splash of milk into the mix. "I had been working for the Duke and Duchess of Gloucester as their butler for two years. One of the best jobs I ever had."

"Where?"

"At Kensington Palace. Their residence in London."

"Sounds amazing! What made you leave?"

"I was ready for a change. I listed my name with the agency and two months ago they called me for an interview."

"Who interviewed you?"

"Mrs. DeGrasse, of course. A butler's job requires close contact. She wanted to make sure that we were a match."

"Clearly, you were. That's why you're here."

"Well, yes. That was a part of the deal. But not all of it…"

"Let me guess. Money talks. Does she pay better than the royals?"

"You bet! And she offered to sponsor me to get a green card." Milton turned on the stove and began cooking. "A dream come true, really. A once-in-a-lifetime opportunity to come to America."

"Awesome. Sounds like this is a long-term commitment for you."

"I'm still on probation, but yes. If all goes well, it will be."

"Do you think you'll miss London?"

"I'm missing it already. But I plan to visit as often as possible."

Within minutes, Milton had sprinkled a handful of shredded cheese over the sizzling mixture in the pan and watched it transform into a hardened layer. With nimble precision, he slid a spatula beneath it and executed a flawless flip, yielding a perfect golden-brown fold. After dividing it into halves, he presented Devin with his steaming creation.

"What do you think?"

"Mm… Smells delicious!"

"Toast? Orange juice?"

"No, thanks. I'm good."

They sat side by side and shared breakfast.

Just as the first fingers of dawn began to come in through the kitchen windows, Milton rose, picked up the empty dishes and placed them in the sink. "You're welcome to sleep over," he said. "There's no one in the house, you know."

"Is that right?" Devin stood, walked over to Milton, wrapped his arms around his waist and gazed into his eyes. "Thank you for breakfast. You *do* make a mean omelet."

They leaned into each other and kissed for the first time.

"Does this mean you're staying?"

"Yes. But, I'm beat. I really need some shuteye."

"Fine. I know what you're saying," Milton winked. "I promise not to ravish you while you're sleeping, my precious princess."

Devin giggled.

Several hours later, Devin woke stirred by bright layers of light streaming through the blinds of a large window. He stretched his arm and found an empty space beside him. Sitting up he called out for Milton. There was no answer. He climbed out of bed and walked into the en-suite bathroom. The shower was warm and damp. A faint scent of shampoo hung in the air. *Where the hell is he?*

While putting on his clothes Devin caught a whiff of a faint, comforting smell. *Coffee!* He stepped out of the bedroom and followed his nose. Making his way down a long hallway with perfectly arrayed photographs hanging on both sides, he passed by several open doors: a laundry room, a gym, a massage suite, an office, a library, and five spacious bedrooms. At the end of the hallway was the kitchen. *Bingo!* Coffeepot in hand, Milton stood by the counter in a pair of lounge shorts and t-shirt, filling two ceramic mugs.

"There you are!" Devin said as he entered the kitchen.

"Good afternoon, Devin! Do you take milk with your coffee?"

"Please. Extra light, no sugar." He yawned and stretched.

"Did you sleep well?"

"Like a baby!"

"Do you know you talk in your sleep?"

"I've been told…"

"You woke me up."

"I'm sorry. What did I say?"

"You kept mumbling something about some kind of bridge. Then, you yelled, "The bastard! They got him!""

Devin rolled his eyes. "I must've been dreaming. But not about a bridge… *Bambridge* is the name of this monster who keeps chasing after me for some odd reason."

"A nightmare."

"Kinda. It's creepy."

"Is he a sexy brute by any chance? Big and hairy?"

"No. Far from it. This is an evil man with awful teeth and breath."

"Does he ever catch up with you?"

"I'm not sure. Although sometimes I feel I get away from him, somehow."

"Good! But you won't get away from me. Not today!" Milton said with a wink.

"Oh! So, I'm *your* jailbird now? Does this mean I get to see the rest of this impressive cage?"

"You want to see the apartment?"

"I wouldn't mind. I've never seen anything like it. How big is it?"

"Sixteen rooms."

"Shit!"

"I suppose I could give you a tour, but only if you promise me to keep what you see to yourself. Unless, you want me to get fired and end up on Page Six."

"Nooo! Of course, I promise!"

"How about a shower first? You smell like The Fort."

They laughed.

"I'd be more than happy to!" Devin said.

"You'll find towels and a basket with toiletries in the closet by my bathroom."

A while later, fresh from the shower, Devin stood beside Milton in the foyer gazing at a bronze sculpture of a young ballerina.

"Mrs. DeGrasse is a serious art collector."

"I can see that."

"This is the *Little Dancer of Fourteen Years*, by Edgar Degas" Milton said. "She welcomes all guests when they come in."

"Beautiful! I remember seeing one just like it at the Met."

"Gorgeous, right? Apparently, there are a number of originals around the world. I was stunned when I saw this one here."

They continued on to a room where a number of colorful paintings hung on the walls.

"This is her collection of impressionist canvases," Milton explained. "She loves Monet."

"Incredible."

"I know. It's a rare privilege to see them in private."

"This one looks very familiar…" said Devin, approaching a painting that caught his attention.

"One of my favorites!" Milton said. "I actually asked Mrs. DeGrasse about it and she told me it's a portrayal of Madame Picard, a high society lady, sitting in a box at the Theatre de la Monnaie, in Brussels."

Devin leaned closer to the canvas. "Weird. The name of that theater strikes a chord…"

Next, they stepped into the library. A Picasso hung above the mantel of an impressive fireplace.

"Mrs. DeGrasse cherishes her quiet time here."

"I can see why. It's so peaceful." Bending slightly, Devin read the titles on the spines of several illustrated books stacked on a white marble table. "So many books about ballet and Venice."

"Two of her passions."

"Venice?"

"She's concerned about it. They say it's sinking."

Leaving the library behind, they made their way to a spacious dining hall and living room area.

"I love the uncluttered look," said Devin, casting a sweeping gaze around the room.

"Mrs. DeGrasse calls it *minimalist style*. Few furnishings and crafts, and a select number of masterpieces on the walls. Simplicity is the key."

"So cool. And the views of Central Park… Just amazing! I'd be happy with half of even one of these windows."

For a moment, the two looked down upon a vast canopy of trees, the wind shaking their late autumn leaves. They walked back to the hallway and headed for the private quarters.

"So how wealthy is Mrs. DeGrasse?" Devin asked.

"Very. She married into big money, but she's divorced now. I heard the settlement was quite substantial. Liquid assets, several homes and cars, a Learjet, etcetera."

"A jet? Geez!"

"Just for domestic travel. She flies the *Concorde* when she goes to Europe."

"She seems to have a lot on her plate."

"Yes, but she's got plenty of help. Every household has its own staff. Here alone, she's got a personal assistant, two maids, a chef, a masseuse, a launderess, a chauffeur, and all kinds of other people catering to her every whim."

"Most importantly, she's got you: a sexy royal butler!"

"You've got it, baby! She hired me to join her in the colonies, and here I am, among the natives, discharging my duties."

"I'd watch out for our native charms if I were you. We might turn you into a rebel Yankee before you know it."

"Mmm… Oh yeah? We'll see about that," he said, pausing outside an open door.

Devin peered in. "Awesome bedroom!"

"It's Mrs. DeGrasse's boudoir."

"Maybe we shouldn't…" said Devin. "It's her intimate space."

"Of course. We won't go in. But take a look at that," Milton said, pointing to a huge framed canvas above the headboard of a four-post king size bed.

Devin froze. Astonished, he gazed at a highly detailed watercolor of a shiny metallic disc casting a powerful beam of light on a nuclear power plant.

"Pretty wild, eh?"

"Definitely…" Devin replied, memories of Venus' visions suddenly parachuting into his head. "I wasn't expecting that."

"I thought you'd find it interesting."

"Yeah! What the hell? A UFO checking out a nuclear station? That's brilliant! Does she believe they're real?"

"UFOs? I have no idea. Maybe one day I'll ask her," said Milton. "Anyway, this was the last stop on the tour, sir."

"I loved it, Milton! Thank you!"

"A measly *thank you*? That's all I get for my effort?"

Devin's eyes twinkled. "I'm your jailbird, remember? I'm at your mercy."

"In that case…" Milton paused, a roguish smile curling his lips. "There's one more thing I'd like to show you." He turned and started for his bedroom.

Moments later Devin and Milton stood wrapped around each other, shirts and shoes on the floor, lips locked, hands and fingers probing eagerly.

"Mmm…Feeling frisky?" Devin asked.

Milton grinned. "And a bit randy, too…"

Devin began nibbling around Milton's neck.

"Ooh! That feels so good," said Milton softly as Devin's warm breath slowly inched closer to his earlobe. He lifted his hands and cradled Devin's face. "So damn handsome. Your Yankee charms are working." He gently pulled him closer until their lips and tongues met again.

Suddenly, Milton withdrew, unbuckled his belt, unzipped, and dropped his pants.

"No underwear?"

"Time-saving strategy," Milton replied, breathing heavily.

Devin's eyes lit up, fixed on Milton's exposed manhood.

Again, they embraced. Touching felt natural, sending waves of pleasure down their spines. Milton's mouth found Devin's chest, his tongue and lips nursing and tickling a perky nipple. Devin moaned, heart pounding.

They tumbled into bed and quickly found themselves anchored in each other's arms again. Devin's hand slowly glided south on Milton's strapping backside, gripping and seizing fleshy landscapes before reaching a pair of beefy mounds. He cupped one, then delivered a gentle thwap on the other.

Milton groaned. "Oh man, you've got me!"

"Do I?"

Milton ran his hand down Devin's lower torso and reached below his navel.

Devin drew a quick breath.

"And now, I got *you!*" Milton said, blue gleams dancing in his eyes.

XXIV. A ROYAL TUB

D evin flashed his ID card to the security officers stationed at the main entrance of the United Nations Headquarters in New York City, walked past the gate and joined a handful of staffers standing by an elevator.

Moments later, he stepped into his office. He set a small brown bag on his desk, took off his blazer, hung it in a wardrobe locker, loosened his tie and sat down. Just then his phone beeped and his extension button flashed. He picked up the handset and pressed the button.

"Good afternoon! UNESCO Internal Operations. Devin Sharp here."

"Hello, sexy!" said a male voice at the other end of the line.

Devin smiled. "What can I do for you, sir?"

"Wouldn't you like to know!" Milton replied.

"Er… Yes, sir. I'll make sure I check out that package later."

Milton giggled. "Busy?"

"It's okay. I'm at lunch."

"Great. I won't keep you. I think I found the perfect place to celebrate our anniversary tonight."

"Fill me in."

"La Petit Auberge. It's a French bistro on Lexington and 28th. Karen recommended it."

"Mrs. DeGrasse's chef?"

"Yes. She was there with her boyfriend and they loved it."

"Must be good then."

"I trust her. She's an expert on French cuisine. Mrs. DeGrasse's favorite. She also mentioned this place is a hit with some of the local celebrities."

"Great. We'll fit right in."

"Please! We're so ready! You and I are pros at casual-chic looks!"

Devin snorted. "You kill me."

"So we're a go then. I'll make the reservation. Wish me luck. It's Friday night."

"Thank you, Milt!"

That evening, Devin and Milton sat in a corner booth, sipping French wine while waiting to be served.

"So cozy and intimate," said Milton, looking around. "The wood paneling and fireplace make all the difference."

"Nice decorations, too," Devin responded.

"From Brittany, I think. They look authentic."

"I love how you know these things, Mister Worldly. I keep learning from you."

"And me from you, Mister Opera Aficionado." Milton reached across the table and squeezed Devin's hand. "Can you believe it's been a year?"

"Crazy, right? Time went so fast."

"Yes, it did. But you made good with it. You got your master's, landed a full-time job, and found a nice flat to call your own."

"You got a thing or two under your belt as well."

"Meaning?"

"For one, you passed your probation. That was a biggie, wasn't it?"

"Mrs. DeGrasse needs me."

"And you've made yourself indispensable. That's nothing to sneeze at."

"I suppose."

"Come on! Mrs. DeGrasse loves you. She wouldn't have taken you to Aspen and La Côte d'Azur with her if that wasn't the case."

"Well, she also took the maid and the chef."

"They must be great at what they do. Just like you."

"Thank you. You're too kind."

"Effort pays! She won't let go of you. And neither will I, Mister," Devin winked.

"You know you got me, Dev. But effort has little to do with us," said Milton. "Our thing is serendipity."

"Or destiny. Who knows?" Devin responded. "I told you about Venus and her visions."

"You need to go back to her pronto, before the next big lotto."

"Shut up. I'm serious."

"So am I."

A waiter approached with appetizers. "Escargot dans la coquille," he said, setting a steaming casserole in front of Milton. He then presented Devin with a small charcuterie board featuring a sliver of country pâté, toast, a bowl of mustard, and a few figs and grapes.

"That smells so much better than it looks," said Devin, eyeing the food on Milton's dish.

"Looks are deceiving. But your nose is right," Milton responded. "You should try it. The garlic butter and the parsley give it a wonderful flavor." He lifted a pair of tongs, deftly removed a snail from its shell and popped it in his mouth. "Mmm... *C'est magnifique*!" he said, after swallowing.

"I'm glad you find the escargot to your satisfaction, Monsieur," said the waiter. "It's one of our most popular *spécialités*. Would you care for anything else, Messieurs?"

"Just a silly question, if I may," said Devin. "I hear rumors this place is frequented by VIPs. True?"

"*Oui, Monsieur*. Of course, we're not at liberty to disclose their identities."

Devin stared at the waiter, eyebrows raised. "No exceptions? Not even on a special occasion? We're celebrating an anniversary here, you know."

The waiter leaned forward. "We have an honored guest who always sits at this very booth."

"Who?"

"Jacqueline Kennedy. She thinks no one will notice her here."

"For real?" Devin whispered. "This is Jackie O's booth?"

The waiter nodded.

"Oh my, my... I think I'll breathe a little deeper now. This is rarefied air."

The waiter smiled.

"So, do people recognize her or not?" asked Devin, casting a quick look around.

The waiter chuckled. "Of course, they do! Even with her sunglasses, everyone knows who she is." He excused himself and returned to his duties.

"I didn't know you were so easily starstruck," Milton said.

"I've learned from the best. Look who you work for. And before that, the royals!"

"*Work* is the key word. Household staff are not allowed to make conversation."

"I see. The rich and the powerful don't talk to mere mortals, eh?"

"It's not that. They're not friends or acquaintances. Speaking of, have you heard from any of yours lately?"

"I spoke to Stella on the phone a couple weeks ago. She's doing fine. Working on her PhD. Ben and Donna are moving in together. And Meg is still Meg, living in D. C."

"Fantastic! What about Penny? You haven't seen her in a while, have you?"

"Nah. None of my friends have seen much of me lately. And that's because now I got *you*, babe!"

"Yes, Cher. I'm glad to be your Sonny Bono!"

"We've got each other!"

"We do. And I love that. But we shouldn't forget our friends, should we?"

"I don't. By the way, I'm a bit worried about Hal."

"Your older friend in Florida? What's up with him?"

"Last time we spoke he sounded awful."

"When was that?"

"About two months ago."

"Is he ill?"

"I'm not sure."

"Didn't you tell me he's a heavy smoker?"

"Yes, he is."

"That could be it. Smoke affects the vocal cords. Maybe you should give him a call and see how he's doing."

"I will."

"Good. So, are we still going to PA tomorrow?" Milton asked.

"Yeah, why? I thought I mentioned our hotel reservations are confirmed for the weekend."

"You did. Just checking."

"We could always cancel and go to my parents, if you like."

"Come on, Dev. This is *our* anniversary. We'll be seeing enough of them during the holidays."

"I was kidding. You know my family loves you, right?"

"They warmed up fast. Must be my accent. The charm that never fails. With one exception, though: Abbey."

"Never mind her. She's a special case."

"By the way, I hope you get to meet my family too, at some point. Do you think you'll be coming to England with me next spring?"

"During Easter break, right?"

"Yes. Mrs. DeGrasse is in Texas that week."

"Cool. I'll just have to feel things out with my boss. I'm pretty sure she'll be on board with it."

"Brilliant!"

Early Saturday afternoon Devin and Milton checked in at a waterfront hotel in New Hope, Pennsylvania. As they entered their suite, they spotted a bottle of Prosecco, two glasses and a card set on a table on their private deck overlooking the Delaware River.

"Smashing!" said Milton. "You did great booking this room, Dev!"

"Glad you like it. Ben and Donna swore by this place. They come here often."

They put down their suitcases and walked out on the balcony.

Milton picked up the card and read it aloud:

"Dear Milton,
They say true love is forever.
Can we make ours last even longer?
Happy anniversary to us!
Love you, Mister!
Devin"

"Sweet! I wasn't expecting all this. Thank you!" They hugged and kissed, then sat quietly, savoring the wine as they watched the river peacefully flow by.

Moments later, while Milton unpacked, Devin sat on the bed, his back resting on the headboard.

"I've been thinking…" Devin started.

"About?"

"My friends. I feel a bit guilty, you know."

"Why?"

"I've been rotten. Especially with Penny."

"What do you mean?"

"Remiss, I guess. I've been kinda ignoring her lately."

"Give her a call."

"Now?"

"Why not? Ask her to join us for dinner or a day trip or something. It'll make you feel better. And her, too."

Devin reached for the phone on the nightstand and dialed Penny's number. After a few rings she answered.

"So now you call me?" she said, when she heard Devin's voice. "What took you so long?"

"I'm sorry Penny. Milton and I—"

"—go ahead, blame Milton. You know, I totally get that you're infatuated."

"What? No, wait. You have no idea. It goes much deeper than that."

"But not returning my calls? It's been months! I thought we were friends."

"We *are* friends! Hear me out. It's been crazy. New job, new apartment. And Milton and I come from different worlds, so it's taken a while just to get to know each other."

"What's going on?" Milton mouthed silently.

"Sorry, I don't take well to vanishing acts from people I consider my friends," Penny carried on.

"I haven't vanished! I'm still here and I happen to be calling you on the day of our anniversary."

"What?"

"Yes. Milton and I have been together for a year now. And we'd like to ask you to join us on a day trip to Atlantic City so we can celebrate and catch up with each other. What do you say?"

Milton smiled and gave Devin a thumbs up.

"I'd love to," Penny replied. "But first things first. We have unfinished business to deal with, you and I."

"What's that? Did I forget to return one of your makeup kits or something?"

"You're such a goofball! You don't remember? You told Doctor Haverhill you would consider signing up for one of his research projects and you never did."

"But *you* did, didn't you?"

"Of course I did! You know that. Thing is, they're recruiting again and they keep asking about you. I didn't want to give them your new phone number until I spoke to you first. Are you still interested?"

"Absolutely. Except, I'm not prepared. I've been neglecting my journal lately."

"Like you've neglected your friends? So, what's your answer? Are you going to join or not?"

"I'll have to give it some thought. To be honest, the issue is not just my journal. Milton and I are planning to take a trip to England together, and that's a priority."

"Oh, that's wonderful. I can tell where this is going! I thought *we* had planned to join this project together way before you met your new boyfriend."

"Come on, Penny! I'm being real. I can't commit to it right now. I need time to think it over."

"Okay, fine. But you'll have to make up your mind real soon. There's a deadline, you know."

"I understand. I'll call you soon with my decision. I promise!"

"What was that all about?" Milton asked after Devin hung up.

"I had completely forgotten about Doctor Haverhill's project."

"I thought you told me you were keen on it."

"I am. But it's not the right time. Still, I don't want to let Penny down."

"Well, at least I'm glad to know our trip to England is now a priority."

"You know it is."

"I'll keep you to your word."

The following week, Devin called Penny from his office.

"I'm sorry to disappoint you Penny, but after speaking with Milton, joining Doctor Haverhill's research group is not an option for me at this time. Not until we return from England."

"I figured," she said, letting out an audible sigh.

"It's an important trip for us. Milton plans to introduce me to his family and friends, and he'll be showing me his hometown and other places that are dear to him."

"When are you leaving?"

"We're shooting for Easter next year."

"That still leaves time to join the project, right?"

"Not really. The holidays are around the corner and I wouldn't want to commit until I know I can show up."

"Okay, fair enough."

"Are we good now?"

"Yes. And Devin, I want you to know I totally respect that Milton is your significant other."

"Thank you, Penny. That means a lot."

"I'll speak to Doctor Haverhill and see if he can save you a spot. I'll also take notes and share them with you when you're ready. Sound good?"

"Wonderful! I appreciate that."

"Meantime, maybe you could go back to working on your dreams journal?"

"I'll try. That's all I can say."

Several months later, Devin and Milton landed at London's Heathrow Airport. Walking briskly, luggage in tow, they advanced toward the underground station at Terminal Four. Along the way, through the airport labyrinths, giant colored eggs and Easter bunnies matched the spring-inspired arts and crafts displayed at every turn.

"Will you please tell me now?" Devin pleaded.

"Tell you what?"

"You know what."

"Where we are staying? It's a surprise, remember?"

"You're driving me nuts! At least tell me how we're getting there."

Milton shook his head. "You're one pesky little rascal, aren't you?"

"Guilty as charged. But fear not, sir. My mischief is of the friendly kind."

"Shush! You win. We're taking the tube to South Kensington, then a taxicab to our final destination. We should be there in forty minutes. Happy?"

"The *tube*?"

"The subway."

"Ah! Thank you! At least I know you're not kidnapping me and taking me to some dungeon in the bowels of London."

"Don't you wish!"

After a thirty-minute train ride, Devin and Milton emerged at South Kensington station and flagged down a traditional black cab.

"Good morning, gentlemen!" said the cab driver. "Where to?"

"Kensington," Milton replied. "Would you please take Queens Gate to Kensington Road, then High Street?"

"If you're going to the hotel, I'm afraid that would not be the best route, sir."

"Sorry, I meant the palace."

Baffled, the driver cast a furtive glance at Milton through the rearview mirror.

Devin leaned on Milton. "Are you serious?"

"Yes. Now you know."

"Holy shit! We're staying at Kensington Palace? How did you do this?"

"I'm blessed with good friends. And one of them is hosting us."

"Who?"

"John McLeish, Princess Margaret's butler."

"The Queen's sister?"

"That's right."

"Oh my God! So, he lives with her *at* the Palace?"

"No, but he's got his own place inside the compound."

"What do you mean *the compound?*"

"A bunch of buildings, all in one place. You'll see when we get there."

"Can't wait!"

"Anyhow, John is a special fellow. He's been in the Princess' service for the past thirty years."

"A lifetime! How old is he?"

"He's in his sixties, I suppose. I never asked. A bachelor. From Scotland."

As the cab rolled into the neighborhood surrounding the Palace, Devin fixed his gaze out the window.

"So much green everywhere. Everything looks lush and manicured."

"It's what's expected. This is one of the most exclusive places in the country, Dev. The whole place is like a huge royal garden."

"I can see that."

The cab driver made a turn onto High Street and drove straight up to a security post by a gate. Milton rolled down the window. An officer promptly came out and approached.

"Milton! You're back!" said the officer, extending his arm to shake Milton's hand.

"I thought you had moved to the States."

"Good to see you, Pete! I'm on vacation for a few days with a friend. We're staying with John."

"Welcome back, mate! Enjoy your visit!" He waved the driver on and returned to his post.

Milton spoke to the driver. "It's up this entryway. I'll let you know."

Briefly, the cabbie turned around and stared at his passengers. Devin and Milton looked at each other.

"I've been through this before," Milton whispered.

"It's so odd," Devin whispered back. "He must think we're celebrities or something."

"We *are* something. Not everyone gets an insider's view of a royal palace."

"You're right."

"Before I forget. I brought a special gift for John."

"Nice. What is it?"

"Rum. The best I could find. It's John's favorite spirit."

"Very thoughtful."

"He's a fine chap. And generous to a fault. Watch him. There's no telling what he may come up with once he gets busy with the bottle."

"Like what?"

"Some kind of favor."

"Another surprise? What is this, a British tradition?"

"No. That's just John. By the way, he and I spoke on the phone before we left the States and he said he would not be home when we arrived. He told me we'd find the key to his apartment under a red flowerpot by the front door."

"Perfect. I'm so jet-lagged. I could use a nap."

"It's the brick cottage with the black door coming up on the right," Milton hollered through the cab's glass partition.

The driver nodded and pulled over. He got out of the car, took the suitcases out of the boot and helped Devin and Milton carry them to the front door of the apartment.

Following a restful nap, with John still away and Milton in the shower, Devin relished a moment alone exploring John's modest yet tastefully decorated home. Exquisitely framed, signed photographs of senior members of the royal family adorned the walls and filled the shelves. Many of these bore handwritten notes addressed to John, extending warm birthday wishes, holidays greetings, or conveying gratitude for his loyalty throughout his years of service.

While examining a signed picture of the Queen Mother sitting in her drawing room at Clarence House, Devin heard someone unlocking the front door. Glancing up he saw a tall, older male coming in.

"Hello there! You must be Devin!" he said smiling, his blue eyes barely visible through a pair of thick-rimmed glasses. "I'm John."

Devin approached for a handshake. "Nice to meet you, John! Milton's in the shower."

"Sorry I couldn't be here earlier," John responded. He took off his suit jacket, hung it in a closet by the entrance and unbuttoned his waistcoat. "How was your flight?"

"Fine, but tiring. We crashed as soon as we got in."

"Crossing the pond can be brutal," John said. He loosened his necktie and rolled up his shirtsleeves. "The time change is part of it, of course. I'm glad you were able to rest."

"It's so kind of you to have us. We're very grateful."

"My pleasure! Are you chaps planning on going out tonight?"

"I don't think so. We'll probably stay in and relax."

"Good! Then how about refreshments in the living room in a little while?"

"Sure!"

"Splendid! I'll get some nibbles ready. See you both in a bit!"

Within a half hour, Devin, Milton and John sat in the living room around a small cocktail table crammed with prawns, devils on horseback and sausage rolls, set around a bottle of whisky, a coke, a bucketful of ice and three crystal glasses.

"Nice spread! Everything looks delicious," Milton said. "Thank you, John!"

"You're most welcome! Please dig in."

"Cheers! Now, if we may," Milton said rising, "Devin and I would like to present you with something we brought you from America." He dashed over to the bedroom and came back with a bottle of Puerto Rican rum. He handed it to John and sat back down.

John examined the label. "Jolly good show!" he said. "I appreciate the gesture. If we're all good with rum we could start with this one."

"Certainly," said Milton.

Devin nodded.

John opened the bottle and decanted a precise measure of liquor into each of the three glasses on the table. "Here's some fizz pop and ice," he said. "I take mine neat."

Toasts and cheers behind, Devin turned to John and gestured toward the walls. "You have an awesome collection of photographs here, John," he said.

"Thank you. They're relics." He paused for a moment and turned to look at them. "That," he said with a sweep of his arm, "is all I have to show for a lifetime of service."

"A treasure trove of wonderful memories," said Milton.

"Some, not so wonderful..." John sighed. He took a generous gulp from his glass and went on. "Did you know I didn't even get to attend Charles and Diana's wedding? I deluded myself into thinking that, as one of the most senior members of staff and close to retirement, my boss might at least get me a standing spot at the back of St. Paul's. But I had no such luck."

"Your *boss?*" said Devin. "You mean, the Princess?"

"Of course!" John replied. "She couldn't bother."

"That must've hurt."

"You think? Some of us have spent our lives in their service. We see them. But they don't always see us."

"On the bright side, it's not like your service has gone unnoticed," said Milton, eyes fixed on the walls.

"I suppose. And yet, do you see me posing with any one of them in these pictures? I might as well have been a ghost."

While John and Milton went on chatting, Devin kept a watchful eye on the bottle of rum on the table. As its contents went down, John's spirits gradually began to lift.

"Ahh… Success!" John said after a while, pointing to a half empty bottle. "I can proudly report I have officially tied one on."

They laughed.

"I should be turning in shortly, gentlemen. But first, if I may, I'd like to inquire about your plans for the week."

"They're tentative," Milton responded. "We thought we could start with a tour of the State Apartments tomorrow here at the Palace, then drop by the Victoria and Albert Museum in the afternoon. And of course, we will be visiting my family in Hastings before we go back later this week. Other than that, we're free and open to suggestions."

"Great plan there, Milton! Exploring the Victorian era is quite fitting, especially since this is Devin's first time staying here at Kensington."

"Queen Victoria's birthplace," Devin chimed in.

"Devin is a history maven," said Milton, poking Devin on the shoulder. "He loves all that stuff. Don't you, Dev?"

Devin flashed a self-effacing smile.

"Then I suggest you take a walk around The Orangery, when you get a chance. An eighteenth-century marvel. You've been there, haven't you, Milton?"

"Oh yes. A few times. The gardens and the restaurant are stunning."

"Stonking good, indeed! The restaurant offers a wide selection of refreshments, teas and all kinds of goodies to treat yourselves with after a hard day being a tourist."

"I'll make sure we don't miss it," said Milton.

"Something else you might not want to miss," John continued, in a low, conspiratorial tone. "Since the royals are away at Balmoral this week, I was wondering if at some point, you blokes might fancy a private tour of Princess Margaret's apartment."

Milton grinned, eyes gleaming. "That's a hard question, John," he said. "Of course, we'd love to!"

"Fantastic! Let's see then… Today is Monday. You're fully booked tomorrow. Would Wednesday morning work for you, my esteemed guests?"

"Sounds perfect!" Milton answered.

—➤◉◄—

The next day, Devin and Milton stood in line outside Kensington Palace's State Apartments, waiting to view the wings open to the public. A blanket of slow-moving clouds, back-lit by a fading sun, hovered above them.

"Are we doing the guided tour?" Devin asked.

"I could be your guide, if you like. I know this place inside and out. And, I'm also well acquainted with its history."

"Awesome! Thank you Milt!"

"Let's get on with it, then," said Milton, as they advanced toward the main entrance. "In a nutshell, this whole area used to be a forest where King Henry VIII went deer hunting. Later on, another monarch, William III of Orange, chose this as his country retreat. He built a mansion and the old hunting grounds became a park."

"Dutch, right? Name rings a bell…"

"That bell in your head is always ringing."

They laughed.

"But you're right. William was Dutch."

They walked into the building.

"Mind you, there were a few royal Dutch princes named William sniffing around the English throne for a while," Milton explained. "But Parliament invited William III to take the Crown."

They entered a large dining room and paused.

"King George II died here in 1760. He was the last reigning monarch to use Kensington as one of his homes."

"How did he die?"

"Quite suddenly, I believe. A heart attack while having breakfast."

"I'm getting goosebumps," Devin responded. He looked above the Palace rooftops through a window and caught a glimpse of a wedge of sunlight passing through a narrow path between the clouds. "I swear I felt a strange vibration the second we stepped in here…"

"You're on a roll today, aren't you? But this time, you may be on to something," said Milton. "There are plenty of stories about Kensington being haunted by King George II."

"I knew it!"

Time flew by between ghost stories and anecdotes about the many notable past residents of the Palace. Before long, the pair completed the tour and headed for The Orangery.

After settling on the terrace, Devin and Milton took in the breathtaking views of the surrounding gardens.

"John was right," Devin said. "This *is* a wonderful place. Too bad all I can think about right now is food." He picked up the menu on the table and began reading it.

"Mmm… Ham hock croquettes."

"Hungry?"

"Famished."

"Let's go then," Milton said, standing. "There's a buffet inside. We pick what we want, pay, and return to the terrace."

"No servers?" asked Devin, as they walked toward the building. "I bet the royals wouldn't put up with this nonsense."

"You'd be surprised. I've seen them roll up their sleeves when others wouldn't, in rather uncomfortable circumstances."

"They also have resources and privileges no other people have, right?"

"And many responsibilities to match," Milton countered. "They didn't choose to be where they are. They were born into it."

They stepped into a spacious and elegant interior, full of natural light, with tall windows, white marble floors and tall pillars.

"Aren't most people born into whatever they're born into? How are the royals any different?"

"They're trapped in a fishbowl! Few know what that's really like. But everyone is quick to judge them."

"Maybe that's the price they pay for getting to live in such a pretty fishbowl," Devin insisted.

"Says who? A fugitive from the colonies? You better watch your mouth or we'll have you sent to The Tower!"

"Fine. I'll just have my ham hock croquettes and keep quiet."

They filled their trays and walked back to the terrace.

———➤·◎·◄———

The following morning, Devin and Milton walked into the kitchen and found John seated at a breakfast nook reading the news. A warm and gentle breeze swept in through a large open window beside him.

"Good morning chaps! Coffee?"

"Good morning John! And yes, thank you!" Milton replied, peering out the window overlooking the entryway to the Palace compound.

John pointed to a French press coffeepot and two empty purple mugs at the center of the table. "Feel free to indulge. There's milk in the fridge," he said. Also on the table, peach jam, clotted cream, and two saucers stacked with scones and crumpets beckoned the hungry.

Devin poured coffee for Milton and himself, then took a seat by the window. "Mmm... Yummy!" he said, eyes locked on the food.

Milton sat beside Devin. "I'm chuffed to bits! It's sunny and warm," he said, still looking out. "We couldn't ask for better."

John nodded. "You're right. You gentlemen are in luck. This weather is unusual this early in the year."

"Do the royals ever hang out in the yard when it's nice outside?" Devin asked, chomping on a cream-covered scone.

"They might take a quick stroll here and there with a guest. But not often," John answered.

"No American-style cookouts for them, huh?"

John chuckled. "Not recently."

Milton gazed at Devin. "Since we're on the subject and about to step out, perhaps we should re-visit the *rules of engagement*."

"Again?"

"Sorry, Dev. Hearing them once more won't hurt you."

"Fine. Go for it."

"No photographs, anywhere, ever. If you happen to encounter any member of the royal family, you do not address them. If you wish, you can bow to acknowledge their presence, but you never *ever* initiate verbal contact. If they wish to speak to you, they will. Then, you can respond."

"But always briefly and to the point," Devin spouted off, as he casually peered out the window. "See? I got it!"

Milton and John broke into a small laugh at Devin's unexpected comment.

At first, nothing about the female figure slowly approaching in the distance with a child by her side caught Devin's attention. Picking up his coffee mug, he took a sip and fiddled with the crumbs on his plate before lifting his eyes and looking out again. This time, however, he took notice of the blonde, tall young woman who had gradually drawn closer, and realized she seemed familiar.

With a bag strapped on her shoulder, dark sunglasses and a straw hat, she strolled casually in a white short-sleeved blouse, wide pink pants and flats. A little boy in shorts, no older than four, held her hand. Suddenly, she veered toward the cottage.

Devin gasped, quickly turning to Milton. Pointing at the window, he stammered. "I—I think… I think that's Diana!"

Milton rose, leaned forward, and looked out the window. "That *is* her. And she's coming our way," he said, glancing at John.

John looked out and nodded. "Yes. That is the Princess with her eldest, William," he said calmly. "She must have decided not to join the rest of the family in Scotland."

Holding his breath, Devin watched Princess Diana and William walk right up to the window.

All three men quickly stood and bowed. She lifted her sunglasses and nestled them on top of her hat.

"Good morning John!" she said softly, flashing a smile. "I'm sorry to interrupt. I didn't know you had company." Using her right hand in a downward motion she subtly bid everyone to sit. "We were just taking a stroll and saw your window was open. I only wanted to wish you a happy Easter."

"Good morning, Your Royal Highnesses!" John responded. "Thank you! How nice to see you both! These are my houseguests, Milton and Devin."

The Princess glanced at them in acknowledgment, then addressed Milton. "I remember you… You were with the Gloucesters, weren't you?"

"Yes, indeed. I was, Your Royal Highness. I'm Milton Keane. I was with the Gloucesters for two years until I moved to the States. I'm here on a short visit."

"Very nice! Enjoy your stay!" she said. Without a word she tilted her head ever so slightly, looked at Devin and smiled again. Devin mirrored her gesture and remained silent.

"Ready, darling?" she asked young Prince William by her side. He nodded. She lowered her sunglasses and looked at the men one last time. "Bye, everyone!" She waived and walked away.

"Someone, please pinch me!" Devin burst out. "Was this one of my dreams or was it real?"

Milton shook his head. "Definitely real. But I just can't believe she remembered *me!* I'm so touched!"

"You're a good egg, Milton," said John. "You must have made an impression on her when you were with the Gloucesters."

"I suppose I did."

"I'm confused," Devin said, raising his hands out with a quizzical look. "If you were with the Gloucesters, how did you get to meet Diana?"

"She came to dinner with Charles and turned up in the kitchen unexpectedly. She said she wanted to thank the staff for making their lovely evening possible."

"She's known for doing that kind of thing," John said.

Milton patted Devin's shoulder. "Your stars must be aligned today Dev!" he said in a playful tone. "On your first visit to Kensington, you got to see Princess Diana and Prince William in person, and now we're off to a private tour of Princess Margaret's apartment. The chances of anything like this ever happening to anyone are nearly zero. But here you are!"

"I have a special type of magnetism," Devin kidded. "Not even Diana could resist me!"

Milton and John chuckled.

"Seriously, I'll never forget this. I also got to see how truly beautiful she is."

"Inside and out, really," said John. "She's kindhearted and caring, through and through."

"I can see that!"

"Come along now, chaps! Let's get a wriggle on," John said, standing up. "We've got another royal engagement to attend."

They quickly cleared the table and walked out.

Within minutes, Devin, Milton and John approached the front entrance of Princess Margaret's apartment. John stepped up to the landing and unlocked the door.

"Welcome to Apartment 1A, gentlemen!" he said, opening the door and motioning for Devin and Milton to come in.

"This is what you guys call an *apartment*?" Devin asked, as they walked into a grand entrance hall. "In my neck of the woods this would be considered a mansion."

"You're right," John responded. "The word 'apartment' to describe this type of housing unit can be rather confusing. In the UK, an apartment is a *flat*. But, the royal apartments at Kensington, or at any other royal palace, are nothing of the sort."

"I'm curious, how big is this place?"

"There are twenty rooms on four floors."

"Just for the Princess?"

"Well, she does have live-in staff. Just a handful, though. Then there's her children, who often spend the night here. They're all grown up now. But of course, I've known them since they were in their nappies."

"So how many royals live at Kensington Palace?"

"Quite a few. Charles and Diana and their two boys, William and Harry, Princess Margaret, the Duke and Duchess of Gloucester, their children, and the Duke's mother, Princess Alice."

"Amazing. All of them in one place."

"This is a sprawling compound. There's plenty of room for each of the royal households to have their own private homes, staff and security."

Following John's lead, Devin and Milton walked into a large room, immediately facing a long glass wall unit. John reached behind one of its ends and flipped a switch that lit it up inside, revealing an extraordinary display of pale blue blown glass.

"This is the Princess' Rene Lalique opalescent glass collection," John said. "Most pieces are precious gifts from family members and close acquaintances."

"Brilliant!" said Milton. "I don't remember seeing this the last time I was here."

"It's been around for a while. You must've missed it. It's got to be lit from within to fully appreciate its contents."

Devin stepped forward for a better look and tripped over a floor rug that was frayed at one edge.

"Oops! Sorry!"

"Don't be," John said. "It wasn't your fault. I should have warned you about how things work around here. She's reluctant to replace things just because they're old or wearing out." He pointed to a table lamp with no shade and a tattered pillow on a weathered armchair.

"Maybe that's why she keeps you around, old bean!" Milton quipped.

John's lips twitched into a half smile. "You're probably right about that!"

"It's odd, though," said Devin. "She clearly has the means."

Milton scoffed. "You people… It's her home! She does as she pleases."

As they walked into a formal dining room Devin spotted a large crystal ashtray overflowing with cigarette butts. Next to it, a single sheet of paper with a handwritten message in capital letters: *DO NOT TOUCH!!!* Each letter traced over and over in blue ink.

Devin stared, mouth agape. "Did the Princess write this?"

John nodded. "Oh yes… She resents my picking up after her."

"Why?"

"She claims I am constantly chasing after her waste. But of course, I'd be remiss if I didn't. Keeping her dining table neat and fresh is a part of my duties. Does this look neat to you? Right. It also smells like death!"

Milton cleared his throat. "But you still love her, don't you?"

"As long as we both shall live."

They laughed.

"Please come along," John said, starting up the steps of a wide staircase. "It's time for the cherry on the cake."

Moments later, they entered the Princess' bedchamber.

"Good God! I didn't expect this at all!" Milton said. "I bet not even her closest friends ever get a chance to venture this far."

"Certainly not," John responded. "This is a special treat for special friends."

"Thank you, John. We're grateful for your kindness."

Astonished, Devin gazed at the crest of an imposing four-post, canopied bed in the center of the room. "A true royal crib, I guess," he said.

"It's a Lit a la Polonaise," said John, nonchalantly.

Devin blinked. "Pardon me?"

"It's a just a fancy name for an extravagant style," John explained. "Notice the upholstery with fringes, cords and tassels. The swags of drapes on the sides are so long, they reach the floor."

"Awesome!" Devin gushed.

"I love the velvet comforters and pillows," said Milton. "I bet you could use them in your bedroom, Dev!"

"Sure! After I see Venus again and win the lotto!"

"It's all part of the style," John carried on. "Take a look at the foot of the bed. That gilded tiara at the canopy's trimming says it all, doesn't it? Could this be anything but a royal princess' bed?"

"You should ask Milton," said Devin. "He's a true savant when it comes to tiaras and princesses."

Milton smiled. "You know it! I picked you, didn't I, Your Highness?"

"So, what's the next surprise?" Devin asked. "I'm starting to get used to this, you know."

"There is one more thing…" John answered. He walked across the room toward a closed door and opened it.

Devin stared in awe as they stepped into the Princess' lavishly-appointed en-suite bathroom. "Wow! Unbelievable!"

Surrounding them, a room that bore a striking resemblance to a hall of mirrors. All the walls had been turned into reflective surfaces, creating an illusion of infinity in endless repetitions. Nestled in a corner, a gleaming oversized porcelain tub, pristine white, with graceful curves and gilded accents paid homage to the grandeur of a bygone era. Four golden lion's paws, meticulously cast in ornate bronze, supported it as if it were a throne.

"Fancy giving it a go?" John asked.

Baffled, Milton stopped. "You mean getting in the tub?"

"Trust me. It's a one-of-a-kind experience."

Just then, the front doorbell rang.

"Must be the florist. The weekly floral arrangements are due for delivery today. Please excuse me. I'll be back in a jiffy!" John walked out and hurried down the stairs.

"Go for it, Dev," Milton said. "I need to use the loo. I'll see where I can find one downstairs."

"Take your time. I'll be here."

Devin climbed into the tub, sat down and stared at the mirrored walls. Running his hands over the cool curving rims, he allowed himself to be cradled in the regal splendor. His reflection repeated itself into infinity making him feel light-headed and oddly drowsy. He closed his eyes and instantly heard bells ringing in the distance. Suddenly, everything around him became vivid and intense. Every sparkle, spot and speck of dust on every surface came into focus. Then, a mysterious force pulled him into one of the mirrors before him, his image liquefying and dissolving as he passed through it.

Deep darkness and silence followed.

Seconds later, the sounds of people chatting and pigeons cooing and flapping their wings prompted him to open his eyes. Blinded by sunlight, he squinted, straining to see what appeared to be statues lined up in a row, resting at the edge of a rooftop. Looming behind them, a colossal dome rose up to the sky with a cross at its apex.

A cathedral? He pressed his hand just above his eyebrows, his forehead warm and moist, as he attempted to shield his eyes from the light.

A familiar female voice resonated in the ether.

"Gio, my darling, are you all right?" He turned and looked at Sheina, her smiling face shining bright as she stood beside him. In the near distance, St. Peter's Basilica glowed in the blazing Roman sun. Around them, Piazza San Pietro bustled with life.

XXV. Baptism in Rome

S urrounded by blooming jasmines, Giovanni and Sheina sat in the shade of an umbrella on a terrace overlooking Piazza Farnese, at the Brigidine Sisters convent in Rome. Two glasses and a water pitcher on a small table between them sparkled in the mid-afternoon sun. Nearby, the convent's age-old bell tower stood tall and proud, its venerable walls thick with ivy.

Sheina relished the sweet floral scent around them as she watched Giovanni from under a flat straw hat, hands folded in her lap. With his legs crossed and his waistcoat partially unbuttoned, he read the headlines on a broadsheet.

"It appears the King of Prussia has decided to compel the peasants to grow a filthy root the Spaniards call *patata*," said Giovanni rubbing his beard.

"Heavens!" Sheina responded. "Whatever for?"

Giovanni put the paper down. "To replace bread, they say, which is becoming quite a luxury."

"In Prussia?"

"And in France, too! Louis XV has made it his mission to make a fancy treat out of this awful tuber. I would not be surprised if 1756 becomes the year people begin eating it everywhere."

"Ghastly tidings! Sometimes being unlettered feels like a blessing."

"Oh, no, no! The written word is wondrous, my dear! It shan't be long before you learn the alphabet. I hear the Mother Superior has been helpful in that regard."

"Indeed. Sister Agnes could not have been more supportive."

"Then, I am certain you shall be reading and writing in no time. Besides, you are gifted! You speak four tongues!"

"Fate bore me such gifts. I learned Chinese and Javanese from my birth family. Then Dutch and English from the Valckeniers."

"You fared well despite all odds. Who could boast of such exploits?"

"You could! Your command of English, Italian, French and Latin is remarkable."

Giovanni placed his hand over his heart. "We make a remarkable pair!"

A gleeful smile played on Sheina's face. "Truth is, preparing for baptism in the past two months has been a joy. I have gained so much in such a short time."

"Clearly, Sister Agnes has taken to you."

"And I to her. We're building a strong bond."

"I've been a witness to it."

"We are so different and yet so much alike. She's twice my age and hails from Sweden. Yet tragedy struck us both at a young age, making us orphans."

"How did such an awful occurrence befall her?"

"Her family perished in a great fire that destroyed Uppsala, her hometown. She was an infant then, but by the grace of God, she survived. Ever since, the Church nursed her and protected her."

"Is that how she wound up in Rome?"

"Verily. Her parish elders sought refuge for her at this very convent during her tender years."

A nun approached.

"Mi scusi. Per lei, Signore," she said, handing Giovanni a letter. He tore the seal and read it.

"Such a pleasant surprise!"

"A letter from your twins?"

"Not this time. This is from my dear friend, Lady Azzoni."

"The wife of Genoa's ambassador to London?"

Giovanni set the letter aside. "The *former* ambassador. The new Doge replaced him quite a while ago, but he and Arabella decided to remain in England."

"What tidings does the letter bring?"

"It appears my old chum and former colleague, Francesco Vanneschi, is in trouble."

"The man who brought you to England?"

"Aye. He was sacked from his post at the King's Theater, went bankrupt and landed at the Fleet. A recurrent theme among a select few..."

"Good Lord!"

"That's not all. Thomas Bambridge is also in hot water. A scandal, by the looks of it. The House of Commons has called for an inquiry to investigate complaints about the manner in which he runs the Fleet."

"Are you taken aback?"

"Not in the least! He is a dark and impious man. I can attest to that."

"Then this could be Divine Justice at work."

"Pray let it be so. Now, on to more pressing matters. "'Tis been two *months* since we arrived in Rome and we have not heard from my cousin."

"Patience, my dear Gio. Niccolo may be your kinsman, but he is also a Marquis and Genoa's envoy to the Pope. To him, our predicament may not be a priority."

"I am aware of that. As vexing as this delay may be, we must endure. I had hoped we would find someone in the clergy to bless our union by now. But it was not to be. And here we are. It took years before we could leave everything behind and make the journey to Rome. Now, we can only hope to be granted an audience and appeal to Niccolo to intervene on our behalf."

"You have always been steadfast that our wedding should be officiated by an ordained Catholic priest, and at a church, in public. Alas, we've been refused again and again with one excuse after another, none of which has ever made any sense to me."

"Or me! And yet, we've persevered and never lost sight of our goal. Our commitment to each other should be dignified and honored."

Sheina reached across the table and touched Giovanni's hand. "We must have faith, my darling."

"I do! I have placed mine in Niccolo. His letters alone restored my hope when I was growing weary. Remember, it was he who upon hearing of our engagement and our plan to come to Rome, offered to arrange our stay at the convent with the Brigidine Sisters."

"'Tis true. He also said the convent would serve as the ideal place for my conversion to the Catholic faith."

"Which put my mind at ease," Giovanni continued. "For I believed this was a sign he would come to our aid."

Sheina sighed. "I have prayed for this to come."

"We both have."

"Shall we get back inside? The sun is setting."

"Aye. 'Tis time." Giovanni folded the newssheet and rose. A ray of light glazed his face as he looked out at a giant ball of fire slowly sinking below the horizon.

A fortnight passed before the morning of Sheina's christening arrived. The couple stood next to each other by the open doors of the convent's modest chapel. Sheina gleamed in a white dress, her hair neatly tucked under a satin day cap with lace lappets gracefully falling on her shoulders.

Inside, white paper bows tied to the ends of each pew made a path on the nave leading to the altar. Around the baptismal font, fresh lilies had been woven into garlands.

"This stirs the heart," Sheina said, peeking inside the humble enclosure. "The Sisters made this happen in the blink of an eye."

Giovanni nodded. "They have been awfully kind to us, considering…"

"Sister Agnes says the convent has always embraced visiting pilgrims," Sheina responded. "'Tis a long-held tradition."

"We are beholden to them. They are aware we're an unmarried couple."

"We have been discreet and judicious. We stay in separate quarters and respect the house rules."

"And yet, they see us," said Giovanni. "They know."

"We have nothing to hide."

"Indeed not. Nothing at all."

"Yet, Sister Agnes probed me…," Sheina said quietly, lowering her head.

"Did she? When?"

"Not long after our arrival."

"You never mentioned it."

"She was keen to know if I…" Sheina paused and cleared her throat.

"Pray continue," Giovanni pressed on.

"She wanted to know if I had lost my innocence."

Suddenly, a stern look swept across Giovanni's face.

"How did you—?"

"—respond? I told the truth. I told her I had not. Yet, I avowed our deep affection for each other."

Placing his hand under her chin, Giovanni gently raised her head and gazed into her eyes.

"My sweet Sheina, we've honored each other since the moment we met. We are without sin. Now Sister Agnes is aware of it."

"You seem assured she approves of us."

"Why would she not? We're but two souls bonded by our sentiments for each other. The purest kind. All the same, we do not require her endorsement. Soon, my cousin shall make everything right."

A hopeful smile lit up Sheina's face. "Have I ever told you how much I admire the strength of your convictions?"

"And I, your poise and grace."

As the Sisters began filing into the chapel, Giovanni checked his pocket watch.

"'Tis time. Let us go in." They walked together to the front pew and took their seats across from the baptismal font.

"Sister Agnes should be here at any moment now," Sheina whispered.

Giovanni gazed at her adoringly as the morning sunlight streamed through a stained-glass window, casting a warm glow over her face. "You must be overjoyed, my dear," he said quietly. "A precious gift is about to be bestowed upon you."

She turned to him. "A kindness I intend to return by bringing myself into full communion with the Church."

"How do you mean?"

"I have decided to receive the next two sacraments. The Holy Eucharist and Confirmation. Sister Agnes said I could begin catechism while we await to hear from the Marquis."

"Sister Agnes seems to have plenty to say about so much..." Giovanni responded. "Did she mention how long it will take for you to prepare to receive the sacraments?"

"She did."

Giovanni leaned back and paused.

"Apologies, for I confess I am baffled," he said, his forehead creased. "Your devotion to the faith is virtuous. Yet, after all we have been through, I feel our commitment to our nuptials should come first."

"Pardon, my darling. Sister Agnes is here."

<hr>

Early the following morning, Giovanni sat by himself in the convent's courtyard. At its center a two-tier white marble fountain stood ready to bear witness to another day in the convent's long life. Transfixed by the gentle bubbling and dripping sounds of water, Giovanni gazed at the basin. A flash of lightening startled him. He looked up. Thick, dark clouds had started to move in.

A nun came up to him and spoke quietly. "The Mother Superior would like a word with you, Signor."

"Sister Agnes wishes to see *me?*" he said, rising.

"In her office chamber, if you please," the nun answered, her arm pointing to a door a few feet away.

Giovanni nodded. He walked up to the door and knocked.

"Entra!" Sister Agnes called. He opened the door and stepped into the room. A tall middle-aged woman rose from behind her desk, wearing a habit with a wool belt around her waist. A large corpus crucifix hung on the wall behind her next to an open window.

"Buon giorno, Impresario!"

Giovanni bowed. "And to you, Sister!"

"This just arrived," she said, handing him a letter. "From your kinsman, the Marquis. The footman from the embassy said it was urgent."

"Obliged." Giovanni opened the letter and read its contents. "I am delighted! At last, we have been granted an audience. It appears my cousin took immediate action upon hearing of Sheina's baptism. I presume it was you who apprised him of it."

"Indeed, 'twas me. I sent word, as he requested. You must be aware the Marquis and his wife, Lady Carlotta, are patrons of our convent and long-time acquaintances of mine."

"I am."

"They are the reason why you and Signorina Valckenier are staying here with us," Sister Agnes continued. "May I ask when you are expected at the embassy?"

"At one, this afternoon."

"So soon!"

"It appears so."

"I hope all goes well, then."

"I expect it shall, in which case, Sheina's catechism will be delayed until after our nuptials. In all likelihood, she will receive the sacraments long after we're gone."

A practiced, steady countenance met Giovanni's eyes. "I am aware of your sentiments for each other," Sister Agnes said.

"Are you?"

"Such affection is an all-pervading mystery, Impresario. I am also aware of your efforts and endeavors through the years to shield and protect the Signorina."

"Since the moment I laid eyes upon her."

"Then, *that* is something we share…"

"We are deeply grateful for your hospitality," Giovanni said. "You have been nothing but gracious and kind to us. We shall be ready for our departure as soon as our nuptials are behind us."

"As I said, I hope all goes well this afternoon…," Sister Agnes repeated in a sober tone.

"I shall apprise Sheina of the auspicious tidings, so she may ready herself for your audience. I bid you a good day, Impresario."

"Much obliged, Mother Superior," Giovanni responded. He bowed and exited the room.

Thunder rumbled as Giovanni and Sheina stepped off the carriage that brought them to Genoa's Embassy to the Papal States. A footman greeted the couple at the entrance and led them to the audience chamber.

"You look radiant, my dear!" Giovanni said, beaming. "My cousin shall be dazzled by my beautiful young princess from Batavia."

"As ever, your compliments are charming, my darling Gio. Yet, I know better. I'm aged over thirty-one and a mere shadow of my former self."

They walked into the chamber, Sheina one step behind Giovanni, and advanced toward the front of the room. There, a middle-aged couple in fancy robes sat next to each other under a red canopy supported by four wooden pillars. Two guards stood behind them. To their right, the Standard of the Republic of Genoa, and to their left, its Coat of Arms.

As Giovanni and Sheina approached, Giovanni removed his tricorn and bowed while Sheina curtsied.

"Benvenuto mio caro cugino!" Niccolo said as he and his wife arose. He walked over to Giovanni and embraced him.

"'Tis good to see you, Niccolo!" Taking his cousin's right hand, Giovanni bent on one knee and kissed the ruby on his ring.

"There is no need for protocol, cousin. We are family. I'm sure you remember Carlotta," he said, indicating the woman standing behind him.

"Most assuredly! Your lovely wife!"

She nodded.

Taking no notice of Sheina, Niccolo and Carlotta stepped back and returned to their seats.

"This is Signorina Sheina Valckenier, my betrothed," Giovanni said, turning to her, standing behind him.

"I am aware," Niccolo responded, looking in Sheina's direction without any sign of acknowledgment.

Wide eyed, Lady Carlotta leaned into her husband and whispered in his ear. "Were you aware of this? I had no notion. I thought she was a servant! How audacious of him to bring her with him!"

"Hush!" Niccolo responded, his attention quickly returning to Giovanni. "'Tis been a long time since we last saw each other, cousin."

"Since 1745, as I recall. Eleven years past. I had lost my Antonia, and my new life in the theater had just begun."

"Of course. You were on our books till then. You had been with us a lifetime."

"I was aged but twelve when my father brought me to uncle Pietro, your dear *papà*."

"We were so young," said Niccolo. "I am aged sixty now, and you?"

"Fifty-six, and eternally obliged to you for your goodwill and generosity during all these years. In truth, I would have been at a loss without your helping hand."

"*My* helping hand?"

"Aye. The bailout from the Fleet and the King's pardon. All due to your graciousness!"

Thunder boomed like cannon fire echoing around the hall. Pouring rain followed.

"The Fleet? What pardon?"

"Surely, you must recall. I had found myself in dire straits and… The Ambassador to London, the Lord Renato Azzoni, forwarded my correspondence to you."

"He did? I fail to recollect ever receiving any such dispatch."

"You jest."

"I certainly do not."

Giovanni's face turned pale.

Again, Lady Carlotta whispered in her husband's ear. "He seems unwell."

"Quiet!" Niccolo whispered back, eyes glaring. He faced Giovanni. "There is no folly here, cousin. No cause to fret. Someone must have bailed you out. Not me."

"Then who?"

"Someone in England, I presume. About that, only you would know."

Giovanni rubbed his temple, his mind whirling. "On reflection, there is someone I know…"

"Might I enquire who?"

"A fair lady. An admirer and supporter of the opera, with means and possessions aplenty."

"A noblewoman?"

"Indeed. Lady Arabella Azzoni, the Ambassador's wife and a dear acquaintance. Knowing her, she must have acted alone. Quietly, behind the scenes."

Niccolo chuckled. "All the while pretending to be me! A brilliant deception! She made the King of England believe that you, a foreign commoner, had the support of a high ranking official from the Republic of Genoa."

"I suppose so…" Giovanni responded, eyes lowered.

"Well, one thing is true, I did receive your letter announcing your visit to Rome. I understand you have been searching for a consecrated church where your nuptials could receive the blessings of an ordained priest."

"We have. Since our engagement in The Hague six years past. Alas, to no avail. No church there, in Amsterdam or in the Austrian Netherlands would indulge us."

"And not *here* either," Niccolo cut in. "There is *no* such church anywhere. And you know the reason. No church will ever approve of this inimitable union."

Giovanni shuddered. *Another nightmare?* He looked down, a cold sweat starting on his face. *Lord Almighty, shake off this noxious malady or strike me dead!*

Sheina's eyes welled up. "Pray let us take our leave, my dear," she pleaded quietly, clinging tightly to Giovanni's arm.

Niccolo carried on. "I could find clergy who may just do this for you, cousin. Privately, of course. And for a hefty price. But you are aware of this already."

Feeling a cold dagger thrust deep into his heart, Giovanni flinched, pain reverberating through his body. "I am. And I shall say no more. Good day to you," he said, jaws clenched as he bowed. He turned, took Sheina's hand, and led her out.

Breaking their long-established rules, they stepped out of the embassy still holding hands. For a moment, they stood together in silence as they watched the raindrops pelting the ground around them. The street seemed deserted, the world around them faded.

"All these years deluding myself into thinking my cousin had been there for me," said Giovanni, his face dripping. "I'm such a fool!"

Sheina leaned her head against his chest, feeling his heartbeat through the clothes plastered to his skin. Giovanni gazed down at her, tenderly pulling her in for a kiss.

"Best to forget who or what you thought you knew," Sheina said as they pulled away from each other.

"Aye. In truth, after today, I may no longer know what is real…"

———— >-☺-<————

In the days that followed, an uncomfortable silence fell between Sheina and Giovanni, each carrying the pain of knowing their day of reckoning could not be far. Sheina found sanctuary in prayer, while Giovanni sought comfort in long walks around the city parks, where he could breathe at ease and rest his mind.

A week after keeping their distance, their eyes met as they crossed paths in the convent's courtyard. Sheina gestured gracefully, bidding Giovanni to accompany her. Quietly, they strolled out of the convent toward Piazza Farnese. There, nestled in the greenery, they found a bench where they could share their thoughts away from curious eyes and ears.

Gently taking Giovanni's hands, Sheina held them together on her lap. "I've been reflecting…" she said softly. Dappled sunlight filtered through the leaves, caressing their faces.

"As have I," Giovanni responded.

"This is God's will," she continued.

Giovanni's eyes lit up. "I have no doubt. His will is clear. The Lord calls upon us to carry on! Besides, we have no choice. Our resources have dwindled down to nothing. We must return. I received word from Filippo. The troupe is now in Turin."

"Not that," said Sheina.

"Then what?"

"I shall remain in Rome."

"What say you, my dear? Your words elude my grasp."

"Sister Agnes made a most gracious proposal, and I have accepted it."

"What proposal?"

"That I stay at the convent and take the sacraments."

"Then what? Become a nun?"

"That is not *her* design."

"I see. 'Tis yours."

"Indeed. And my mind is made up. After much prayer and meditation, I have concluded I belong among the Sisters, doing the Lord's work."

"A confounding conclusion. What about us?"

"Our fondness for each other is true and real, my dear Gio," Sheina responded as tears began to flow. "Alas, so is the world we live in. It would be reckless to ignore this any longer. We've suffered long enough. We simply cannot go on pretending we're impervious to the scorn hurled at us at every turn and every time we're seen together."

Giovanni closed his eyes and breathed in. A voice arose from deep within him, carrying with it a sense of rightful indignation…

"Why give a care what those who scorn us say or do?" he said. "They cannot win! Our sentiments are pure and timeless. Our affection for each other shall endure!"

"And so it shall," Sheina responded. "In our hearts and through the ages."

"Clearly, I have failed you."

"Nonsense. You have not. Your purpose was to protect me, and that you did. When you proffered the safest of all havens for me. In your heart."

"A broken heart, now."

"The Lord shall provide a means for it to heal. Who knows? He may have had a different scheme for us all along."

"How do you mean?"

"Perhaps we met too soon. Perhaps our souls belong together in another place and time…"

"Do you believe we're not where we're supposed to be?"

"Who could say for certain? I entreat you to consider, if you may. If it is true we were created in the Lord's image, then wherefore are we imperfect?"

"Elucidate, my dear. Such thoughts evade me."

"I venture the Lord himself may be imperfect! In which case, a divine lapse every so often would not be so uncommon."

"A mystery, no doubt. And one I'd keep from Sister Agnes. But what now?"

"We carry on. As for me, I am resolved. I shall spend the rest of my days with the Sisters, serving the poor and the weak. I cannot forget I was once one of them, and not so long ago. I beseech you to think of me as I was when we first chanced upon each other, if just for a moment. And you shall see what I mean."

Giovanni closed his eyes as the wind murmured. Images of a younger and vulnerable Sheina on the Bredenhoft flashed through his mind. He recalled the horrible ordeals she endured as a child and how she rose above the pain to become the resilient young woman that he knew.

"I see you, my darling Sheina. I really do. You've grown stronger through the years and shall be stronger still. I expect Sister Agnes shall become like a true mother to you, and the Sisters, your family. I hope and pray that you shall find true happiness here in your new home."

Sheina nodded as she wiped her tears.

Giovanni continued. "One day, the pain of not having you beside me shall vanish, as it did once before, when my Antonia left me for eternity. For now, knowing you are safe and well provided for shall suffice."

"We shall write to each other," said Sheina. "Surely I will need the practice."

Giovanni wrestled to muster a smile. "We shall endeavor to maintain a steady correspondence," he said with tepid acquiescense.

"I promise you. I will."

"Something else," said Giovanni. Reaching into his coat pocket he pulled out a small blue velvet box and handed it to Sheina.

She opened it and gasped. Inside lay a round silver pendant, engraved with images of dragons and swallows.

"Precious!" she said, as she examined it.

"I had it made especially for you. From the lid of one of my favorite snuffboxes. I intended to gift it to you after our wedding."

"I shall treasure it, my darling Gio! It will serve as a reminder of our time together."

— ➤ ◉ ◄ —

The very next morning, Giovanni boarded a six-horse stagecoach packed with seven other passengers. The carriage lurched along the rutted roads that would take it to Turin. Nothing on the long and arduous journey assuaged the pain and grief lodged in the center of his chest.

As twilight approached, the coach made one last stop at an inn somewhere near the Duchy of Modena. Upon arrival, Giovanni spotted a copy of *Il Messagieri*, a newssheet, on the counter in the reception parlor. Someone had left it behind. He picked it up and took it with him to his chamber. Settled in and in bed for the night, he rested his back on the headboard and began reading it.

House of Commons Inquiry Ends with Jail for the Jailer! read a headline that caught his eye. As he went on reading, a sense of vindication overwhelmed him. His nemesis, Thomas Bambridge, had been publicly exposed:

> *Sufficient evidence was found indicating that through the years, as the Fleet's Warden, Bambridge willfully used his position to feather his own nest, permitted several inmates to escape, extorted money and stole prisoners' goods and charitable bequests, bribed or frightened the barristers who came to defend them, and committed torture and murder. As a result, he was dismissed from his office, arrested and imprisoned at the Fleet for a short time, after which he was tried. He was acquitted of the murder charges, but was found guilty of abuse.*

Giovanni pondered. *Curious fate… The fox got caught in the henhouse with feathers stuck to his chops. He got off easy!*

In time, Giovanni nodded off. The newssheet fell onto his lap as his mind began sinking to the bottom of a dark, watery pit. A timeless void engulfed him. He looked up and saw a ray of light piercing the water above. An irresistible magnetic energy pulled him toward it. He ascended faster and faster, clusters of tiny air bubbles rising alongside him, visible from the corners of his eyes. At last, he emerged. Out of breath, he gasped for air and opened his eyes to a bright and breezy day.

In the distance, a familiar voice beckoned: "Devin! Come on! Let's go! It's lunchtime!" His eyes clearing, he could see Milton standing on the shoreline, waving for him to come out of the water.

XXVI. SHARED DREAMS

A brief mid-morning break found Milton and Karen, Mrs. DeGrasse's perky young chef, chatting in the kitchen. A white orchid on a windowsill cast delicate shadows on the polished hardwood floors. The scent of freshly-brewed coffee lingered in the air.

Seated across from Karen at the kitchen island, Milton watched her tuck a loose red curl beneath her net cap, and lean against the countertop beside the range.

"So how long has it been with you and Devin?" she asked.

Milton crossed his fingers and smiled. "Almost four years now, and still going strong."

"Good for you! I'm not surprised. You guys really click."

"We do."

A timer beeped.

Karen put on a pair of mitts and pulled the oven door open. A wave of heat rolled out, bringing with it a delicious aroma that quickly filled the room.

Closing his eyes, Milton drew a deep breath. "Mmm-mmm! That smells amazing!"

"Wise words, Milton!" Karen responded. "If you seek a taste of heaven, befriend the cook." She took a baking pan out of the oven and carefully placed it on the stove to cool.

"Duly noted. Looks like I've just found my way to culinary bliss."

Karen removed her mitts, grabbed her mug and sat across from Milton. "You know," she said with a quick eye roll, "since Charlie and I moved in together, it's a miracle we haven't murdered each other."

"I don't know about Charlie, but you're a redhead," said Milton, grinning. "Your murderous tendencies come with your factory default settings."

They laughed.

"So how do you and Devin make it work?"

"Lots of hanky-panky."

"Come on! Be serious."

"I am. It's part of it. We also keep things light and fun. And, of course, we have our *baby*…"

"You mean your cabin in the Catskills?"

"Yes, our *Earth Angel*. That's what we call it. A shared dream, really."

"Sweet! You've had that for a while, haven't you?"

"Since 1986, when we got back from our first trip to England. We were looking for a place for our weekend getaways. We thought the Catskills would be perfect. Devin grew up there."

"How did you find it?"

"His parents knew a savvy local realtor. It was love at first sight."

Karen took a sip. "I've been to the Catskills. It's a special place."

"That's how we feel."

"Where is your cabin?"

"In the woods, on the slope of a mountain, near a tiny village called Pine Hill."

"Beautiful views, I bet."

"Oh yeah. And very peaceful. A great place to relax. We're there every weekend. Especially during the warmer months."

"Sounds like a paradise."

"To us, it is. Cookouts on the deck, swimming at the lake, and starry nights around the fire pit. Couldn't ask for more."

"A lake? Nice. I love to swim! Wink, wink."

"You and Charlie are welcome to join us anytime!"

"Just kidding! We wouldn't want your love nest to become a crime scene."

"Stop. I'll talk to Devin and we'll set something up."

"That's very kind of you, Milton." Karen rose, walked to the pantry, and retrieved a large Tupperware container from a cabinet. "Will you be there this weekend?"

"That's the plan. Devin should be picking me up around noon."

Karen began loading the Tupperware with the contents of the baking pan. "Do you guys like seafood lasagna?"

"Sure! Especially if *you* made it!" Milton replied, eyes on the food.

"Then you're welcome to it. It was supposed to be Mrs. DeGrasse's lunch, but she left a note saying she'd be out for the day. You know how she is. She won't have anything reheated."

"Yummy! Devin's gonna love it."

Karen put the lid on the container and placed it in the refrigerator.

"Thank you, Karen! I'll make sure I take it with me when I'm done."

"Enjoy! The weekend sure looks promising." She pointed toward the window overlooking Central Park.

Outside, the sun shone down on Manhattan's urban forest.

———➤◉◄———

A half hour past noon, Devin sat at the wheel with Milton riding shotgun as they crossed the Hudson to the New Jersey shore. A Pet Shop Boys tape played on the cassette deck of their new 1988 Dodge Shadow America.

Milton rolled down his window and took in the fresh, earthy scent of the woods along the Palisades Parkway. "All this green makes me feel lighter every time," he said, with a deep sigh.

"It's soothing," said Devin. "I love the city, but there's something about being surrounded by nature."

"You would say that, you sexy Catskills boy."

Devin faced Milton and winked. "You got my number, baby!"

A few miles down the road, Milton glanced at the clock on the dashboard. "Are we stopping for a bite somewhere? I'm peckish. Don't ask me why but I'm craving chips."

"You, french fries? An au gratin potato kinda guy?"

"No, not *puh TAY tow* but *puh TAH tow*."

"We're in America, Mister! Here we say *puh TAY tow!*"

"Sure! And the word potato is spelled with an *e* at the end, right?"

"What?"

"Didn't the Vice President say that to a sixth-grader on national TV just a few days ago?"

"You're right. But that was Dan Quayle's potato, on a day that will live in infamy."

Milton laughed.

Seeing a sign for a rest area, Devin took the ramp and pulled into a parking lot. "You know, you got me thinking…" he said, echoes of words from a dream about kings, peasants and a filthy tuber whirling in his head. "I'm also up for french fries."

"Must be my bewitching charms working on you!"

After a couple hours driving on the interstate followed by a swim at the lake, Devin and Milton settled into their cabin.

Sitting in the shade of an umbrella on the sundeck, Devin watched Milton through the kitchen's open glass doors. "The water was so cold and dark today," he said. He lifted a pitcher from the table and poured himself a glass of fresh lemonade.

"You were out there for a while," Milton responded, carefully loading their lunch onto two plates.

"It was amazing. It totally re-energized me."

"Good! I hope it also made you hungry," said Milton, placing a plate into the microwave.

"We've got a big lunch today."

"I'm always hungry. What is that? It looks yummy."

"Seafood lasagna. Karen made it. I'm sure it's delicious."

Within minutes, Milton placed the dishes on the table and sat across from Devin. "All yours!" he said. "Bon appétit!"

"Thank you! What a feast!" Devin picked up a fork and helped himself to a mouthful. "Mmm… so good!"

"Karen is a master chef."

"No doubt."

"So, what does your after-work schedule look like next week? Mrs. DeGrasse is away for a few days. I was thinking we could do something special."

"Oh yeah? I thought we tried everything in the *Kama Sutra*."

"I'm serious. *The Barber of Seville* opens this week at the City Opera. I thought you might be interested."

"I'd love to see it. As long as it's not on Thursday. I have my session with Doctor Haverhill after I leave the office."

"Right. You never miss."

"You know how long it took me to sign up with him. I don't want to disappoint."

"Of course not. Is Penny still part of that?"

"You bet. She's been devoted to the project from day one."

"Long-term commitment. Must be working for her."

"I hope so. We haven't talked about it in a while. Our schedules don't mesh. But I'm sure she's gone much further with it than I have."

"At least you've been keeping your journal."

"Sort of. I haven't had much to write about lately."

"Don't you need to share your entries for your sessions?"

"Yes. But that's only part of what's required."

"What else? The surveys?"

"Yeah. They use them to track our sleep habits and detect any additional details we might remember from our dreams."

"I get it. They're data vampires."

"Well, they need as much as they can get. They cross-reference everything and try to connect the dots. Doctor Haverhill says they're looking for patterns."

"What exactly are they trying to find out?"

"I guess they're trying to make sense out of all the fragmentary data they keep gathering."

"If you ask me, *The Barber of Seville* sounds like a lot more fun."

"You're right. Let's go ahead and get tickets. As long as it's not for Thursday."

"Will do. Now it's your turn to wash the dishes, sweetheart."

"Fine. I knew *that* was coming!"

>-©-<

The following Thursday evening, Devin headed for Doctor Haverhill's office. When he arrived, he found Penny sitting in the waiting area. "Lady Penny! What a surprise!"

She rose. "Look what the gorilla dragged in, like a lost piece of luggage!"

They hugged.

"Yep, that's me all right, a little beat up but definitely well-travelled," Devin said. "It's so nice to see you! What are you doing here tonight? Isn't your session on Fridays?"

"I had to switch this week. I'm babysitting for my sister. How have you guys been?"

"We're good! But you and I definitely need to catch up. It's been way too long."

"I'd love to! Are you and Milton still going upstate every weekend?"

"Religiously. We were there just last weekend."

"How was it?"

"Peaceful. The way we like it. How are you spending *your* weekends nowadays?"

"Oh, you know me. Always involved with one thing or another."

"I see you're still working on your journal." Devin pointed to a thick binder on her lap.

"*Religiously,*" she responded, playfully.

"Looks like you got an impressive record there, Penny. You could write a book, you know!"

She chuckled. "Maybe I will one day."

"Will you be doing the regression hypnotherapy tonight?" Devin asked.

"I did already. I was just taking a few notes before going home."

"How's it going lately with your sessions?"

"Can't complain. I've had great results, and they keep coming. Do you think you'll ever give it a try?"

"Maybe. I don't know," Devin answered, flashing a grin. "Could you turn me into a believer?"

"I can take a shot at it, if you like. Wanna go for a bite?"

"When?"

"Tonight, if you're free. I wouldn't mind waiting for you."

"Sure thing! My sessions are short."

"Great! I'll be right here when you're done."

A half hour later, Devin and Penny walked out onto Sixth Avenue bathing in the gentle hues of a waning summer evening. Around them, a vibrant scene unfolded: a mix of cars, taxis, buses and cyclists navigating the city's concrete canyons. Pedestrians strolled by, some pausing to watch a dancer showcase his talents under neon signs with a boom box blaring, skyscrapers towering overhead.

Devin stared at a food truck. "I got a hankering for a corndog. Sound good?"

Penny stopped. "What? Are you nuts? Do I look like a corn-fed Midwestern *dude* to you? Look at me! I'm a delicate Asian *flower* and you wanna feed me street food?"

"Oh my God! You're such a crybaby! Fine, let's find a restaurant somewhere."

"I'm kidding, you twerp! Of course, I'll have a corndog! I love them! It's sooo damn easy to get to you!"

"Smartass!"

After a quick stop at the food truck, they walked to nearby Washington Square Park and sat on a bench.

Devin popped open a can of ginger ale and pulled the corndog from a brown paper bag.

"Now please tell me everything about your hypnotherapy sessions with Doctor Haverhill," he said, then took a generous bite.

"They're fun!"

"Any big revelations?" Devin asked, still chewing.

"There's always something new that comes up."

"So, how does it work?"

Penny wiped her mouth with a napkin. "They're one-hour sessions. The focus is one dream from my journal at a time. During the first thirty minutes Doctor Haverhill guides me, through hypnosis, to go back in time to any particular word, image, or event of interest that he thinks needs to be examined. He encourages me to recall specific memories surrounding it, through targeted questions. Everything gets videotaped."

"Huh. Tell me more." Devin reached for his ginger ale.

"During the second half hour, we review the tape."

"Can anyone be hypnotized?"

"As long as they're willing. You just have to be open to suggestion. If you're not receptive, it probably won't work for you. At least, that's what Doctor Haverhill says."

"I know you've been doing this for a while now. Has it paid off? From our last phone conversations, you sounded like you had learned so much about the girl in your dreams."

"It's taking me a long time to piece it all together. And I'm not done yet. But yeah, in a nutshell, I found out she was a real flesh-and-blood person and her name was Sheena or Sheina."

Devin's face flushed. "*Sheina?* This is insane! I recognize that name…"

"What? How?"

"From *my own* dreams!"

"Are you kidding me? How does she fit into *your* dreams?"

"I know it makes no sense, but the name Sheina has come up in my journals."

"You never mentioned it before."

"Neither did you. I mean, this is the first time you told me her name. So what else did you find out about her?"

Penny took a sip from her soda can and cleared her throat. "First a recap. Sheina and at least one of her male siblings were rescued by a Dutch military officer named Valckenier during the massacre of 1740. He took them to live with his family as servants within the fortress in Batavia. You remember Batavia, don't you? Jakarta's Old City, from our trip to Indonesia?"

"How could I ever forget? Please go on."

"Years later, this officer retired and decided to move his family to South Africa. The ship they were on sank. Sheina and her brother apparently survived, but her adoptive family didn't."

"I remember we talked about this years ago," Devin said. "Didn't I tell you that one of her brothers must have made it alive? Otherwise, your last name would have never survived."

"Yes. And, it made sense. Still does. The thing is, there's hardly anything in my dreams about him."

"Even so, Sheina's brother would have been a Valckenier, and so you and your father would be his direct descendants."

"Exactly."

"Anything else you learned about Sheina?"

"I know she fell for someone significantly older than her. His name was *Gio*. Apparently, they were together for a while. Then, for some reason, they split up. That was an intense moment in her life. The last few sessions have been about what happened to her after that."

Devin shook his head. "This is so wacky... Do you realize that years ago, a psychic told me that *Gio* was the name of the guy in *my* dreams?"

"Oh yeah! That woman in Woodstock, right?"

"Yes. Venus. She was incredible. Actually, she said his name was *Giovanni*."

"Okay, this is insane! What's going on here?" Penny stood up and cast an intense gaze at Devin.

Devin shrugged. "I wish I knew!"

"It's funny," Penny sighed. "Sometimes I feel what I remember about Sheina are *her own* memories, not mine."

"I feel the same about Giovanni."

"No way in hell this is a fluke," said Penny, frowning. "We should share this with Doctor Haverhill."

"Wait, wait... What if we let *him* discover these connections on his own?"

"What do you mean?"

"We wait until I go through hypnotherapy myself."

"Oh, wow! I'm glad you finally made up your mind."

"So am I. Talking with you helped."

"What are friends for?" said Penny, breaking into a smile. "Now, I should get going. It's getting late."

"I'll walk you to the subway."

———————>-☉-<———————

A week later, Devin sat across from Doctor Haverhill at his office. A framed caricature of Sigmund Freud on the wall behind the doctor added a touch of playful charm to the décor. Wearing a pink tie, the famous psychiatrist peered out through matching eyeglasses, the words PINK FREUD superimposed on one of his renowned handwritten letters.

"New decorations?" said Devin, pointing and smiling.

"A gift from Wren for our wedding anniversary a few days ago. I love Pink Floyd. Anyway, she thought it was funny."

"Congratulations! And yes, it is funny." Devin leaned forward and took a close look at a photo on the doctor's desk. "And this?"

"That was taken at Epcot just recently. We were celebrating Eric's birthday."

"Your older son."

"Yes, he turned fifteen."

"I remember when I was his age and still haunted by my dreams."

"Must have been tough."

Devin nodded. "It was. I had so many questions and nobody to talk to."

"I believe you."

"And I never stopped wondering about certain things…"

"I know. All those recurring images you describe in your journal."

"I've been seeing them ever since I was a child. But then, there's so much more… I was wondering if maybe regression hypnotherapy could help."

Doctor Haverhill stared, an incredulous look on his face. "Why now, Devin? It's been a while since I offered."

"I wasn't up to it. Then, for a long time, I thought maybe I could just move on."

"What changed?"

"I need to know why I see these things, and if they're real."

"Fair. But, are you prepared for what you may find out? Often what comes out of hypnotherapy is unexpected. Sometimes, even traumatic. Are you sure you're willing to accept the risks?"

"I am."

The doctor proceeded to go over the protocols, then gave Devin a form. "I need you to sign this before we can begin," he said. "It's a consent agreement. We will be videotaping the sessions. Is that okay with you?"

"Of course." Devin filled out the form, signed it and handed it back.

"Thank you, Devin. Would you like to start today?"

"Sure."

"Okay. Let's move to the therapy couch."

Devin lay on the couch while the doctor set up a videotape recorder on a tripod stand. He then connected the recorder to a monitor on a coffee table next to the couch. "Perfect. We're ready," he said. He aimed the camera lens at Devin and took a seat. "Let's get started. I see you brought your journal. Let's pick a target for today's session. Your choice."

"Okay, hm… My freshman year in college. I was experimenting with psychedelics."

"Your roommate introduced you to mescaline, correct?"

"LSD."

"Remind me, what was your roommate's name?"

"Matt. Matt Shultz."

"Okay, now close your eyes and relax."

The doctor walked up to the tripod stand, pressed the RECORD button and sat down in an armchair next to the couch.

"Now that your eyes are closed, you're becoming more and more relaxed. You're so comfy, you're starting to feel a bit drowsy, a bit sleepy, and you begin to drift. Focus on the sound of my voice as I start counting down. Slowly, with each number you hear, you will let yourself fall deeper and deeper into sleep. Yet, you will be able to hear me and respond. Ten, nine, eight, seven, six, five, four, three, two, and… one."

The doctor paused for a moment, then continued. "Can you hear me, Devin?"

"Yes, I can."

"You are now with Matt, your roommate in the dorms."

"Yes."

"You have taken a powerful drug and you're starting to feel its effects."

"Yes, I feel that…"

"What happens next, Devin? Tell me what you see."

Thirty minutes later Devin opened his eyes and sat up. "How did I do?"

"Let me show you." The doctor turned on the monitor on the coffee table and played the tape.

Over the next half hour Devin heard himself narrating the beginning of an incredible tale that placed him in the year 1750.

"Could this be real, Doc? I'm not sure what to make of it."

"Your account of what occurred points to at least two possible scenarios. You either have an extremely fertile subconscious or we may have something substantial here. We've only examined *one* of your entries under hypnosis. We still have a long way to go. We must assess and evaluate all of the data we can before we construct a theory."

"Is there a chance I actually travelled to the past?" Devin insisted.

"As I recall, when I first met you and Penny years ago, I mentioned that there are theorists who have suggested there may be a number of parallel worlds or dimensions that interact with each other by allowing energy to pass between them."

"Just energy?"

"*Everything* is energy, Devin. We know this. It's a scientific fact. Every cell in every organism is energy, and every speck of dust in the universe is energy. So, hypothetically, conscious entities like us could come in and out of different worlds and communicate with each other. But of course, it's all speculation at this point."

"Still a fascinating concept, Doc. But what would that mean, though? What if it's true?"

XXVII. TEMPUS FUGIT

S ix weeks of regression hypnotherapy had wrought a profound impact on Devin. Fragments of elusive memories scribbled on the pages of his dreams journal had unfolded into richly detailed oral narratives. The veil of his early childhood visions had finally lifted, and the dreaded shadows behind it had vanished, revealing a world strangely familiar.

Reviewing the videotapes at the end of every session filled Devin with a sense of vindication every time. "It feels good to know my 'silly dreams' were always real," he told Doctor Haverhill as he prepared to leave his office on a balmy Thursday evening in late September.

The Doctor stopped him. "About that… Can you spare a few more minutes?"

"Sure. Is everything okay?"

"Of course. Nothing to worry about. Let's sit at my desk." He motioned for Devin to follow.

They sat across from each other.

The doctor cleared his throat. "The extent and quality of the material you have produced under hypnosis is staggering," he said. "It's an overwhelming task for just one person."

"Are you giving up on me, Doc?"

"On the contrary. I'm only saying I can no longer manage this all by myself. At this point, I think calling in my colleagues to join us would be helpful."

"How do you mean?"

"They would act as advisors and assist me in conducting an in-depth analysis of all the data. They could help me discern facts from fantasies, and filter every detail that's being put on the record."

"Oh… So, you're skeptical. You think I made all this up?"

"No one is questioning your integrity, Devin. All this information was obtained while you were in a hypnotic trance. Of course, I believe you!"

"But you used the word *fantasies,* and frankly, that's offensive to me. I heard plenty of that kind of talk when I was a child. They said I suffered from nightmares and hallucinations, and shut me down."

"I'm sorry. I apologize. I used the wrong word. Please believe me, Devin, I don't mean to offend. Still, the fact is, dreams are complex mental structures made up of all kinds of things, including images, sounds, and emotions that most of the time make no sense at all. Our subconscious can and will play tricks on us."

"*Tricks?* Like what?"

"There may be people and situations in your dreams that represent something very different from what you think they are. Take Thomas Bambridge, for instance. I looked him up, and in fact, there *was* a warden by that name at the Fleet Penitentiary. He was a real person, but he was *not* present at the time your Giovanni was imprisoned there."

"He wasn't?"

"No. You must've picked up what you knew about him from books you read, or things you heard when you visited England with your family in your late teens. You mentioned you were in a neighborhood where a prison used to be, and you heard stories about what went on in there. Or then again, it could be something else."

"Are you suggesting I subconsciously incorporated Bambridge into my dreams?"

"It's possible. Bambridge and his dungeons could represent your own worst fears. But we don't know that for sure. And we don't have time to get into it just now."

"I see your point. I'm sorry I overreacted."

"It's okay. At this stage, we just want to make sure we know which parts of your story jibe with the historical records and which don't, that's all." He opened a drawer and started rummaging through files. "Ah… here it is." He pulled out a piece of paper and handed it to Devin.

"A Liability Release Form? What for?"

"It states that you grant me and three senior members of my staff permission to examine all data gathered during our sessions. Please take your time to review it carefully. If you agree with the terms, from now on we will conduct this research collectively."

Devin read the document and paused. "What exactly is this liability?"

"After signing, you'll be unable to file a lawsuit against us for using confidential data obtained during our sessions for research purposes."

"I'd never do that anyway, Doc."

"I know that. This is just protocol."

"Who are the staff members who will be part of this?"

"You probably know them already. They work at the office."

"Fine. It's all good, then." Devin signed the form and handed it back.

"Thank you, Devin. I'll make you a copy for your records." The doctor rose, walked over to a Xerox machine just outside his office and returned with a manila envelope. "Here you go," he said. "See you next week?"

"Sorry Doctor, I meant to tell you I won't be able to make it next week. A dear friend of mine will be in the city for a few hours on Thursday, and I'll be hosting a small gathering to welcome her."

"No problem, Devin. We'll see you in two weeks then. Enjoy your friend's visit!"

"Thank you, Doc!"

————⟩-☻-⟨————

A week passed, marked by the steady rhythm of daily routines, until Thursday evening rolled in and the doorbell rang at Devin's apartment on the East Side.

"She's heeere!" Devin shouted, dashing to the door.

Drinks in hand, Milton and Penny sat on a couch in the living room. Before them was a coffee table with a tempting array of appetizers and an uncorked bottle of wine.

Devin opened the door. Stella Hayes stood in the hallway holding a bottle of champagne.

"Welcome to the Big Apple, Miss Ottawa! Come on in!" Devin threw his arms around her, embracing her warmly. "You look great! I love the longer hair!"

"Thanks, gorgeous! It's so good to see you!"

"Same here! It's been way too long!"

"Here, sweetie!" she said, handing him the champagne. "I saw this at the duty-free at the airport and thought we might enjoy it."

"Oh my God! *Cristal!* Class-y!" Devin gushed as he read the label. "Thank you so much!"

"Well, we have much to celebrate," she responded as she began to take her coat off. "Nine years of friendship. Time flies!"

"You're right. *Tempus fugit.* Let me take your coat. We'll let this chill for a while and savor it after dinner." Devin hung Stella's coat, quickly stepped into the kitchen to put the champagne in an ice bucket and rejoined her. "Please come meet Milton and Penny," he said. "I wanted this to be a surprise. That's why I didn't tell you they'd be here tonight."

Stella followed Devin into the living room. "What an honor! I finally get to meet the marvelous *Sir* Milton and *Lady* Penny in person?"

Milton rose to greet her. "I feel like I know you already, Stella!" he said, giving her a quick kiss on each cheek. "I've heard so much about you."

"As have I!" said Penny, also rising.

"I know what you mean!" Stella responded. "Devin has always kept me in the know about who's who in his inner circle."

Devin's lips curved into a gentle smile. "And you, Doctor Hayes, happen to be a significant who in *my* circle!" he said. He turned to Milton. "Did you know we have *two* doctors in the house tonight? Both these honorable ladies completed their PhDs years ago."

Milton bowed to them in an exaggerated gesture. "Congratulations, ladies! By the way, I'll have you know, I received my PhD in fabulosity ages ago!"

They laughed.

Milton lifted the wine on the table and pointed it at Stella. "A glass of wine for our esteemed guest? It's a Bordeaux."

"Absolutely! Much obliged, Sir Milton!"

Milton poured and handed her the glass.

"Anyone need a top off? This bottle is nearly finished." No one took the offer. He poured himself the rest and took a sip.

Still standing, Stella's eyes wandered to the surrounding furnishings and decorations. "I love what you've done with this apartment, Devin. My goodness! Your taste is flawless!"

"Thanks, but this wasn't all me. Milton had a lot to do with it. He knows all about taste and style."

"That's positively delightful for you to say so, good sir!" said Milton, grinning. "But the truth is, over the years I picked up a few clues from my illustrious employers."

"Then both of you did a great job!" Stella said. "I expect your home upstate must be a palace."

"A rustic one," Milton responded, returning to his seat. "But charming. And after two years, still a work in progress."

"A labor of love," Devin said, eyes shifting to Milton.

Stella walked up to the living room window. "Oh, wow! What a view! The Empire State Building, no less!"

"Yeah, it's one of the perks here," Devin responded. "It compensates for the reduced living space."

He and Stella took their seats.

"So, how was your flight?" Devin asked.

"Short and sweet, as expected. You know, Ottawa is not that far."

"Where are you staying?"

"At the Empire Hotel across from Lincoln Center. Steps away from Fordham University. All paid for by Ottawa U, my employer."

"Awesome!"

"We have a joint project with them."

"With Fordham?"

"Yes. That's why they sent me here."

"And then you're off to Milan, I hear," Penny said. "How wonderful is that?"

"I'm looking forward to it. I'll be on my way there tomorrow, early in the morning."

"Fantastic!"

"It's also work-related. I'm attending a seminar."

"About?" Devin asked.

"The evolution of the theater in Europe during the Renaissance and beyond."

"That should be fun!"

"Yes. But not as much as being here with you and your friends. *This* is the highlight of my trip!"

"Can you see why I love this lady?" Devin said, looking at Milton and Penny, his hand on his heart.

"Speaking of friends, how are Ben and Donna doing?"

"Great! Still very much together. Visiting Meg in D. C. at the moment."

"I was sorry to hear about Hal. I know how much you cared for him."

"Yes…" Devin paused, eyes glistening. "That was a big blow. HIV has been merciless. I never expected he would be gone so fast."

"How old was he?"

"Forty, I believe. We met in '81 when he was thirty-three, and he passed back in March of this year. So, yeah, he was forty."

"Such a shame. So young."

Devin lowered his eyes. "Yes, *young*," he sighed. "Funny thing, I used to call him Grandma."

Milton patted Devin on the shoulder and rose. "Our lovely guests," he said, "please excuse us for a moment. There's food in the oven that requires our attention."

"Holler if you need me," Penny responded.

"Same here," said Stella. She then turned to Penny and winked. "Not that I can cook if my life depended on it."

Penny giggled.

Devin stood. "Thank you, ladies. We got this. Feel free to take your seats at the dining table whenever you're ready. We'll be serving dinner shortly."

Several minutes later, Devin and Milton walked into the dining area, each carrying a steaming tray of food.

"Wow! What have you been cooking, Milton?" Penny asked as the pair set the main dish, a gravy boat, and serving spoons on the table. "We *know* who the chef is around here."

Milton smiled. "Flattery will get you everywhere, Penny! You're now excused from helping with the dishes."

Everyone laughed.

"Now, about dinner…" Milton continued. "The main course is *Yorkshire Pudding*, a traditional British dish you may have heard about. Nothing fancy really, just popovers, beef, roasted potatoes, veggies and gravy."

Stella leaned in and eyed the food. "It smells delicious!"

"Thank you, ma'am!" said Milton. "You first." He handed Stella one of the serving spoons.

"That's very sweet of you," she responded.

As everyone settled down, Devin looked around the table. For a moment, he sensed a warm energy flowing in the air. A special rhythm had emerged from the lighthearted chatter and had turned into a hum, vibrating softly along some sort of timeless groove.

"How are your parents doing these days, Stella?" Devin asked. "I heard from my mom they were thinking of coming to visit next spring."

"Yes, that's the idea. By the way, it was lovely seeing yours when they came to Ottawa last summer."

"They said they had a blast."

"I'm not surprised. The four of them get along so well. And they love to travel."

"We take after them, don't we?" said Devin. "I can't wait for my next trip *anywhere*. I'm long overdue. My last one was to England with Milton, over three years ago."

"Come visit me in Ottawa! You know you're welcome anytime."

"Thank you. We'd love to. We'll have to catch you when you're at home, though. Look at you, travelling to Milan at this time of the year. And it's not your first time. You must be so excited."

"Well, it's not exactly a vacation."

"Right. So, what are you doing at this seminar? Will you be attending or giving lectures this time around?"

"Both. We're learning new things all the time, either way. I'll be training newbies on the latest techniques being used to verify the authenticity of Renaissance and Enlightenment-era documents."

"What kind of documents?"

"Mostly theater-related manuscripts about staging, costume design, musical instruments... You name it."

"Sounds like a plateful," said Penny. "How did you get into this line of research?"

"I've always been interested in the history of the theater. Particularly in Italy and France. It can be challenging sometimes, but fun."

"In that case," Devin jumped in, "I'm sure you'll want to see this."

Stella's eyes sparkled with curiosity. "See what?"

"Hang on." Devin dashed to the bedroom and returned with a folder in his hands. He pulled two carefully wrapped documents out of it and passed them to Stella. "A gift my parents brought me from Italy when they were there with your folks in 1984."

Stella gently unwrapped them. "Goodness! These look like the real McCoy," she said, holding a libretto and a pamphlet in her hands. "Rare finds. And in excellent condition."

"I thought you might be able to enlighten us a bit about the pamphlet," Devin said. "I have a general idea what it is, but you're the expert."

Stella held it up for scrutiny. "It's an ad for a play in a Turin theater in 1766. The company in charge of staging it was the *Commedia dell'Arte Crossa,* one of the Italian troupes that introduced comic opera to England and several cities in Northern Europe in the mid-1700s."

"Wow, that was quick! So, is *Crossa* a name? That's what my parents were told."

"Yes. It's the surname of the man who owned and managed the troupe."

"For sure?"

"Definitely. It's a well-documented fact. The academics who study this particular genre are very much aware who he was. His full name was *Giovanni Francis Crossa.*"

Suddenly the room fell silent. Devin and Penny stared at each other.

Baffled, Stella looked at them. "Did I say something wrong?"

"So, this *is* my Giovanni..." Devin said, his voice dropping. "The Giovanni in my dreams."

"Oh, right!" Stella said. "That psychic we saw in Woodstock years ago told you his name."

"Venus actually confirmed his *first* name," said Devin. "I had jotted it down in my journal well before we went to see her. She blew my mind! I had *never* shared this with anyone!"

Milton looked at Devin. "That psychic was one-of-a-kind," he said. "She was also right when she predicted you'd be meeting someone like me, wasn't she?"

"She sure was."

"What just happened here?" Stella asked. "Did I unwittingly become the key that unlocked some other kind of mystery?"

"I think you did!" said Devin smiling. "You confirmed that *Crossa* was Giovanni's *last* name! I wasn't really sure until now. What are the odds that these documents would end up in my hands?"

"Weird, to say the least," Penny broke in. "More so when you think the name *Giovanni* has a familiar ring to it for me too."

"I know! And then, there's Sheina," said Devin. "Another person who keeps showing up in *both* our dreams!"

Incredulous, Stella's eyes grew wide. "What???" she shrieked. "Are you two shitting me? You share *dreams* now?"

"It's a long story, Stella... I know it sounds incredible, but every word is true."

Penny nodded. "I wonder what Flora would say about all this?"

Stella blinked. "Flora?"

"A medium we met in Jakarta," Penny replied. "She was unbelievable."

"My guess is, both Flora and Venus would probably agree on this," said Devin. "Maybe everyone's dreams are connected at some level."

"Well, I think it's time we bring this to Doctor Haverhill," said Penny. "We now have solid evidence we're not making this up."

"I agree. We should fill him in the next time we see him."

"If I may, my lord and ladies," Milton interrupted. "I am certain nothing could top your amazing otherworldly revelations. Except, maybe dessert."

Penny sat up. "Something sweet! Yay! What is it Milton?"

"Eton Mess," he responded. "It's a surprise." He stood and walked into the kitchen.

"He does this all the time," said Devin with a wink. "He specializes in surprises."

Moments later Milton returned carrying the chilled bottle of champagne in one hand and a tray with four dessert cups piled high with a mix of meringue, strawberries and whipped cream.

"Sinful!" said Stella with a mischievous smile. "Now, *and* in 1766!"

"We're heathens! What can you expect?" Milton set the bottle and tray on the table. "Wait till you taste the strawberry sauce I drizzled all over these!" He turned to Devin. "Will you get the champagne flutes please, Dev?"

"I'm on it!"

Over dessert, Devin noticed Stella, spoon poised, rapt in thought. "Something on your mind, Miss Ottawa?" he asked.

"I was just wondering… Have you ever thought Giovanni and Sheina could somehow be yourselves in the past?"

"More than once," Devin replied.

"We've always considered reincarnation as a possibility," said Penny.

"What about *your* past life, Stella?" Devin asked. "I remember Venus telling you about a Charlotte Hayes…"

"Yes, she did. The high-class whore who hung out at the tavern near the jail. I never paid much attention to that. It's not like I ever dreamt about her or anything, like you guys have about Giovanni and Sheina."

"Well, if you're ever curious," Penny chimed in, "you may want to give regression hypnotherapy a try."

"Long shot. Maybe one day. What about you, Milton? You've been quiet about this. Do you think you had a past life?"

"Hmm… I never gave that a thought," he replied. "Then again, who knows? I could've been someone with close access to a king."

"A member of his privy council, no doubt!" Penny joked.

"No, no… More like the Groom of the Stool, the king's private parts wiper."

"Stop!" Devin shouted. "You were probably a royal fairy with a knack for making cupcakes."

Everyone laughed.

Milton rose and grabbed the unopened bottle of champagne. "On that whimsical note, may I propose a toast to both our past *and* current lives?"

Applause followed as Milton popped the cork and filled everyone's glasses.

"May our days be long, our friendships strong, and our hearts forever young!" he said, with glee. "Cheers!"

XXVIII. A Trance Within a Trance

S tanding by his office window as if perched inside a glass birdcage, Doctor Haverhill observed MacDougal Street below, dressed for the holidays. Bundled up with coats, scarves and hats, people walked along the frosty sidewalks as night fell early on the city. Lining the curb, vendors sold roasted nuts and trinkets opposite dazzling displays on storefront windows, restaurants and cafes. All around, the glow of Christmas lights floated like a magical veil, delicate and ethereal.

Doctor Haverhill took a quick look at his watch, picked up a folder from his desk and stepped out of the room. On his way to the conference room next door, he glanced over the festive décor. A miniature Christmas tree bedecked with sparkling ornaments and a dainty star topper graced a corner of the room. Tinsel garlands and holiday-themed decals were plastered on the walls. Light holiday music played in the background, the smell of spiced apple cider in the air.

"Great job with the decorations, Jasper!" the doctor said to a young assistant as he passed by his desk.

"Thank you, Doctor! I left a few sugary treats in the conference room. Goodies from the office party earlier. People brought so much."

Doctor Haverhill paused. "Very thoughtful of you!"

"Oh, and I heated some apple cider, too."

"Much appreciated!"

The doctor walked into the conference room. Two middle-aged men wearing sweaters and jeans and a younger woman in a jumpsuit sat at one end of a long table, chatting leisurely and sipping apple cider. Within arms' reach, chunks of chocolate fudge and cinnamon donuts teased their senses.

"Greetings everyone!" said Doctor Haverhill. He took a seat at the head of the table and opened his folder. Doctors Dennis Gault, William Woodruff and Ellie Atkinson greeted him with warm smiles and acknowledging nods.

"Did you forget today is Casual Friday?" asked Doctor Atkinson. "That plum jacket looks great on you, by the way. Very Christmassy." She picked up a donut and took a bite.

"Thank you, Ellie! We're going to see *The Nutcracker* tonight."

"Lucky you!"

"Wren got tickets for the whole family months ago. So, I'm committed to show up or face execution in the public square."

"Come on, Stephen! Your wife deserves a medal."

"She really does," he said smiling, then turned to Doctor Woodruff. "Bill, I believe it's your turn to take the minutes?"

"Yes, it is," Doctor Woodruff responded. He opened a brown leather portfolio, leafed through the notebook to the most recent entry and pulled out a pen.

"Thank you, Bill. Without further ado… This is the eighth time this panel has convened to review Devin Sharp's videotaped sessions. As usual, we have a full agenda. Today, however, in keeping with the holiday spirit, we should try to be as brief as possible with our individual feedback."

Everyone nodded.

"Our main goal remains to compare the content of Devin's videotaped sessions with the historical data we have been collecting through our own research. Is there anything we need to discuss before we view the most recent videotape?"

Doctor Atkinson raised her hand.

"Ellie?"

"Just a brief observation. We often equate consciousness with a sense of personal awareness and a feeling of ownership and control over our thoughts, actions and emotions. Since Freud's theory of the unconscious, the conventional view is that conscious awareness is, to a certain extent, determined by our subconscious. Yet, Devin's experiences, as evidenced by the data we've collected so far, seem to indicate that both conscious awareness and the subconscious coexist and often interact with each other within the mind-stream."

"Right," Doctor Woodruff responded. "In Devin's case, there seems to be a hyper- dynamic flux between the two levels. His subconscious seems to seep into conscious awareness often and consistently over time."

"So, how does this affect his memories?" asked Doctor Gault. "Do they become degraded over time because of this dynamic?"

"At this stage we can't be sure," Doctor Haverhill answered. "What we do know is that whether we're awake or asleep, our brains behave like non-stop video cameras, constantly registering everything that's occurring in our mind streams. All of our experiences are linked into sequences that are stored as episodic memories."

Doctor Atkinson jumped in. "Yes, but… We also know that our brains can register events that never happened."

"Unfortunately, that's true," said Doctor Haverhill.

"So how can we be certain that Devin's memories are reliable?"

"That is indeed a concern, Ellie. Decoding how he has been able to generate such intricate memories is a serious challenge. We cannot rule out the notion that countless possibilities may be available to the subconscious mind, including remote viewing and the ability to connect to higher states of awareness. But, we should also keep in mind that, *a priori*, every memory is subjective."

"That, plus the elephant in the room…" said Doctor Atkinson.

"You mean the issue of possible cross-contamination in Devin and Penny Valchenier's dream recollections?"

"Precisely. Shared dreaming is a highly unusual occurrence. Add to that a close personal connection, and a bias could render our data completely unreliable."

"Clearly, Devin and Penny's friendship is an issue. But, this is why we're here," said Doctor Haverhill. "Our mission is to discern what is objective and accurate about their narratives and what is not."

Doctor Woodruff raised his hand. "Just one more thing, if I may. While we have factual evidence provided by Penny that reflects a possible ancestral connection between her and Sheina, we have nothing of the sort linking Devin to Giovanni. How relevant is this to our research?"

Doctor Haverhill responded. "Our analysis of the data shows that genetic links are not prevalent in the accounts of individuals claiming to have a connection to past lives during hypnotherapy. Penny's case is an exception."

An hour later, the group had finished reviewing the contents of Devin's most recent videotaped session, and Doctor Haverhill was delivering his closing remarks.

"Human perception is essentially subjective, limited by our senses, and tainted by our emotions. Take sight for instance. We only see what we can see, and for the most part, what we want to see. Meantime, bats can see in the dark, butterflies can see ultraviolet light, and some snakes can see infrared. And we're not much better off when it comes to other senses. Dogs' sense of smell is 100,000 times more sensitive than ours. They can also hear sounds in frequencies that are imperceptible to humans. If other species see different realities than we do, then which one of them is true?"

"Maybe this is not a question of truth, but perspective," said Doctor Gault. "Devin and Penny's memories may be subjective like everyone else's, but that does not automatically invalidate them."

"Absolutely! That is exactly my view, Dennis," Doctor Haverhill responded rising from his seat. "Now, something's telling me we're all ready to head off to our holiday revels."

"Hear, hear!" said Doctor Gault.

They quickly gathered their belongings, bid each other goodnight and headed for the exit.

———————>⊙<———————

At the end of Devin's next hypnotherapy session, just before New Year's Eve, Doctor Haverhill briefed him on the panel's preliminary assessment of his progress. "First, you should know that our research team is very grateful for your contributions. We've learned so much in such a short time. It's truly astonishing. Our sessions are yielding enough data that we're now able to see patterns which explain some of the complexities of your experiences."

"What did you find out, Doc?"

"Let me give you a bit of context before we dive into the nitty gritty."

"Of course. Fill me in."

"Well, here it is: Everyone's dreams are concoctions of experiences, real and imagined. In that sense, yours are no different from anyone else's, except for the richness of detail. The quality and the extent of your recollections go far beyond anything my colleagues and I have ever seen. We've cross-referenced and checked the accuracy of most of the historical aspects that are central to your narrative, and nearly everything seems to fit."

"*Nearly* everything? What fits, and what doesn't?"

"Let's take Giovanni, for example. He was a real person, but not exactly the same individual that you have described."

"How do you mean?"

"You talk about a man who had been wronged. Yet, the historical accounts tell us quite a different story. As early as Giovanni's first season at the King's Theater, several London newspapers of the day reported growing public resentment toward him due to last-minute program changes, recurring delays, and inflated ticket prices for what were thought to be mediocre performances."

"Really?"

"That's right. Then, during the second season, things took a turn for the worse. Some of the principal singers left his troupe and rumors were rampant about his despotic management style. The papers referred to him as 'tyrannical and iniquitous' in the treatment of his subordinates."

"Hmm… So, he wasn't such a great guy after all," Devin said, lowering his head. "I'm disappointed."

"Apparently not. Then, one of his dancers filed a lawsuit against him sometime in the year 1749."

"Why?"

"Unpaid wages. Giovanni denied he was responsible, but a Court ordered him to pay 800 pounds to the plaintiff. He delayed meeting his legal obligations, which landed him in debtors' jail."

"Yikes!"

"In your narrative, Giovanni blamed someone by the name of David Garrick for his arrest and imprisonment at the Fleet."

"Was Garrick not involved at all?"

"There is nothing that points to his direct involvement. Giovanni must have known *about* him, but he might have never even met him in person."

"Seriously? Then why did he detest him?"

"We can only guess. At the time, Garrick was a well-known and respected actor and theater manager. An Englishman through and through. Well-to-do, and rather handsome by most accounts. On the other hand, Giovanni was described by the local press as an ill-mannered, snuff-addicted, and repulsive-looking foreign Papist. Do you think *that* might have made him resentful of someone like David Garrick?"

"Maybe. Then again, the fact is, Giovanni *was* different. People could have made assumptions about him based on his appearance, his accent, his lifestyle, and his religion. I know from personal experience that people who are different can fall victim to this type of prejudice."

"Are you saying Giovanni may have been a victim?"

"Possibly. For all we know, Garrick could have been the true source of that lawsuit. Bankrupting Giovanni and taking his troupe could have been his motive. That would've made sense. After all, Giovanni's company was Garrick's competition."

"That's true. It was."

"Then why would Giovanni *not* be resentful when he was being publicly maligned and humiliated?"

"You have a point there, Devin. We don't have all the facts."

"What about the other individuals mentioned in the videotapes? Do they check out?"

"Some do, and some don't. Vanneschi and all the members of Giovanni's troupe were clearly within his circle. Lord Fielding, the magistrate, and John

Cleland, his chamber mate at the Fleet, could have certainly had something to do with him in one way or another. Even some of the senior members of the English royal family, the Hanovers, may have had some contact with him, because of their connections to the theater."

"What about his powerful Dutch friend, Sir Richard Westerbeek?"

"There are no written records to prove or disprove that Giovanni had friends in high places who ever came to his rescue."

"Not even Niccolo or the Azzonis?"

"Niccolo Crossa was certainly Giovanni's cousin. He was also the King of Sardinia's Emissary to the Papal States for years. The Kingdom of Sardinia at the time included Genoa, Niccolo's ancestral home. However, we found no evidence that Niccolo and Giovanni were ever in contact. About the Azzonis, there was never a Genoan Embassy in London, although there may have been an official representative there. We just don't know."

"And, Sheina? Was she real?"

"She's an enigma," the Doctor replied.

"I can imagine why…" Devin responded, eyes wandering. "Sheina is in my dreams as well as Penny's."

"Yes, we now know this, Devin. The difference is that Penny figured out who Sheina was through years of research and hypnotherapy, long before you ever brought her up."

"Are there two Sheinas, then?"

"We don't think so. The details you and Penny provided about her have been nothing short of extraordinary. Everything you've told us fits perfectly. So, my colleagues and I have concluded that the Sheina in your narrative is the same person as Penny's Sheina. Nonetheless, it will be a while before we can explain the correlation."

"Are shared dreams common?"

"As far as we know, they're extremely rare."

"I've heard people say souls travel in clusters. Could it be that Penny and I are reincarnations of Sheina and Giovanni who keep finding each other in successive lifetimes?"

"I don't know about souls, Devin. I guess religions, spiritualists, and psychics are the experts on that subject. Although we are exploring areas outside the boundaries of mainstream science, our research remains based on the scientific method."

"So, what do you think is happening here, Doc?"

"Well, so far we've come up with two possible theories. The first one suggests that your memories are, in fact, Giovanni's memories *of himself*, whether they're real or not."

"Why would they *not* be real?"

"For several reasons. We all choose which memories we retain and which ones we discard or block out. It's a normal process. Then, some people create their own memories and use them to replace unwanted ones. This could well be what happened in Giovanni's case."

Devin frowned. "But how?"

"Well, say the papers were right and he was indeed a tyrant toward his employees. If he managed to block all that from his memory and replace it with a kinder version of himself, then *you* would not be aware of the former version, only the latter."

"I think I understand…"

"This theory implies that your consciousness becomes *his* every time you cross the threshold, and his becomes yours when you return. Another possibility would be that these inconsistencies are a product of random *distortions* that could occur every time energy travels between dimensions. I believe I mentioned this to you and Penny once before."

"Yes, you did. You also called them *disturbances*. But what exactly are they?"

"We're referring to events that, on the surface, could appear to be inconsequential. However, once they're set in motion, they could have rippling effects, causing much more significant changes to take place."

"Hmm… Like how?"

"Well, imagine that your presence in Giovanni's subconscious had somehow caused him *not* to board the Bredenhoft in Calais. In that scenario, he would have never met Sheina."

"I'm having a hard time wrapping my head around all this," Devin responded. "Which one of these theories do you believe is more likely to be right?"

"Honestly, I can't say. It's all conjecture at this stage. We just don't know enough yet. However, there's an experiment we're considering that could possibly shed some light…"

"An *experiment*?"

Doctor Haverhill's desk phone beeped, his direct line flashing. He pressed the button and picked up the handset. "Hello. Yes, sweetheart. I'm with a patient. Of course, I'll be there on time. Don't worry. See you soon." He returned the receiver to the cradle.

"Sorry, Devin. I had to take that. It was Wren. We have a dinner reservation at eight-thirty at Windows on the World."

"Of course, I understand. We can finish next week, if you like."

"Not at all. We have plenty of time. Let's continue."

"You were saying about an experiment you are considering," Devin said. "What's that about?"

"We're contemplating having you go through that rabbit hole or threshold you've described so often. But *in real time*. While you're under the effects of hypnosis."

"How? This doesn't happen at will. I've never had any control over it. It's always been a random thing. It happens when it happens."

"We're aware of that. Yet, we believe we could possibly induce a trance within a trance."

"What? What do you mean?"

"While under hypnosis, we would attempt to recreate the theta waves that we believe are crucial in prompting you to conjure up the portal on your own."

"Theta waves?"

"Yes. The soundwaves that you hear just before you drift into deep sleep."

"Oh yeah. I forgot that's what they're called. And then?"

"And then we hope you'd just go through it."

"The portal?"

"Yes. We have no guarantee that this will work. But if it does, we might have a chance to witness things *live*, while gathering data at a much faster rate."

"Sounds promising, but weird…"

"You can take your time to think about it. Nothing will take place without your full approval."

"Thank you, Doc!"

"There's one more thing I'd like to share with you."

"I'm with you."

"My colleagues recently dug up a compelling document confirming that Giovanni was in Milan in the year 1771. He would've been 71 at the time."

"What kind of document?"

"An excerpt from a handwritten letter by Leopold Mozart to his wife, dated February of that year. He mentions seeing the Impresario. In Milan."

"Mozart? The famous composer saw Giovanni?"

"Yes. Apparently, they knew each other. Mind you, Leopold is not to be confused with his son, the great Wolfgang Amadeus, who at the time was just fifteen."

Doctor Haverhill pulled a sheet of paper from a folder on his desk and began reading. "It says here that Leopold saw a scruffy Giovanni Crossa in the streets, wretchedly clad and begging alms. Yet, he was hardly sympathetic toward him. He wrote: *This is how God punishes cheats!*"

Devin stared.

"The last entry in your journal places Giovanni in Rome in 1756. Through our sessions, we learned what took place while he was there with Sheina. But we have nothing at all *after* that. Except for Mozart's letter. We're curious about what occurred between 1756 and 1771."

"Yeah, that's a fifteen-year blackout."

"Exactly. We also know nothing about Sheina's fate after Giovanni left Rome for Turin."

"What about Penny's recollections of her?"

"She hit a dead end a while ago. The last she could recall were minor events related to Sheina's stay at the convent. That's why earlier I referred to her as an *enigma*. The experiment we are proposing could reveal what happened to her."

"Well, even if it worked, I can't choose what year I land on, Doc."

"True. But by your own accounts, you consistently go back to the mid-1700s. The pattern is clear."

"So, if I do this, what are the risks?"

The doctor rubbed his temple. "Uh... Barring the distortions we've discussed, I would say none. Except for a few minor procedural details, everything should be just like it is during any another session."

"I trust you, Doc."

"I know you do. I promise you, we'll keep things safe. Every member of our advisory panel will be there, right next to you. If we notice anything unusual, we'll end the session immediately."

"Cool. I'm in."

———➤⊙◄———

On the first Thursday of the new year, Devin walked into Doctor Haverhill's office, where he and his colleagues were awaiting him. As usual, a video camera had been set up on a tripod stand across from the therapy couch.

"Please take a seat," said Doctor Haverhill softly.

Devin sat on the couch, leaned back and stretched his legs. "Is this for me?" he asked, glancing at a crystal wine glass half-filled with water set on an end table next to him.

"Yes, but it's not for drinking," the doctor replied. "Now, let's start getting you ready." He turned to Doctor Atkinson. "Ellie?"

Doctor Atkinson approached. "Okay, Devin," she said calmly, "Today we're going to do an EEG while you're under hypnosis." Using a special gel, she began attaching a number of small sticky patches on Devin's head. "These will help us monitor the electrical activity in your brain. The wires will transmit the signals."

Devin glanced at the monitor. "Good luck with that. I hope it won't explode."

She giggled. "Don't worry. It's all very safe."

When Doctor Atkinson finished wiring Devin's head, Doctor Gault wrapped an inflatable cuff around his upper arm. "This is to check your blood pressure," he said.

"How are you feeling, Devin?" asked Doctor Haverhill.

"I'm fine."

"Good! You know the drill. Please lie down, make yourself comfortable and close your eyes." He motioned his colleagues to turn on the ceiling fan and the videotape recorder. After everyone was seated, he continued. "Okay, Devin. Please focus on the sound of my voice and the humming of the ceiling fan above us."

Devin nodded, his hands folded and resting on his chest.

"Now that you're relaxed and at ease, you may begin to feel sleepy, slowly sinking into the couch, letting yourself go, deeper and deeper… At the count of one you will be completely asleep. Yet, you will still be able to hear and respond to me." He paused for a moment then continued at a slower pace. "Five… four… three… two… and… one. Can you hear me, Devin?"

"Yes."

"Where are you?"

"I'm here."

The doctor picked up the crystal wine glass that was on the table by the couch, stuck his index finger in the water, and began rubbing its rim with it. As the glass began to emit a soft sound wave, he resumed the questioning.

"Devin, what do you hear?"

"I hear a ringing tone."

"Take a moment to immerse yourself in the vibrations."

Timing himself while looking at his watch, the doctor paused again.

Fifteen seconds went by.

"Are you still here, Devin?"

"Yes."

"What do you see?"

"I see everything…"

"Please describe what you see."

"Your office, your desk, the plants by the window, you and your colleagues watching me… lying on the couch… down below."

Doctor Atkinson gasped. Doctors Woodruff and Gault glared at her, then turned their attention back to Devin.

"*Down below?*" Doctor Haverhill continued.

"Yes. I'm right above you."

"Do you see anything else in the room?"

"I do. I see… er… I—I see the eye of a twister, spinning and whirling."

"The eye of a *tornado?*"

"Yes. Flashing and shimmering, and… pulling me into it."

"Go to it, Devin. You're safe."

For a brief moment, the room fell silent.

"Devin?"

There was no response.

"He seems inert," said Doctor Woodruff. "Except for his eyes. They keep darting back and forth under his lids."

Doctor Haverhill checked Devin's heart rate and blood pressure. "Everything's fine. He's in deep sleep, in REM." He glanced at the EEG. "His brain is in high gear, though. There's lots of activity going on. He must be dreaming. We should wait."

Several minutes went by before Devin's face began to twitch.

"Seems like he's waking," Doctor Woodruff observed.

"Devin, can you hear me?" Doctor Haverhill asked.

His eyes still closed, his body motionless, a garbled stream of words slowly began to flow out of Devin's mouth: "It weighs a ton… Ascanto in Alba… It made no sense."

"He's incoherent," Doctor Gault said.

"He's still in a trance," Doctor Haverhill responded, leaning in. "Devin, this is Doctor Haverhill. If you can hear me, please respond."

At last, Devin responded: "I can hear you."

"Where are you?"

"I'm here. In your office."

"Please tell me what happened."

"I was at the Carignano."

"What is that?"

"A theater in Turin."

"What were you doing there?"

"I was backstage, about to leave. The curtains were drawn. No one was there. On my way out, I glanced at a large mirror among the props and saw a shadow. I was curious so I walked up to it to take a closer look."

"What was it?"

"It was me, I thought. Until I saw *his* necktie… That's when the wrinkles and the spots appeared on my face. And then, his beard."

"Who was it?"

"Giovanni. It's always *him*…"

"What about you? Where did *you* go?

"I guess I was still there, somewhere… I couldn't tell."

"And then? What happened next?"

"The same as usual. I lived his life, as *him*."

"What did you do?"

"I led the troupe. We travelled from town to town for years, as we had always done."

"Did you… I mean, did *he* ever go back to Rome?"

"There was nothing more that I desired! I longed to see my fair Sheina! But it was not to be. Sister Agnes forbade it. She offered to write to me on her behalf and I, foolishly, accepted."

"Did she write?"

"Once a year, twice at most. And only but a few words."

"What did she say?"

"She never veered from her account that my sweet Sheina had found her bliss in prayer, and in the service of the Lord. 'Twas clear to me then, that after we parted, life within the convent's walls was all she knew. Until she drew her final breath…"

"She died?"

"Aye. She ascended to heaven. That is what Sister Agnes said in her last letter."

"When? How?"

"In the midst of wintry slumber, in the year 1769. She was aged forty-four. *That* was the start of my unraveling. Having sworn off love and marriage, I was a wretch. I left the troupe in Turin, this time for good, and made my way to Milan."

"Why Milan?"

"I can't explain. I felt an urge. Perhaps, 'twas a call from destiny…"

"What did you do in Milan?"

"I was adrift, living in the streets, playing my flute for coins and begging alms, till—"

Silence hung in the air for a moment.

"Yes? Till what?"

"Until someone stole my flute, and then…"

Another pause.

"And?"

"And then, I *died*."

"*You* died? But you're alive! You're here!"

"Well, yes I am…"

"Then, how could you be dead?"

"My heart gave out on a bench at *Piazza del Duomo* in the late autumn. I had been there for a while, ill and in rags. Passersby would offer alms. It was too late. No one could save me. Not at that point. On my last day on earth, a whooshing sound awoke me. Falling leaves, I thought. But no, a cold wind had blown a newssheet that landed on my chest. I reached for it and tried to lift it. It weighed a ton. I struggled to read the headlines. *Ascanto in Alba* had opened in Milan to great acclaim. The composer, they said, was Wolfgang Mozart. It made no sense. He was aged but fifteen!"

Doctor Haverhill glanced at his watch, then looked at his colleagues.

Doctor Gault gave the hand signal: *Time out*.

Doctor Haverhill nodded, then proceeded with the last few questions. "Were you aware of your last few moments?"

"It all happened in a trice. One moment I was awake, and then I wasn't.

I heard my heart when it finally stopped beating. Then, it all went dark and silent. It could have been a second or a century. I wouldn't know. Then I heard a voice in the distance calling my name."

"Calling Giovanni?"

"No. Devin."

"Whose voice?"

"I believe it was yours. But I could not respond."

"Then what?"

"I felt a mighty force lifting me upward. I soared, then hovered for a moment above Giovanni's body. I looked down and saw his sightless eyes, still open. I gazed at him once more before the same twister that brought me there swept me away into the ether. Then suddenly, I was back here."

XXIX. 2043

L ike a proud African queen with a bright orange turban as her crown, Venus held court seated beneath a pergola on a large patio surrounded by flowerbeds brimming with purple spikes of catmint reaching for the sun. By her side, Devin and Luuk listened intently as a mellow summer breeze blew gently on their faces.

"In the end, is my beginning," Venus declared solemnly. Perched on her lap, De Groot, her Himalayan kitty, purred contentedly. "*That* was Mary Queen of Scots before her head rolled off the chopping block," she added, adjusting her gold-rimmed sunglasses.

"That sums it up!" said Devin. "We're stuck in some eternal rut."

"Well, in a way… The here and now is an instant that will last forever."

"No past or future?"

"Just in our minds. We're built to see the world as a sequence of events that our minds weave together as reality. But, in fact, everything is happening in a single moment."

"Ah! So, we're exceptional!" Flooding in, Devin saw his own reflection repeated into infinity on the mirrored walls of a royal bath chamber.

"Of course we are!" Venus raised her right arm and gestured in the direction of others who were seated on the patio. "For *them*, this is the end, or so they think. But we're like Mary Queen of Scots. We know our physical constraints are just illusions. *We,* have choices!" She gently stroked her teardrop amber pendant with one hand and petted De Groot with the other.

"Even in our sleep?"

"We are always awake, Devin. Especially, when we're deep inside our dreams."

"Oh, my dear Venus! Listening to you is so refreshing. Your visions rejuvenate me!"

"I'm glad they do."

"Truth is, at eighty-three, it's not too often I get to feel this way." Devin's eyes shifted toward the hum of a postal drone making its descent onto the rooftop of a nearby building.

"John, is that the post?"

"My name is Luuk. And yes, that's the mail."

"Then, we shall have Hawley fetch it for us. I am expecting a letter from Rome."

"What?"

"From Sister Agnes."

"Sister *who?* Please Devin, let's not do this."

"Do... Do what?"

"Never mind. We have a visitor," Luuk answered, indicating a fast approaching tall and slender middle-aged man in a business suit.

Moments later, the man stood by their table, his long black hair in a braided pony tail. "How's everyone doing today?" he asked with a smile.

"Great!" Luuk replied. "Thank you, Mr. Vanneschi!"

"It's lovely to see you all. Especially you two lovebirds on your special day," Vanneschi said, his gaze falling on Devin and Luuk. "Congratulations!"

Luuk beamed. "Much appreciated!"

Devin leaned toward Venus and whispered. "What is he saying?"

Venus took Devin's hand. "Don't you worry, sweetie. It's nothing."

"The nurses will be here soon with your afternoon pills," said Vanneschi. "See you at the party later. Have a great afternoon!" He smiled, nodded slightly and walked over to the next table.

Venus turned to Luuk. "I didn't know he worked on weekends."

"Me neither."

"He must be here for the special occasion."

"Probably. He's the Big Banana."

"He and Ms. Davis. They run this place."

"True. They're the top administrators."

"She's nothing like him, though."

"Right. No airs," Devin chimed in. "That silly pony tail of his... It's obvious he's trying to look younger than his age."

Luuk frowned. "Come on, Dev. We don't judge."

"I guess I should be going," Venus announced, placing De Groot in her pet carrier bag. "It's time to feed my furry friend here. Come on baby, momma has your favorite treat waiting for you at home. Sardines! I'll see you boys later!" She grabbed her cane, rose, and slowly walked away.

"Later!" Devin waved, as he and Luuk watched her probe her way forward in the distance.

"I'll never understand how that woman can get around with just that cane," said Luuk. "She's as blind as a bat. She should have a guide dog instead of a cat."

"She doesn't need one. She may be blind but she can see things better than anyone else. Anyway, what's with Mr. Vanneschi's *lovebirds* insinuation? Where the hell did he pick *that* up?"

"For heaven's sake, Devin! Not again. Not on our anniversary!"

Baffled, Devin grimaced. "*Our* anniversary?"

"Come on, Dev! We've been married forty years!"

"I'm—I'm sorry! I just—"

Luuk patted Devin on the shoulder. "I know, I know, my Sweet Pea. It just slipped your mind."

Within minutes, two nurses stood by Devin and Luuk's table. Embroidered on their green scrubs, the name of the establishment: *Thomas Bambridge Senior Living Community.*

Pinned directly below it, tags with their names and titles: Stella Hayes, RN and Penny Valckenier, CNA.

"Good afternoon, gentlemen!" said Stella, her green eyes sparkling. "Ready for your meds and blood pressure check?"

Running his hand through his thinning grey hair, Devin replied. "I'll wash my pills down with a porter, Miss. Extra stout, please."

"Oh Mr. Sharp, you're hilarious! Just so you know, Doctor Kessler will be dropping by to see you both later. Short visit, just to say hello."

"Thanks for the heads up," Luuk responded. He popped a pill, took a sip of water and swallowed.

"By the way, happy anniversary! We won't be able to make it tonight, but we left a little something for you on the gifts table. It's from both of us."

"So thoughtful of you, ladies!"

"You're most welcome, Mr. Westerbeek."

"Enjoy yourselves this evening!" said Penny, picking up the empty plastic cups on the table.

"Lovely girls," said Devin, watching the pair walk away. "What are their names?"

"You know who they are. Penny and Stella. They've been around for years."

"Yes, yes... Of course!" Devin responded with a muddled look on his face.

Seated at a table nearby, two ladies wearing fancy hats enjoyed chilled tea and assorted delicacies. A pair of leashed white mini poodles lay at their feet.

"Amelia, darling, I adore the vintage brooch you're wearing!" Mrs. DeGrasse told Dame Hanover, leaning forward to take a closer look. "It's a golden harp, isn't it?"

"Thank you, dear! Yes, it's an heirloom. One of my favorites." Lowering her sunglasses, Dame Hanover squinted as she strained to see in the distance. "Is that George coming in?"

Mrs. DeGrasse turned to look. "Yes, that's him."

"He looks good for his age, doesn't he?"

"How old is he?"

"Ninety-something. He's the most senior resident here." Dame Hanover replied. "You know, sometimes I can't help thinking of him as a father figure." She lifted a treat from a small serving saucer and took a nibble.

"Charming man. He seems so happy with his parakeets."

"He is! Caroline and Henrietta are gorgeous. And he adores them. Their cage is a royal palace!"

They giggled.

"Did you know that George used to be a coin dealer?" Dame Hanover asked.

"I figured. He has a thing for eighteenth-century Guineas. Last time at Bridge, he told everyone he keeps a number of them in a safe somewhere."

"I'd love to see them. Maybe one day he'll show them to us. He's a friend."

Mrs. DeGrasse took a napkin and gently wiped the corners of her mouth. "Speaking of friends, is Bella coming today?"

"Arabella? Yes, she said she would. She'll be taking an air cab this time."

"Isn't that a bit pricey?"

"She doesn't mind. She's tired of the hyperloop. She prefers the privacy of an air cab. It's also door-to-door and just fifteen minutes from Manhattan. Worth the price."

"When do you expect her to arrive?"

"She didn't say," Dame Hanover replied. "But she wants to get here before the party begins. Don't forget that today, she's more Devin and Luuk's guest than mine."

"I hear the Sunshine Committee did a wonderful job with the ballroom. Apparently, it's a red fairyland in there."

"Makes sense. It's their ruby wedding anniversary."

"Milton was very much involved," said Mrs. DeGrasse.

"I would expect so. He wouldn't fail them. He's not just the chef, you know."

"Absolutely. When duty calls, he becomes our special events coordinator extraordinaire. He did a great job organizing your last birthday party. The decorations and the food were superb. I'm sure he'll do the same for them. I just hope Venus keeps De Groot away. That stinky cat never fails to unsettle my poor little puppies. Garrick and Rousseau detest her!"

"You're right about the stink. She smells like tobacco. It's uncanny. Venus doesn't smoke."

"It must be something in the food. Who knows what that woman feeds it?"

"I know how much you adore your poodles, Julienne. But it's Devin and Luuk's party, so maybe this time you might consider keeping Garrick and Rousseau away?"

"Fat chance! This may be *their* anniversary, but it's also a community event and my pets have every right to be a part of it."

"Very well, I'll say no more," said Dame Hanover. She lifted the pitcher on the table, filled her glass, and took a sip. "Mmm… This strawberry basil iced tea is to die for! Ready for a top off?"

"No. Thank you, dear," Mrs. DeGrasse responded. "So, please remind me, how did Bella end up making friends with Devin and Luuk? Remember, I moved in here after they had already met."

"During one of her visits. She and I were having brunch in the dining room and Devin and Luuk happened to be at the table next to us. Devin kept staring at her. It was odd. After a while, he came over and introduced himself to her. He told Bella she reminded him of someone."

"Odd indeed. How did she react?"

"She told him she felt the same way about him. I was flabbergasted! Honestly, I thought she was flirting with him. They've been chums ever since."

"That's rather peculiar, isn't it? Those two have little in common."

"You'd be surprised…"

"Really? What do they talk about?"

"She says they talk about Niccolo."

"I believe it. She's constantly talking to *everyone* about him. Especially since he moved to Rome."

"Well, he's her only child. But there's more there than meets the eye, Julienne."

"What do you mean?"

"Arabella raised Nick to be a straight arrow. Even more so after her husband passed when he was just a child. She sent him to Catholic school, took him to Mass every Sunday, and so on. But, life is life… The fact is, he turned out to be a bit *different* from what she expected."

"How did he turn out?" Mrs. DeGrasse asked raising an eyebrow.

"Like Devin and Luuk. You know…"

One of Mrs. DeGrasse's poodles jumped on her lap, nose fixated on the crumbs at the edge of the table.

"You mean Nick is gay?"

"She never actually said it," Dame Hanover replied. "But it was in the air."

"She must've known all along. Mothers always know, Amelia."

"Here's the thing: Bella didn't *want* to know. There's a reason why she steered him into the priesthood."

"You think she did that on purpose?" asked Mrs. DeGrasse, ignoring Rousseau standing on her lap licking the table.

"I'm pretty sure."

"Well, we should not forget the world was quite a different place back then. People did such things. She must've thought it was a way to protect him. I mean, it was the perfect cover."

"True. But there was always the risk it could backfire."

"Did it? How old is Nick now? Forty? He could've changed course long ago."

"This is not just about Nick, my dear. I think Bella may have come to regret her role in encouraging him to take the cloth."

"Really? What makes you think so?"

"Ever since she met Devin and Luuk she began to see how things could have been different for him."

"In what way?"

"She witnessed firsthand their love and commitment to each other."

"Well, I'm sure she's also aware that Nick is a grown man and perfectly capable to make his own decisions."

"I hope so. She adores him and the feeling is mutual."

"Good! In the end, that's all that matters."

Back at Devin and Luuk's table, the couple was engaged in a recurrent squabble.

"Would you please quit ogling at Adam?" Devin complained.

Luuk made a face. "Hawley?"

"Yes, the groundskeeper. Every time he's around your eyes pop out of their sockets!"

"Look who's talking! You stare at Sheina whenever she's around!"

"Who's *Sheina?*"

"Don't play stupid. You know exactly who she is. The Asian cleaning lady. You make her uncomfortable."

"I'd never think of her that way. You're the one looking South. I keep a North view."

"Are you aware she's a married woman with five kids?"

"Bless her heart then! She's got a full plate. Anything else I should know about her?"

"Yes! Her husband Gio is a card-carrying member of *La Cosa Nostra*, and if you don't quit your nonsense, he'll have you whacked!"

They laughed.

"I happen to know Gio!" Devin said. "Sheina introduced me to him and her sister Flora on a day they came together to pick her up. Did you know he works as a stagehand at the Met?"

"There you go, then. You should know better!" Luuk said, wagging his index finger. "His wife should not be an object of your wandering eye!"

They laughed again.

A fit young man in a tight pair of jeans and a casual shirt rolled up at the sleeves approached with a food tray.

"Good afternoon, gentlemen," he said in a British accent. "And happy anniversary to you! Please excuse me." He set the tray on the table and stood before them, his short blond hair shining in the sun.

Luuk greeted him with a broad smile. "Hello, Milton! What are all these delights?"

"I've taken the liberty of preparing a few treats to kick off the celebrations on your special day. I hope you don't mind."

"Mind? You're kidding!" Devin responded. "It looks amazing!"

"Just a few tidbits, that's all. Please help yourselves."

"We appreciate the effort, Milton!" Luuk said. "What do we have here?"

"A little of everything: water boatman pâté spread, grilled mealworms with pureed russet apples, an arugula salad topped with roasted beetles drizzled in a citrusy lemon sauce, and a small basket of light and flaky handmade sourdough flatbread. Perfect for the pâté!"

"I'll have some pâté," Luuk said. "You, Devin?"

"Same, please."

Luuk lifted two empty saucers and a butter knife from the tray, placed a few pieces of bread on one of them and a generous portion of pâté on the other.

"Is that chocolate?" Devin asked, seeing a small bowl filled with dark brown sticks.

"They're California grasshoppers, covered in chocolate."

Devin sampled one. "Mmm… Yummy! You couldn't have picked healthier goodies, Milton!" he gushed, eyes admiring the athletic, gentle-mannered English chef.

"We've all had to learn to adjust to healthier diets, Mr. Sharp."

"I know what you mean. I was still working at the UN when we began urging people to shift to edible insects as a primary food source. Of course, no one paid much attention to us then. Not until the global droughts began and everything went the way of wilting petals."

"I was a child living in England then, but I remember my parents going on about it."

"Very sad indeed," said Luuk.

"Is there anything else I can offer you gentlemen?"

Devin reached for the chocolate grasshoppers. "Just a few more of these. Thank you."

"You're very welcome. Now, if you'll excuse me, I must keep moving. Enjoy!" He flashed a smile, picked up the tray and walked away.

"He's adorable, isn't he?" said Devin, eyes trailing Milton as he sauntered on to the next table.

Luuk scoffed. "Yes, he is. And you're a drooling old goat."

"Why? For stating the obvious? He's attractive and very charismatic." For a fraction of a second, an image flickered before Devin's eyes: A perfectly cooked omelet and a kind smile from a new acquaintance in the kitchen of a grand Fifth Avenue apartment.

"I was kidding. I knew what you meant. Look at him now, turning his magic on Julienne and Amelia."

"Those two should take lessons from him," Devin smirked. "They could use a bit more charm and shed some of their vanity."

"No need to be so harsh, Dev."

"Well, take Amelia, for instance. Is she actually a Dame, or did she give herself that title? 'Dame Hanover.' The nerve!"

"Why do you care? You know you outrank her. You're a Queen!"

Devin chuckled. "Very funny. Julienne, on the other hand, is actually quite classy. Did you see the oil painting she donated to the library?"

"Not another one of Garrick and Rousseau, I hope. No one can stand those dogs."

"No, no. This one is different. Some kinda UFO."

"Odd. Must be an old one. From the time before the *Big Disclosure*."

"Probably. People were still skeptical then."

"Not anymore," said Luuk, casting a gaze at a few thin clouds drifting languidly in the sky.

Devin reached for another chocolate. "I wonder if Amelia and Julienne will show up tonight."

"I'm sure they will! They'll sit among us mortals while fancying themselves feasting on Beluga caviar at Petrossian or the Russian Tea Room."

"Caviar? You have a long memory, Luuk! If only the Caspian Sea hadn't dried up…"

Luuk cast his sight toward the threshold ramps at the entrance to the patio. "Check it out. Bella's coming in!"

Devin turned to look. "The wonderful Arabella! I'm so glad she could make it."

"She definitely has an aura about her. Remember a few years back when she helped Mr. Vanneschi organize a day trip to Woodstock?"

"Vaguely."

"She brought along her son Niccolo, the priest. So handsome."

For a moment, Devin closed his eyes, fingertips rubbing his temples. "Of course I am aware who the lady is! A dear friend and a great personage. Lady Azzoni, the wife of the Ambassador."

"Oh, sweet mother of pearl! Here you go again, speaking in tongues. Please, Devin, let's focus. Did you ever hear from your family? Will they be joining us later?"

Devin shook his head. "Um… I'm not sure. We haven't seen each other since Kyle's funeral. She's eighty-seven now, you know. Must not be easy without him."

"Kyle passed away five years ago, Devin. Abbey has been living with Meg in the city, remember? She's doing fine."

"Oh, right… She's with Meg, my lovely niece. She must be in her sixties now."

"Yes, she is. Now about Paige and Frank…"

"I don't expect them to show up, Milton. They're in Kingston. Too far to drive."

"Milton?"

"What's wrong?"

"You called me *Milton* again! You keep doing this!"

"Sorry! I didn't mean to!"

Luuk drew a deep breath and sighed. "About Paige and Frank, they might still come. We mailed everyone the invitations."

"Then if they come, they come. What about your brother? Will he be here?"

"Richard is here already. He flew in this morning from The Hague. He made it in two hours to JFK. Hypersonic jets. Incredible."

"Is he staying the night?"

"Yes, at a hotel nearby."

"Can't wait to see him."

Moments later, a bulky, rosy-cheeked, middle-aged man with grey bushy sideburns walked over to Devin and Luuk's table.

"Hello there! Happy, happy to you both!" he said, blue eyes smiling over thick-rimmed glasses. "Ready to let the good times roll?"

"You bet!" Luuk responded. "Thank you, Doctor Kessler!"

"All's well otherwise, I gather?"

"Tip-top!" Devin replied.

"Super! How are you doing with your new prescription, Mr. Sharp?"

"Better. My memory's coming back."

"Good, good! Anything specific you'd like to share?"

"Hmm… Yeah. Actually, just yesterday while playing cards with John and Henry, I remembered John used to be a hairdresser and Henry a lawyer."

"You mean, Mr. John Cleland and Mr. Henry Fielding?" the doctor asked, discreetly glancing at their table.

"Yes. That would be them. John is the one with the toupee and Henry—"

"—I know them well. They're long-time residents."

"Then you know about John's cologne. He reeks of it! It's not fair. Some of us are allergic."

Doctor Kessler rubbed his forehead. "I understand your concern, Mr. Sharp," he said. "Everyone should be considerate. I've raised the issue with Mr. Vanneschi. I'll see what else I can do." He turned to Luuk. "How about you, Mr. Westerbeek? How have you been?"

"Can't complain," Luuk replied. "Everyone is so friendly and helpful.

Given the circumstances…"

Doctor Kessler leaned in. "Could I steal you for a moment?" he asked in a low voice. "It won't take long."

"Sure."

"Excuse us, Mr. Sharp," the doctor said as he began to walk away from the table.

Devin nodded.

Luuk stood and followed him to a quiet corner of the patio.

"I'm glad you both continue to be comfortable here," the doctor began. "I understand how concerned you are about Mr. Sharp's condition."

"It's not easy. Sometimes he seems to forget who I am altogether. He calls me 'Milton' or some other name. Worse, there are times when he demands that everyone call him 'Giovanni' and he takes on a different personality."

"Sorry to hear."

"The latest is this fascination he's developed for Sheina."

"Who is that?"

"She's on the cleaning staff."

"It's expected. Remember what his neuropsychologist has been saying all along…"

"Yes, of course. Devin loves Doctor Haverhill. He has been treating him for years."

"He's an authority in the field. And he's been unequivocal," Doctor Kessler responded. "Dementia is an insidious disease. Progressive, and almost always irreversible. Distortions in the way patients perceive things around them are unavoidable."

Luuk nodded. "I know. I am a witness to that on a daily basis."

"Let's also keep in mind that Mr. Sharp has exhibited signs he may be suffering from split personality disorder. Needless to say, an added challenge."

Luuk lowered his head.

"He's fortunate to have you, Mr. Westerbeek," Doctor Kessler went on. "Your patience and support at this stage are crucial. Without you next to him, the scenario could be very different."

"Thank you, Doctor. I appreciate your words, but the truth is, we're fortunate to have each other."

"You are! You built a life together! Sorry, I didn't mean to—"

"No, no. It's okay. I know what you meant."

"Well, I should be going. Unfortunately, my schedule won't allow me to stay for the party."

"We understand."

Back with Devin, the doctor bid his farewells and walked toward the ramps and the main building. As he exited, he crossed paths with Milton, coming out to the patio for a brief announcement.

"May I have everyone's attention, please?" Milton called out. "Just a friendly reminder that tonight's festivities will begin at 6 p.m., in the ballroom. Residents and their registered guests should receive their table numbers via text. Anyone in a wheelchair or using a walker will have priority access. Our staff will be here to assist you. Enjoy the rest of the afternoon and see you all later." He then approached Devin and Luuk and spoke quietly: "Are you ready for a great evening, gentleman?"

Devin grinned. "Super stoked for it!"

"We just need a little time to freshen up and we'll be ready to rumble," said Luuk. "I'm hoping we'll all be at our very best," he added, glancing at Devin with tender eyes.

"You'll have plenty of time to rest and make yourselves look wonderful. Just so you know, as our guests of honor, you will be the last to enter the ballroom, after I introduce you."

"We'll be happy to follow your lead, Milton," Luuk responded.

The couple rose and headed for the main building.

XXX. THE SEER

"T rue Colors" played in the background in Devin and Luuk's studio, their cozy home within the senior living facility. Curtains drawn, two scented candles on a dresser cast a warm glow around their modestly appointed bedroom.

Wearing white tuxedos, red bow ties and shoes polished to high shine, Devin and Luuk stood side by side gazing at each other's reflection before a full-length mirror.

Devin beamed. "Timeless elegance," he said, running his hand over his silver hair neatly combed back.

Luuk turned to straighten Devin's bow tie. "Absolutely. We're experts at making us look fab."

They chuckled, years of shared laughter etched into the wrinkles on their faces.

"And now, for the cherries on the cake," said Luuk, glancing at two red sashes lying on their bed. He picked one up and carefully draped it over Devin's shoulder. "Looks great!"

Devin grabbed the other one and attempted to return Luuk's favor.

"Come on, Sweet Pea. You gotta get this right. You know the red in that sash brings out the sparkle in my eyes."

"True," Devin replied, hands shaking slightly. "Same devilish eyes that charmed me all those years ago, back in Jakarta."

They kissed, stepped back, and one last time, admired their reflection in the mirror.

"Bennet, darling," said Luuk, addressing their AI personal assistant. "What time is it?"

Instantly, a floor-to-ceiling translucent screen lit up on a wall showing: 5:55 p.m., EST.

"Our guests should all be seated by now," said Luuk, facing Devin. "Ready?"

"As ever."

They linked arms and strolled with measured steps toward the ballroom.

Milton awaited their arrival by the entrance. "My oh my! You gents look so dapper!" he said as they approached.

Luuk smiled. "Thank you, Milton!"

"Everyone's inside. Shall we?" Milton stepped into the ballroom, signaled an attendant to stop the music, and grabbed the microphone. Devin and Luuk remained just outside the doorway.

"Distinguished guests," Milton began. "Several decades ago, destiny brought together two young men hailing from distant corners of the world to the heart of a bustling flea market on the island of Java. Since then, they embarked on an amazing journey. Today, we gather to celebrate their enduring love and commitment to each other as they proudly and joyfully mark their Ruby Wedding Anniversary. Let us extend a warm welcome to our charming couple, Devin and Luuk!"

A wave of applause and cheers greeted the pair as they entered the ballroom holding hands. Across the room, photos and videos of their time together played in sequence on a giant screen. Out of nowhere, a banner hologram appeared in the midst of an explosion of digital confetti raining down from the ceiling: *40 Years Down, Forever to Go!* it read, in bright red letters.

Basking in the warmth of the people who surrounded them, the couple advanced toward the sweetheart table. Twinkling lights shone on familiar faces, the scent of fragrant flowers wafting through the air.

Devin looked around the room. *They're all here,* he thought as they settled. Everything seemed perfect. Turning to Luuk, he gazed into his eyes. Memories of scenes from a nightclub flowed in and out like sea waves, advancing and retreating as time started to collapse.

Suddenly, loud hissing, snarls and growls startled Devin out of his reverie. A cream-colored fuzzy ball the size of a small watermelon flew by. Chasing after it, Rousseau and Garrick ran under chairs and tables, leashes trailing behind them.

"What's the ruckus?" Devin asked.

"Looks like De Groot got spooked and jumped out of Venus' bag," Luuk replied. "Julienne's poodles are going after her."

Devin pointed to an open double-door exit in the distance. "There she is!"

Luuk rose. "You see De Groot?" he said, looking toward the doors. "I'm afraid she might get hurt." Seeing Mrs. DeGrasse in pursuit of her poodles, he followed.

Oblivious to the mayhem in their midst, the guests engaged in light conversation as the music played on. Before long, De Groot was safe in her bag, Garrick and Rousseau had been restrained, and everyone was back in their seats.

Except Devin.

"Where's Devin?" Luuk asked. "Has anyone seen him?" He was in his seat a minute ago."

Standing nearby, Mr. Vanneschi noticed Luuk's distress. He rushed over. "He's not in the ballroom," he said, scanning the room. "He might be in the restroom. You stay here, Mr. Westerbeek. I'll go look." Within minutes he returned with Devin at his side. "Mr. Sharp is fine. I found him in the kitchen."

"Thank you!"

Vanneschi nodded. "We're happy to assist. I'll be around if you need me." He turned and walked away.

Devin took his seat next to Luuk.

"You had me worried sick!" Luuk whispered in Devin's ear. "People are standing in line waiting to see us. What were you doing in the kitchen?"

"Apologies! When I caught sight of *her* inside the galley I could no longer disavow my sentiments. I yearn for her."

"What are you talking about?"

"Pray, forgive me. I am weary," Devin answered, then briefly closed his eyes. Instantly, a flurry of images rushed in: A radiant Sheina in a white dress stood on the main deck of the *Bredenhoft* with a crown of jasmines on her head. Facing her, Adam Hawley held her hands as Captain van Der Zee pronounced them man and wife. Devin frowned and pouted.

Suddenly, a loud voice jolted him. "Devin, you're dreaming again!"

Devin shook his head, opened his eyes and stared. "You mistake me for someone else, Signore! My birth name is Giovanni Crossa. You may inquire at the Gate House if you wish. I assure you, the Warden shall sustain my claim."

"Look, Dev! Your family's here."

Seeing Paige and Frank approach brought Devin him back to his senses. "You came!" he said, standing to greet them.

Paige rushed to embrace him. "We wouldn't miss this for the world!" she responded with a warm smile, her silver hair shimmering under the lights.

"We appreciate the effort," said Luuk. "It's a long drive from Kingston."

"Stress-free, though," Frank replied. "We hired a driverless pod."

"Ah! Smart choice!"

"We left you a small planter with flowers on the gifts table," said Paige. "White dahlias. Offshoots from the ones on Mom and Pop's patio. We saved what we could after mom passed, remember? You took some too, didn't you

Devin?"

"Er… Not dahlias. A few tiger lilies, maybe. We must've taken them upstate," Devin responded, his pleading eyes falling on Luuk.

Luuk furrowed his brow. *"Upstate?"*

"Yes. To our cabin in the woods."

"Oh, Devin… We've never had a cabin. You must be thinking of our apartment in the city. We had a view of the Hudson. Our windowsills were packed with plants from your parents' patio."

"Well, the dahlias are beautiful," said Paige. "Mom's favorite. They'll need plenty of sunshine."

"We should get back to our table, honey," Frank said. "These gentlemen have a small crowd waiting to see them."

Next in line, Abbey and Meg stepped forward.

"How was the drive from Manhattan?" Luuk asked Meg, sporting a full military uniform and a perfect crew cut.

"We took the hyperloop. Driving was not an option. We're having issues with our EV charger."

"Still riding your Harriet?" Devin asked.

"Every time I get a chance, Uncle," Meg winked. "She's my one and only."

Devin chuckled.

"We brought you and Luuk something I found in my basement around the time I moved in with Meg five years ago," said Abbey.

"Torture tools?"

"Ha. Very funny. It's from Mom and Pop's house. I had forgotten all about it."

"What is it?"

"A special decorative piece. You'll see…"

Meg took Abbey's hand and tugged her gently. "Let's have a seat, Mom. I'm starved." They walked away.

The line moved forward. Devin's gaze shifted to a female figure making her way up to the sweethearts table. As she drew closer, he recognized her face. *An old friend*, he thought. *Still so youthful after all these years!*

"Bella! It's so nice to see you!" Luuk said. "It's been a while."

She kissed them each in turn.

"I've missed you both! Yes, it *has* been quite a while."

"Where have you been hiding?" asked Devin.

"In Rome, with Niccolo, helping him settle. He was assigned to the Vatican a few months ago. He's there with the U. S. Mission."

"You mentioned it the last time we spoke," said Luuk. "He's such a bright young man! He'll do very well in the Vatican."

"It's all very different there now with Pope Sarafina on the Throne of Saint Peter."

"I'd expect so," Luuk responded. "First female Pope from Africa. Must be a challenge for her."

"That's nothing! The relief effort to aid the refugees from Venice is what weighs heavy on her. Nobody expected it would sink so fast."

"It's been tragic all around, Bella. Even here in America. Who could have imagined the Great Floods of 2035? To think that in our youth, Devin and I used to be regulars at Fire Island and Provincetown during the summer. Now, these places no longer exist. Permanently submerged, they say."

"I pray there's still time to reverse things somehow."

"People have been saying that for decades, yet here we are. I'm afraid prayers can only do so much."

Arabella sighed, then turned to Devin. "How's my sweet Devin? Have you been to the opera lately? I hear *Tuscany* is back on at the Met."

Caught in a whirlwind of emotions, Devin stared. A rush of excitement morphed into a broad smile and prompted him to bow. "My dearest Lady Azzoni! What a pleasant surprise!" he said, eyes gleaming. "We finally see each other again. Where is His Excellency?"

Baffled, Arabella arched her eyebrows. "Who?"

"Your husband. The Ambasciatore."

"Pardon me?"

Devin carried on. "He must be engaged, I presume. Matters of state?"

"I—I don't know what you mean."

"Then, I shall make myself plain, my lady. I am very much obliged to you. I learned all about your merciful deeds on my behalf during an audience with my cousin Niccolo in Rome."

"*Your cousin?* You must be thinking of my son."

"Sorry, Bella," Luuk interjected. "It's been a long day. He's not himself."

"Of course. I understand. And I've taken too much of your time already. I should be getting back to Amelia and Julienne. Oh, before I forget…" she said, reaching inside of her pocketbook. "This is from all three of us." She handed Luuk an envelope, smiled and walked away.

John Cleland and his longtime partner Henry Fielding approached next. Two younger men accompanied them.

"We're so very happy for you!" John said, adjusting the hairpiece on his head. "You remember Hal, my nephew?"

"Of course!" Luuk reached out and shook his hand. "Hello, Hal! Good to see you!"

Devin nodded, his eyes locked on the tassels on Hal's moccasins.

"Same here! And, congratulations to you both!"

"Still managing the jewelry shop at Bergdorf's?" asked Luuk.

"Every day for the past ten years, Mr. Westerbeek."

"Wonderful!"

"This is Ben, my grandson," said Henry, gesturing toward the muscular twenty-something standing beside him. "You've met, I believe. He's been here a few times."

"Nice to see you, Ben!" said Luuk. "How's the law firm treating you?"

"Let's just say I'd rather be scuba diving in Tahiti."

Henry cast an affectionate gaze upon his grandson. "Ben carries our family name well," he said. "We're proud of him. He is a true Fielding."

Devin glared. "We are fully aware who you are, Signore!" he said, jumping in. "You are Lord Fielding, the Magistrate."

"I'm no *lord*… but of course, you know who I am, Devin!" Henry replied. "We've been living side by side for years, my friend. I'm your neighbor and your favorite Bridge partner."

"You delude yourself! You are no friend of mine! Twice you locked me up, once in London, and then again, in The Hague. You unleashed Bambridge, that vile dog, to chase after me. There was no rhyme or reason. You knew I was paid up! And now, after all these years, you appear here with your minions, at my abode, as if nothing happened? I take exception to that!"

Luuk placed his arm around Devin's shoulders. "Please, Sweet Pea. It's only Henry, our next-door neighbor."

"Nonsense! I know precisely who he is!"

"So sorry. Please accept our apologies. All this excitement flusters him."

"No need for apologies," Henry responded. "We know how it is." He took Luuk's hand and squeezed it gently, then joined Ben, Hal and John on their way back to their table.

Luuk's younger brother, came next. Devin's eyes lit up when he saw him. "Richard! My dear and loyal friend!" he said, bowing. "What an honor it is to welcome you at this momentous occasion! I'm so verily obliged by your call!"

Richard blinked. "I am glad to see you too, Mijnheer Sharp!" he responded. *"Gefeliciteerd!"* He leaned on Luuk and spoke softly. "Is he all right?"

"He's a bit frazzled and confused right now, but fine," Luuk said quietly.

"Just go along with him."

Devin went on. "Without your helping hand, I would have never made it this far. You were always there when I needed you. You saved me *and* my Sheina! For that alone, I shall be forever obliged."

"You're welcome. Glad I could help," Richard responded. Again, he reached for Luuk, and whispered. "Who's *Sheina*?"

"A cleaning lady. He's been obsessed with her lately."

As the evening unfolded, the ballroom brimmed with warmth. Heartfelt toasts, laughter and music filled the air until the gentle strains of a familiar lullaby brought the party to a close.

"Don't you love 'Moon River'?" asked Luuk as he and Devin waved to the last guests exiting the ballroom. "Feels like the lyrics were written just for us."

"Oh yeah?" said Devin, wearing a playful grin. "Show me. You, sexy crooner."

Luuk cast a tender gaze at Devin and began singing: *"Oh, dream maker, you heart breaker. Wherever you're going, I'm going your way."*

Devin followed: *"Two drifters, off to see the world. There's such a lot of world to see."*

They finished the song together as they made their way to the gifts table.

"I feel it was only yesterday since we said our vows," said Devin, carefully lifting a large wicker basket filled with presents from family and friends. "Maybe Venus is right. Maybe we're timeless beings. We just don't know it."

"Well, if there's one thing I know for sure," Luuk responded, "it's that you're the best thing that ever happened to me."

Devin faced Luuk. *"We* are the best thing that ever happened to *us.*"

They held each other in a long embrace.

Just then a cleaning crew came in, Sheina among them.

She approached. "Excuse me," she said. "I heard Mr. Sharp was in the kitchen looking for me."

Instantly, the physical world around Devin crumbled, his heart racing. "My precious!" he said, stretching his arms out to her. "You come at last!"

Sheina took a step back. "I'm sorry. I didn't mean to…"

"No, no. It's okay," Luuk responded. "He's a bit tired. He got lost earlier, that's all."

"I see. Well, I hope you had a wonderful evening. Forty years is a lifetime. Just so you know, I dropped a little something in your basket when I came in today."

"That's very kind of you, Sheina," Luuk said. "We appreciate the gesture."

"You're welcome, Mr. Westerbeek. I should get back to work now."

"Pray tarry, my dear. I beseech you!" Devin pleaded, gripped by a relentless spell. "This time I shall not fail to keep you by my side!"

"Have a good night, Mr. Sharp!" Sheina responded, compassion in her eyes.

Luuk took Devin's hand. "Come on, Sweet Pea. Let's go. We need to rest."

The following morning, Devin and Luuk sat on their living room sofa. Coffee mugs in hand, they watched quietly as specks of dust scintillated in the first streams of sunlight. Directly across from them on a low table, a pile of gift-wrapped boxes awaited their attention.

"How are you feeling, Dev? Ready to start opening the gifts?"

"Good! Let's get to it."

"Should we begin with the cards?"

"Sure."

"This one is from Bella, Amelia and Julienne," said Luuk, sliding the card out of the envelope. "A lovely drawing: Two gold rings set with rubies and framed by rose-cut diamonds."

Devin leaned in. "Awesome!" he said, images of a scene somewhere in a royal palace blazing through his mind.

Luuk opened the card. "And, two tickets to the Met, for *Tuscany!* Wow! So generous of them!" He lifted the next card. "From George. Feels a bit heavy." He opened it and pulled out a vintage gold coin and a short, handwritten note. He handed the coin to Devin.

"Beautiful!" said Devin. "A mid-eighteenth-century guinea. The English royal coat of arms on one side, and the king's name on the other. From his private collection, I imagine."

"Extremely generous of him," Luuk said.

Devin nodded. "And very much in character. He's obsessed with coinage from the reign of King George II."

"Not just with coinage," Luuk chuckled. "We know he named his parakeets after the King's wife, Queen Caroline, and his long-time lover, Lady Henrietta Howard."

"What does the note say?"

"Happy Anniversary! From George, Caroline and Henrietta."

"What a nut!"

They laughed.

Luuk removed the wrapping from a tiny box. "Now this is from Penny and Stella, the nurses." He opened it and looked inside. "Nice! A silver pillbox."

Devin gazed at it. "It's a snuffbox," he said, goosebumps rising on his skin.

"Really? How can you tell the difference?"

"I've always had a thing for snuffboxes… Some have elaborate designs."

"Sounds right. This has a wonderful engraving. A bit tarnished, though."

"A sign it's aged," said Devin. "But you can still see the two dragons and the birds flying around them. Swallows, I believe."

"A typical Asian motif, for sure," Luuk responded. "Penny must've picked it. She lives in Chinatown, you know."

"So very kind of her."

Luuk handed Devin a black velvet box with a card attached to it, picked up his coffee mug and rose. "I'm ready for a refill. You?"

"Not yet."

Luuk walked over to the kitchenette. While he replenished his mug, Devin read the card aloud: "True Love is Timeless. But keep these for the ride! All the best, your Bridge partners, John and Henry."

"Nice! What's in the box?" Luuk asked, returning to the couch.

Devin opened it. "Take a look. A pair of wristwatches," he said, passing one to Luuk. He turned a watch over and examined its back. "Amazing! These are authentic 1940s Longines." Waves of holographic images of a dashing, brown-haired man sitting beside him at a bar somewhere flickered in his mind.

"Fancy!" Luuk said. "I bet John's nephew Hal, the jewelry man, had a hand in this."

"Probably." Devin then proceeded to unwrap a gift no larger than a shoebox. "Ahh, here it is," he said. "Abbey's *special decorative piece*."

"A model sailboat?"

"Yeah. *The Bredenhoft*," Devin replied, eyes glistening. "A birthday gift from my parents when I turned five."

"Sweet. It's in great condition. We'll need to find a good place for it." Pulling a small box out of a plastic bag, Luuk continued. "This is Sheina's gift. I'm sure you'll want to do the honors."

Devin opened the box and removed from it a red votive candle along with two folded pieces of paper. "Pretty!" He held up the candle, then handed it to Luuk.

"It sure is. And the papers?"

"One is a note from Sheina. She says the candle came from an ancient Buddhist temple in her home country. The other one sounds like a prayer." He read it aloud:

"Like the rain that fills the streams, the rivers and the oceans, may the love of those around you, those gone before you, and those who are yet to join you, flow into your heart and awaken your eternal self."

"Wonderful! But what does it really mean?"

"We'll have to ask Venus to enlighten us on this one," Devin said. "By the way, she should be here any moment now. She told me she'd come by this morning to drop off her gift for us."

Luuk's cell phone beeped.

"A text from Richard. He's on his way."

"Great! What's the plan?"

"He wants to see us again before he goes back to Holland. I'm thinking he and I could meet in the patio before all three of us have lunch together. That should give you and Venus time to talk."

"Sounds good."

Luuk sent Richard a voice message then got back to Devin.

"Remember, there's a can of sardines in the pantry for De Groot. In case she gets hungry. We know she has an appetite for them."

"She sure does! She's lucky that's one fish species that still thrives."

"Bennet, darling. Make a fresh pot of coffee," said Luuk, as he prepared to leave.

"You think of everything," Devin said. "Thank you. I'm sure Venus will enjoy a cup or two."

A few minutes later, a knock startled Devin, dozing on the couch. He checked the video camera on his cell phone and ordered Bennet to unlock the front door. He clicked the speaker icon on his screen and told Venus to come in.

As the door opened, Devin saw De Groot's head sticking out of Venus' pet carrier bag.

"There you are! Good morning!" he said. "You look wonderful! That blue turban really suits you."

"Greetings, sweetie! And thank you!" Venus responded. "A gift from my sister." She raised her head and took a deep breath. "Mmm… What's this deliciousness in the air?"

"You *know* what! I got a fresh pot of coffee on the table. Please come join me."

Venus walked slowly, her white cane leading the way. As she approached,

Devin caught a faint whiff of tangerines and apples. "Can I pour you a cup?" he asked.

"Please." She sat beside him and placed De Groot's bag by her feet. "Where's Luuk?"

"He went to meet Richard for a visit out on the patio. They'll be joining us later."

"Good."

"Did you enjoy yourself at the party last night?"

"I did. At least, until those dreadful dogs started chasing my poor De Groot. Clearly, Julienne has no control over them. I couldn't stay much longer after that. My blood pressure went through the roof."

"Well, I'm glad you're here today. There's a couple things I'd like to show you."

"What's that?"

"First this," he said. He picked up the snuffbox and handed it to Venus. "From our nurses."

"Intricate design," Venus said, feeling the lid with her fingers.

"It's a snuffbox. Beautiful. Dragons and swallows."

"Asian. Very traditional."

"Any special meaning or vibe?"

"Oh yes. Coming from you. Not from the snuffbox."

"Really? I do feel a connection…"

"Dragons are symbols of power. Gigantic and frightening. But here's the thing: at least in our dimension, they don't exist. Swallows are small, delicate birds. In some Asian cultures people believe they're messengers from lost loved ones."

"I've heard that before…"

"In any case, they're very much a part of our physical world."

"Another version of the Yin and Yang?"

"No. Dragons and swallows are not opposing energies. Just different."

"Funny how they appear together."

"Why not? Mythical creatures have always been around the living."

"And my connection to them?"

"You tell me."

"Sometimes I feel so small. Like a swallow facing a dragon."

"There you go. We all do. It's in our nature. We create fear. So we can also vanish it."

"Thank you, Venus. Something to think about. Now, here's a Buddhist prayer that came with Sheina's gift. Can I read it to you?"

"Please do."

"Like the rain that fills the streams, the rivers and the oceans, may the love of those around you, those gone before you, and those who are yet to join you, flow into your heart and awaken your eternal self."

"What's your take on this?"

"It's beautiful! We are embodiments of shared essences across different lifetimes. In our purest state we're much like dolphins, forever plunging into and out of the sea of eternity."

"There you go again, speaking in riddles."

Venus chuckled. "The prayer is about love. Timeless and everlasting."

"Ah, yes. You think we're eternal. I wish I had your confidence."

"It wasn't always that way for me... When leukemia took my daughter Tara, I thought I was finished. She was my life."

"I can only imagine."

"She had just turned four. We were living in Woodstock then, just the two of us and Nixon, our Great Dane."

"How did you manage to cope after Tara was gone?"

"I was a wreck. I thought I had lost her forever. Until the day I found her."

"You found her? How? Where?"

"Where she had always been, from the beginning. In my dreams."

"You mean, in your memories."

"No. In my dreams. The same old place we used to meet for centuries. And then I remembered: In this lifetime, we chose to be mother and daughter."

"And then?"

"I painted my house purple and turned it into a spiritual boutique."

"What did you sell?"

"My craft."

"Your visions?"

"That's all I had. Save for a little ingenuity."

"How do you mean?"

"I'll show you." She reached inside De Groot's carrier bag, pulled out a small four-sided crystal pyramid, and set it on the table.

"It's gorgeous."

"I'm glad you like it. It's your anniversary gift. It's served a special purpose for years. I used to call it The Seer."

"Thank you so much, Venus! What was its special purpose?"

"I used it in sessions with my clients. It was an aid that helped them focus and see within themselves."

"What did they see?"

"All kinds of things. But mostly, their memories and dreams."

"Funny you should mention… Sometimes, I fear my own memories are vanishing. And my dreams, too! They keep fading, leaving no trace."

"No need to worry, Devin. Your memories and dreams are safe! They're stored inside the mind and soul of the Divinity."

"*Stored?*"

"Yes. Deep within Her core. Like nesting dolls, they exist inside each other. Each doll is different, but in the end, they're the same entity. You see?"

"I—I am not sure… Are these *Her* memories or *ours*?"

"They're both one and the same," Venus replied just as De Groot jumped on her lap.

Devin rubbed his eyes. "Sounds like another riddle."

"Well, as they say," Venus responded as she petted DeGroot, "Reality is in the eye of the beholder. You can draw your own conclusions, sweetie."

De Groot purred.

"The eye of the beholder? Then, what is *real*?"

"The universe *within!*"

"So, my dreams are real after all?"

"They always have been! People dismiss their dreams because they seem to end when they wake up. But you and I know better."

Devin's eyes widened. "What about time? Is time real? Have I been travelling back and forth through the centuries for all these years?"

"We are the architects of our own reality, my dear. Including space and time. We can be and do anything we can conceive, anywhere!"

De Groot meowed and jumped off Venus' lap.

"Don't worry," said Devin. "She's rubbing herself on my leg. And purring like crazy."

"I can hear her. She likes you."

"Or I smell like sardines."

They giggled.

Venus took a sip from her mug, then continued. "What else is on your mind,

Devin?"

"Frankly, all this talk about the Divinity and eternity makes me wonder if we, as individuals, matter."

"Of course we do! Without each individual brushstroke there wouldn't be a painting!"

Devin sighed. "I guess I'm a bit of nitwit about these things but…" He stood up and made his way to the pantry. "I *do* know that this kitty is positively hungry and I have the perfect treat for her!" He took a can of sardines from a cupboard and snapped it open. Circling his feet, De Groot meowed persistently.

"Just *one* sardine will do, Devin, only one," Venus said. "She can be very greedy and voracious, you know."

Devin stared, dazed and confused. "D-Devin, say you? A name that strikes a chord… Yet, certainly not mine. And you, Signora? Pray forgive me, your name escapes me…" He placed the fish on a saucer and set it on the floor.

Venus smiled. "Oh, I am known as Lady Woodstock, good sir. We have been acquainted with each other for some time now."

"Of course, of course. My folly," Devin responded. "Apologies. I digressed." Suddenly, he snapped out of his spell and continued. "So do you think we'll ever get to see God?"

Venus chuckled. "You're kidding! Look at who you're talking to?"

"Sorry. I never think of you as being blind."

"Not that! I mean, why wait? When God wants me to see Her, I do."

"It figures. You have a special connection."

"Maybe I do. Now that I think about it… The Seer might be the answer to your question."

"You think so?" Devin responded, standing with an open can of sardines in one hand and a fork in the other.

"Why not? Wanna try it?"

"Okay."

"When you're ready, please sit down and close your eyes."

"Done."

"Good! Let me move closer to you." She edged toward him and reached for his hands. "Take a deep breath. Fill your lungs. Good… Slowly let the air out, emptying your chest. And again. Deep breath in, and out. Let the world around you slow down. Very good… You are now relaxed and calm. Keeping your eyes closed, picture the pyramid as a prism. Focus on the refracting light as it goes through it."

"I can see it…" said Devin, feeling the warmth of Venus' age-mottled hands resting on his.

"Now take your time to peer into each of its faces."

"I am…"

"What do you see, Devin?"

"I—I see… I see myself as a child, then in my teens, as a young man, and now—"

"—now what?"

"The images keep changing!"

"How? Who else is there?"

"My parents, my sisters, Giovanni, Sheina, Stella, Penny, Luuk and Milton… Everyone! Even De Groot is there!"

"De Groot?"

"Yes, devouring the sardine I gave her."

"Very good!" Venus laughed. "Then, you've seen Her!"

"Who?"

"The Divinity!"

9 798869 210777